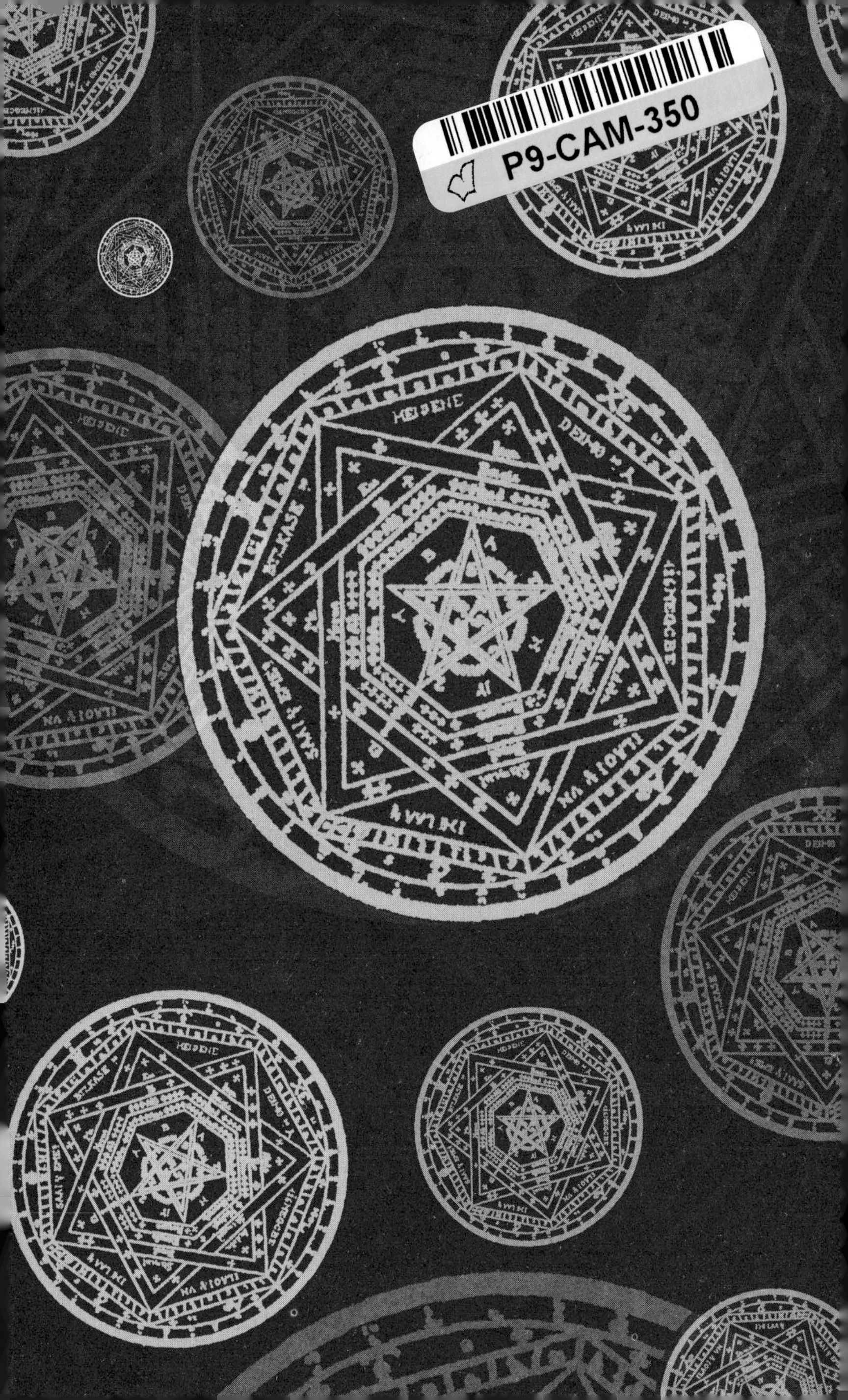

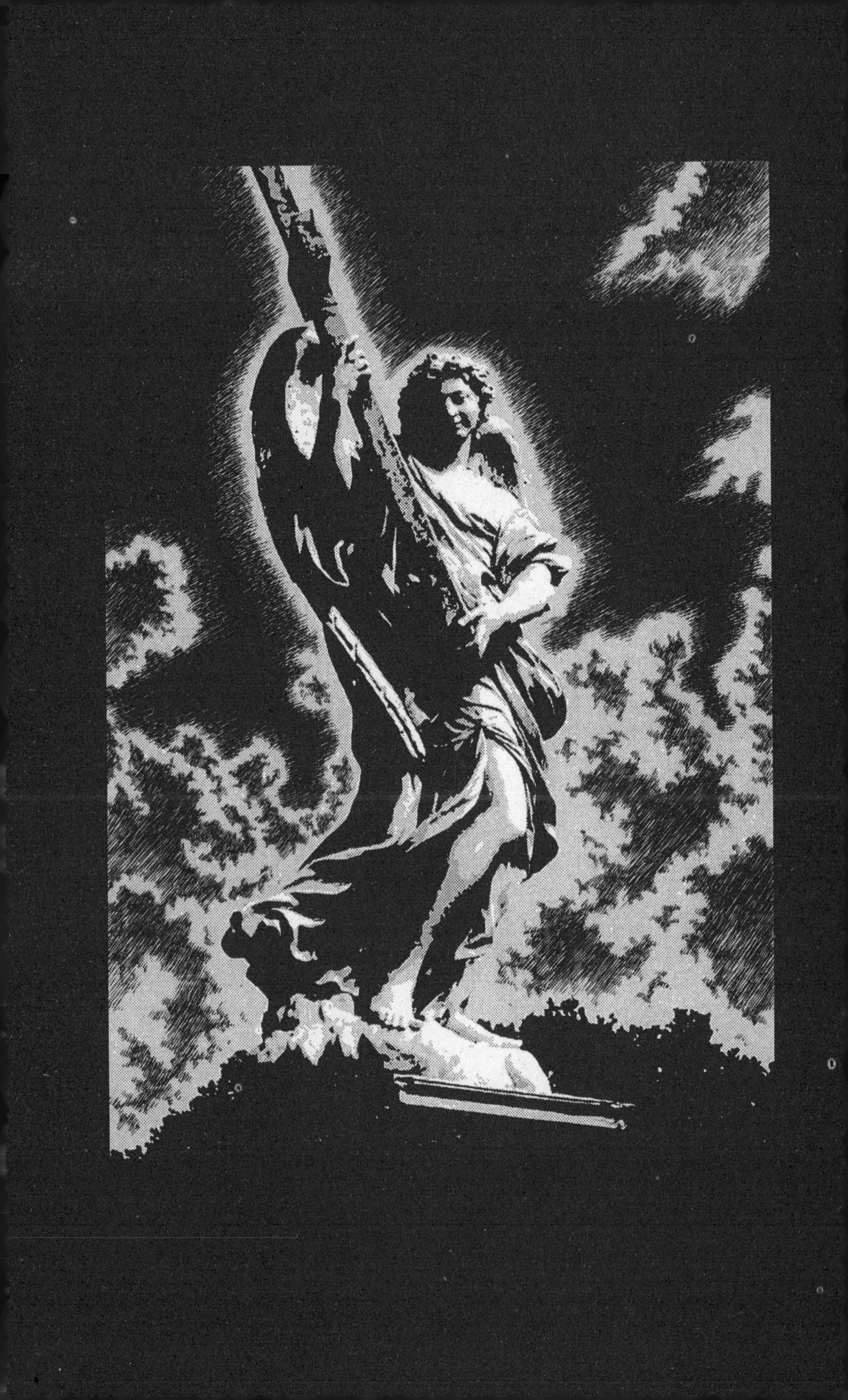

VOLUME 18

STORY and ART BY
WOO

HAMBURG // LONDON // LOS ANGELES // TOKYO

Rebirth Vol. 18
created by Woo

Translation - Jennifer Hahm
English Adaptation - Aaron Sparrow
Copy Editor - Hope Donovan
Retouch and Lettering - Bowen Park
Production Artist - Camellia Cox
Cover Design - Jose Macasocol, Jr.

Editor - Bryce P. Coleman
Digital Imaging Manager - Chris Buford
Production Manager - Elizabeth Brizzi
Managing Editor - Lindsey Johnston
VP of Production - Ron Klamert
Editor-in-Chief - Rob Tokar
Publisher - Mike Kiley
President and C.O.O. - John Parker
C.E.O. and Chief Creative Officer - Stuart Levy

A  Manga

TOKYOPOP Inc.
5900 Wilshire Blvd. Suite 2000
Los Angeles, CA 90036

E-mail: info@TOKYOPOP.com
Come visit us online at www.TOKYOPOP.com

ISBN: 1-59532-662-6

First TOKYOPOP printing: July 2006
10 9 8 7 6 5 4 3 2 1
Printed in the USA

STORY THUS FAR

Mysteriously transported from the ring of the Vampire Lord Tournament, Deshwitat finds himself reliving the worst night of his life—the moment when Kalutika murdered his beloved Lilith. But it is only an illusion, cast by Poison Ash, one that Desh soon overcomes. Meanwhile, at Vatican City, Remi and Eiji learn from a perverted priest that the members of the Order of St. Michael are being held in the deadly Tower of Trials, a place few ever return from. And as the next round of the tournament is about to begin, a massive explosion eliminates nearly all of the combatants, leaving only Deshwitat, Grey and Millenear to compete...

REBIRTH™

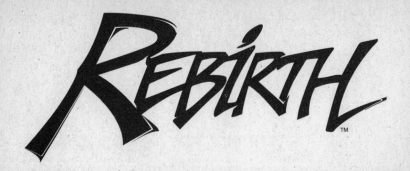

Vol 18

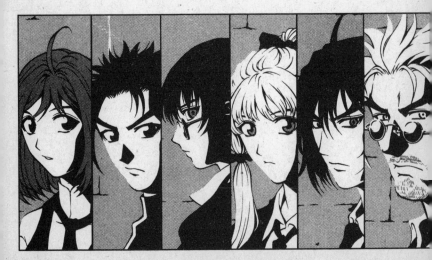

Chapter 71: Tower of Trials

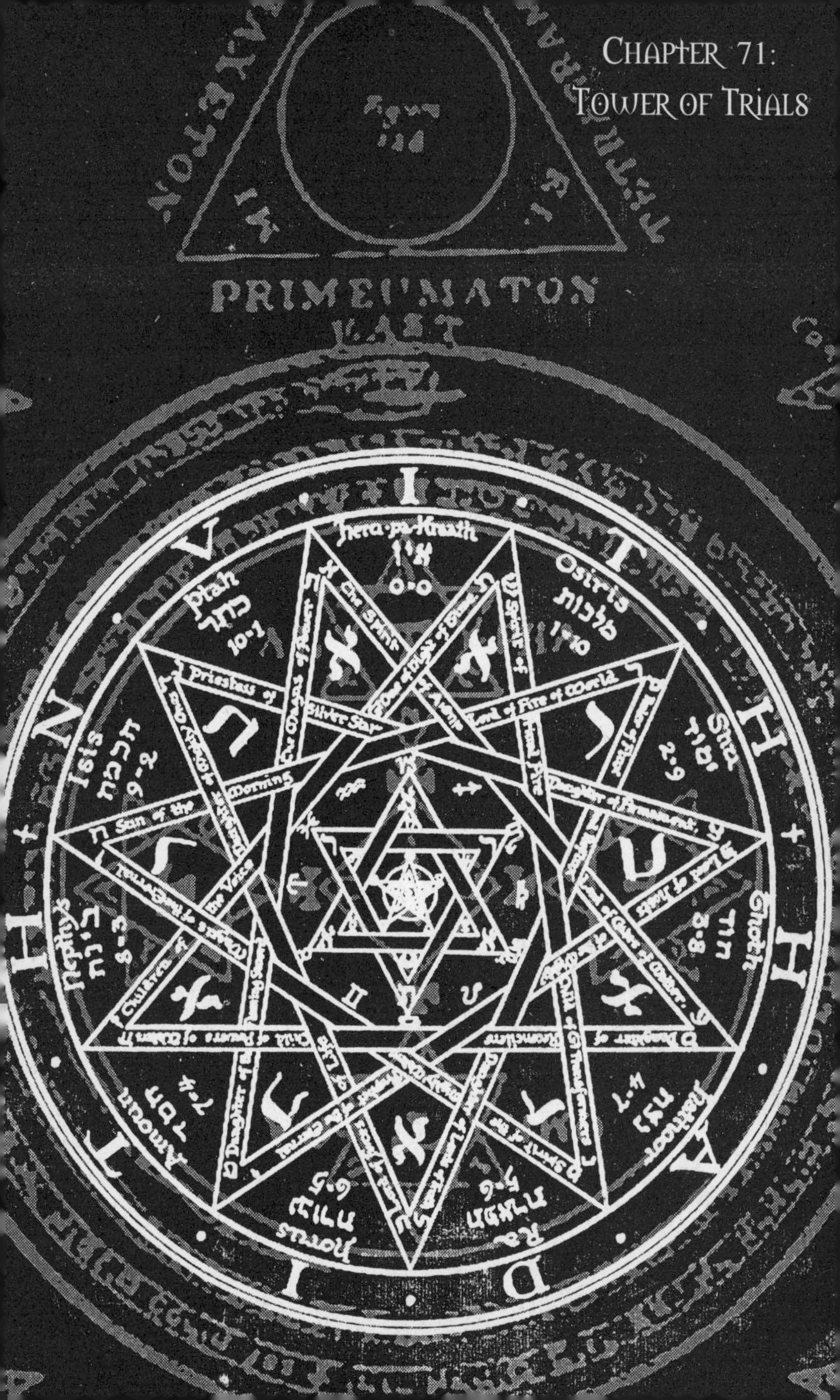
PRIMEU'MATON
Ptah
Osiris
Isis
Nephthys
Thoth
Amoun
Horus
Priestess of
Silver Star
Son of the
Morning
Daughter of Firmament

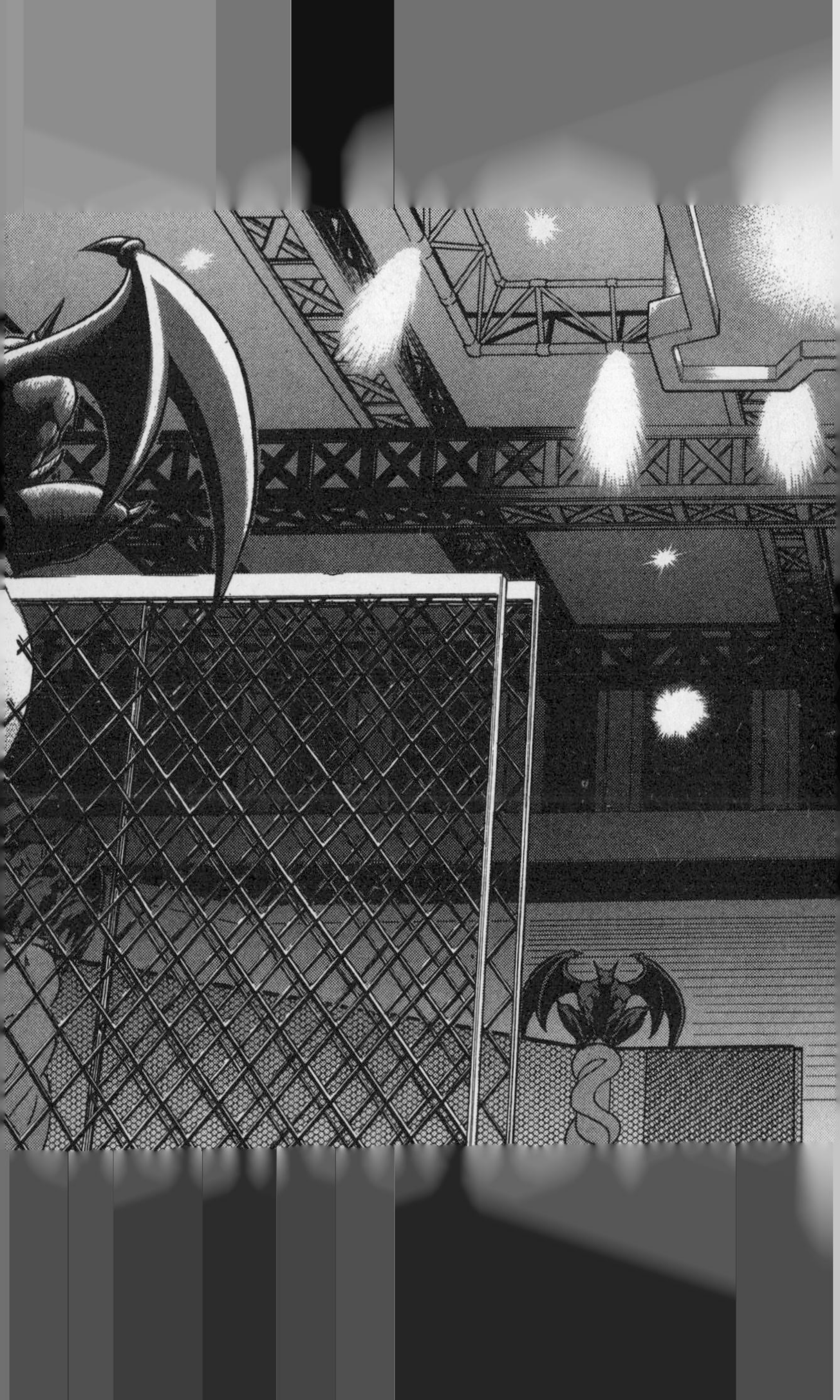

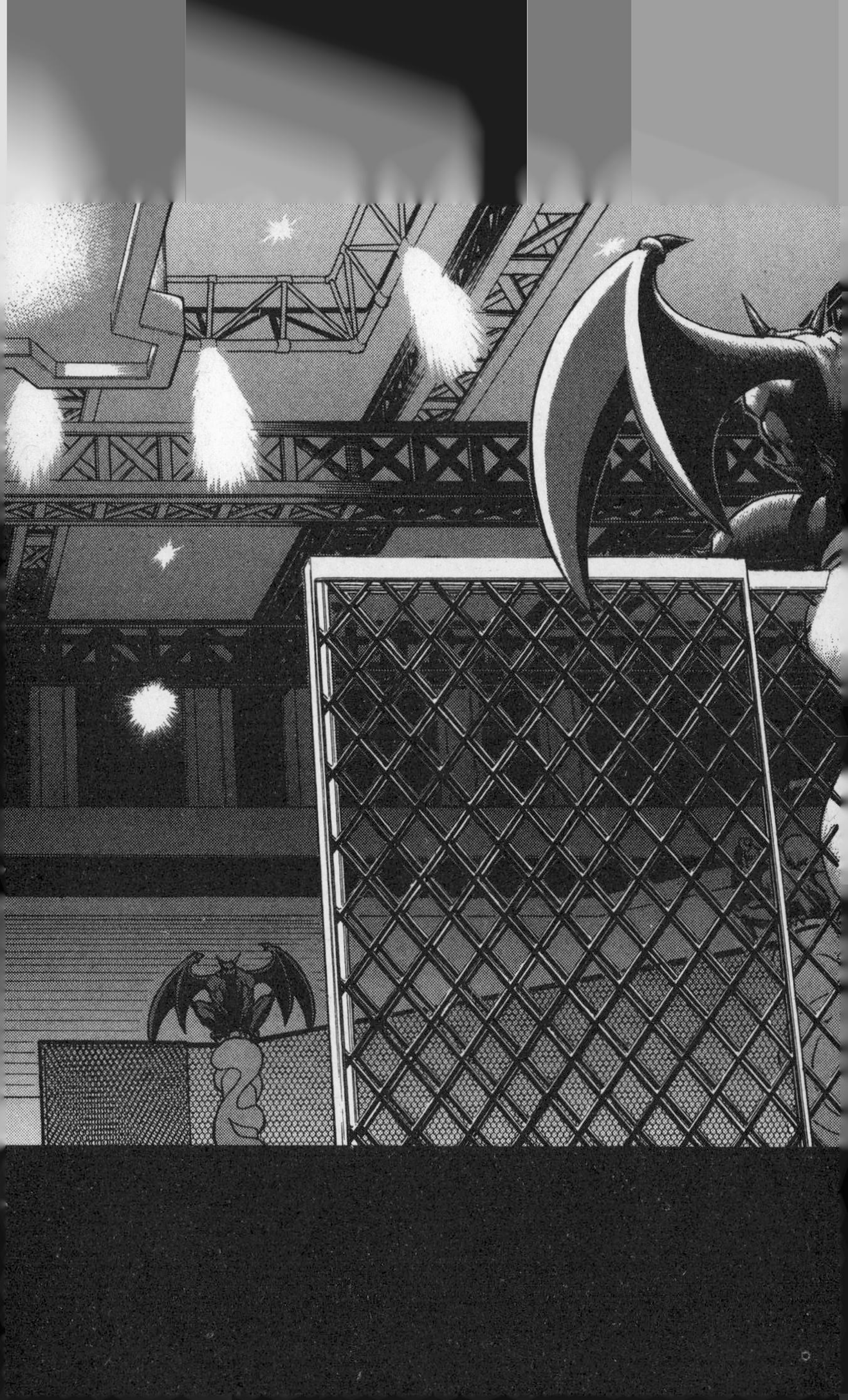

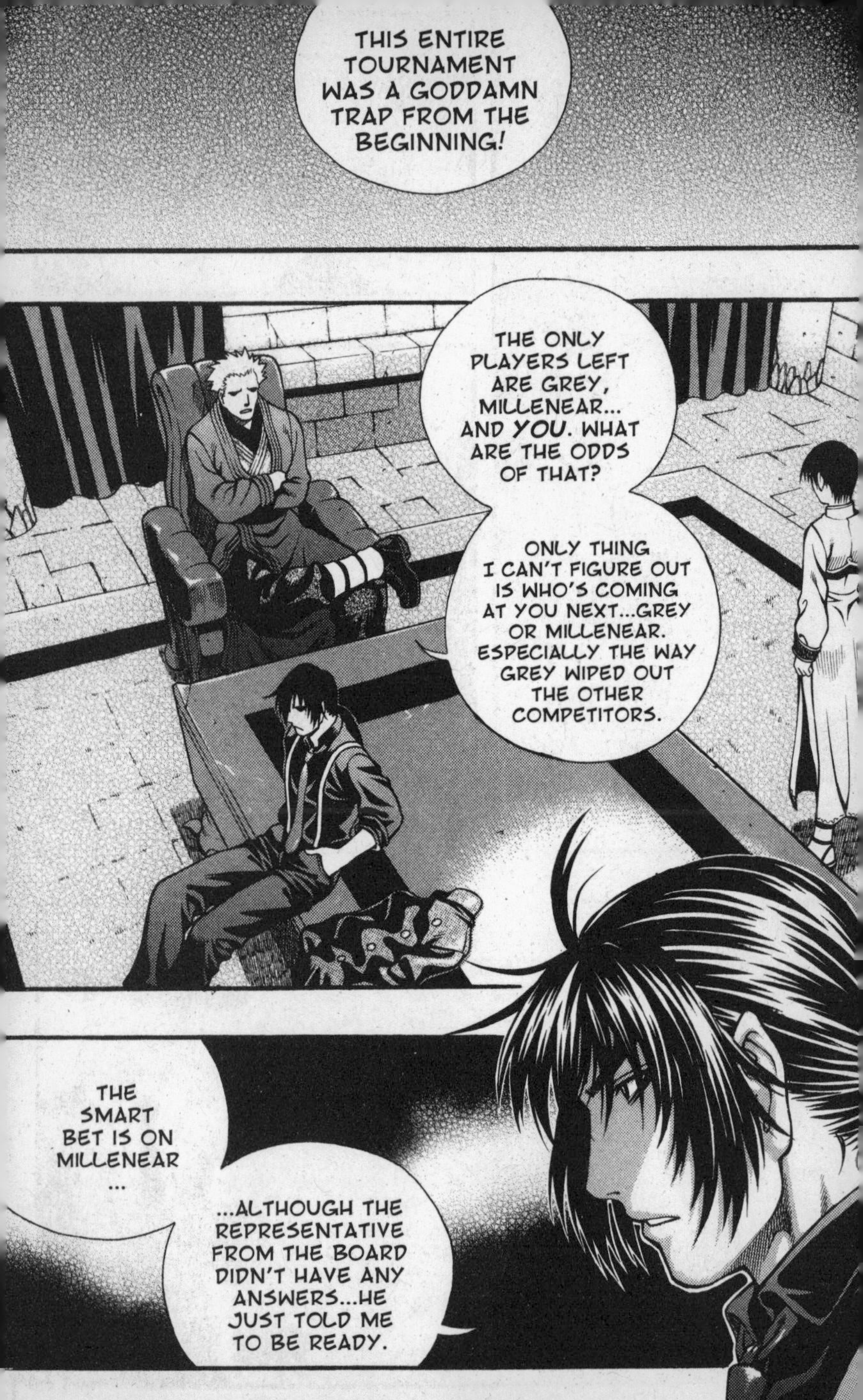
THIS ENTIRE TOURNAMENT WAS A GODDAMN TRAP FROM THE BEGINNING!
THE ONLY PLAYERS LEFT ARE GREY, MILLENEAR... AND YOU. WHAT ARE THE ODDS OF THAT?
ONLY THING I CAN'T FIGURE OUT IS WHO'S COMING AT YOU NEXT...GREY OR MILLENEAR. ESPECIALLY THE WAY GREY WIPED OUT THE OTHER COMPETITORS.
THE SMART BET IS ON MILLENEAR ...
...ALTHOUGH THE REPRESENTATIVE FROM THE BOARD DIDN'T HAVE ANY ANSWERS...HE JUST TOLD ME TO BE READY.

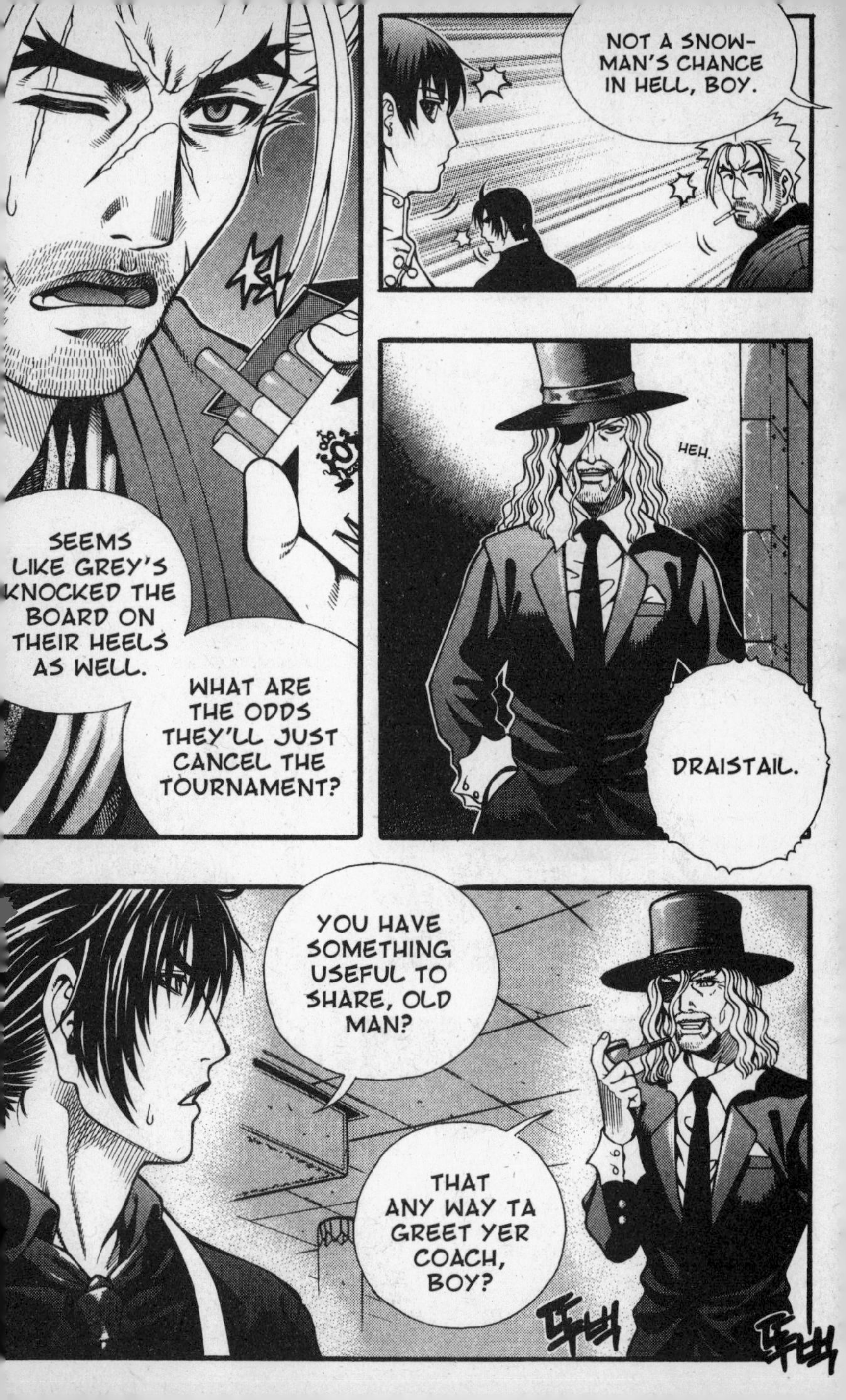
SEEMS LIKE GREY'S KNOCKED THE BOARD ON THEIR HEELS AS WELL.
WHAT ARE THE ODDS THEY'LL JUST CANCEL THE TOURNAMENT?
NOT A SNOW-MAN'S CHANCE IN HELL, BOY.
HEH.
DRAISTAIL.
YOU HAVE SOMETHING USEFUL TO SHARE, OLD MAN?
THAT ANY WAY TA GREET YER COACH, BOY?

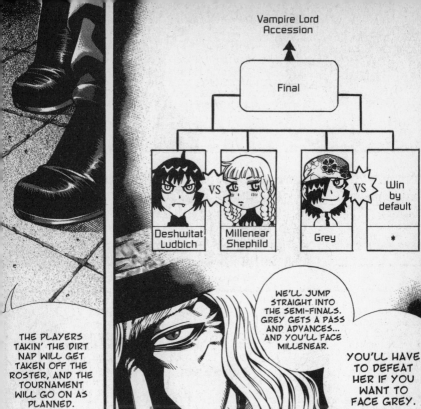

Vampire Lord
Accession

Final

Deshwitat Ludbich VS Millenear Shephild

Grey VS Win by default

*

THE PLAYERS TAKIN' THE DIRT NAP WILL GET TAKEN OFF THE ROSTER, AND THE TOURNAMENT WILL GO ON AS PLANNED.

WE'LL JUMP STRAIGHT INTO THE SEMI-FINALS. GREY GETS A PASS AND ADVANCES... AND YOU'LL FACE MILLENEAR.

YOU'LL HAVE TO DEFEAT HER IF YOU WANT TO FACE GREY.

HOW CAN THE BOARD RECOGNIZE GREY AS A COMPETITOR?

DIDN'T HE BREAK THE RULES WHEN HE KILLED THE OTHER 16 COMPETITORS? HE SHOULD BE DISQUALIFIED, AT THE VERY LEAST!

......

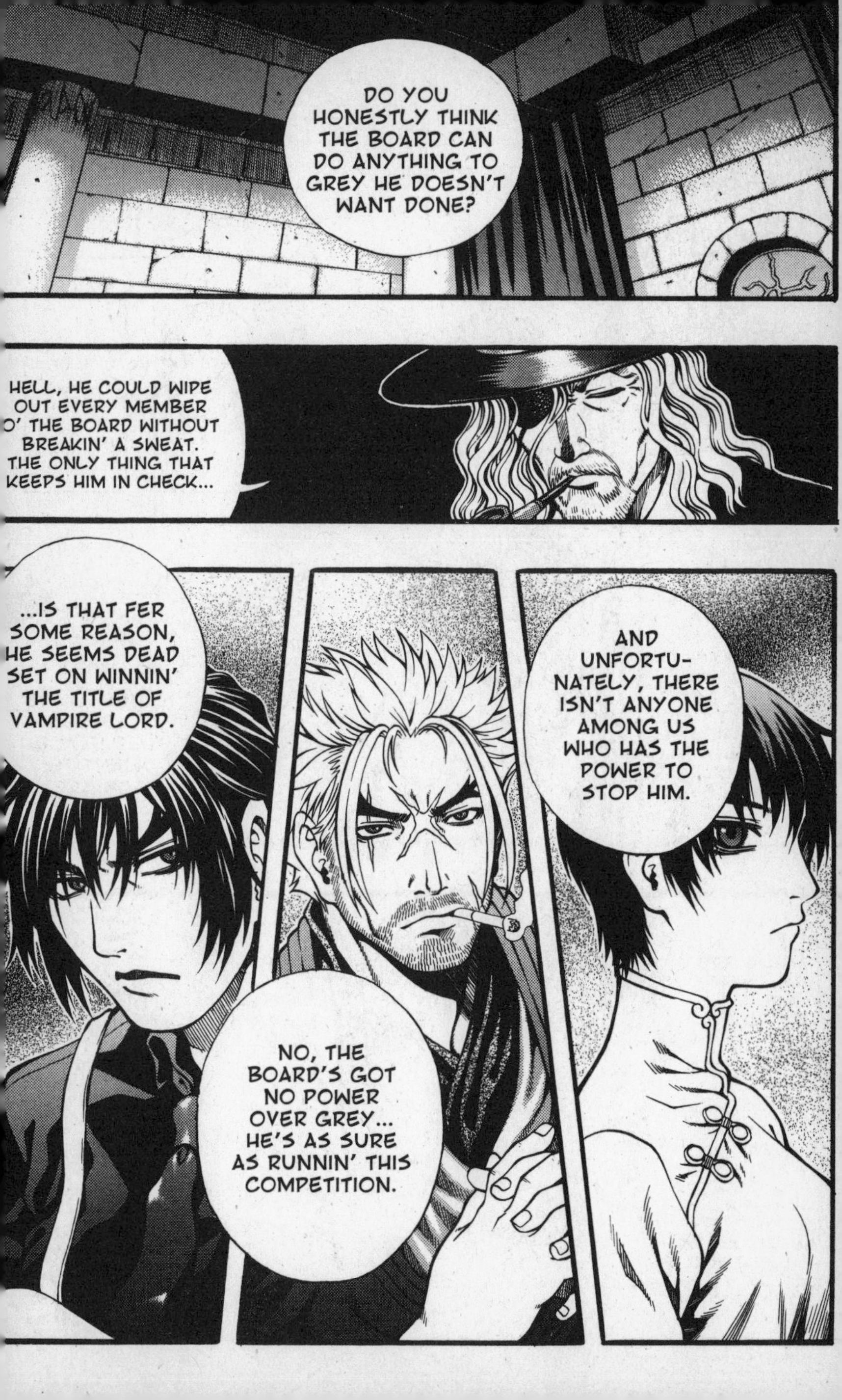
DO YOU HONESTLY THINK THE BOARD CAN DO ANYTHING TO GREY HE DOESN'T WANT DONE?
HELL, HE COULD WIPE OUT EVERY MEMBER O' THE BOARD WITHOUT BREAKIN' A SWEAT. THE ONLY THING THAT KEEPS HIM IN CHECK...
...IS THAT FER SOME REASON, HE SEEMS DEAD SET ON WINNIN' THE TITLE OF VAMPIRE LORD.
NO, THE BOARD'S GOT NO POWER OVER GREY... HE'S AS SURE AS RUNNIN' THIS COMPETITION.
AND UNFORTU-NATELY, THERE ISN'T ANYONE AMONG US WHO HAS THE POWER TO STOP HIM.

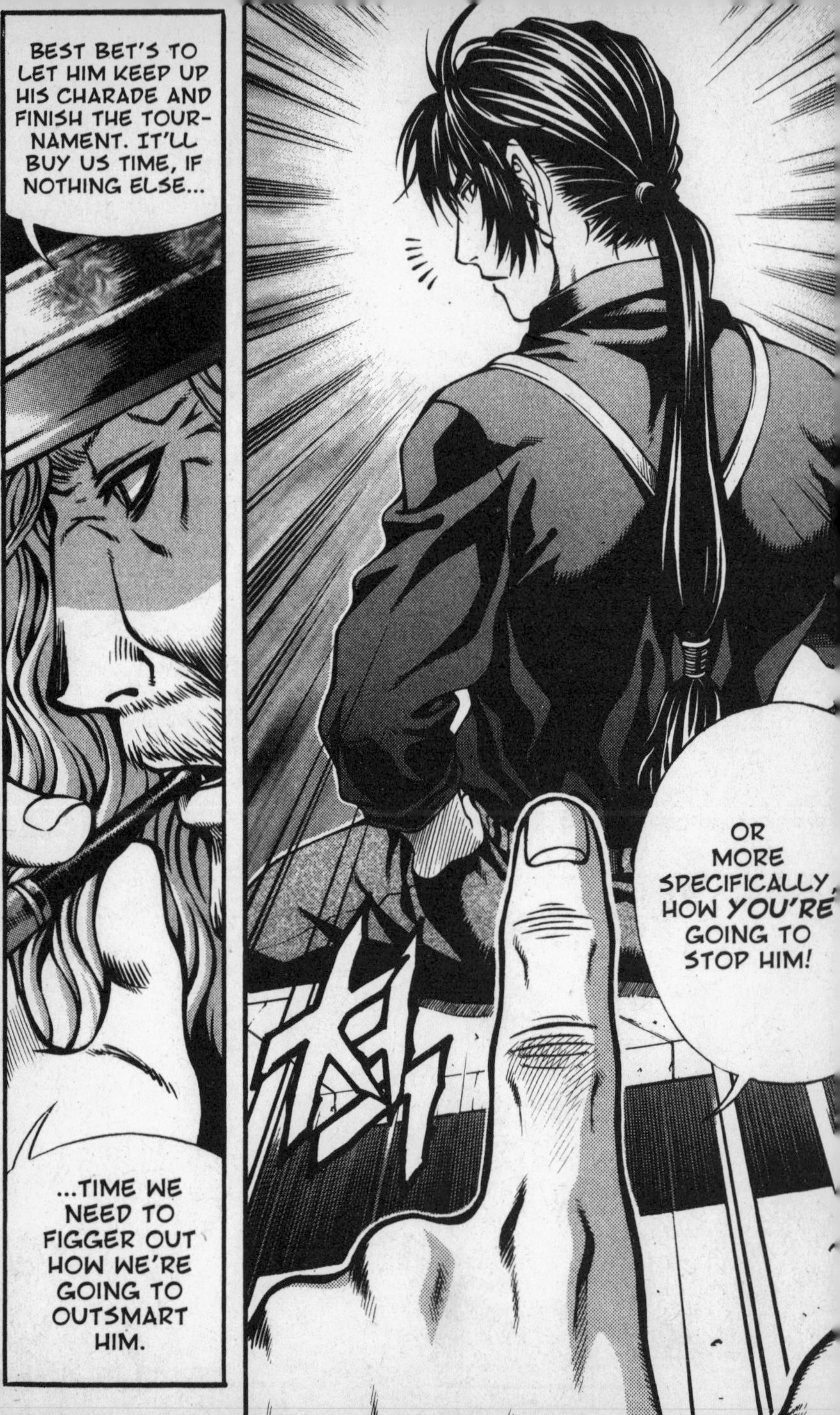
BEST BET'S TO LET HIM KEEP UP HIS CHARADE AND FINISH THE TOURNAMENT. IT'LL BUY US TIME, IF NOTHING ELSE...
...TIME WE NEED TO FIGGER OUT HOW WE'RE GOING TO OUTSMART HIM.
OR MORE SPECIFICALLY, HOW *YOU'RE* GOING TO STOP HIM!

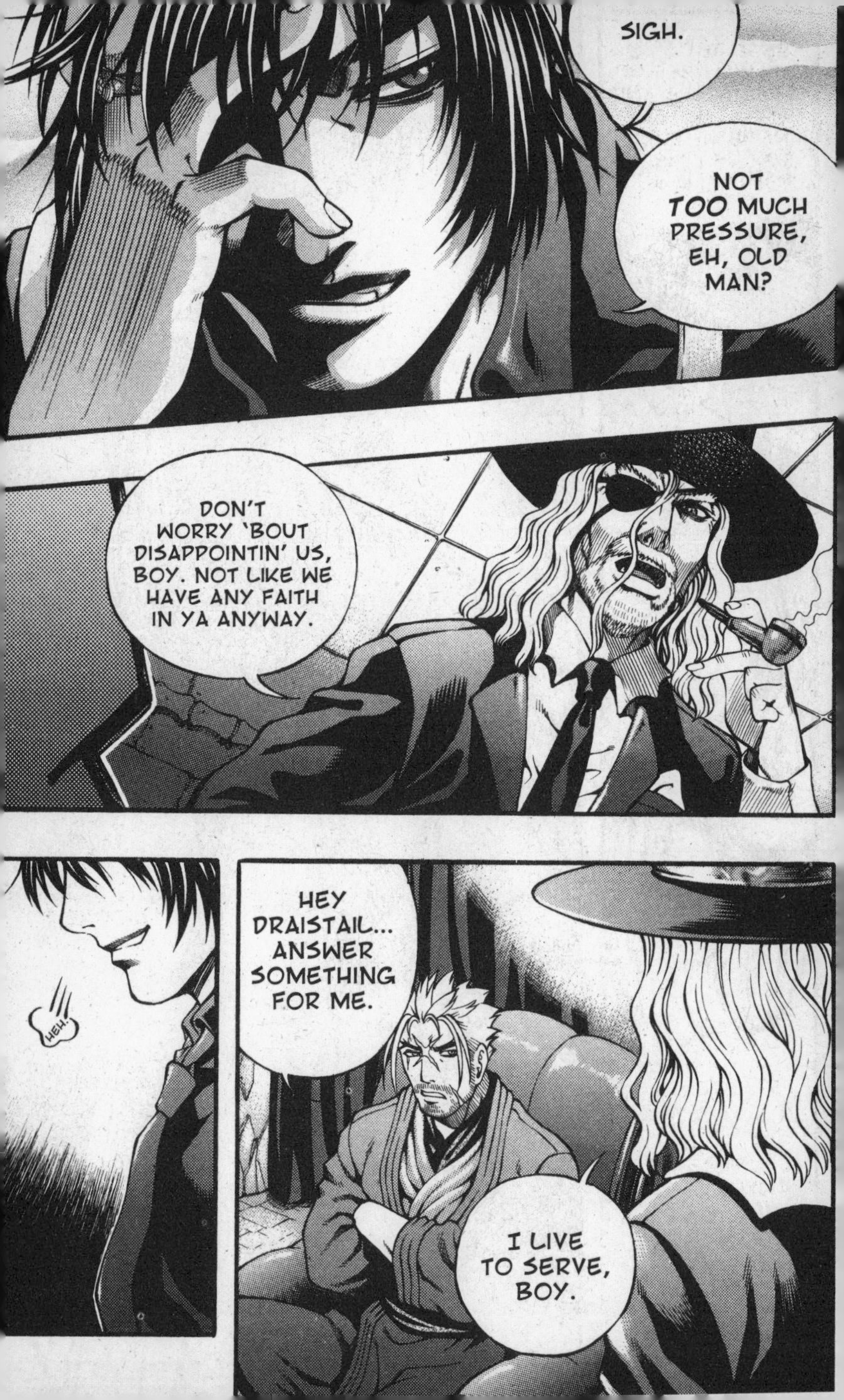
SIGH.
NOT TOO MUCH PRESSURE, EH, OLD MAN?
DON'T WORRY 'BOUT DISAPPOINTIN' US, BOY. NOT LIKE WE HAVE ANY FAITH IN YA ANYWAY.
HEH.
HEY DRAISTAIL... ANSWER SOMETHING FOR ME.
I LIVE TO SERVE, BOY.

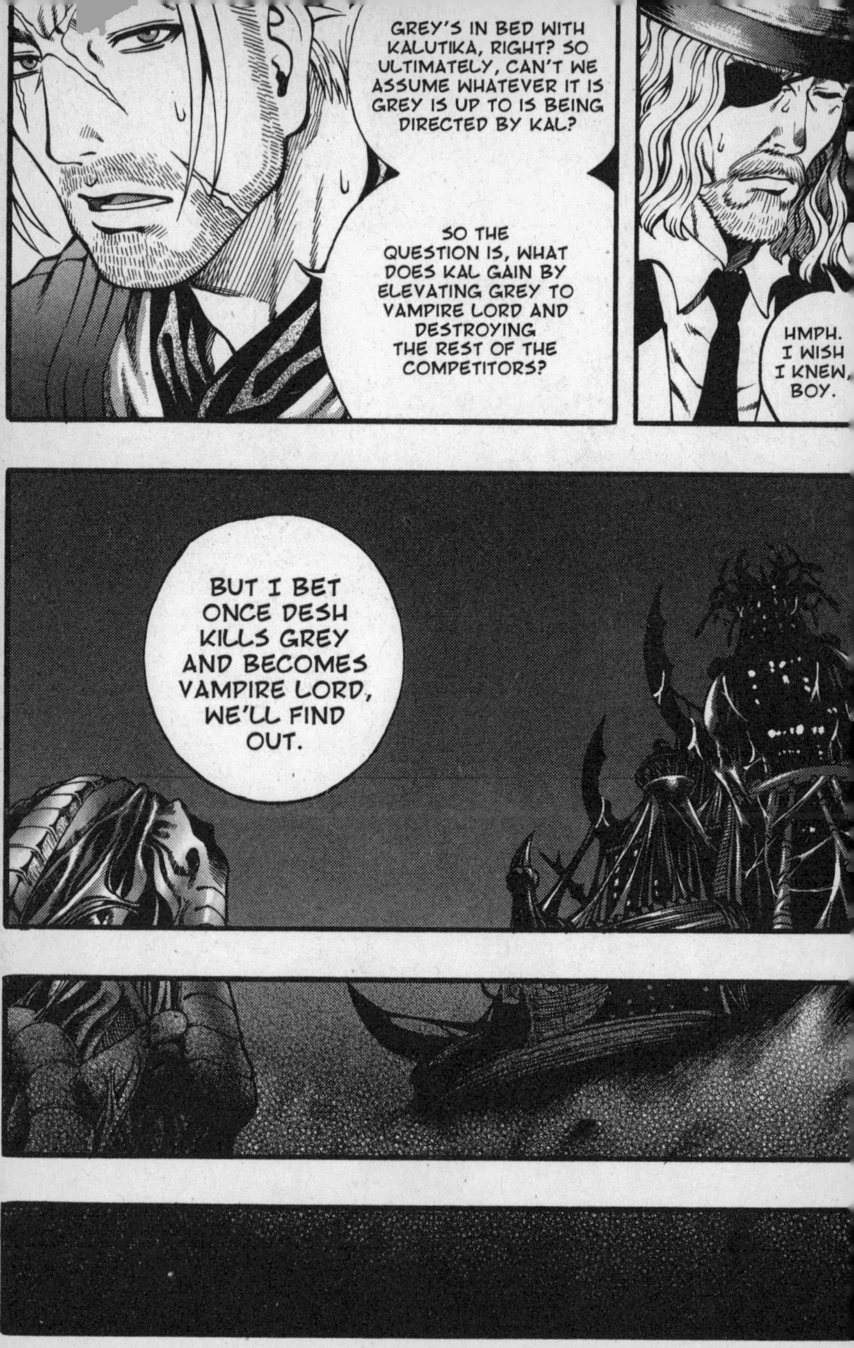
GREY'S IN BED WITH KALUTIKA, RIGHT? SO ULTIMATELY, CAN'T WE ASSUME WHATEVER IT IS GREY IS UP TO IS BEING DIRECTED BY KAL?
SO THE QUESTION IS, WHAT DOES KAL GAIN BY ELEVATING GREY TO VAMPIRE LORD AND DESTROYING THE REST OF THE COMPETITORS?
HMPH. I WISH I KNEW, BOY.
BUT I BET ONCE DESH KILLS GREY AND BECOMES VAMPIRE LORD, WE'LL FIND OUT.

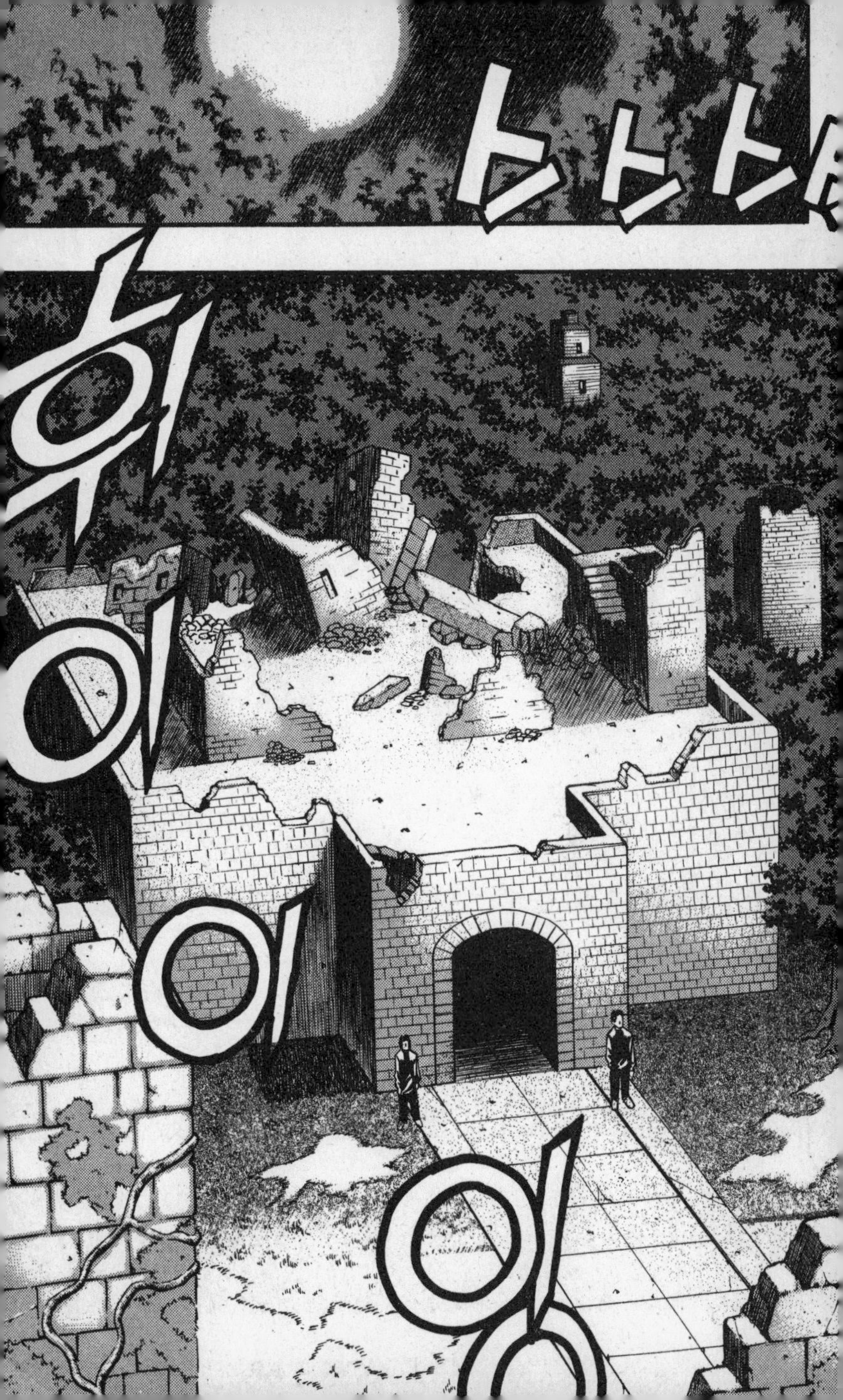
화아아앙

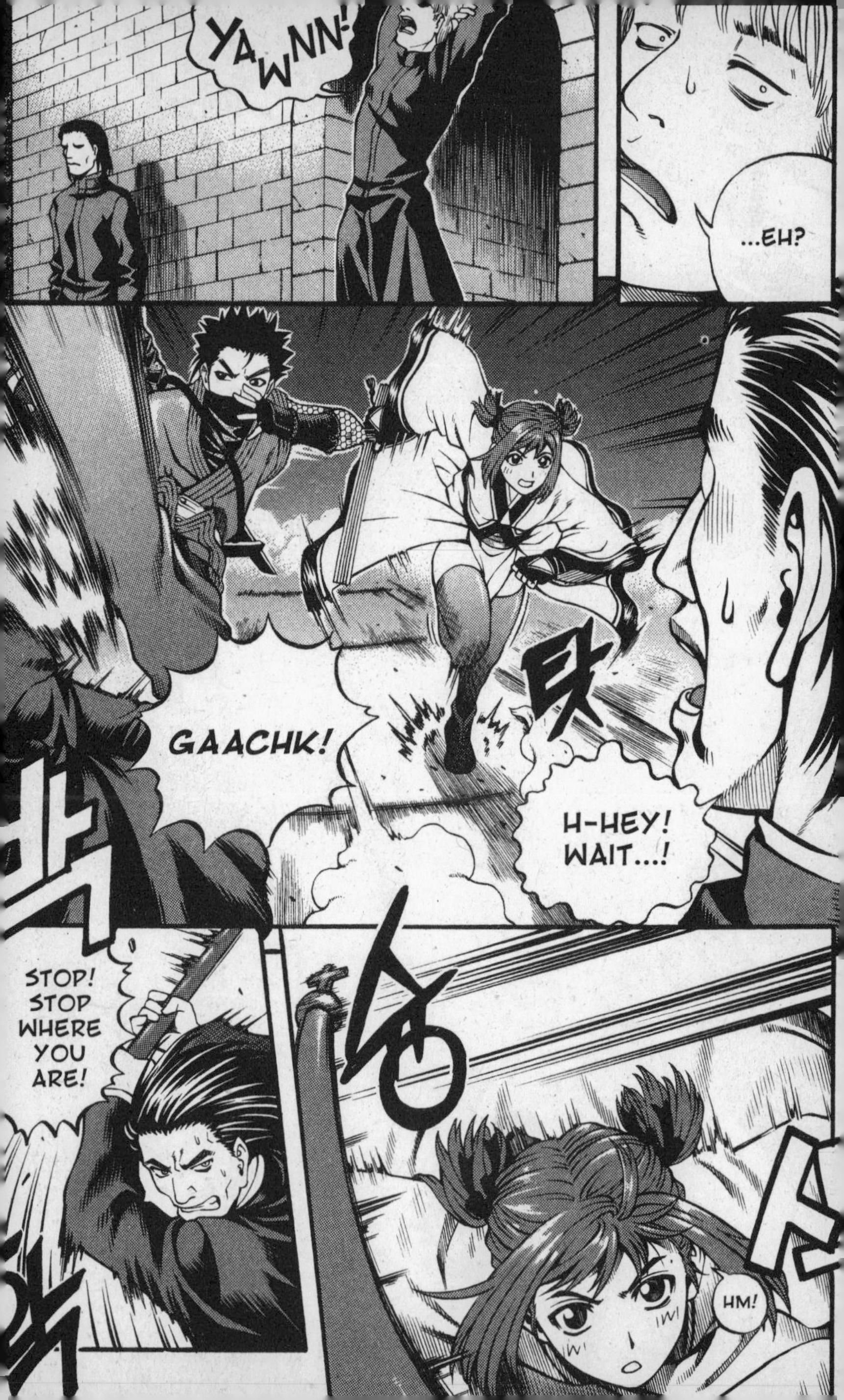
YAWNN!
...EH?
GAACHK!
H-HEY! WAIT...!
STOP! STOP WHERE YOU ARE!
HM!

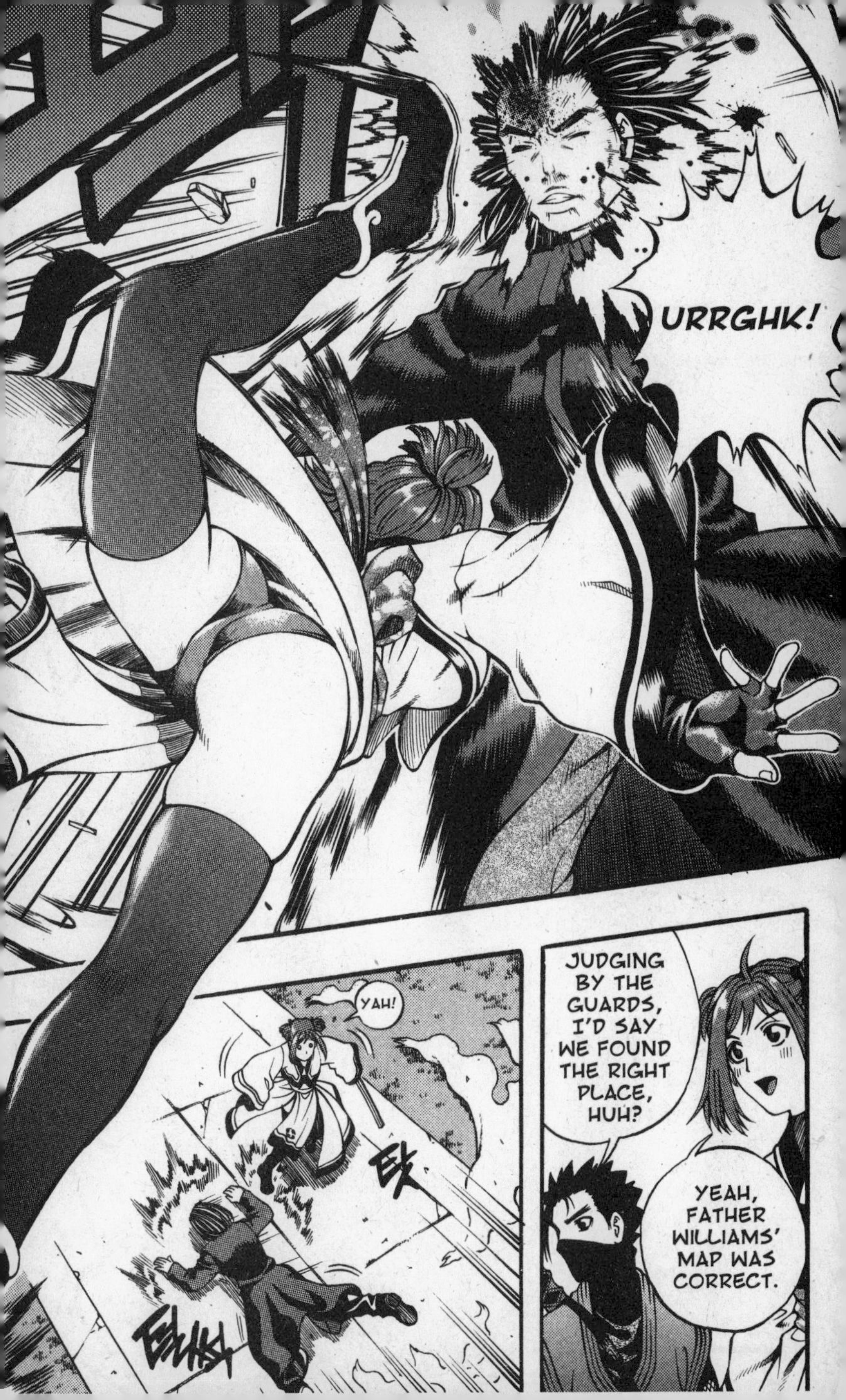
URRGHK!
JUDGING BY THE GUARDS, I'D SAY WE FOUND THE RIGHT PLACE, HUH?
YEAH, FATHER WILLIAMS' MAP WAS CORRECT.
YAH!

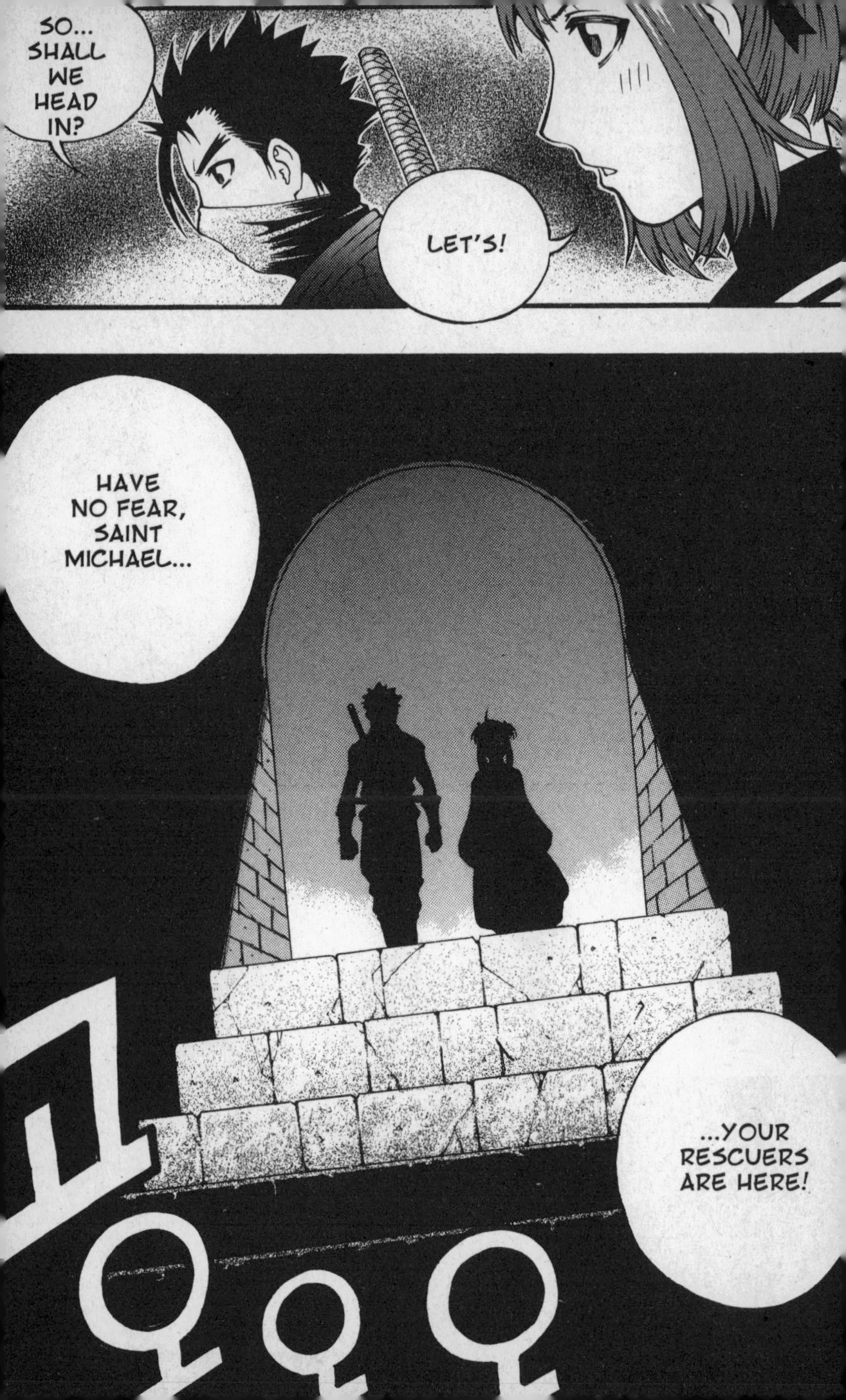
SO... SHALL WE HEAD IN?
LET'S!
HAVE NO FEAR, SAINT MICHAEL...
...YOUR RESCUERS ARE HERE!

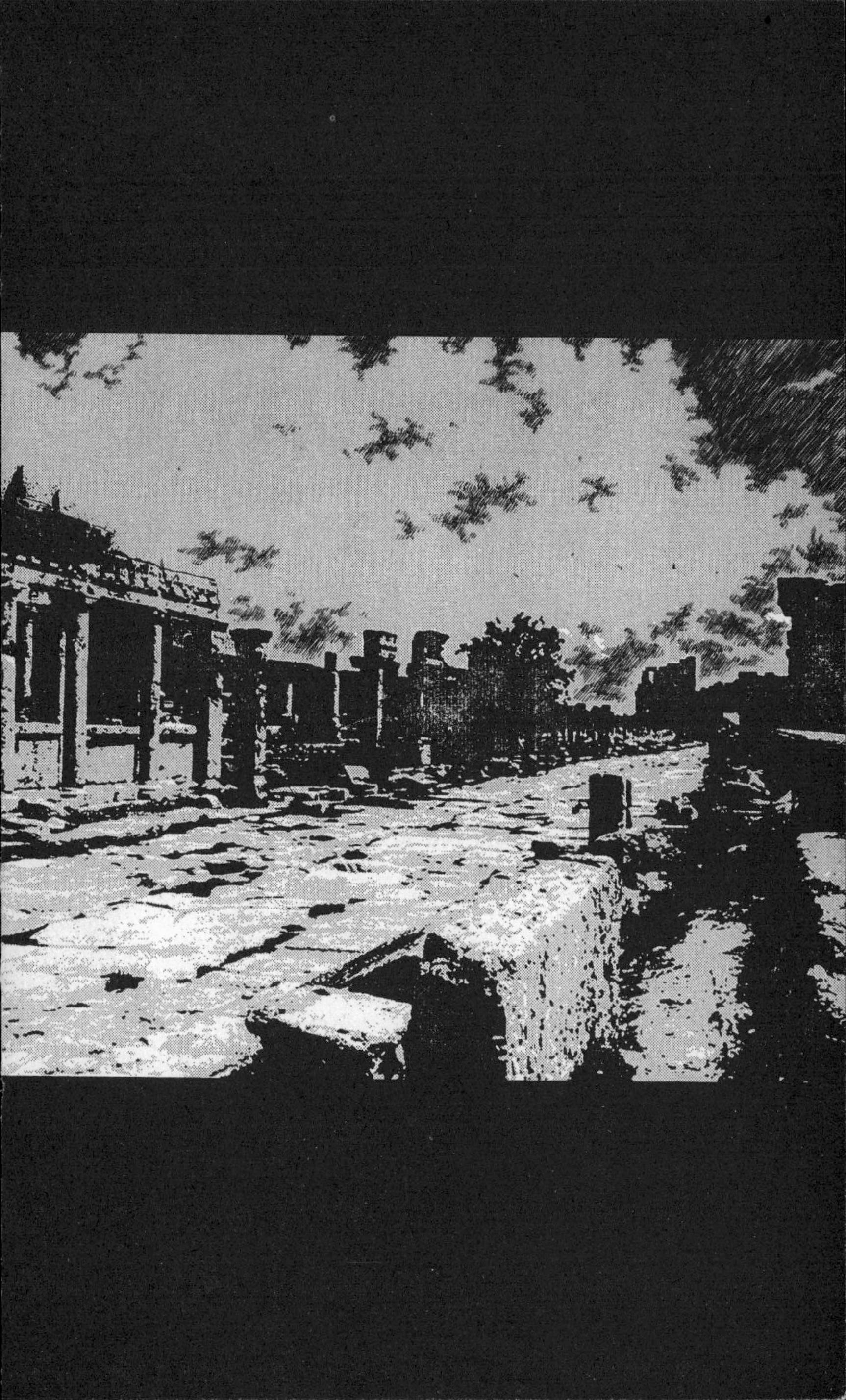

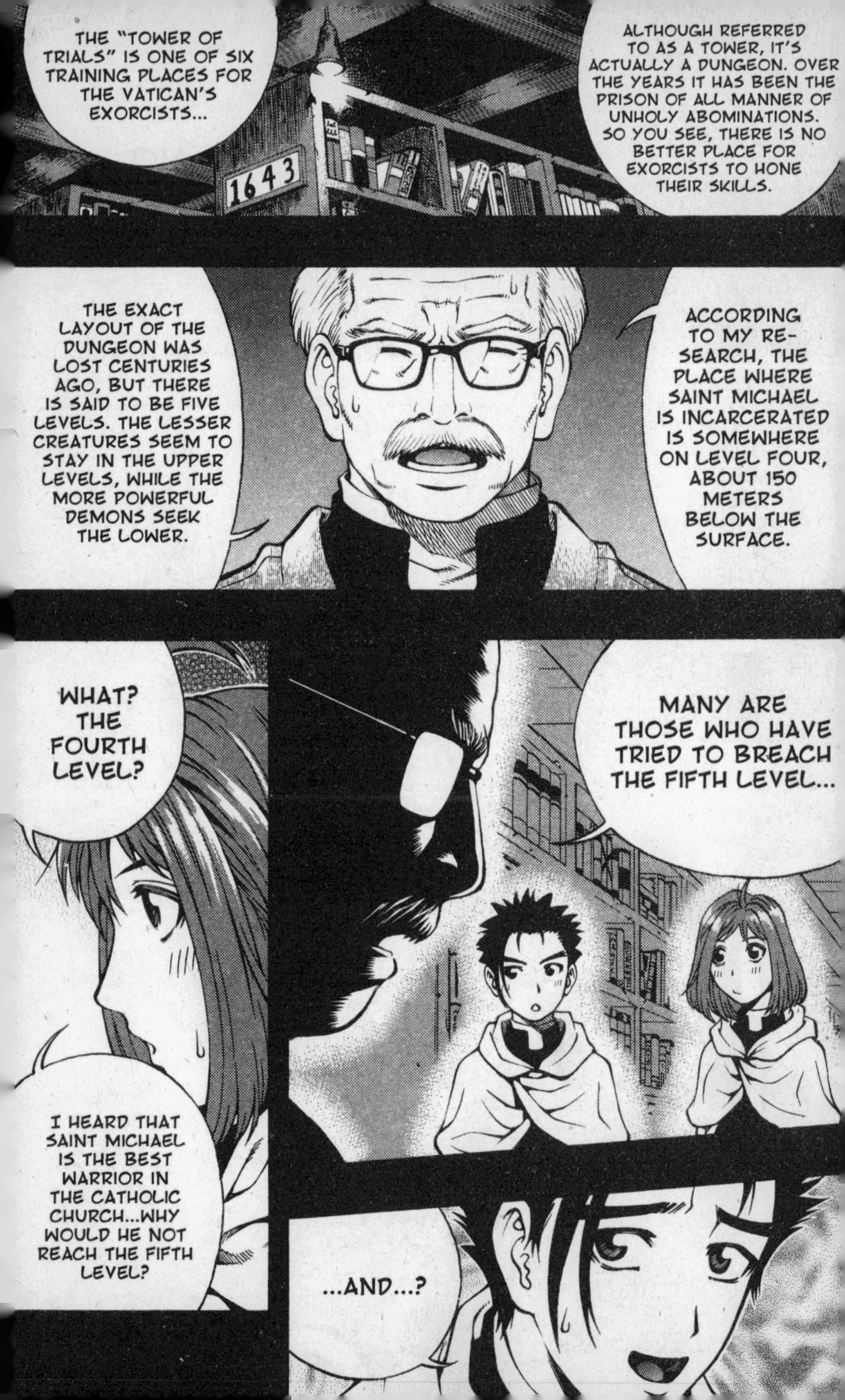

THE "TOWER OF TRIALS" IS ONE OF SIX TRAINING PLACES FOR THE VATICAN'S EXORCISTS...
ALTHOUGH REFERRED TO AS A TOWER, IT'S ACTUALLY A DUNGEON. OVER THE YEARS IT HAS BEEN THE PRISON OF ALL MANNER OF UNHOLY ABOMINATIONS. SO YOU SEE, THERE IS NO BETTER PLACE FOR EXORCISTS TO HONE THEIR SKILLS.
1643
THE EXACT LAYOUT OF THE DUNGEON WAS LOST CENTURIES AGO, BUT THERE IS SAID TO BE FIVE LEVELS. THE LESSER CREATURES SEEM TO STAY IN THE UPPER LEVELS, WHILE THE MORE POWERFUL DEMONS SEEK THE LOWER.
ACCORDING TO MY RE-SEARCH, THE PLACE WHERE SAINT MICHAEL IS INCARCERATED IS SOMEWHERE ON LEVEL FOUR, ABOUT 150 METERS BELOW THE SURFACE.
WHAT? THE FOURTH LEVEL?
I HEARD THAT SAINT MICHAEL IS THE BEST WARRIOR IN THE CATHOLIC CHURCH...WHY WOULD HE NOT REACH THE FIFTH LEVEL?
MANY ARE THOSE WHO HAVE TRIED TO BREACH THE FIFTH LEVEL...
...AND...?

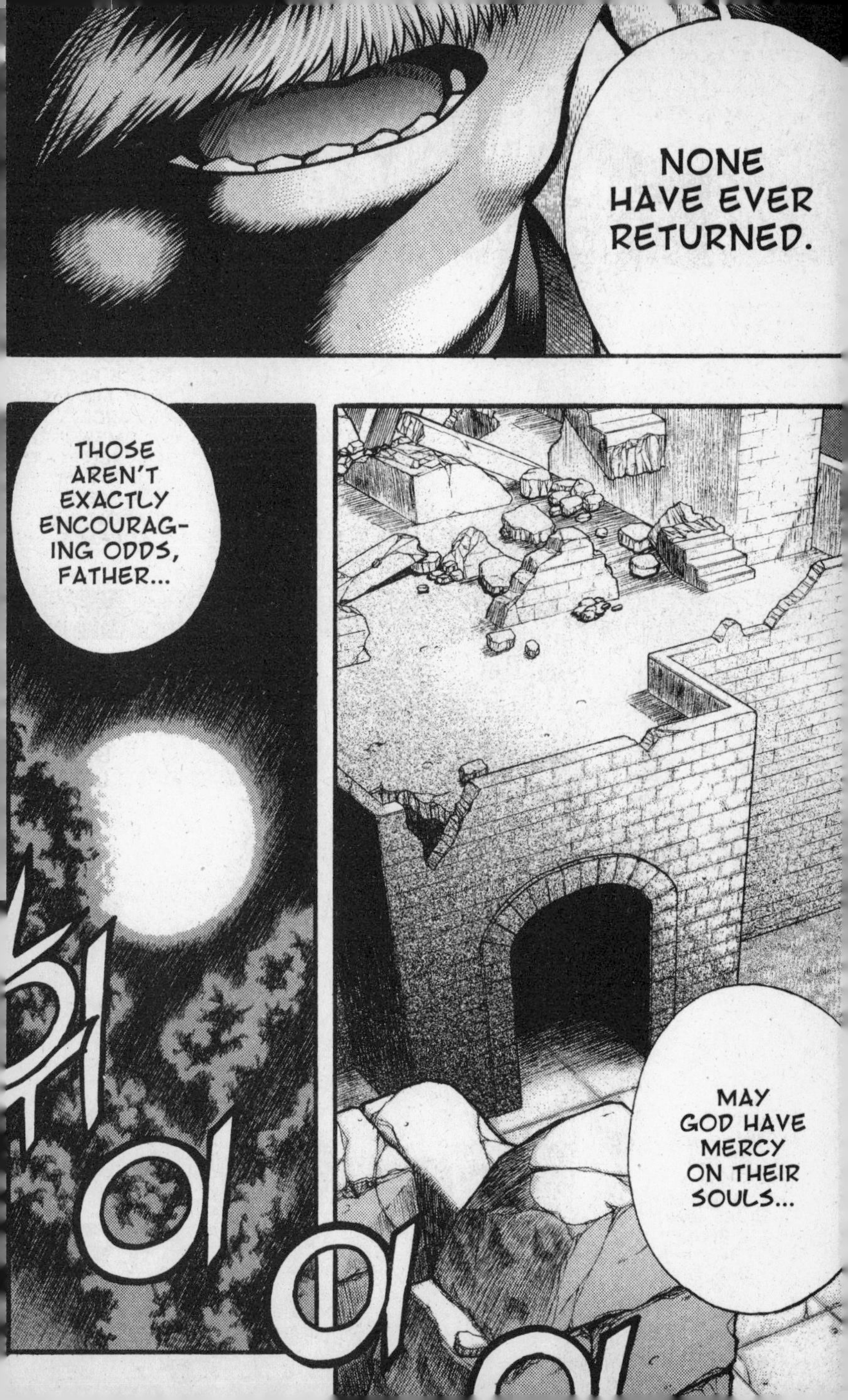
NONE HAVE EVER RETURNED.
THOSE AREN'T EXACTLY ENCOURAG-ING ODDS, FATHER...
MAY GOD HAVE MERCY ON THEIR SOULS...

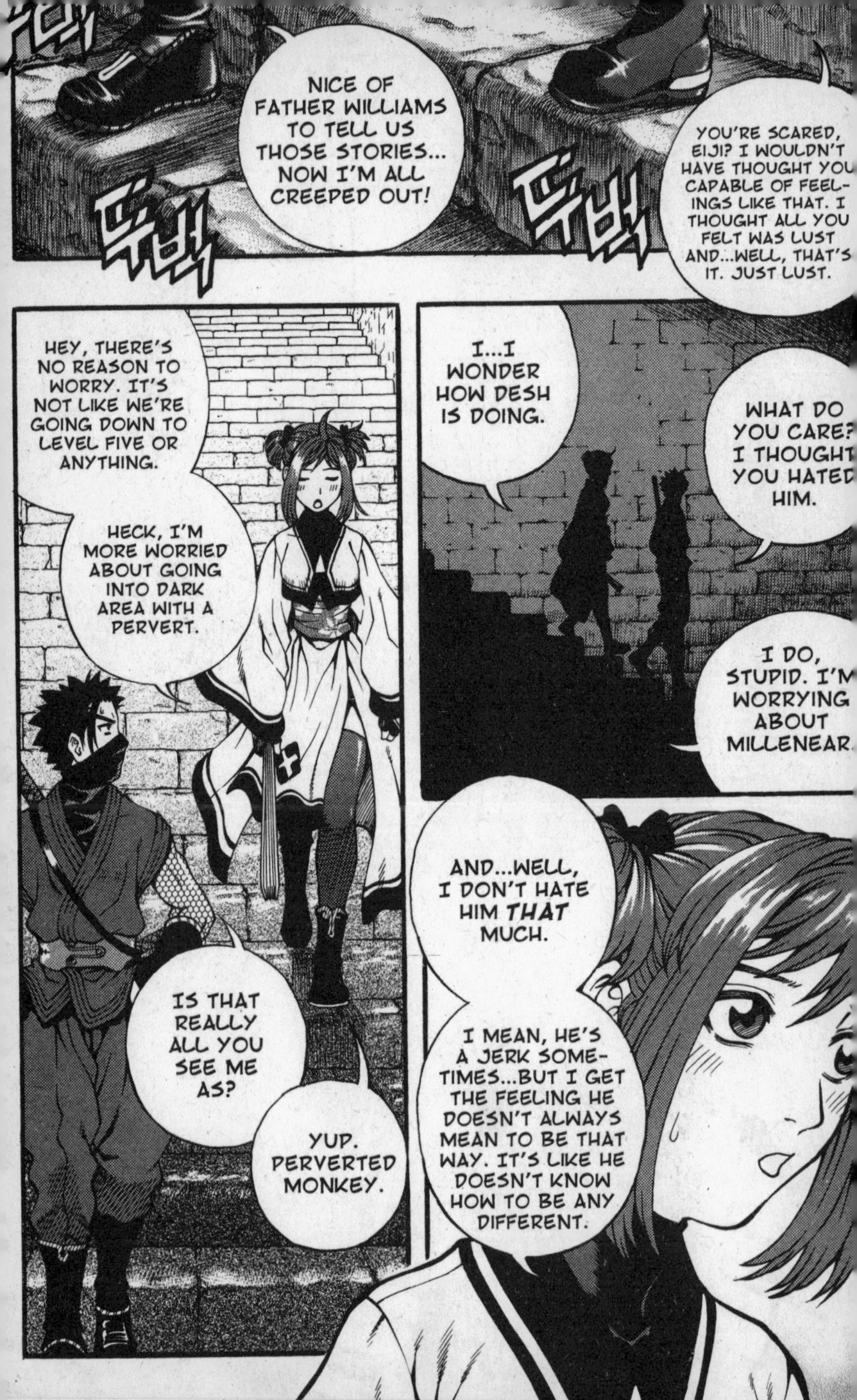
NICE OF FATHER WILLIAMS TO TELL US THOSE STORIES... NOW I'M ALL CREEPED OUT!
YOU'RE SCARED, EIJI? I WOULDN'T HAVE THOUGHT YOU CAPABLE OF FEEL-INGS LIKE THAT. I THOUGHT ALL YOU FELT WAS LUST AND...WELL, THAT'S IT. JUST LUST.
HEY, THERE'S NO REASON TO WORRY. IT'S NOT LIKE WE'RE GOING DOWN TO LEVEL FIVE OR ANYTHING.
HECK, I'M MORE WORRIED ABOUT GOING INTO DARK AREA WITH A PERVERT.
IS THAT REALLY ALL YOU SEE ME AS?
YUP. PERVERTED MONKEY.
I...I WONDER HOW DESH IS DOING.
WHAT DO YOU CARE? I THOUGHT YOU HATED HIM.
I DO, STUPID. I'M WORRYING ABOUT MILLENEAR.
AND...WELL, I DON'T HATE HIM *THAT* MUCH.
I MEAN, HE'S A JERK SOME-TIMES...BUT I GET THE FEELING HE DOESN'T ALWAYS MEAN TO BE THAT WAY. IT'S LIKE HE DOESN'T KNOW HOW TO BE ANY DIFFERENT.

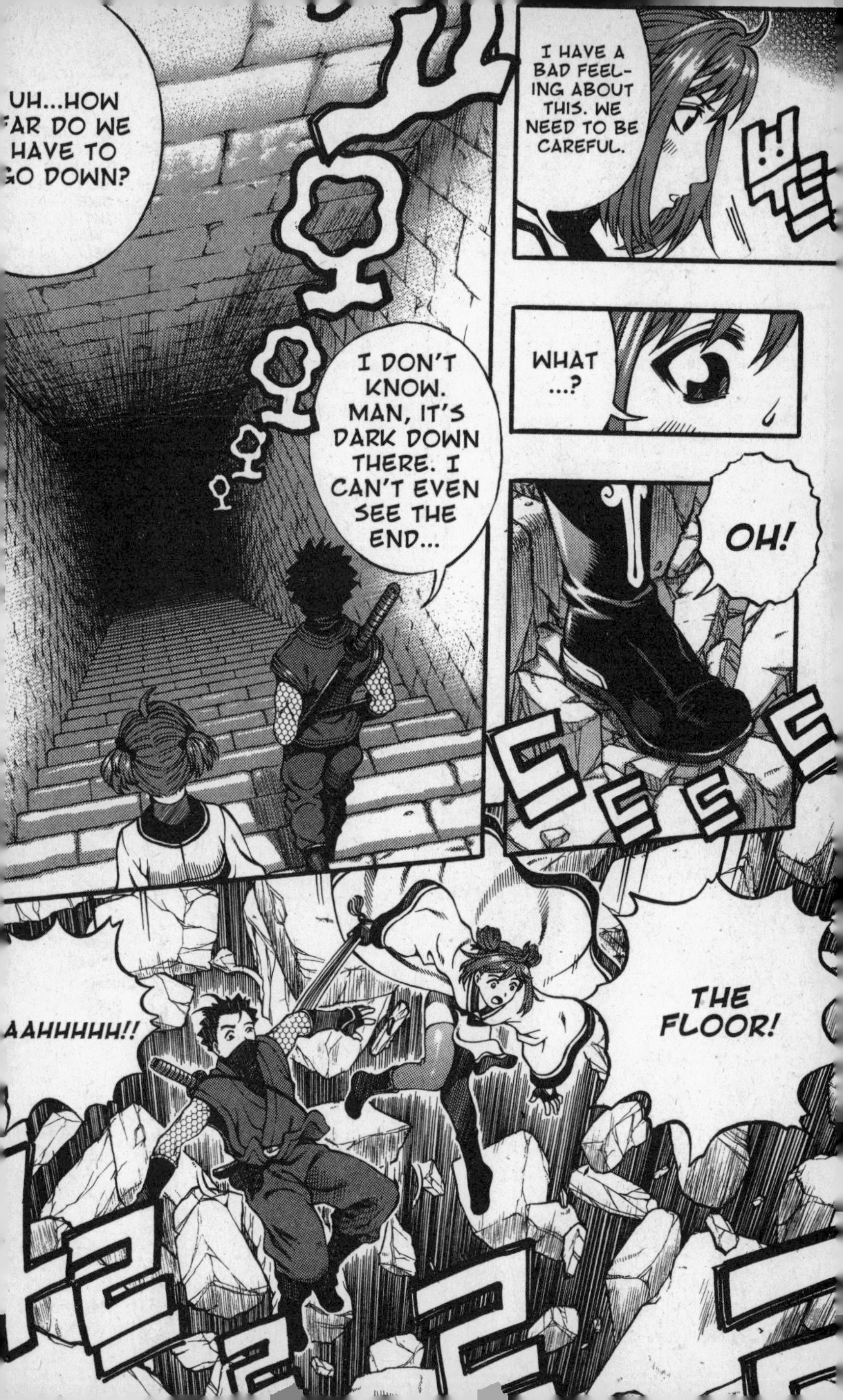
I HAVE A BAD FEEL-ING ABOUT THIS. WE NEED TO BE CAREFUL.
UH...HOW FAR DO WE HAVE TO GO DOWN?
I DON'T KNOW. MAN, IT'S DARK DOWN THERE. I CAN'T EVEN SEE THE END...
WHAT ...?
OH!
THE FLOOR!
AAHHHHH!!

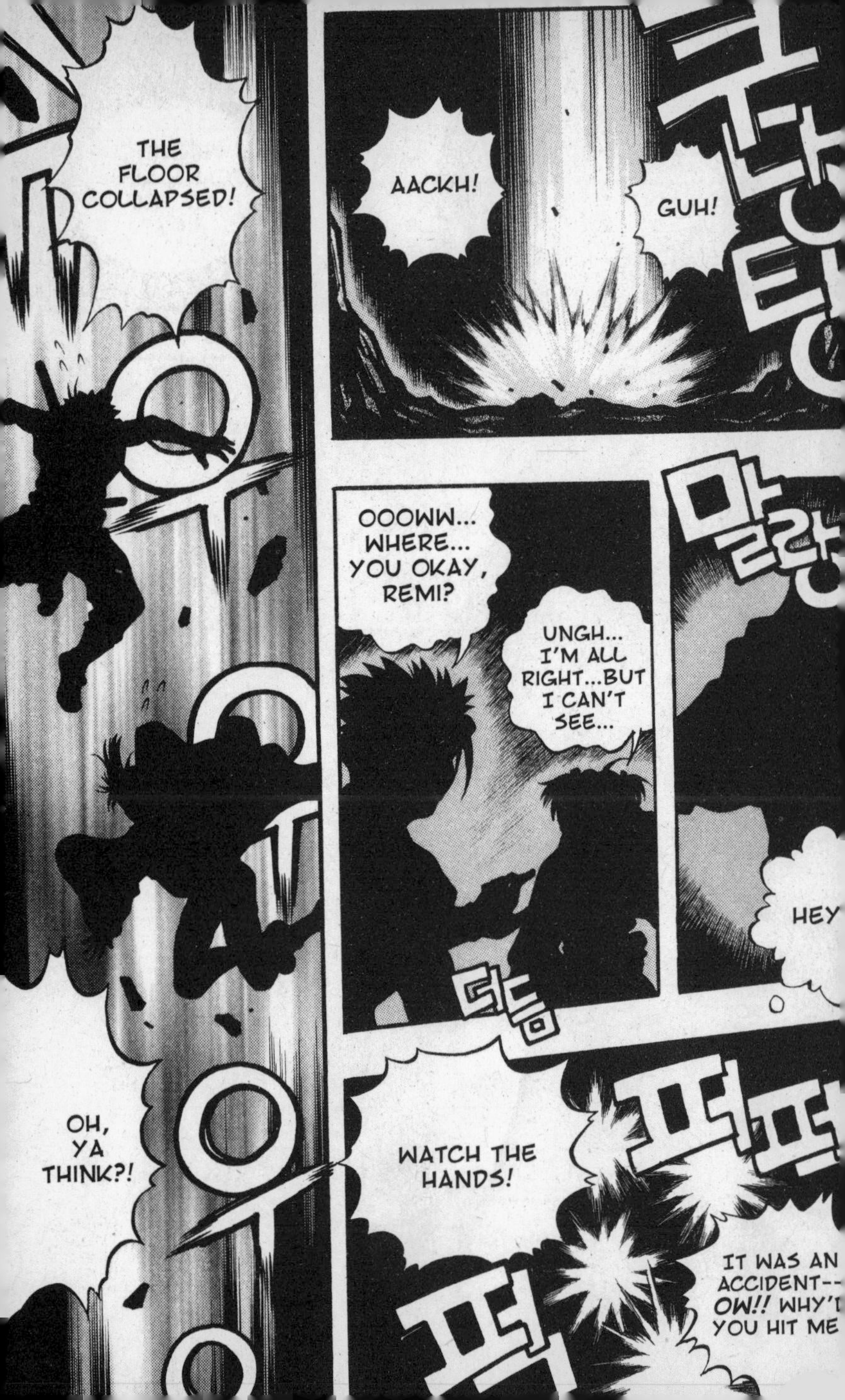
THE FLOOR COLLAPSED!
OH, YA THINK?!
AACKH!
GUH!
OOOWW... WHERE... YOU OKAY, REMI?
UNGH... I'M ALL RIGHT...BUT I CAN'T SEE...
더듬
HEY
WATCH THE HANDS!
퍽
IT WAS AN ACCIDENT-- *OW!!* WHY'
YOU HIT ME

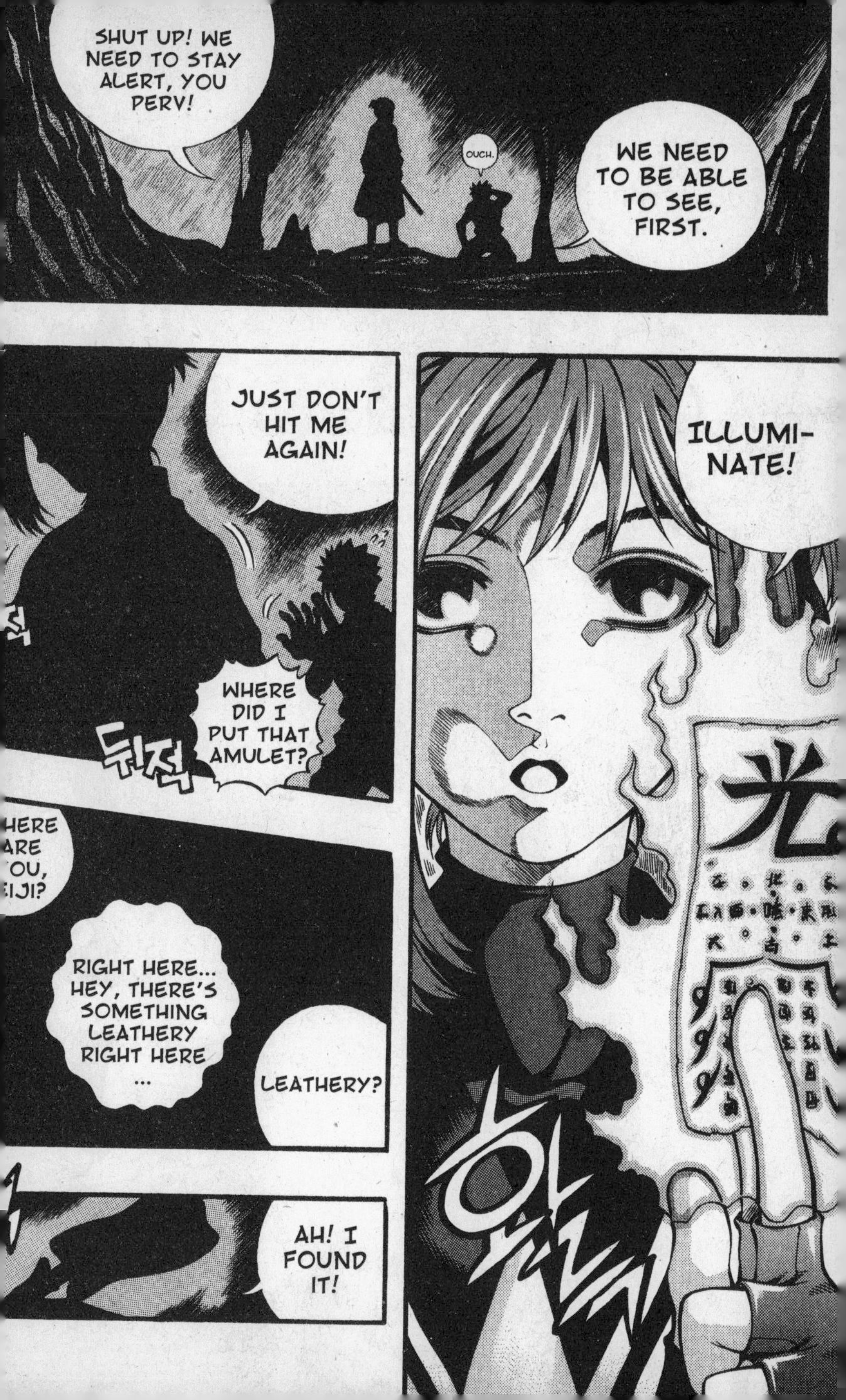

SHUT UP! WE NEED TO STAY ALERT, YOU PERV!
OUCH.
WE NEED TO BE ABLE TO SEE, FIRST.
JUST DON'T HIT ME AGAIN!
WHERE DID I PUT THAT AMULET?
HERE ARE OU, EIJI?
RIGHT HERE... HEY, THERE'S SOMETHING LEATHERY RIGHT HERE ...
LEATHERY?
AH! I FOUND IT!
ILLUMI-NATE!
光

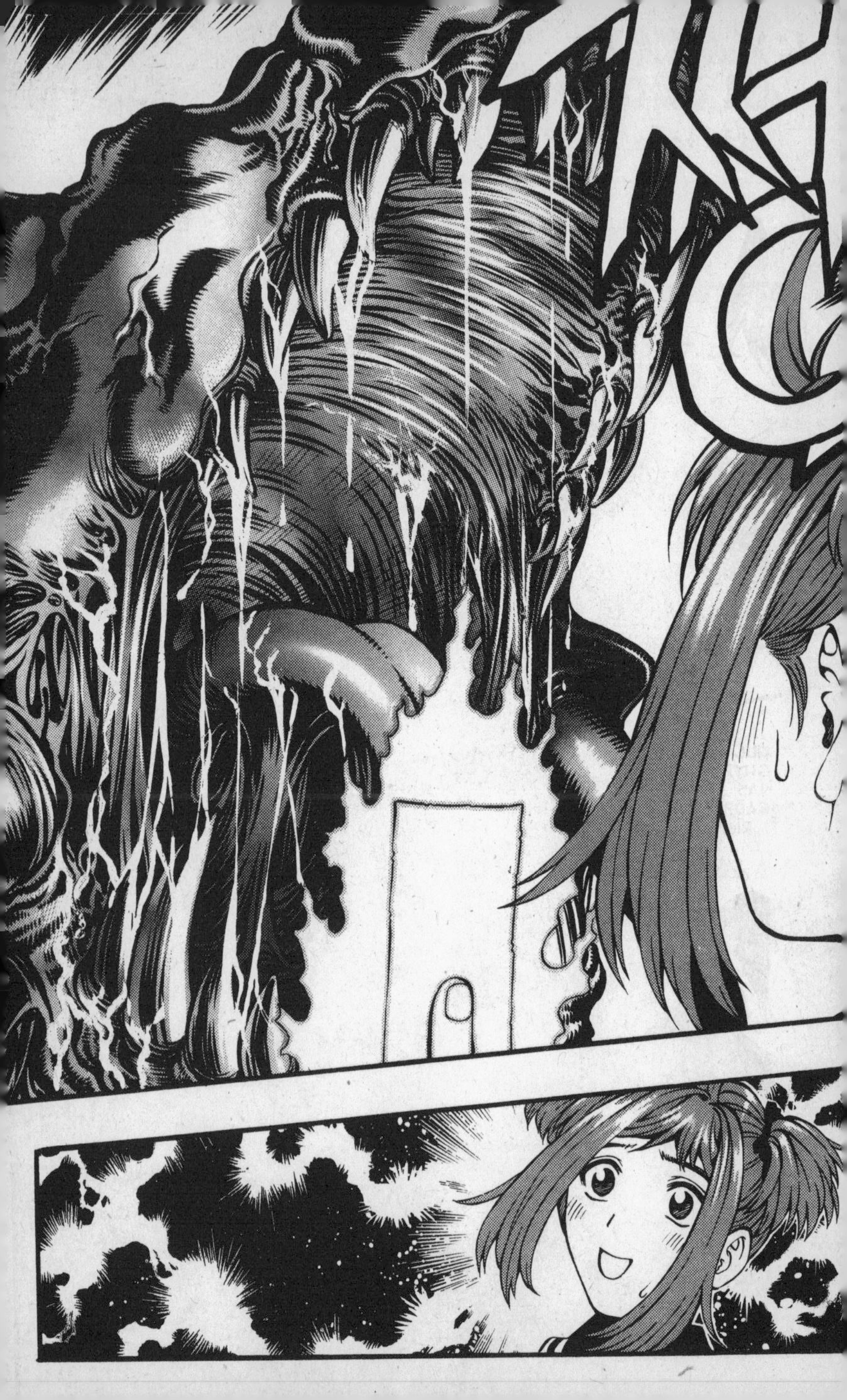

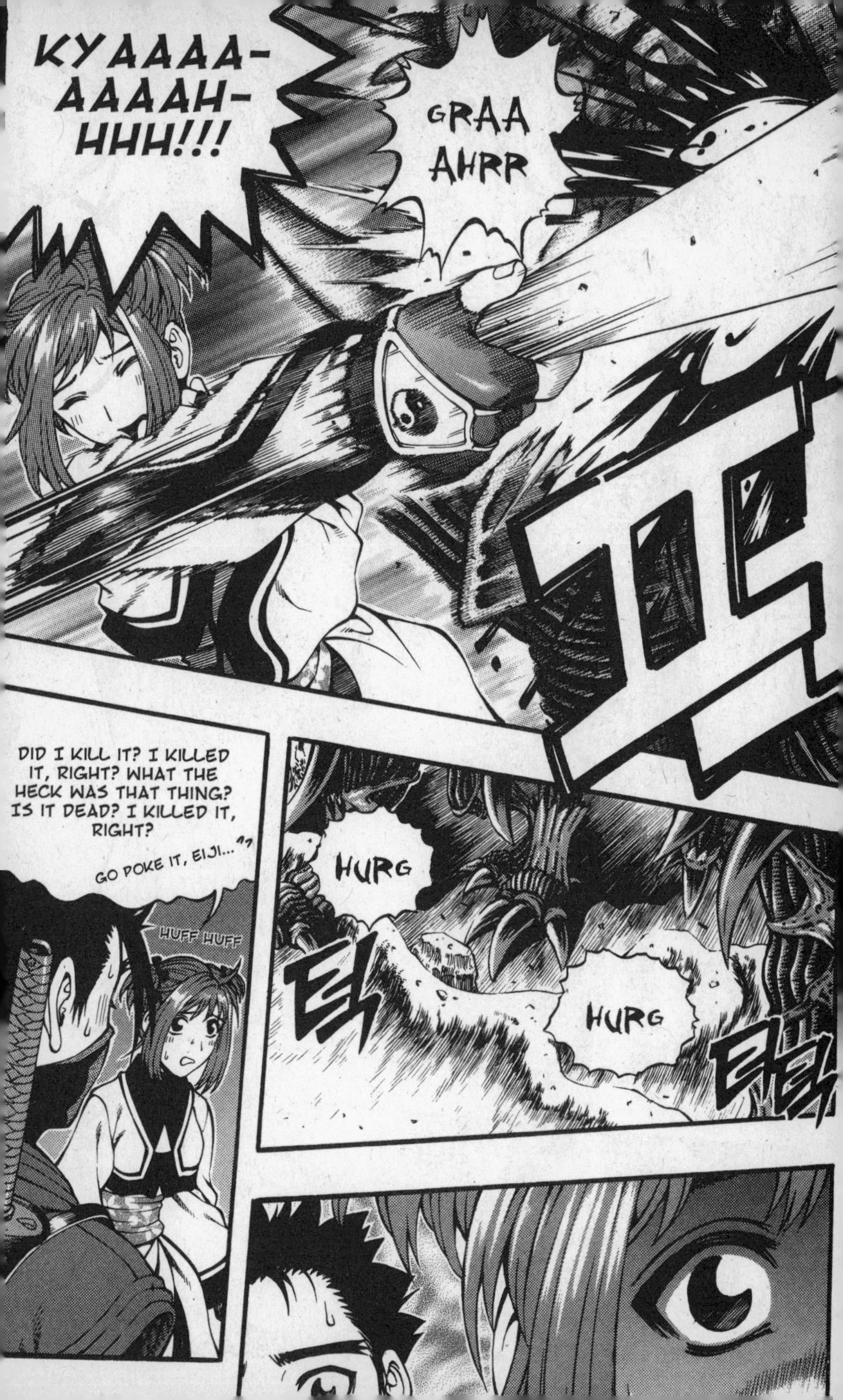
KYAAAA-AAAAH-HHH!!!
GRAA AHRR
DID I KILL IT? I KILLED IT, RIGHT? WHAT THE HECK WAS THAT THING? IS IT DEAD? I KILLED IT, RIGHT?
GO POKE IT, EIJI...
HUFF HUFF
HURG
HURG

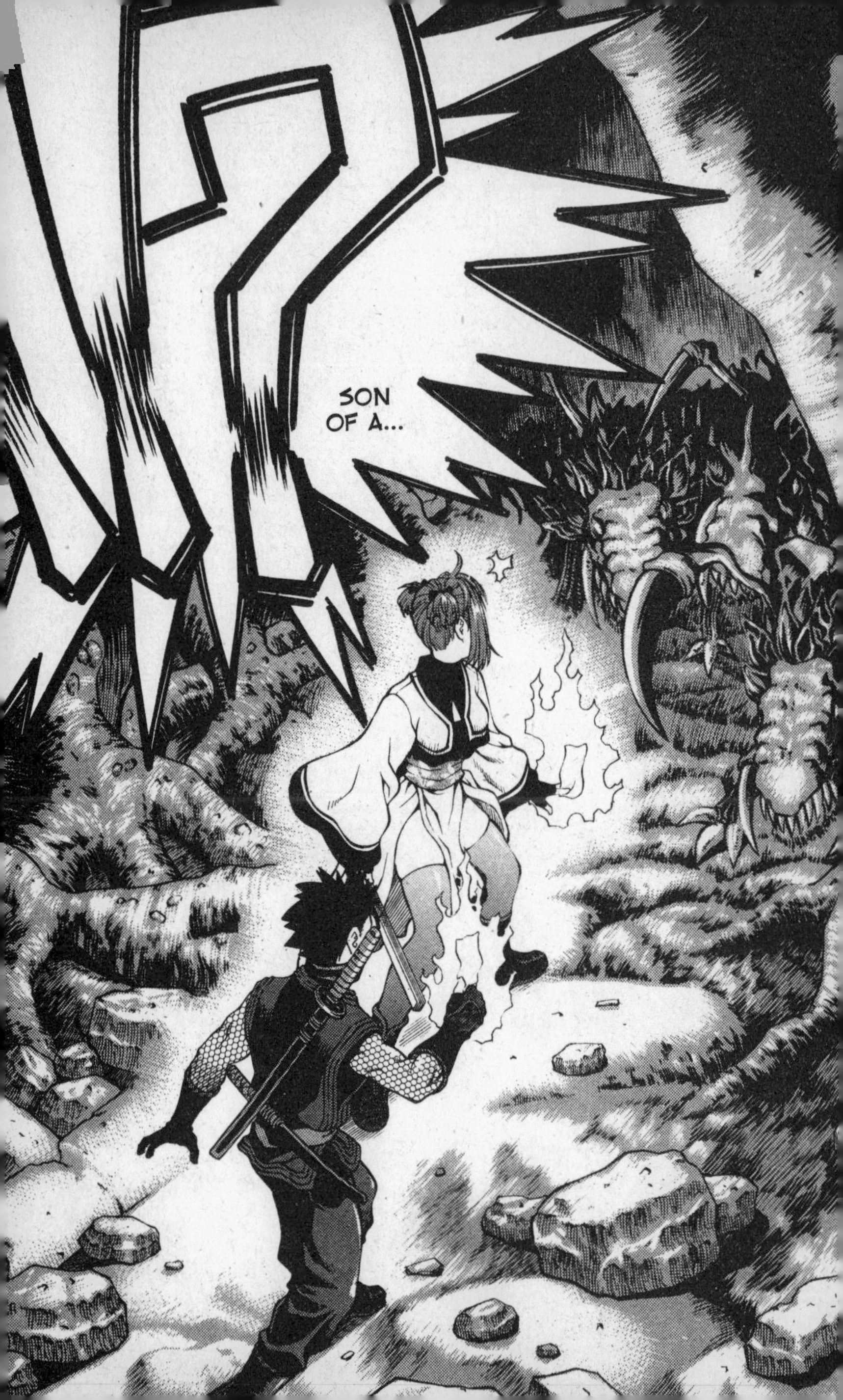
SON
OF A...

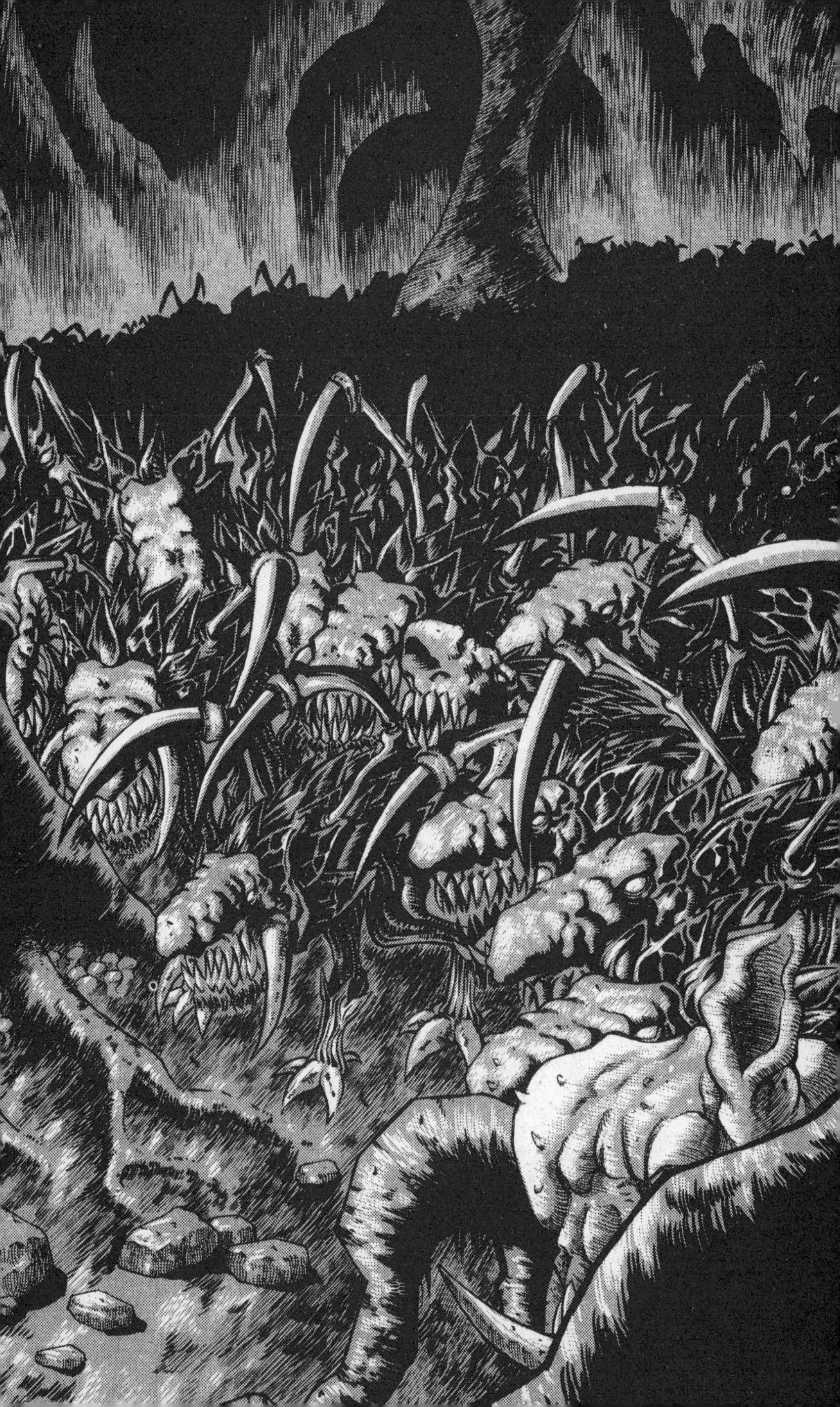

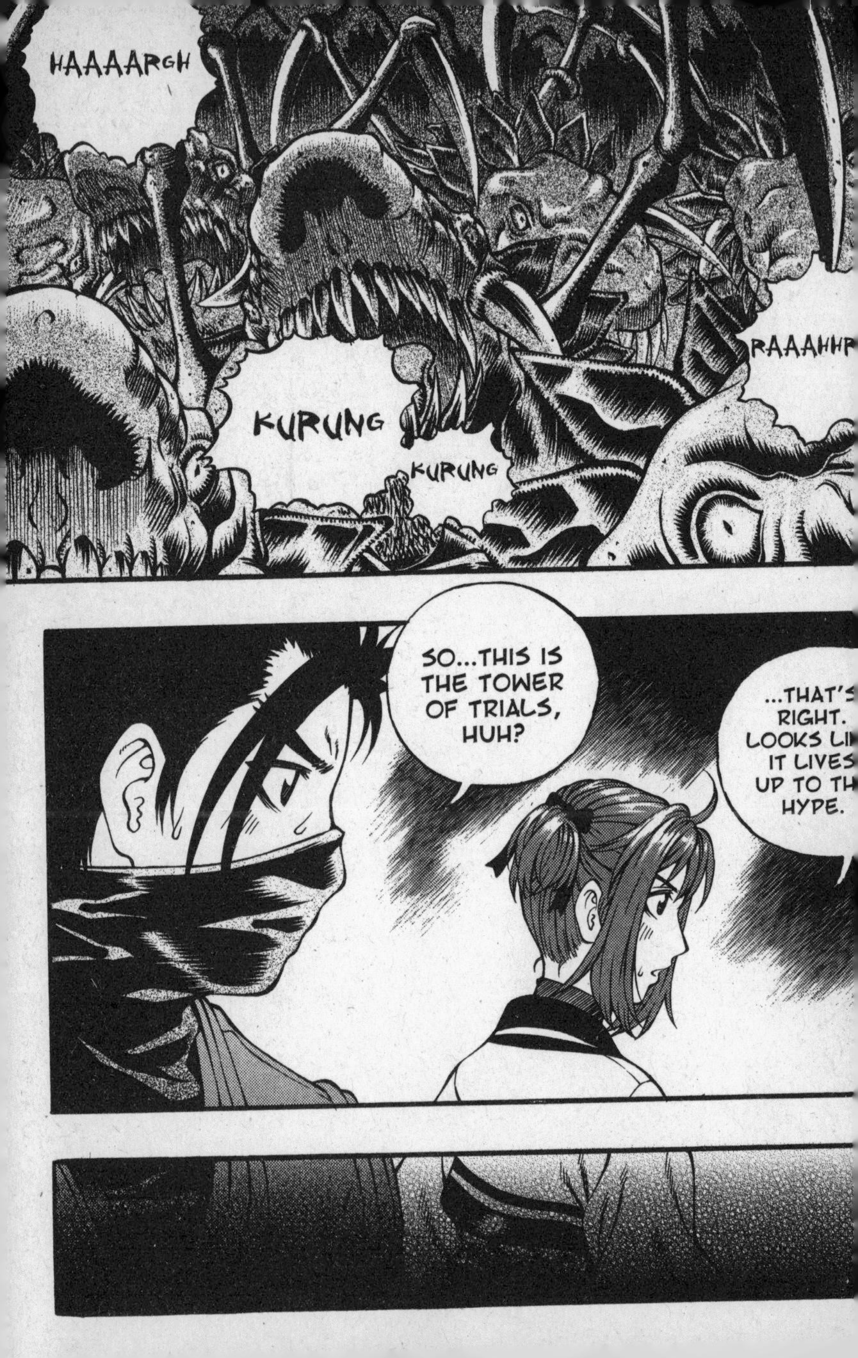
HAAAARGH
RAAAHHP
KURUNG
KURUNG
SO...THIS IS THE TOWER OF TRIALS, HUH?
...THAT'S RIGHT. LOOKS LI IT LIVES UP TO TH HYPE.

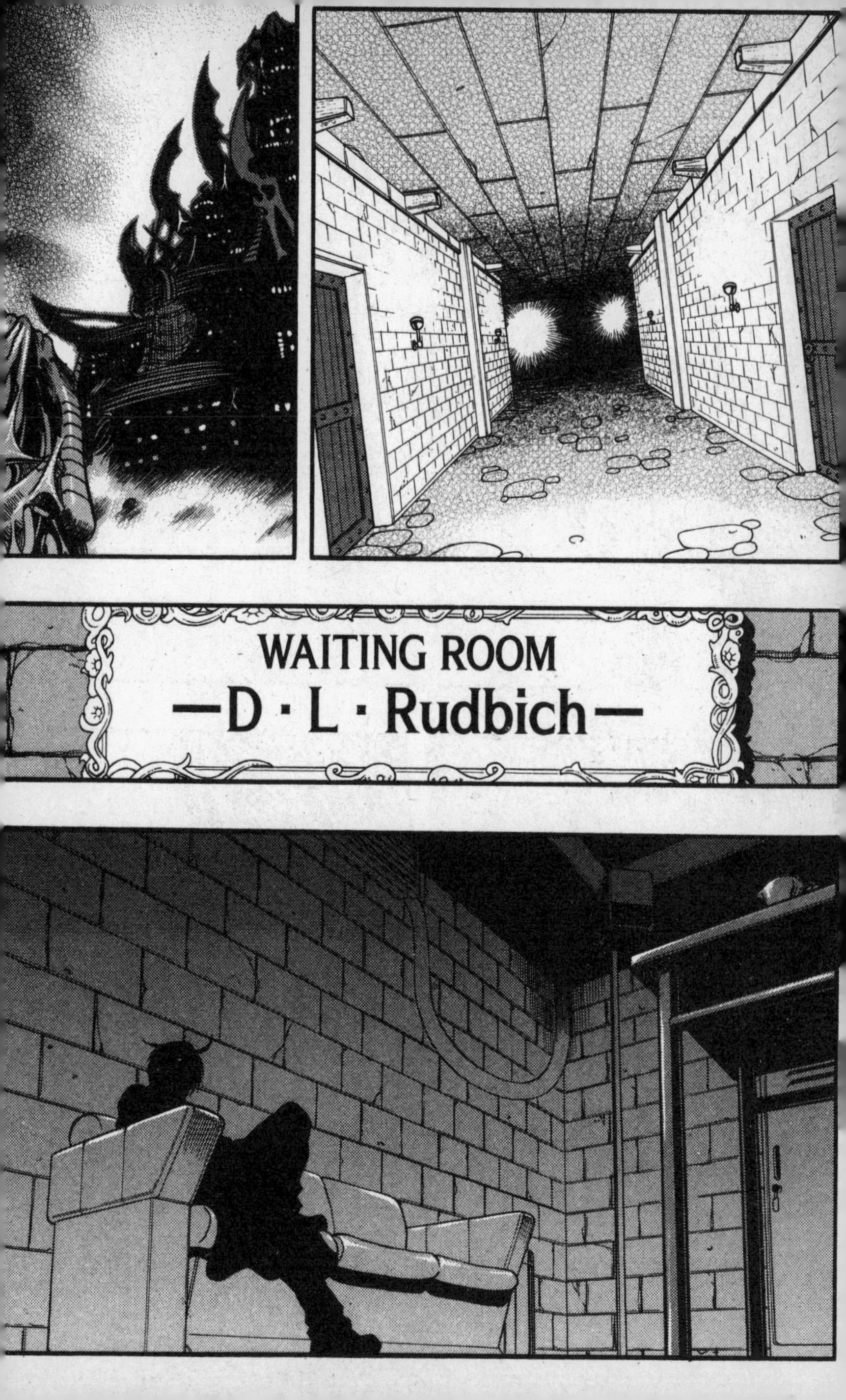
WAITING ROOM
—D · L · Rudbich—

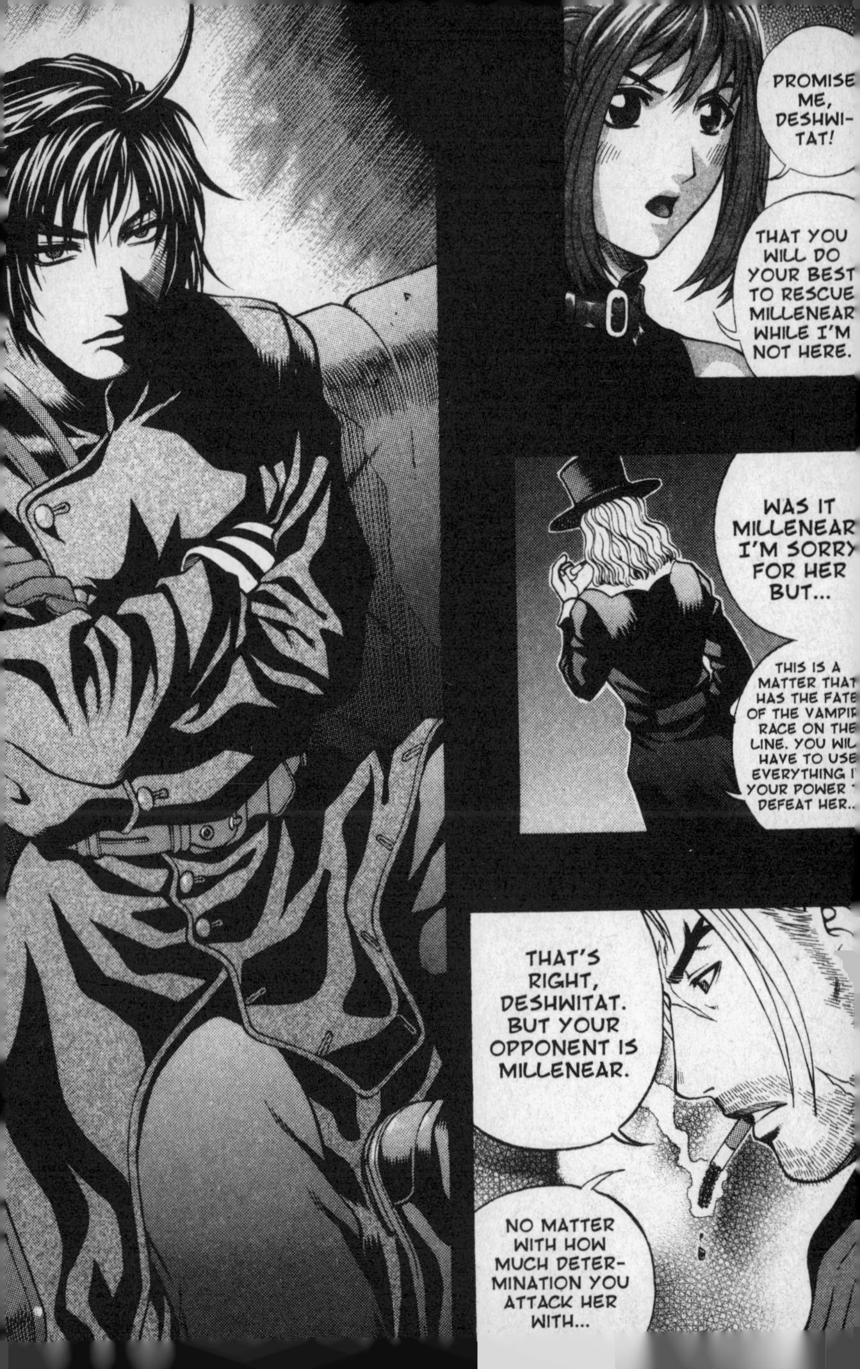
PROMISE ME, DESHWI-TAT!
THAT YOU WILL DO YOUR BEST TO RESCUE MILLENEAR WHILE I'M NOT HERE.
WAS IT MILLENEAR I'M SORRY FOR HER BUT...
THIS IS A MATTER THAT HAS THE FATE OF THE VAMPIR RACE ON THE LINE. YOU WIL HAVE TO USE EVERYTHING I YOUR POWER DEFEAT HER..
THAT'S RIGHT, DESHWITAT. BUT YOUR OPPONENT IS MILLENEAR.
NO MATTER WITH HOW MUCH DETER-MINATION YOU ATTACK HER WITH...

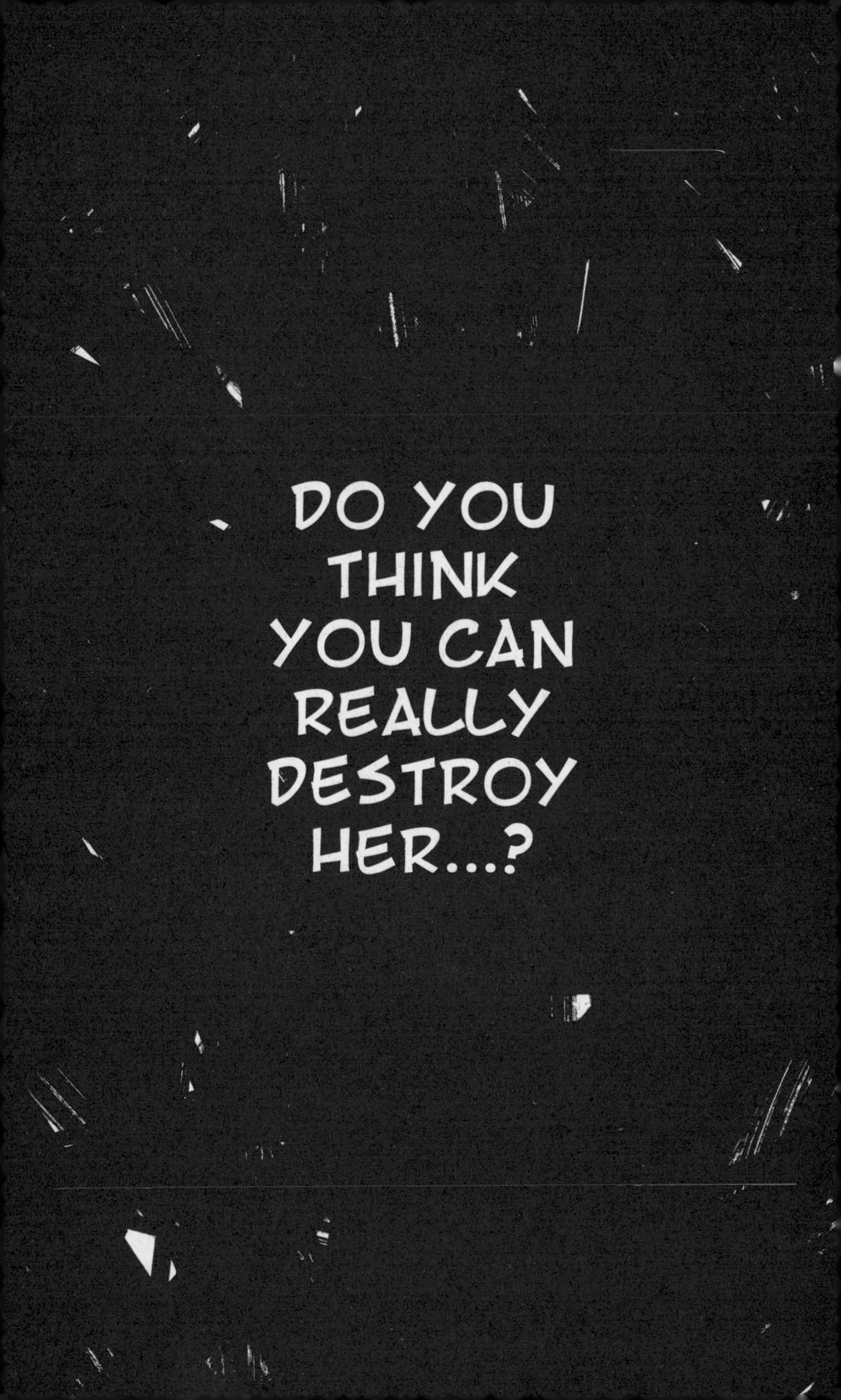
DO YOU THINK YOU CAN REALLY DESTROY HER...?

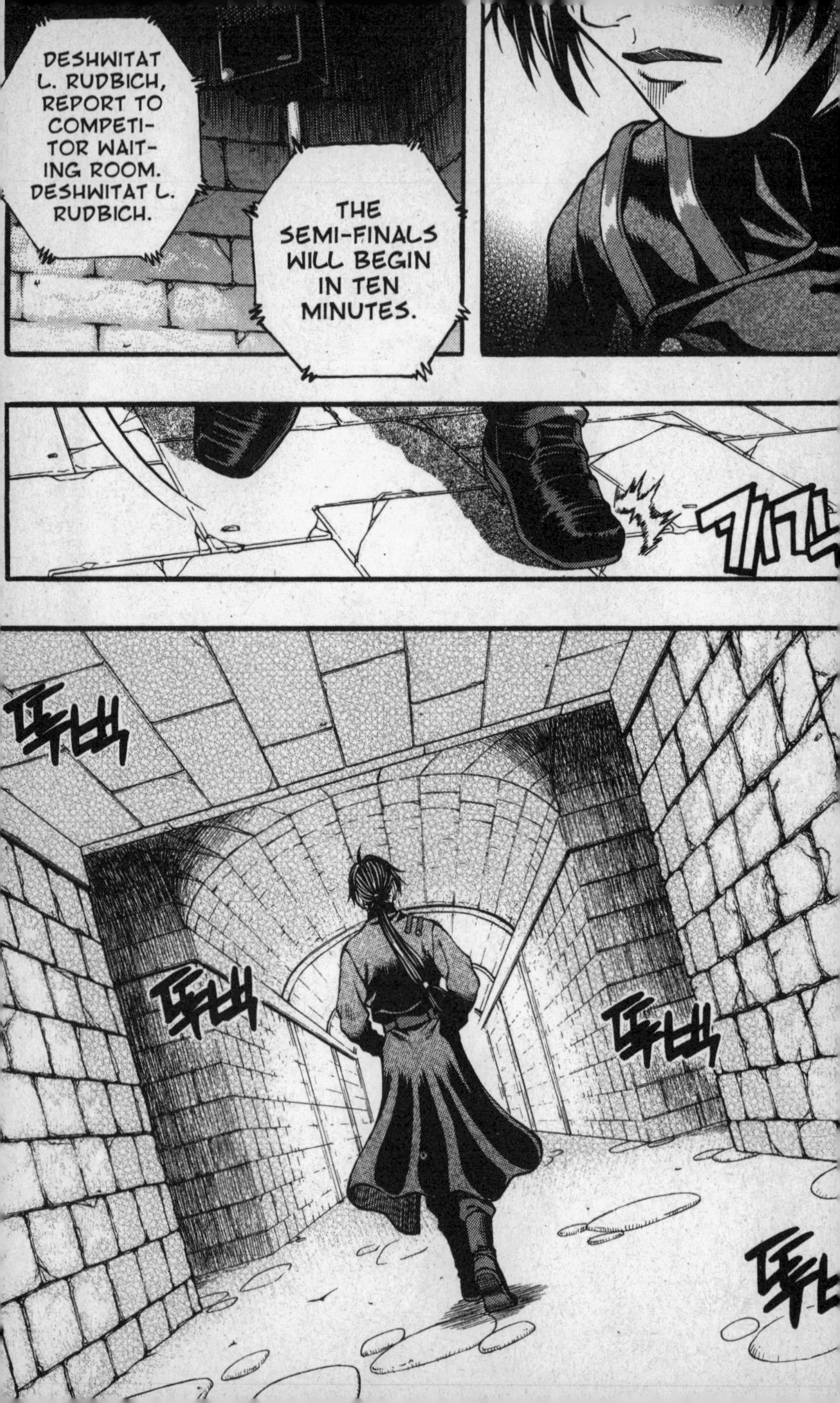
DESHWITAT L. RUDBICH, REPORT TO COMPETITOR WAITING ROOM. DESHWITAT L. RUDBICH.
THE SEMI-FINALS WILL BEGIN IN TEN MINUTES.
뚜벅
뚜벅
뚜벅
뚜벅

Chapter 72: Love and Hate

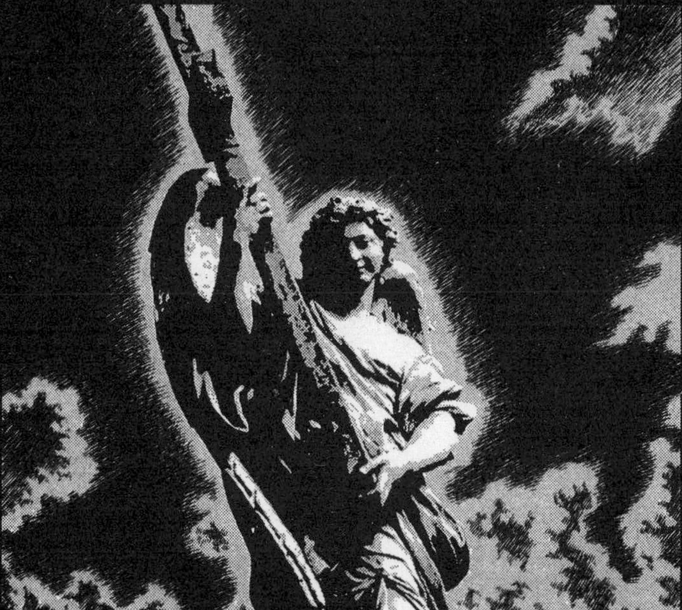

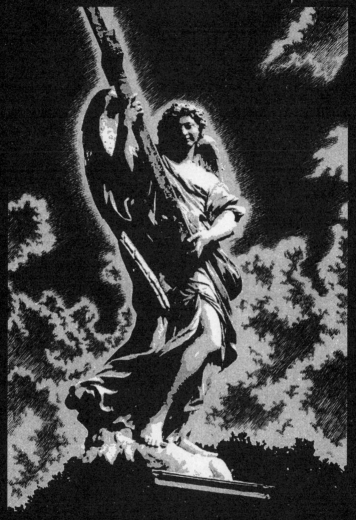

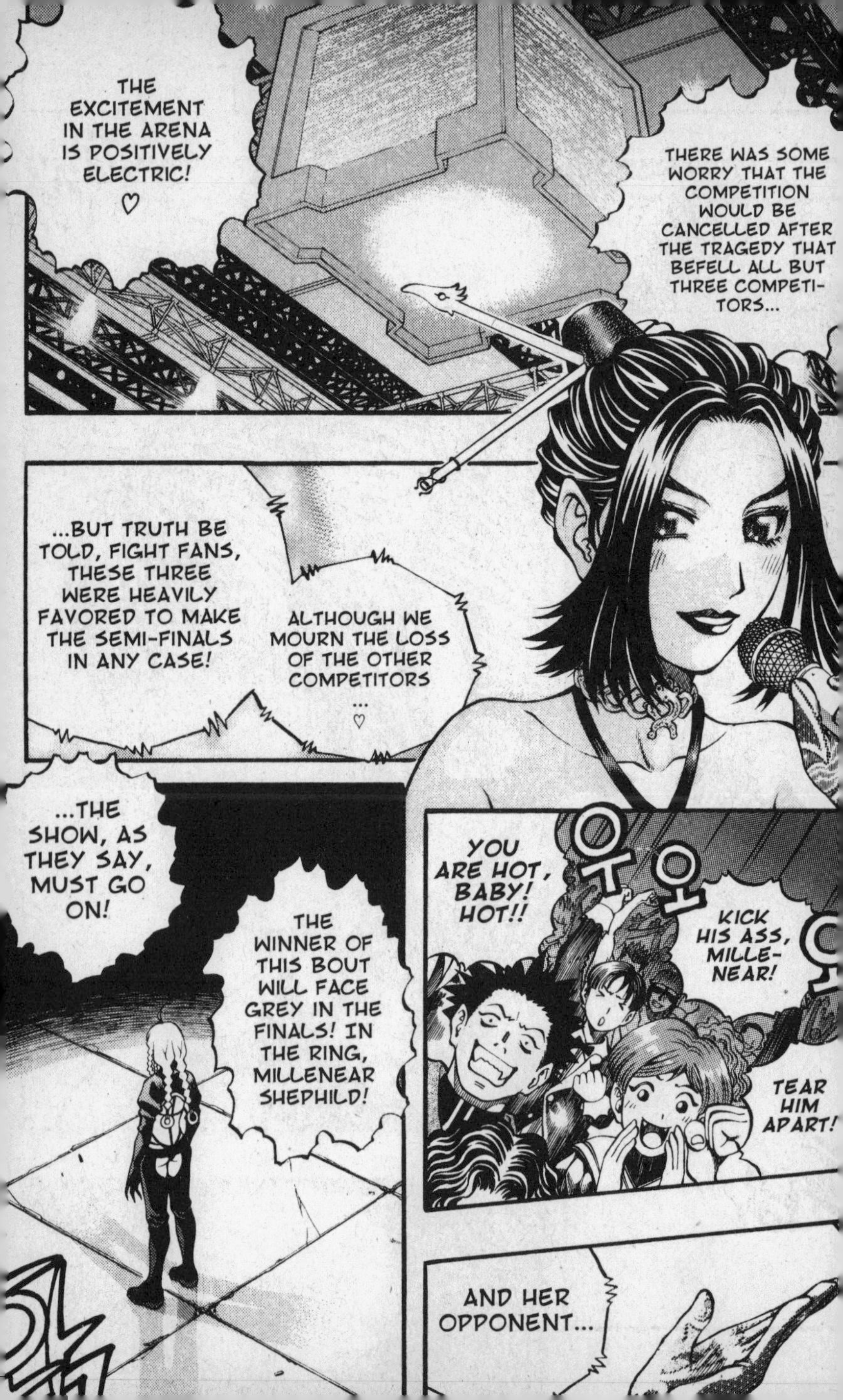

THE EXCITEMENT IN THE ARENA IS POSITIVELY ELECTRIC! ♡
THERE WAS SOME WORRY THAT THE COMPETITION WOULD BE CANCELLED AFTER THE TRAGEDY THAT BEFELL ALL BUT THREE COMPETITORS...
...BUT TRUTH BE TOLD, FIGHT FANS, THESE THREE WERE HEAVILY FAVORED TO MAKE THE SEMI-FINALS IN ANY CASE!
ALTHOUGH WE MOURN THE LOSS OF THE OTHER COMPETITORS ... ♡
...THE SHOW, AS THEY SAY, MUST GO ON!
THE WINNER OF THIS BOUT WILL FACE GREY IN THE FINALS! IN THE RING, MILLENEAR SHEPHILD!
YOU ARE HOT, BABY! HOT!!
KICK HIS ASS, MILLE-NEAR!
TEAR HIM APART!
AND HER OPPONENT...

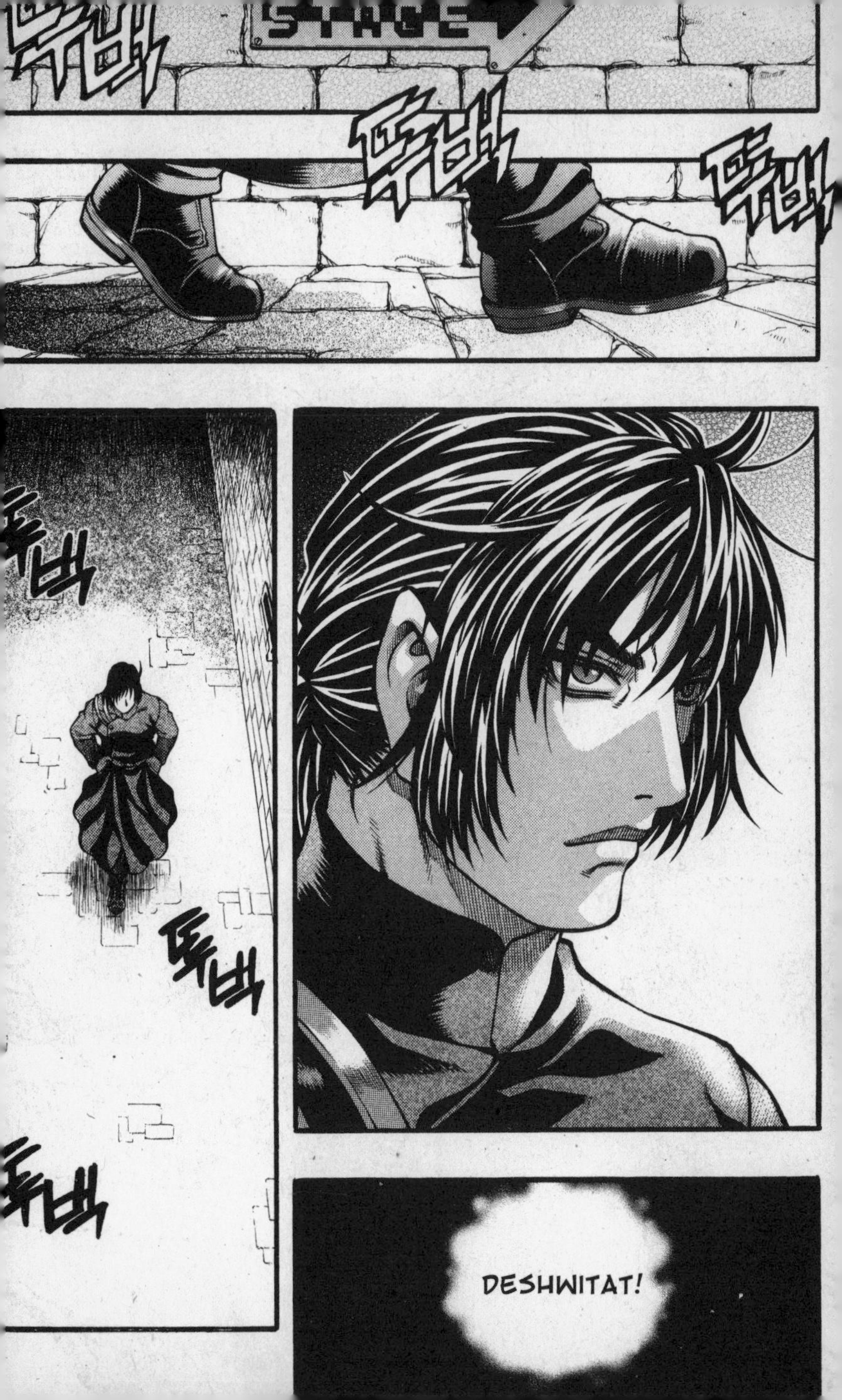

STAGE
뚜벅
뚜벅
뚜벅
뚜벅
뚜벅
뚜벅
DESHWITAT!

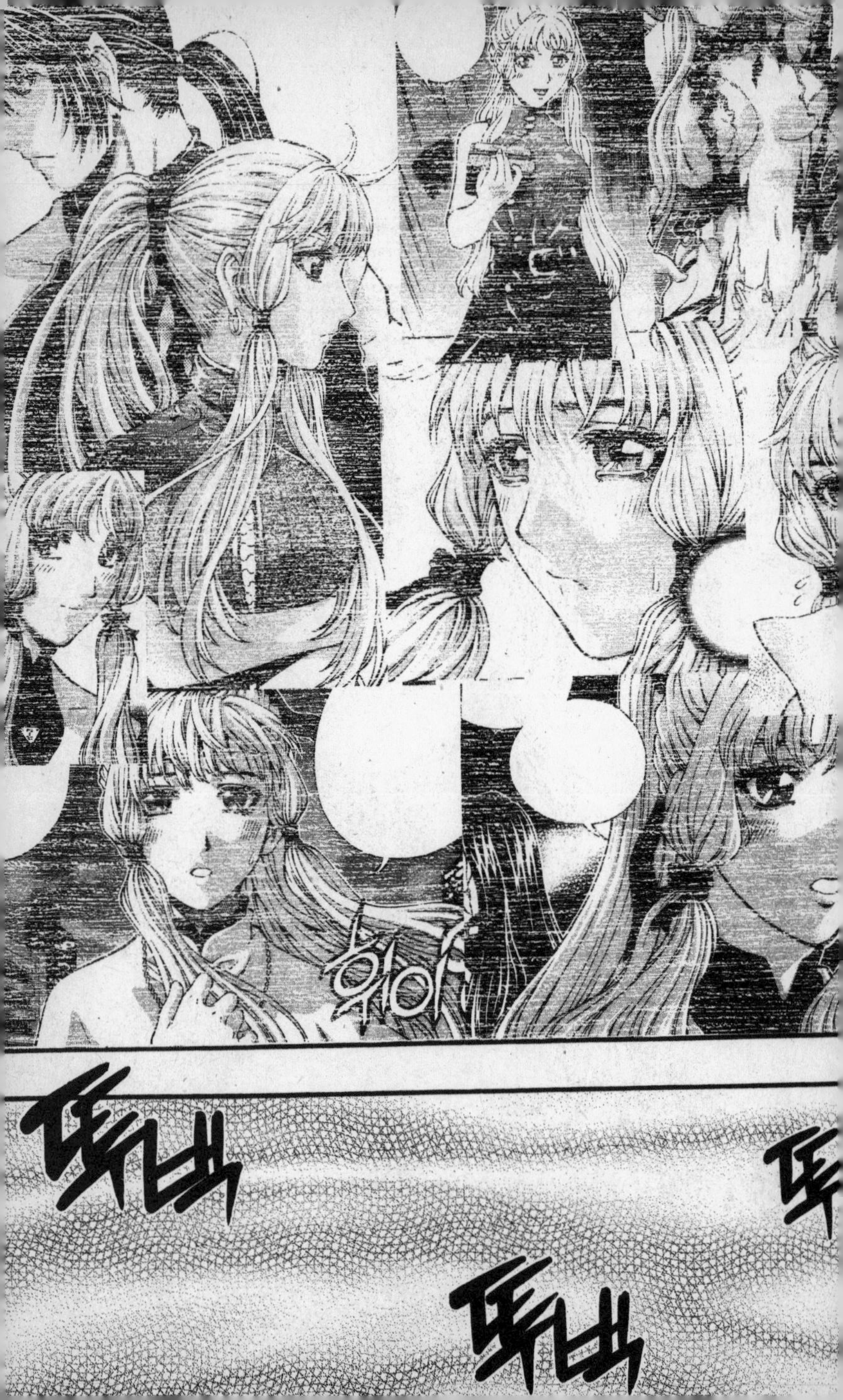
하아
뚜벅
뚜
뚜벅

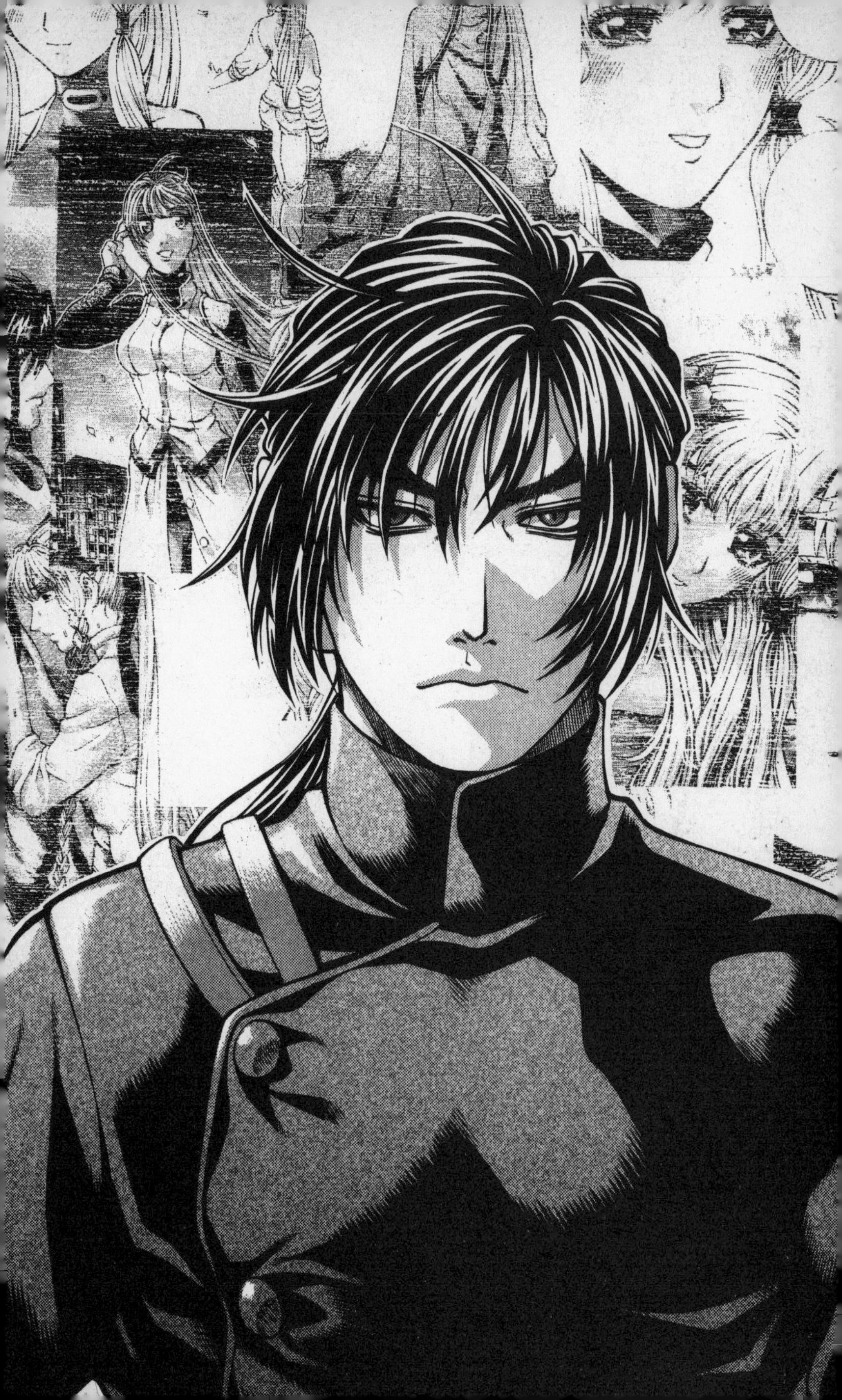

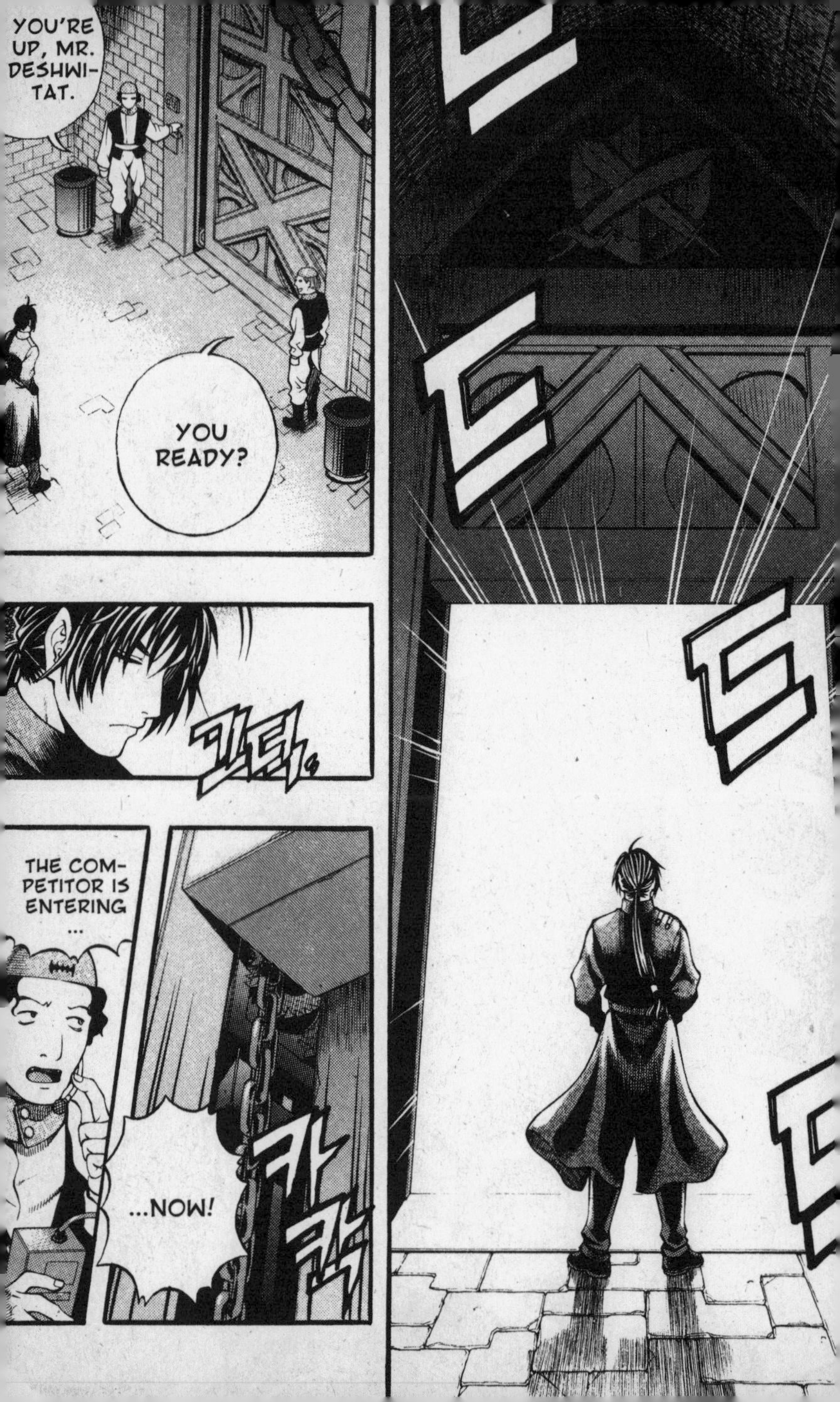
YOU'RE UP, MR. DESHWI-TAT.
YOU READY?
THE COM-PETITOR IS ENTERING ...
...NOW!

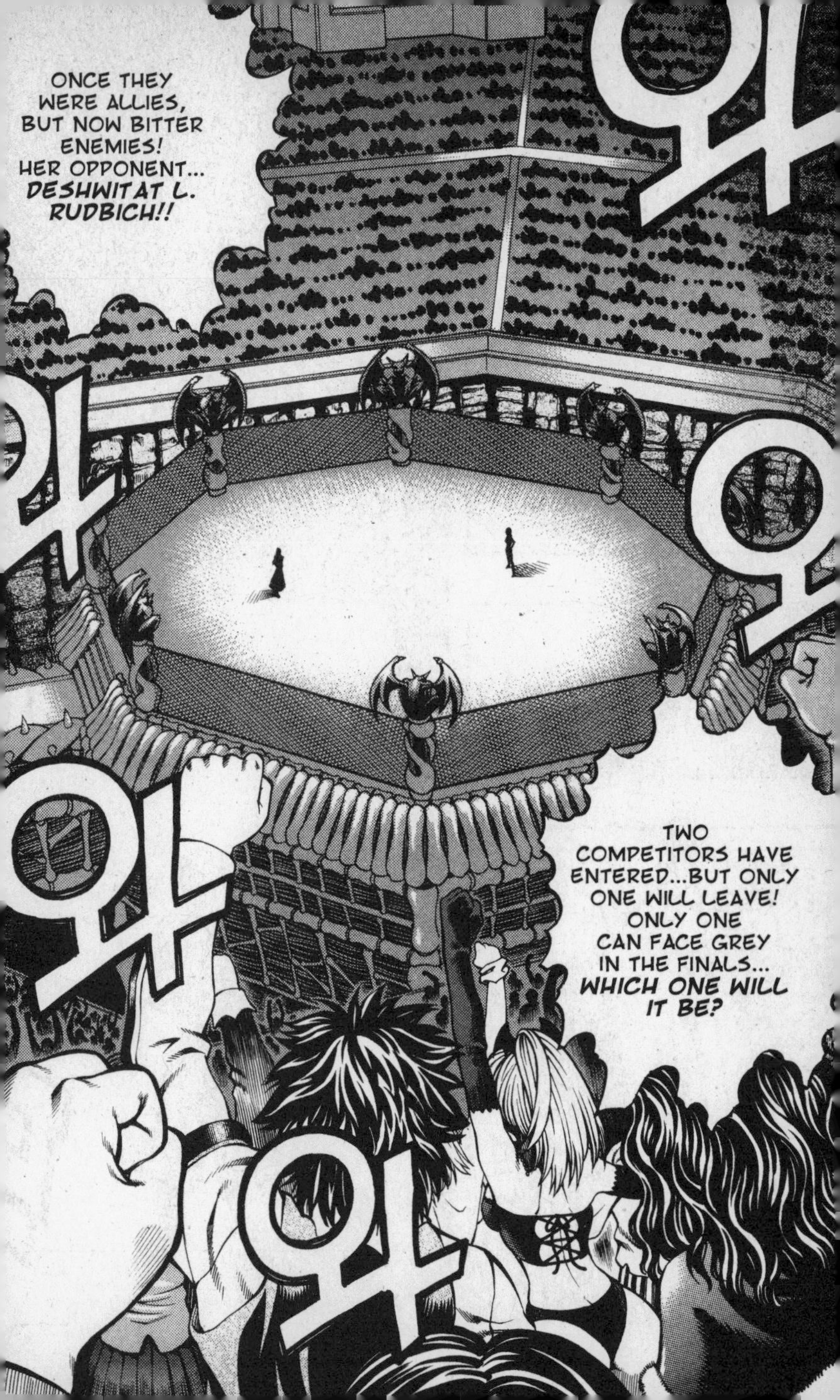
ONCE THEY WERE ALLIES, BUT NOW BITTER ENEMIES! HER OPPONENT... DESHWITAT L. RUDBICH!!
TWO COMPETITORS HAVE ENTERED...BUT ONLY ONE WILL LEAVE! ONLY ONE CAN FACE GREY IN THE FINALS... WHICH ONE WILL IT BE?

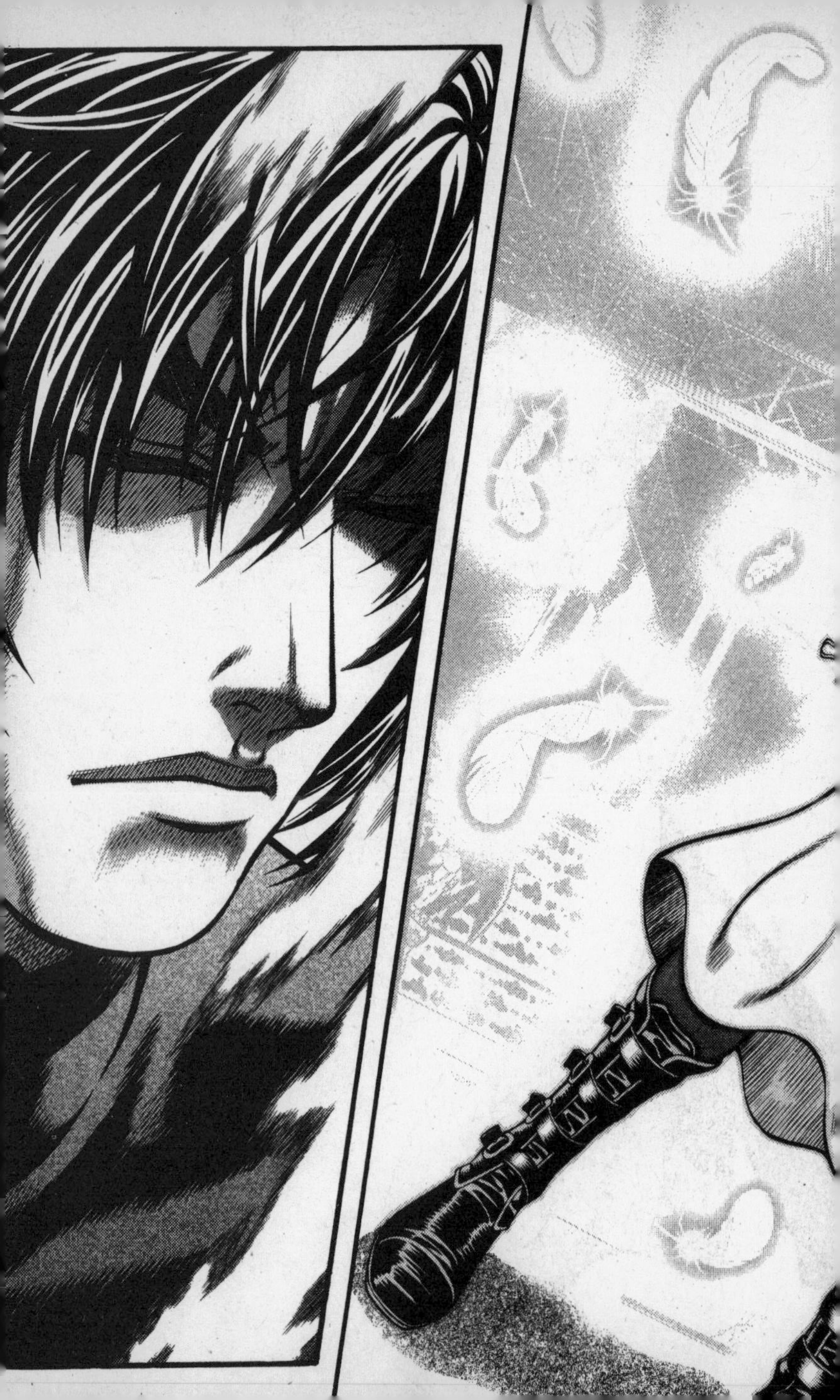

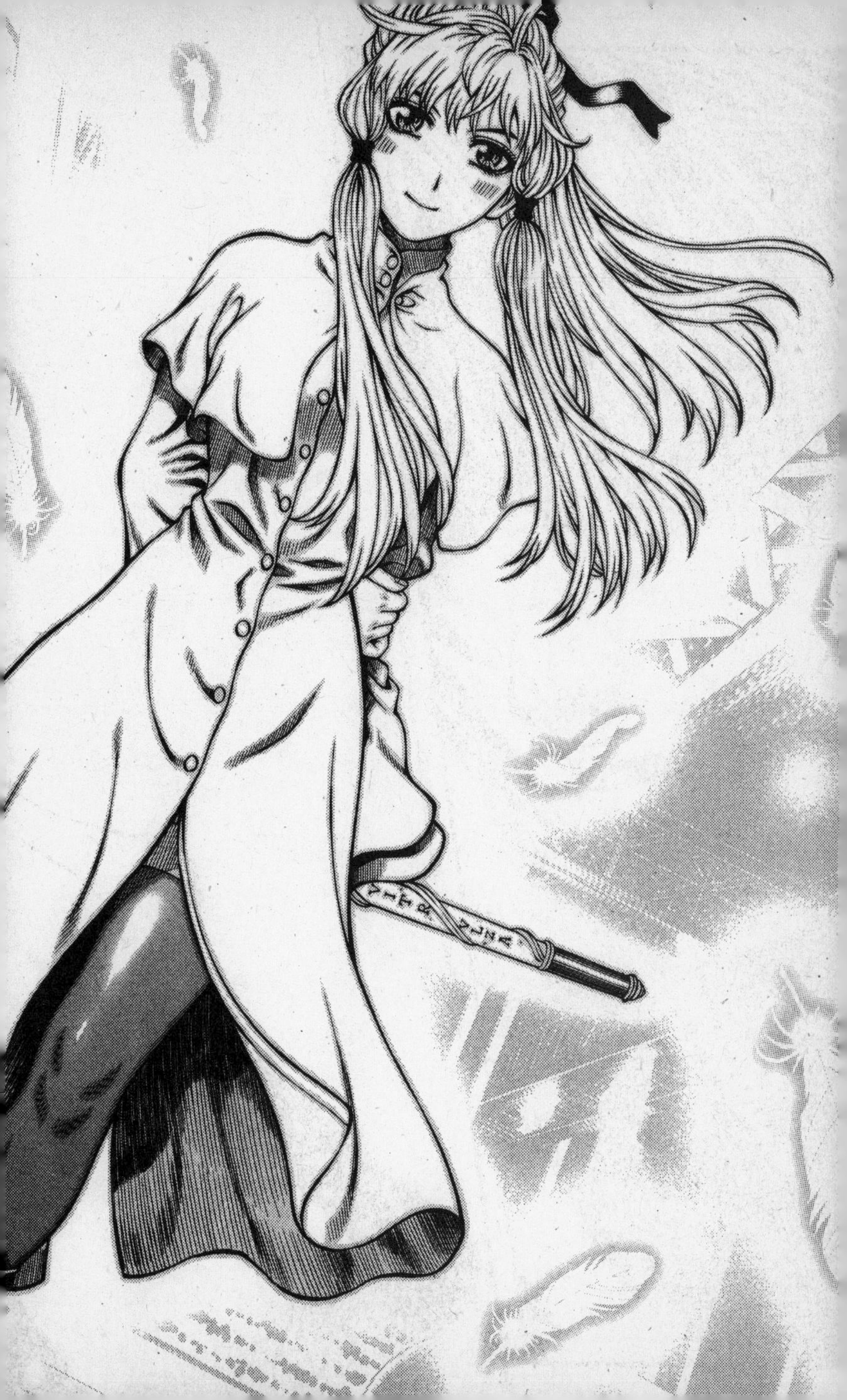

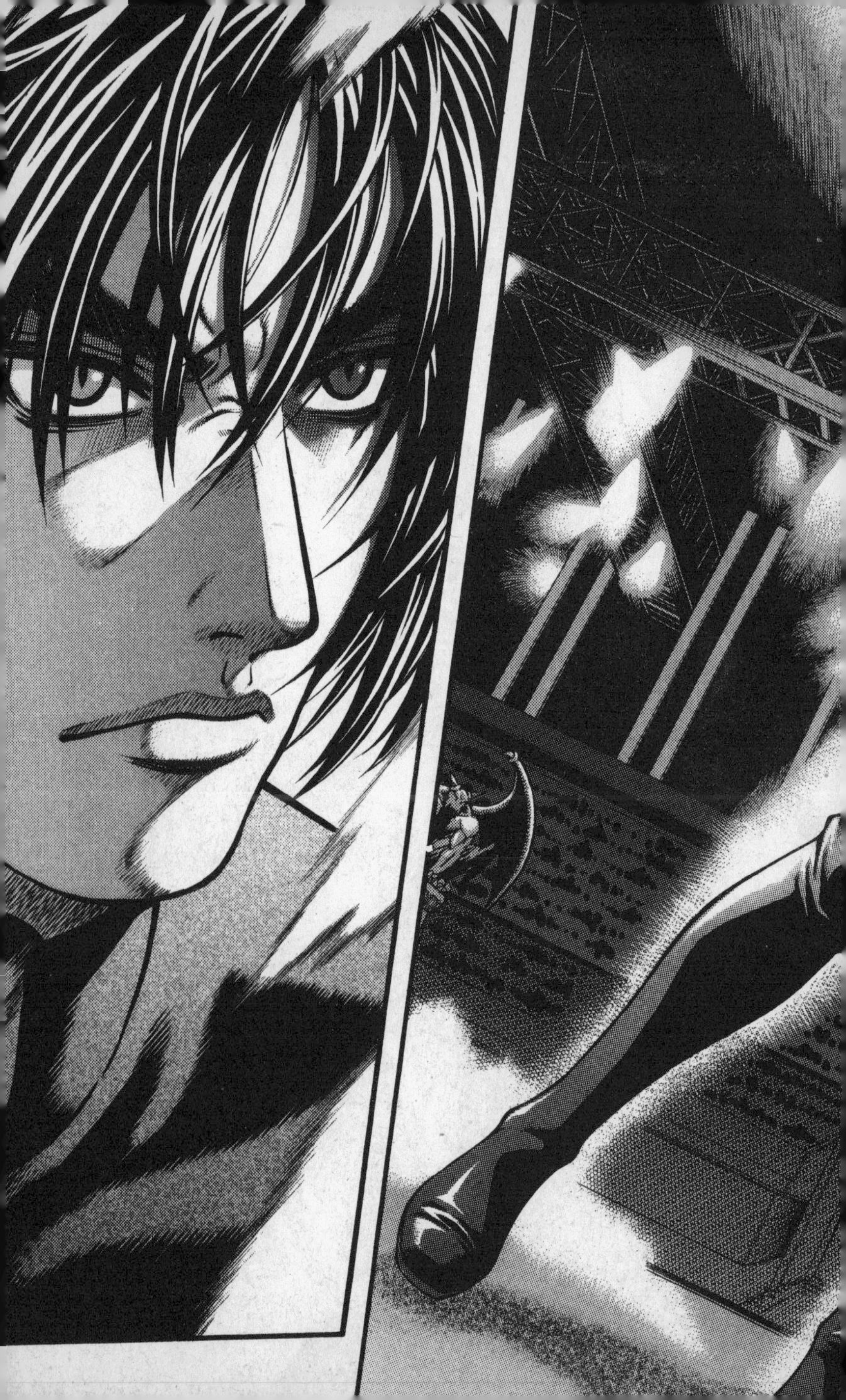

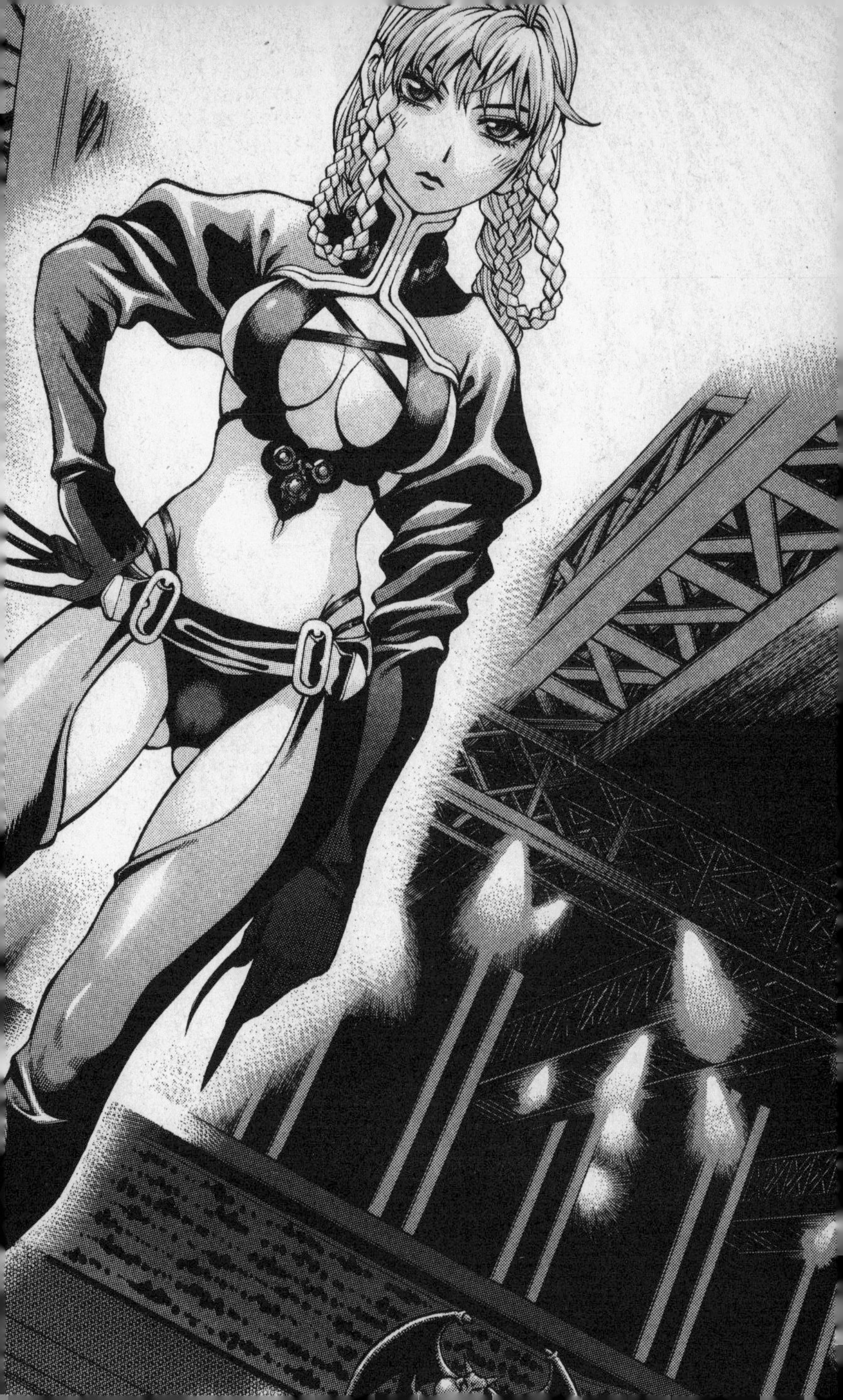

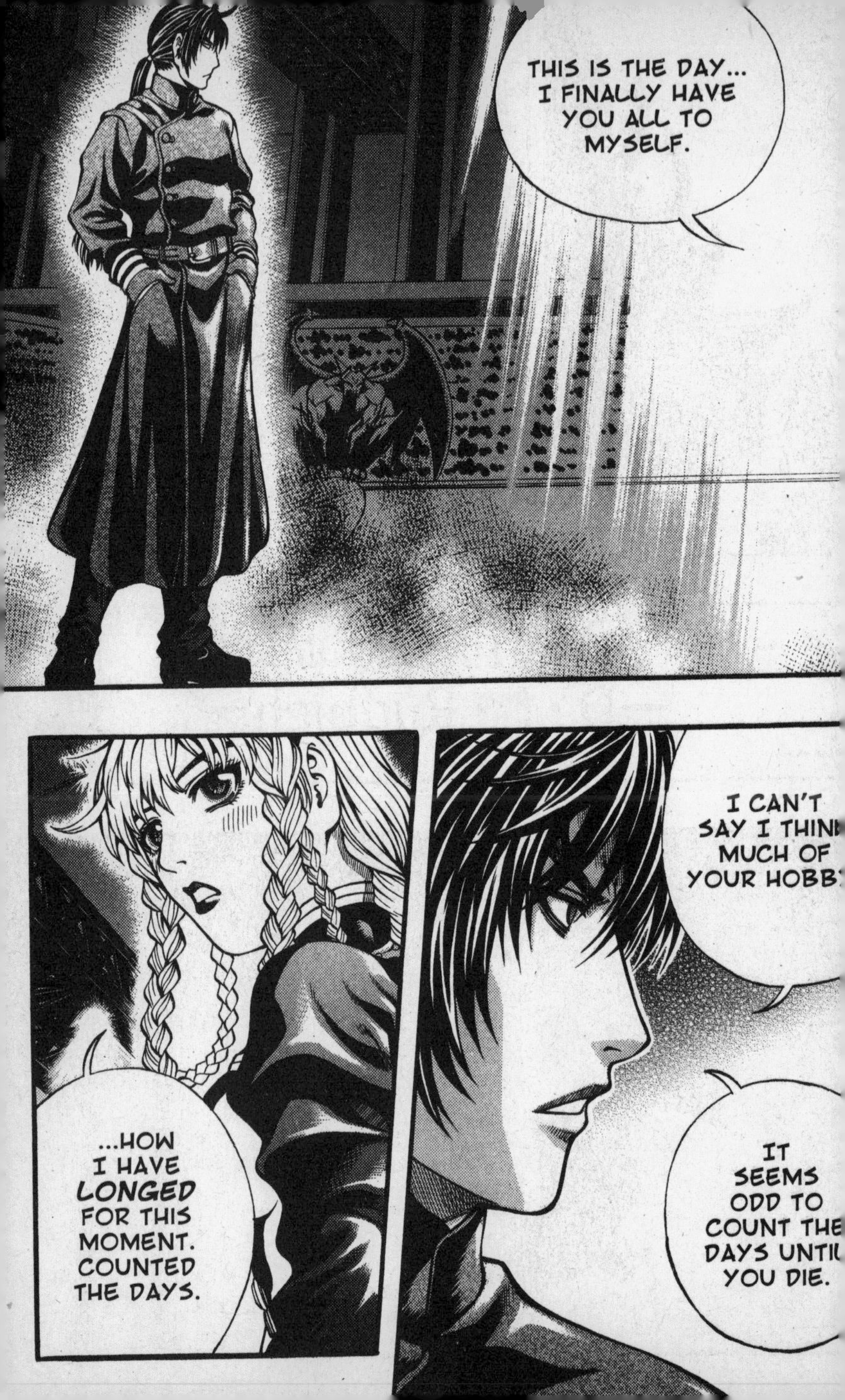
THIS IS THE DAY... I FINALLY HAVE YOU ALL TO MYSELF.
...HOW I HAVE **LONGED** FOR THIS MOMENT. COUNTED THE DAYS.
I CAN'T SAY I THIN MUCH OF YOUR HOBB
IT SEEMS ODD TO COUNT THE DAYS UNTI YOU DIE.

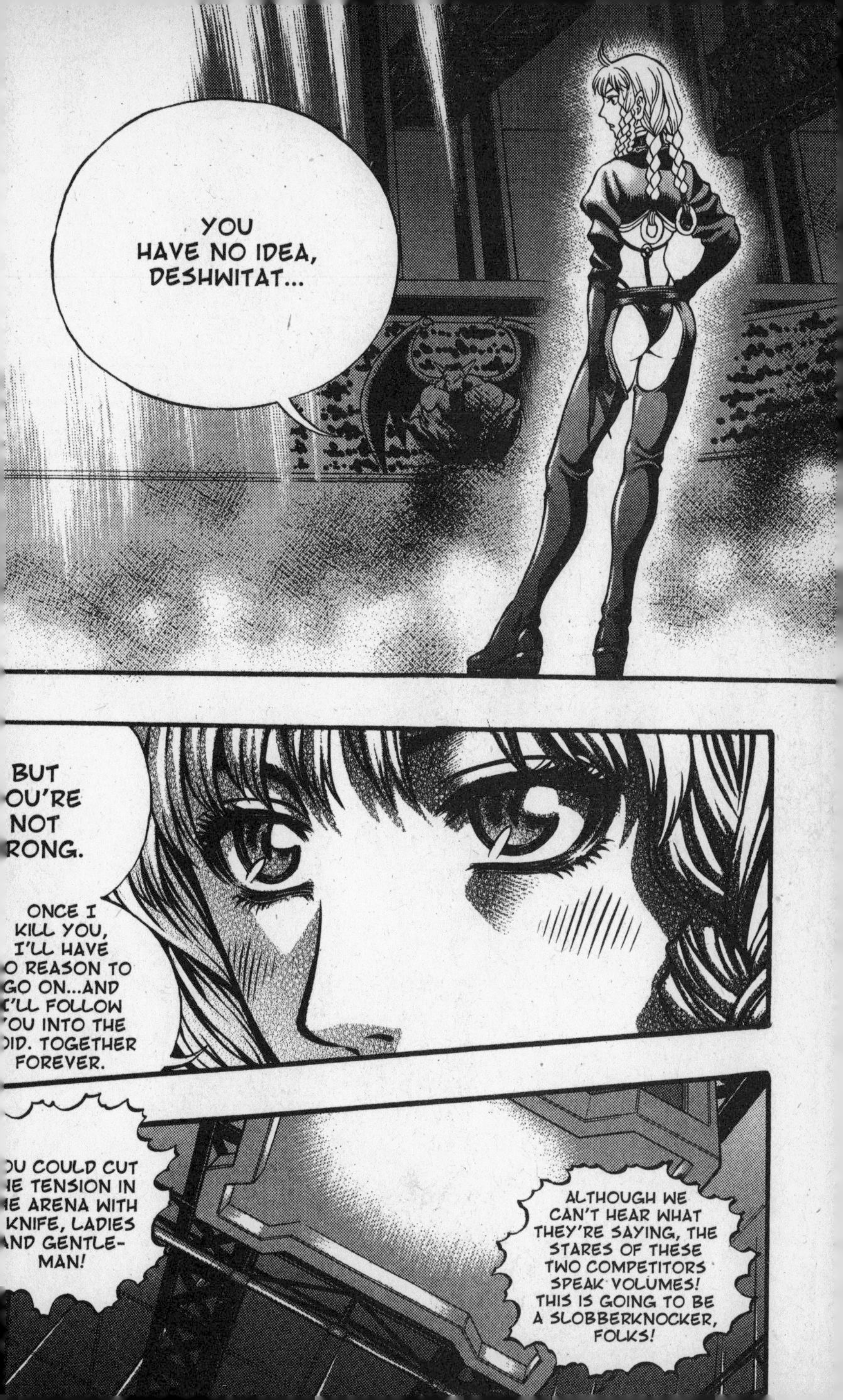

YOU HAVE NO IDEA, DESHWITAT...
BUT OU'RE NOT RONG.
ONCE I KILL YOU, I'LL HAVE O REASON TO GO ON...AND I'LL FOLLOW OU INTO THE OID. TOGETHER FOREVER.
OU COULD CUT E TENSION IN E ARENA WITH KNIFE, LADIES AND GENTLE-MAN!
ALTHOUGH WE CAN'T HEAR WHAT THEY'RE SAYING, THE STARES OF THESE TWO COMPETITORS SPEAK VOLUMES! THIS IS GOING TO BE A SLOBBERKNOCKER, FOLKS!

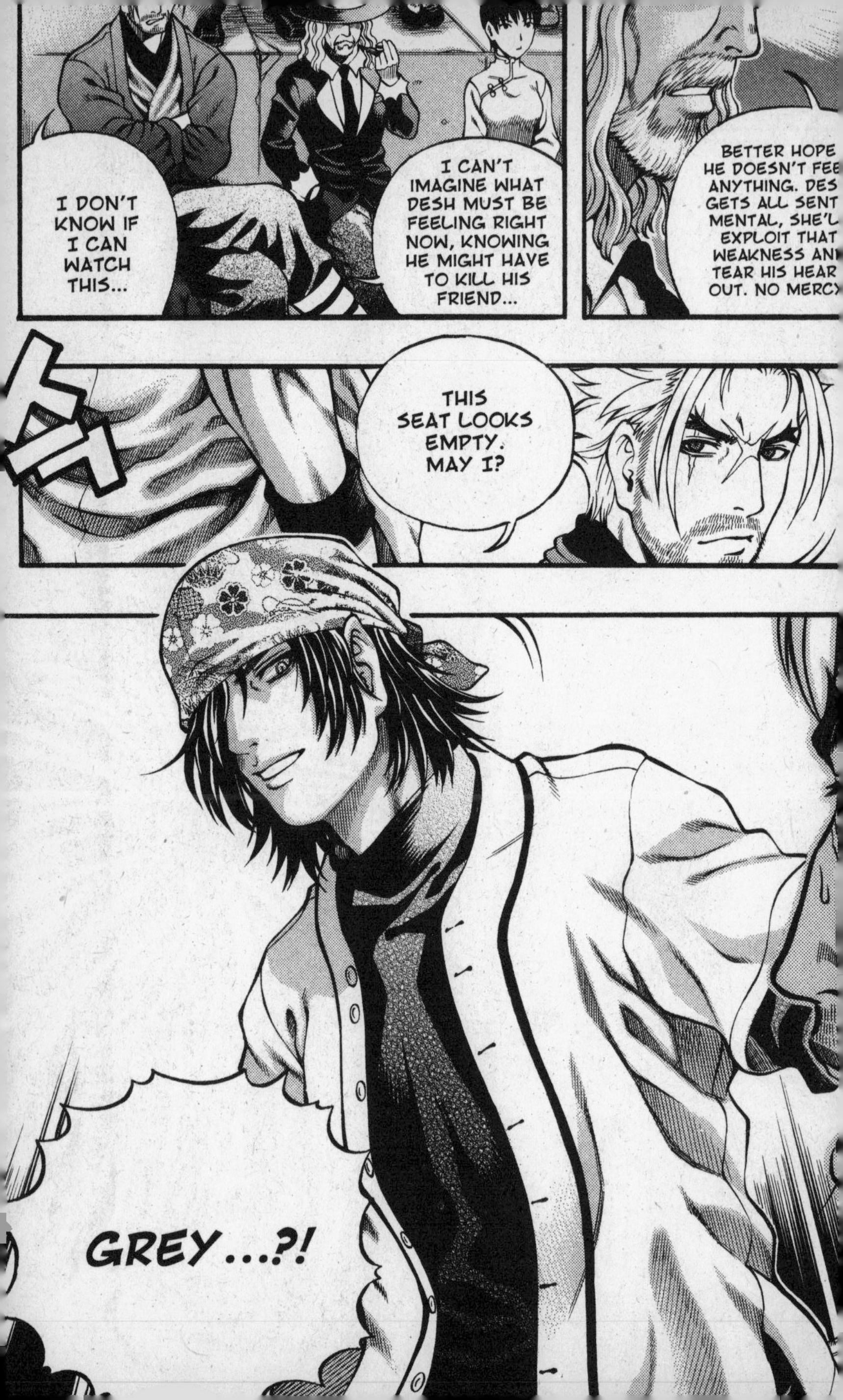
BETTER HOPE HE DOESN'T FEE ANYTHING. DES GETS ALL SENT MENTAL, SHE'L EXPLOIT THAT WEAKNESS AN TEAR HIS HEAR OUT. NO MERC
I CAN'T IMAGINE WHAT DESH MUST BE FEELING RIGHT NOW, KNOWING HE MIGHT HAVE TO KILL HIS FRIEND...
I DON'T KNOW IF I CAN WATCH THIS...
THIS SEAT LOOKS EMPTY. MAY I?
GREY...?!

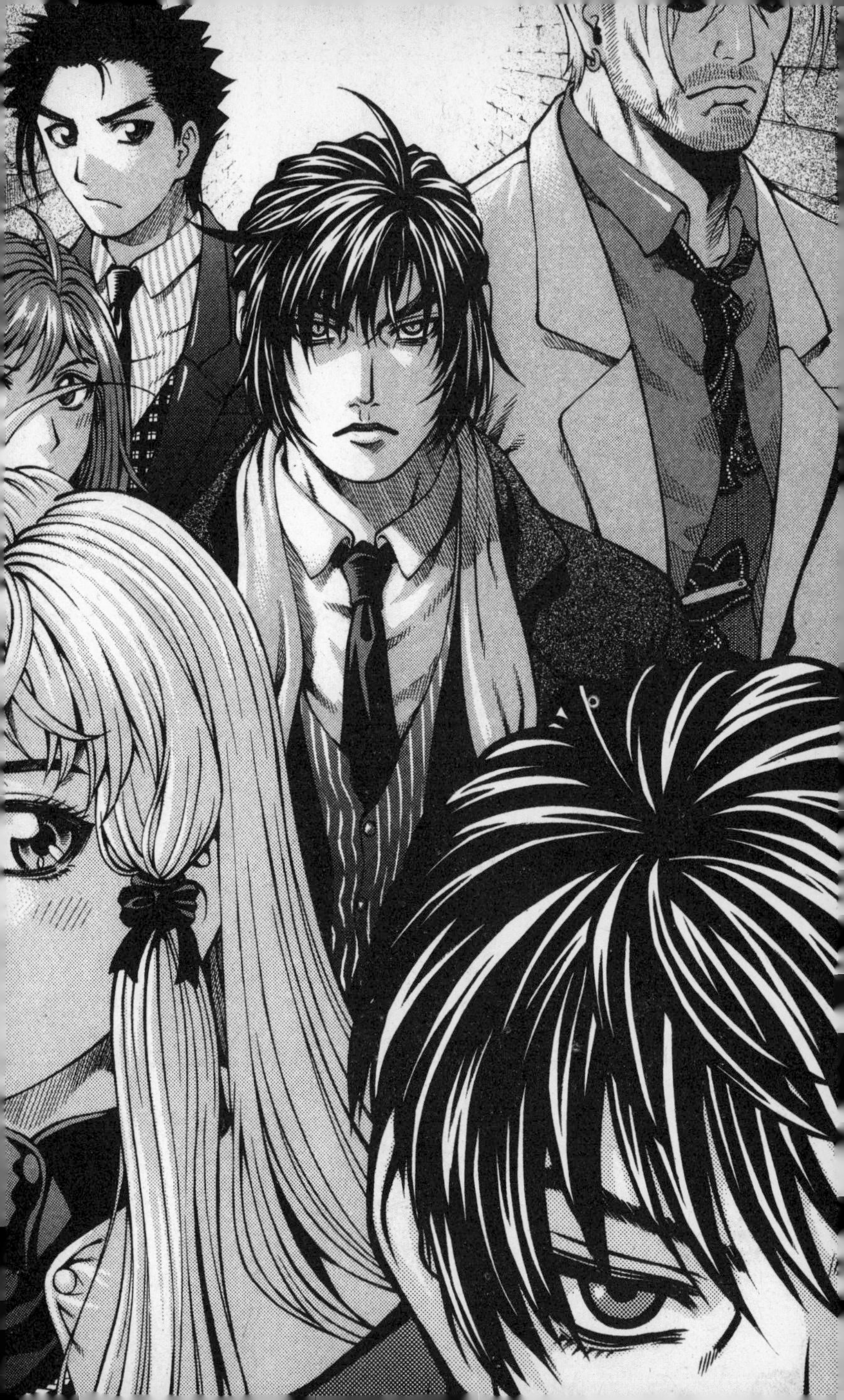

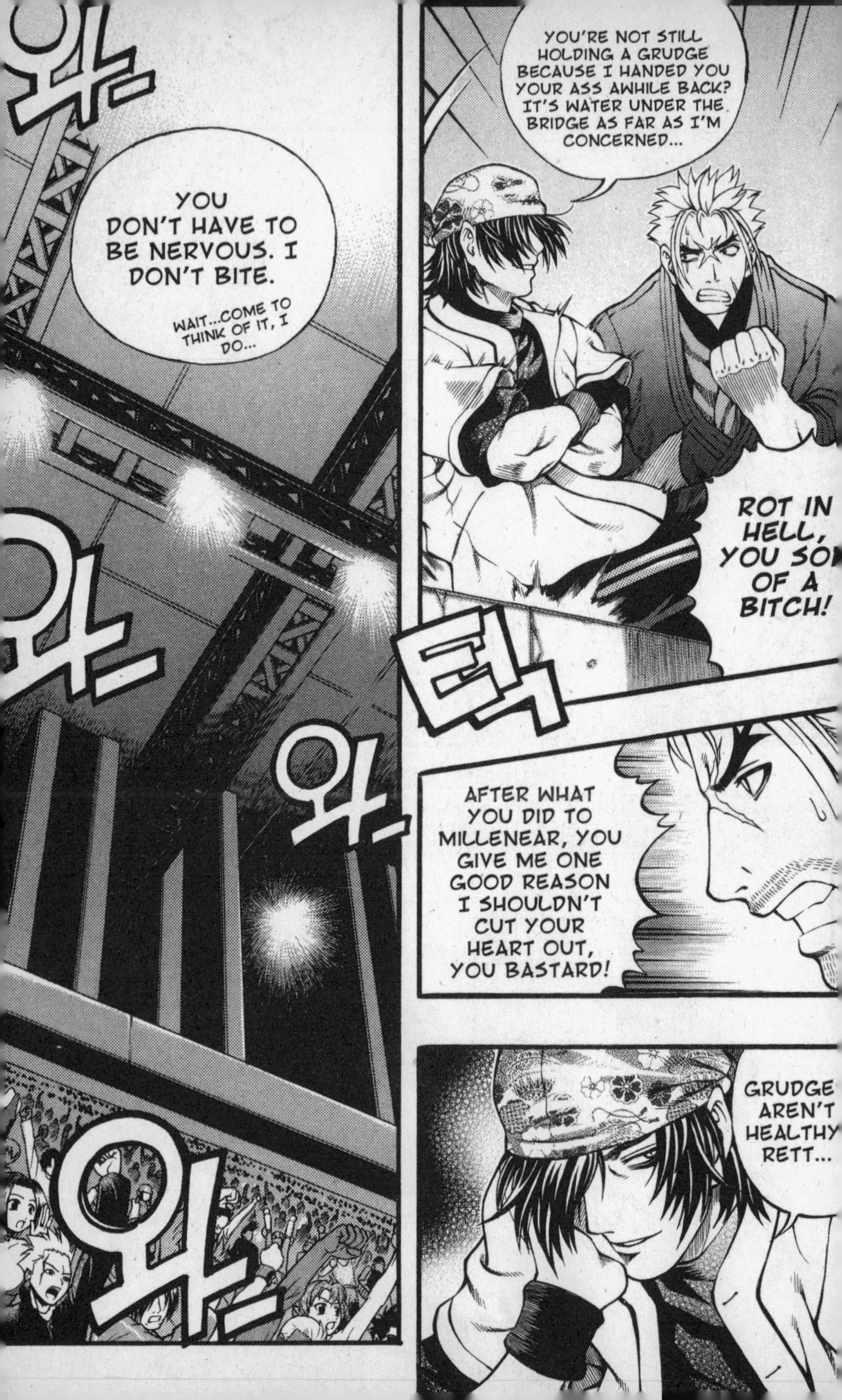
와
YOU DON'T HAVE TO BE NERVOUS. I DON'T BITE.
WAIT...COME TO THINK OF IT, I DO...
와
와
와
YOU'RE NOT STILL HOLDING A GRUDGE BECAUSE I HANDED YOU YOUR ASS AWHILE BACK? IT'S WATER UNDER THE BRIDGE AS FAR AS I'M CONCERNED...
ROT IN HELL, YOU SO OF A BITCH!
AFTER WHAT YOU DID TO MILLENEAR, YOU GIVE ME ONE GOOD REASON I SHOULDN'T CUT YOUR HEART OUT, YOU BASTARD!
GRUDGE AREN'T HEALTHY RETT...

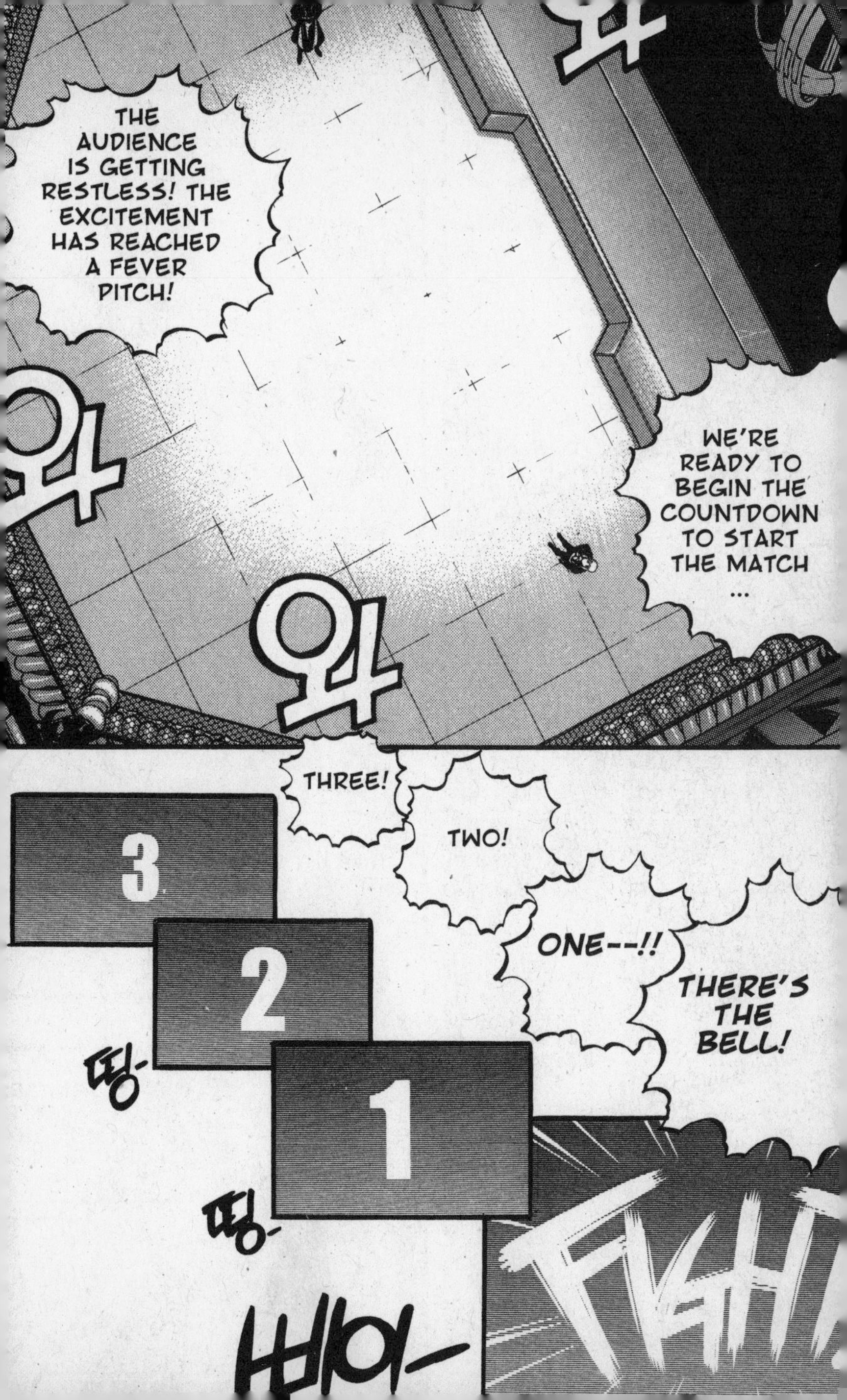

THE AUDIENCE IS GETTING RESTLESS! THE EXCITEMENT HAS REACHED A FEVER PITCH!
WE'RE READY TO BEGIN THE COUNTDOWN TO START THE MATCH ...
THREE!
TWO!
ONE--!!
THERE'S THE BELL!
3
2
1
땡-
땡-
FASH!

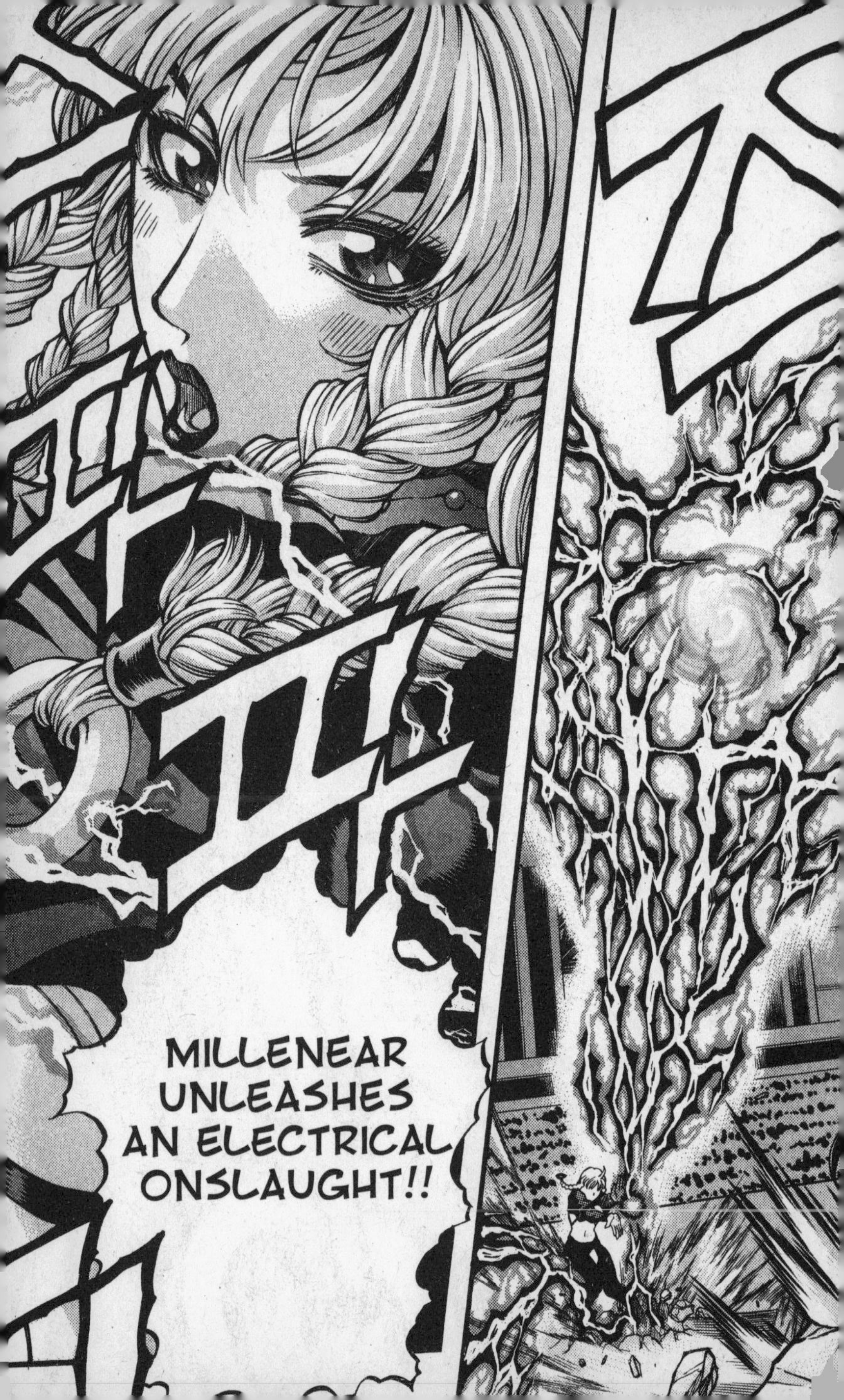
MILLENEAR UNLEASHES AN ELECTRICAL ONSLAUGHT!!

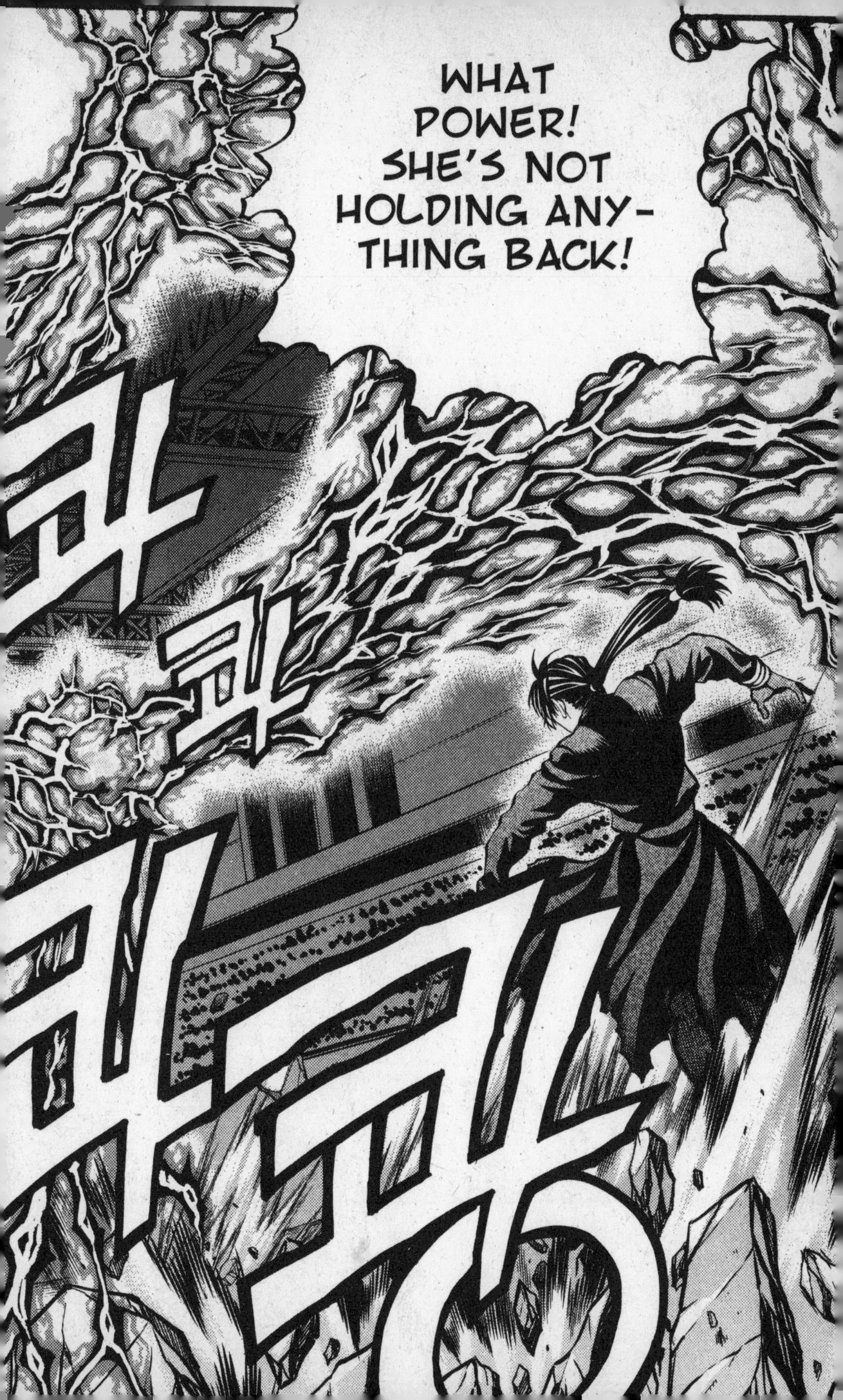
WHAT POWER! SHE'S NOT HOLDING ANYTHING BACK!

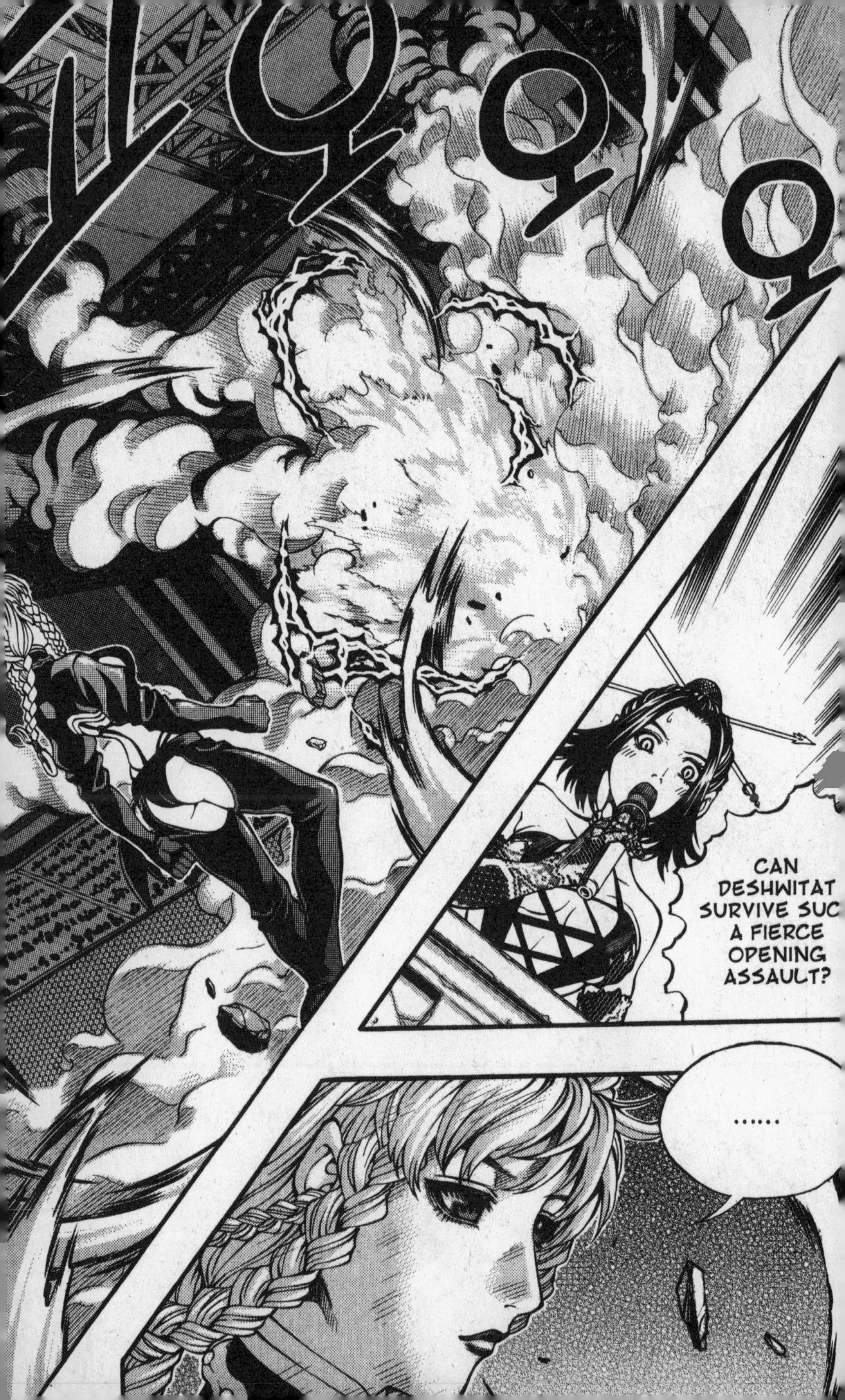

ZGOGOGO
CAN DESHWITAT SURVIVE SUC A FIERCE OPENING ASSAULT?
......

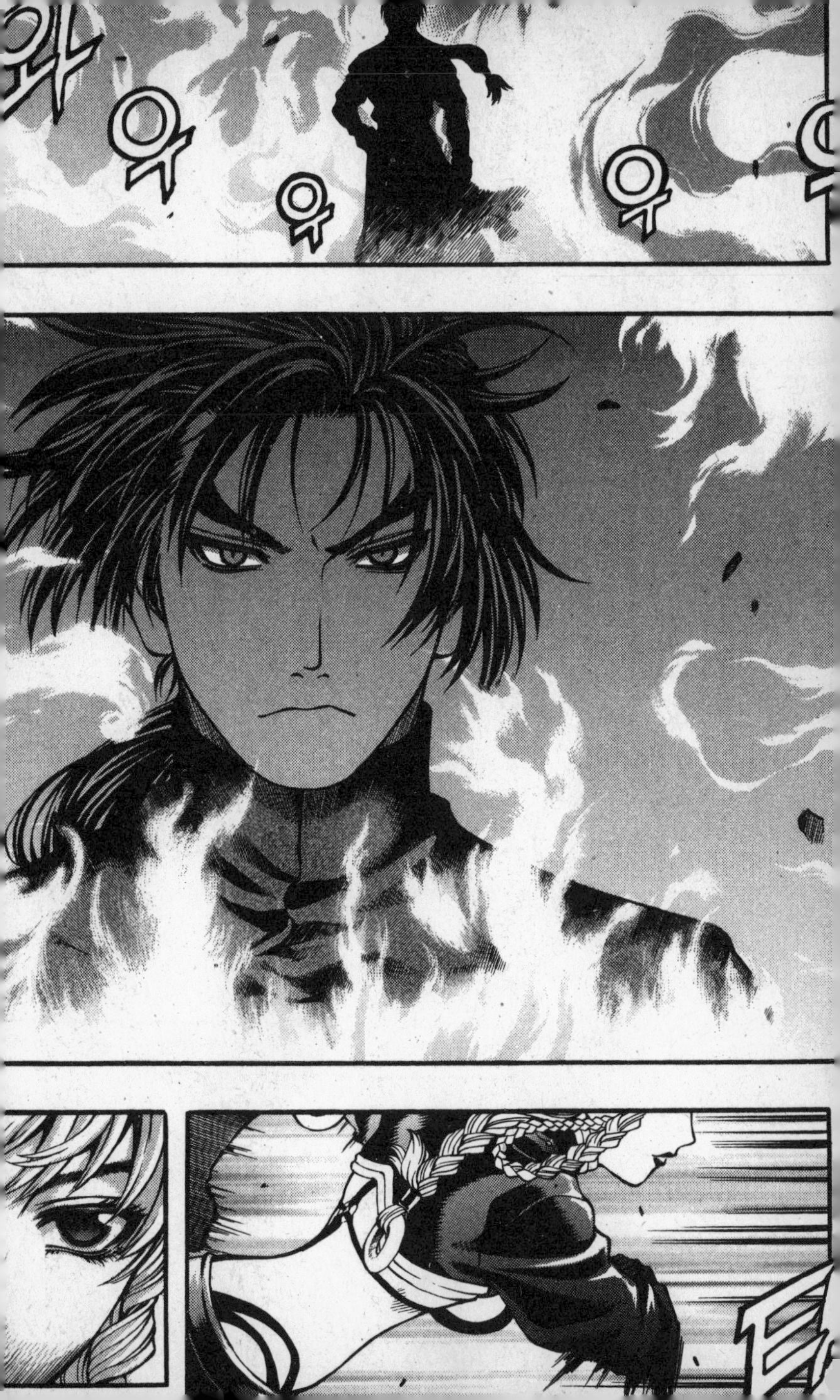
콰우우우

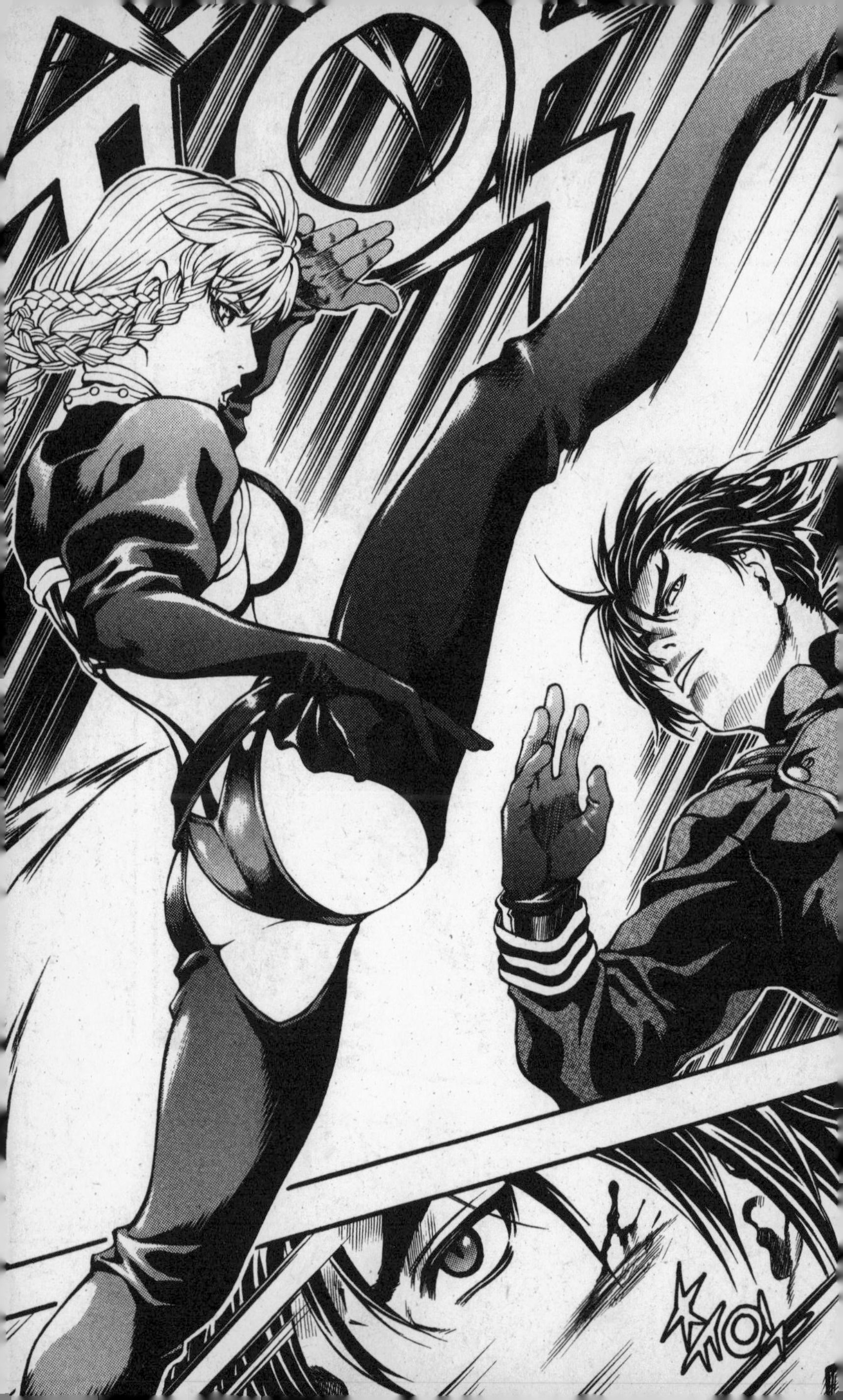

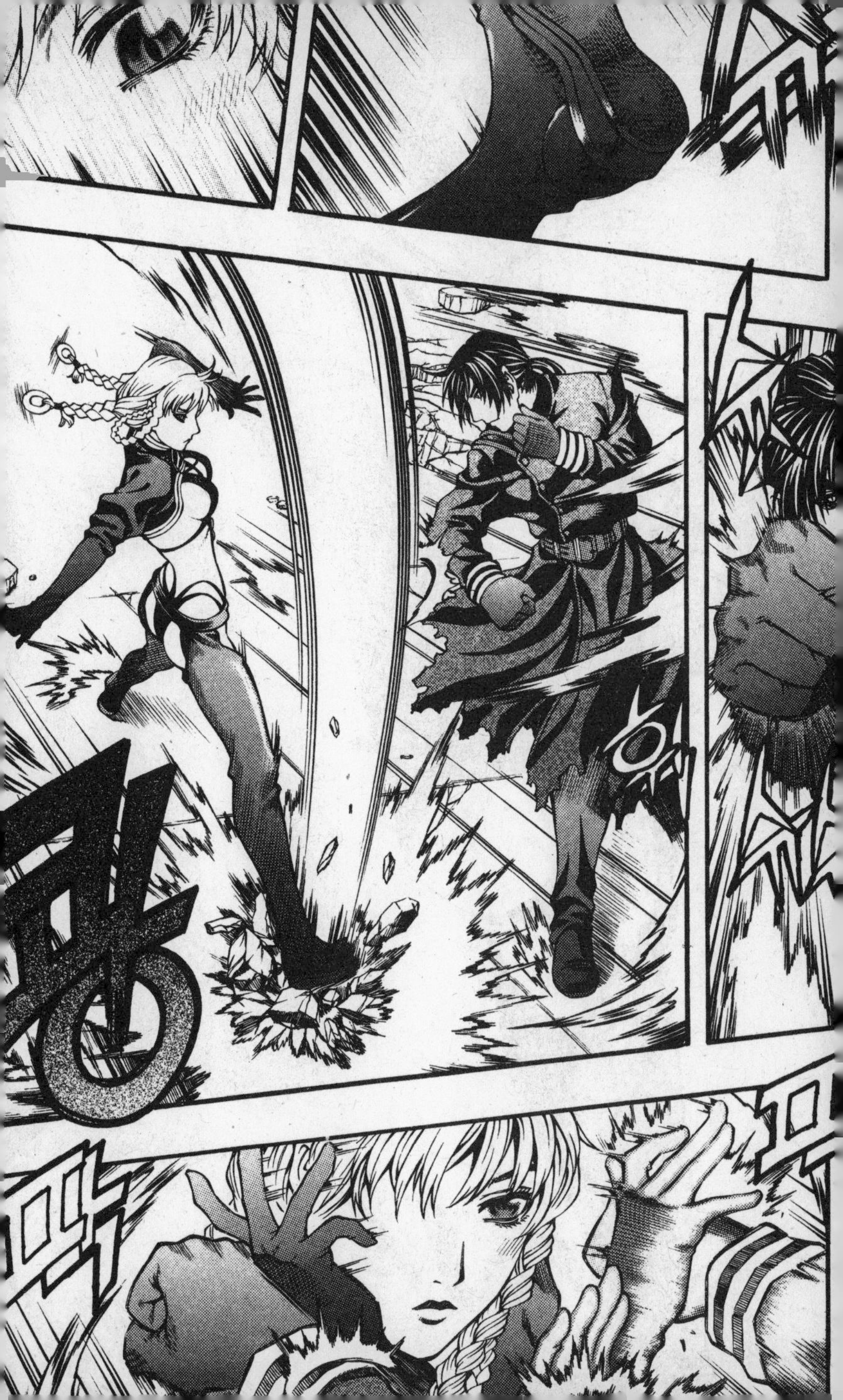

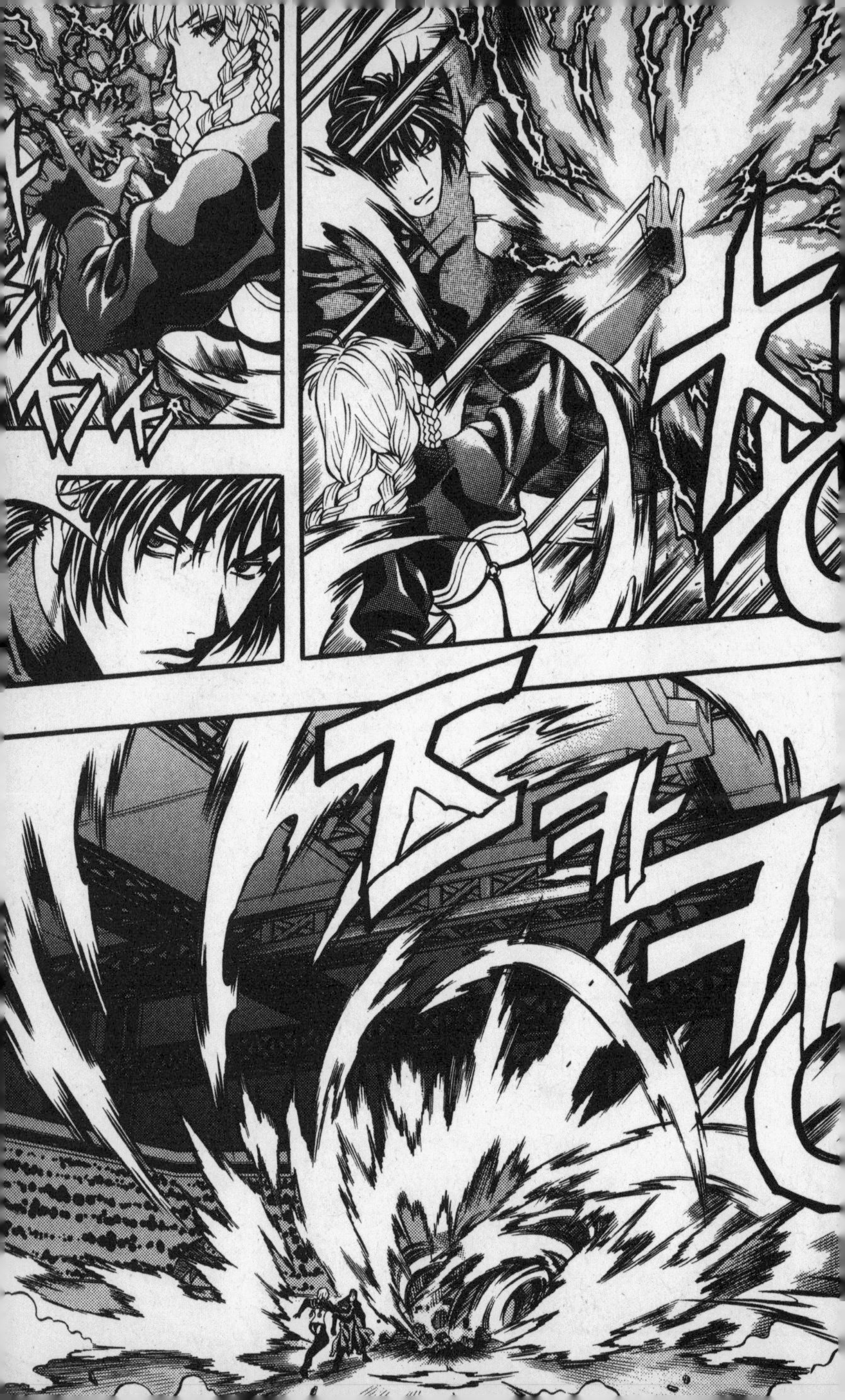

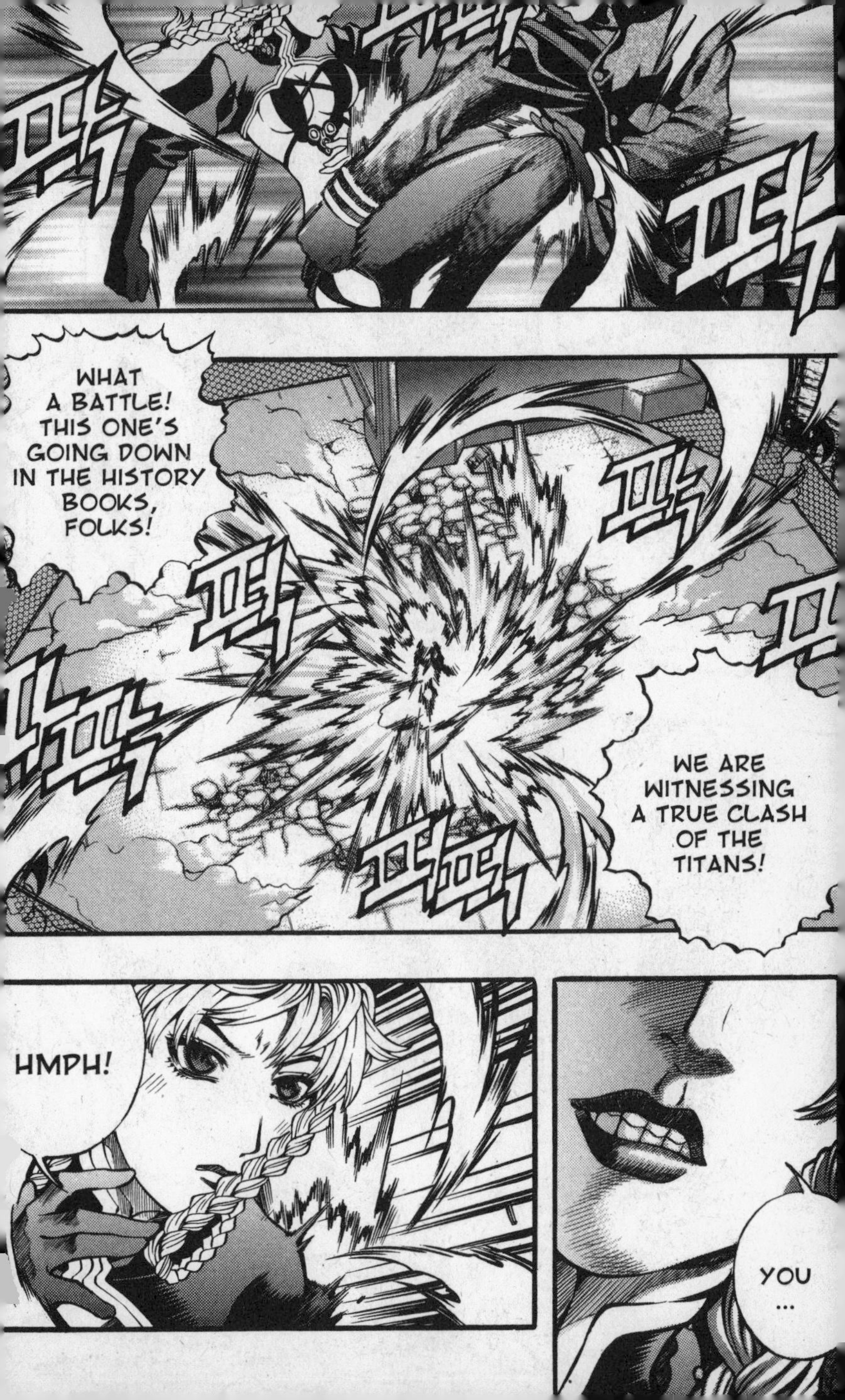

WHAT A BATTLE! THIS ONE'S GOING DOWN IN THE HISTORY BOOKS, FOLKS!
WE ARE WITNESSING A TRUE CLASH OF THE TITANS!
HMPH!
YOU ...

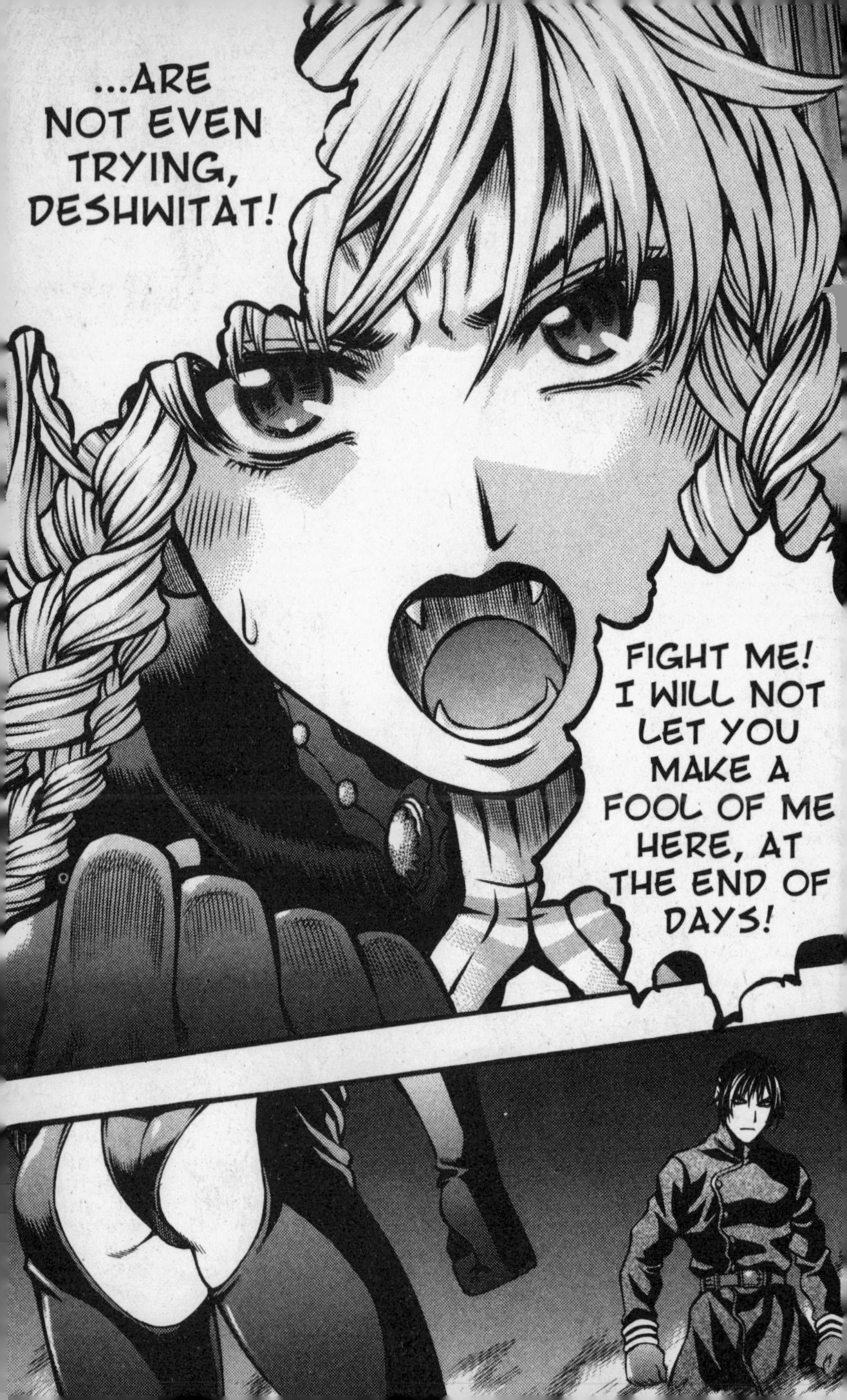
...ARE NOT EVEN TRYING, DESHWITAT!
FIGHT ME! I WILL NOT LET YOU MAKE A FOOL OF ME HERE, AT THE END OF DAYS!

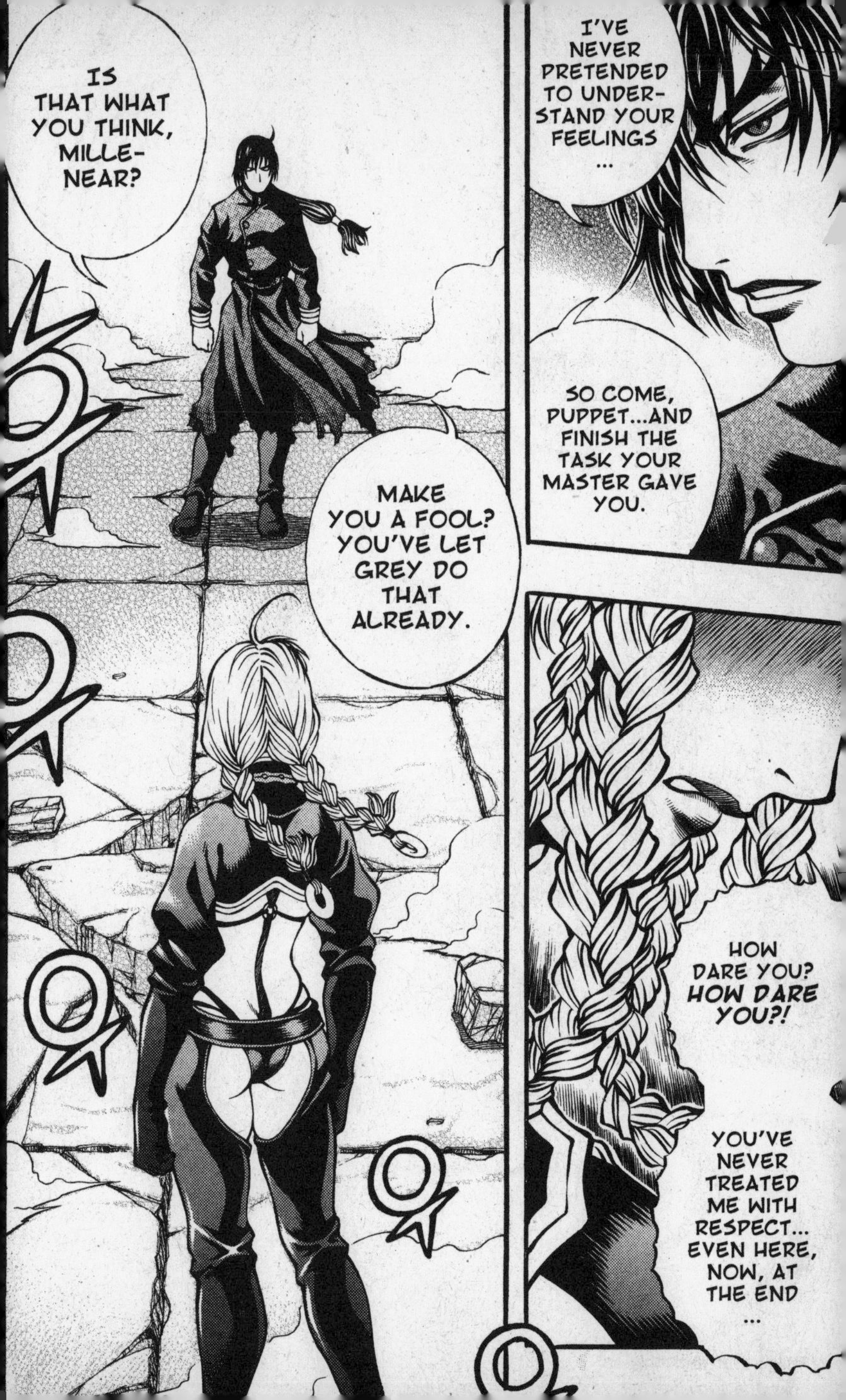
IS THAT WHAT YOU THINK, MILLE-NEAR?
MAKE YOU A FOOL? YOU'VE LET GREY DO THAT ALREADY.
I'VE NEVER PRETENDED TO UNDER-STAND YOUR FEELINGS ...
SO COME, PUPPET...AND FINISH THE TASK YOUR MASTER GAVE YOU.
HOW DARE YOU? HOW DARE YOU?!
YOU'VE NEVER TREATED ME WITH RESPECT... EVEN HERE, NOW, AT THE END ...

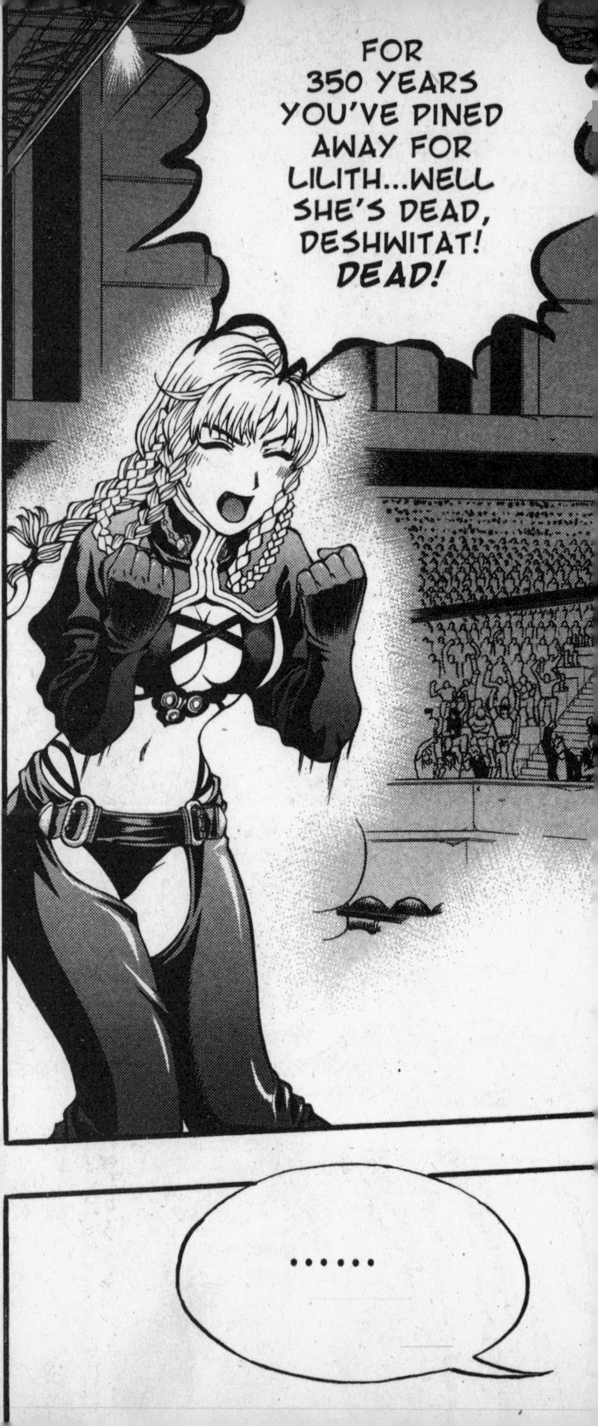
FOR 350 YEARS YOU'VE PINED AWAY FOR LILITH...WELL SHE'S DEAD, DESHWITAT! DEAD!
......

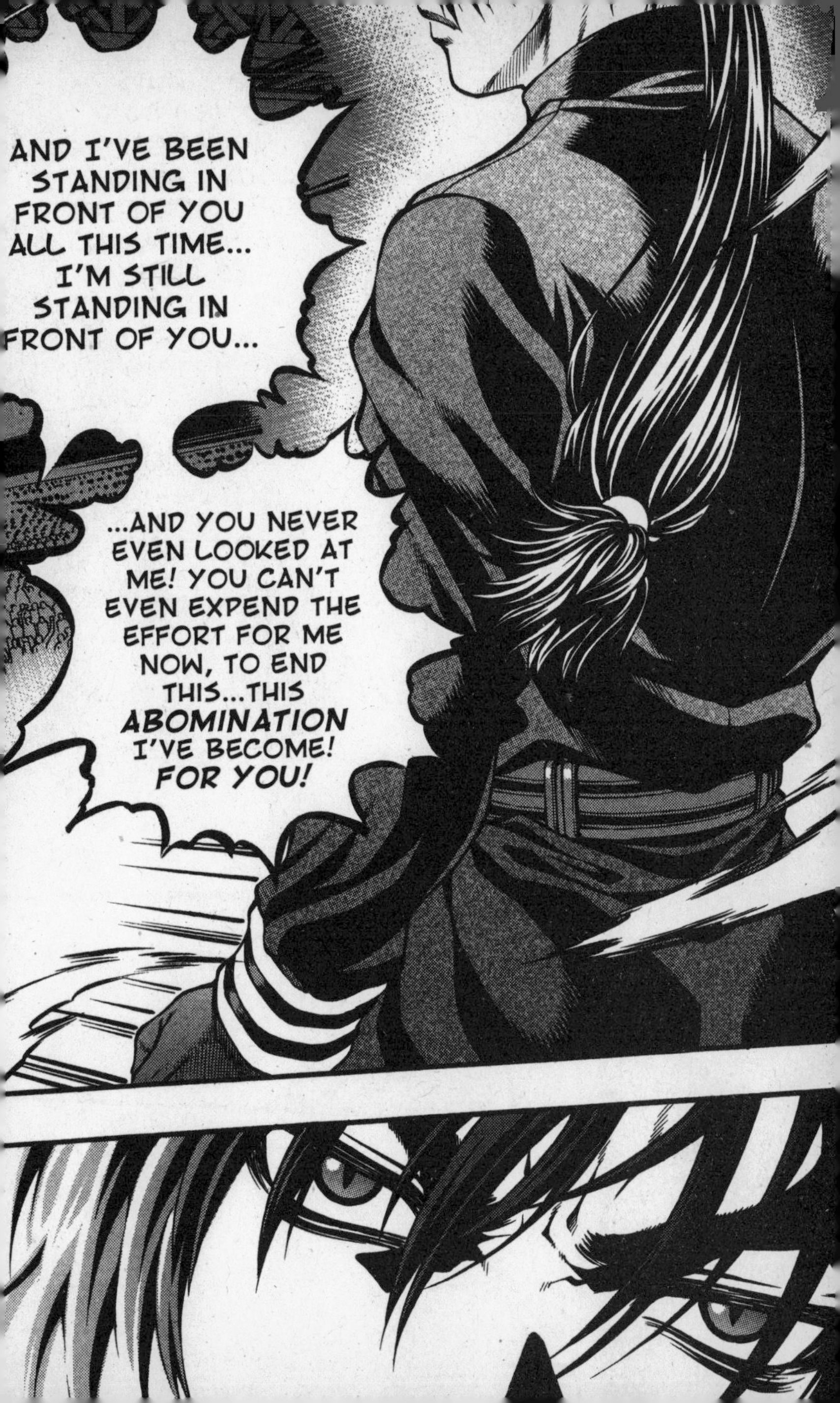
AND I'VE BEEN STANDING IN FRONT OF YOU ALL THIS TIME... I'M STILL STANDING IN FRONT OF YOU...
...AND YOU NEVER EVEN LOOKED AT ME! YOU CAN'T EVEN EXPEND THE EFFORT FOR ME NOW, TO END THIS...THIS ABOMINATION I'VE BECOME! FOR YOU!

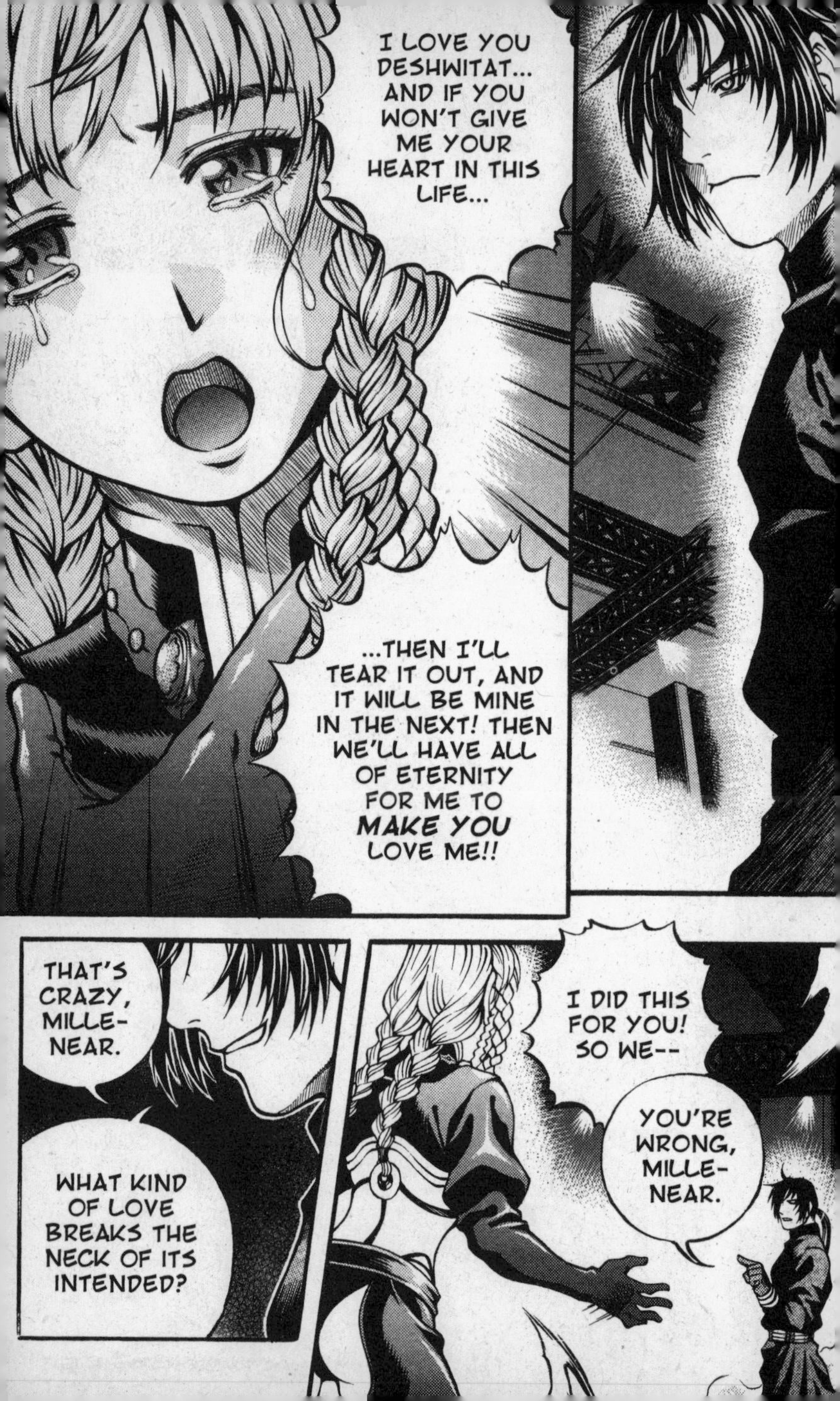
I LOVE YOU DESHWITAT... AND IF YOU WON'T GIVE ME YOUR HEART IN THIS LIFE...
...THEN I'LL TEAR IT OUT, AND IT WILL BE MINE IN THE NEXT! THEN WE'LL HAVE ALL OF ETERNITY FOR ME TO *MAKE YOU* LOVE ME!!
I DID THIS FOR YOU! SO WE--
YOU'RE WRONG, MILLE-NEAR.
THAT'S CRAZY, MILLE-NEAR.
WHAT KIND OF LOVE BREAKS THE NECK OF ITS INTENDED?

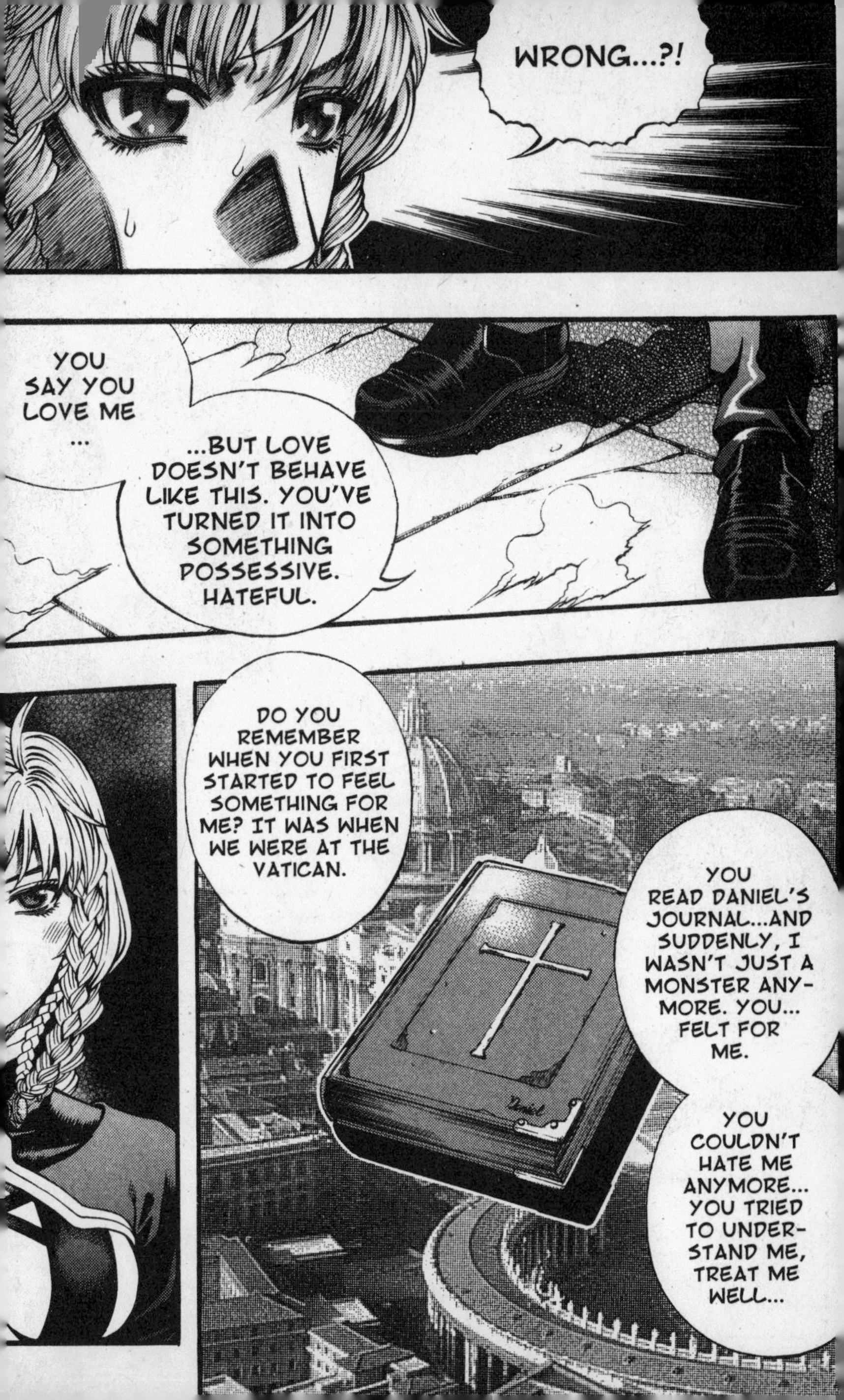
WRONG...?!
YOU SAY YOU LOVE ME ...
...BUT LOVE DOESN'T BEHAVE LIKE THIS. YOU'VE TURNED IT INTO SOMETHING POSSESSIVE. HATEFUL.
DO YOU REMEMBER WHEN YOU FIRST STARTED TO FEEL SOMETHING FOR ME? IT WAS WHEN WE WERE AT THE VATICAN.
YOU READ DANIEL'S JOURNAL...AND SUDDENLY, I WASN'T JUST A MONSTER ANY-MORE. YOU... FELT FOR ME.
YOU COULDN'T HATE ME ANYMORE... YOU TRIED TO UNDER-STAND ME, TREAT ME WELL...

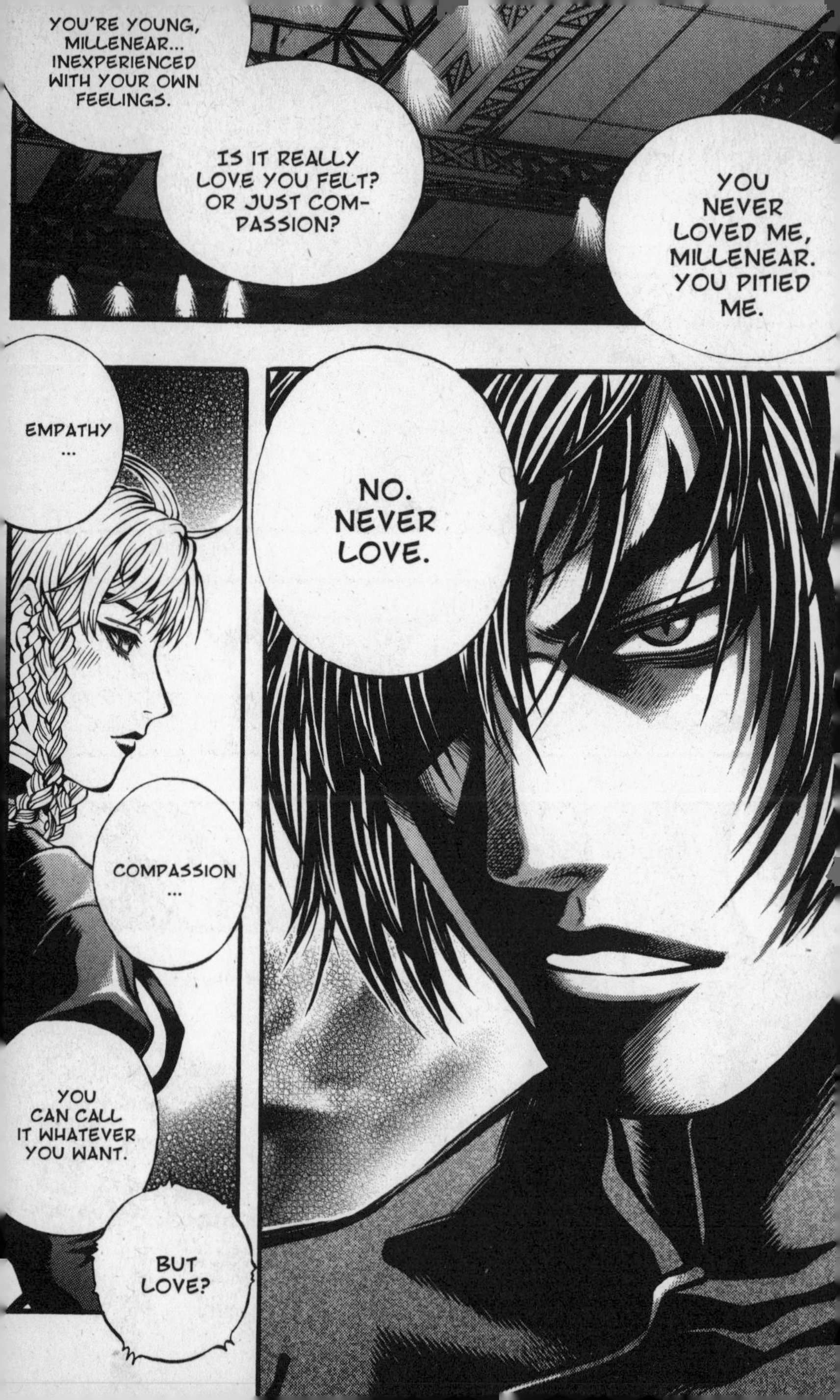
YOU'RE YOUNG, MILLENEAR... INEXPERIENCED WITH YOUR OWN FEELINGS.
IS IT REALLY LOVE YOU FELT? OR JUST COM-PASSION?
YOU NEVER LOVED ME, MILLENEAR. YOU PITIED ME.
EMPATHY ...
NO. NEVER LOVE.
COMPASSION ...
YOU CAN CALL IT WHATEVER YOU WANT.
BUT LOVE?

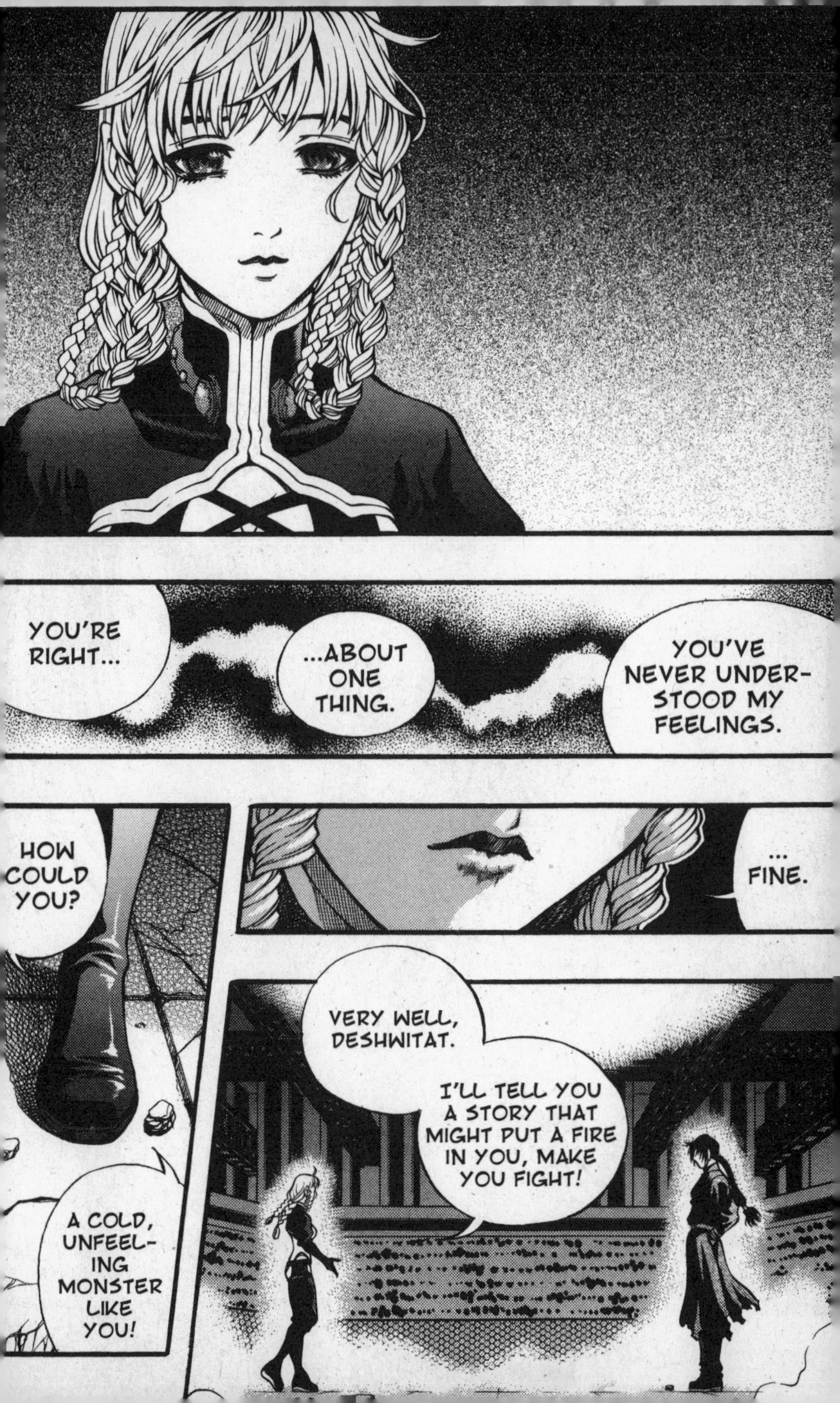

YOU'RE RIGHT...
...ABOUT ONE THING.
YOU'VE NEVER UNDER-STOOD MY FEELINGS.
...FINE.
HOW COULD YOU?
A COLD, UNFEEL-ING MONSTER LIKE YOU!
VERY WELL, DESHWITAT.
I'LL TELL YOU A STORY THAT MIGHT PUT A FIRE IN YOU, MAKE YOU FIGHT!

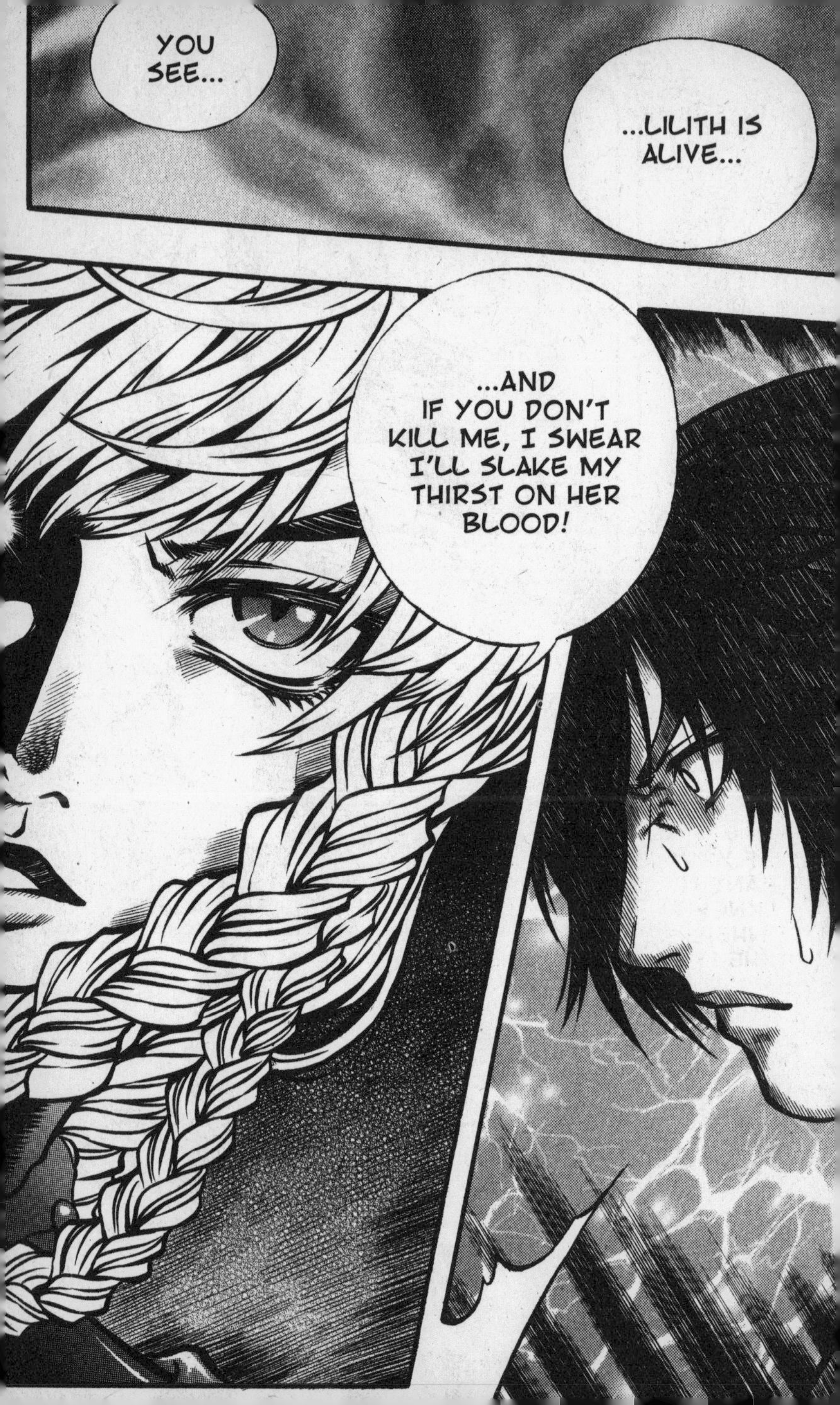

YOU SEE...
...LILITH IS ALIVE...
...AND IF YOU DON'T KILL ME, I SWEAR I'LL SLAKE MY THIRST ON HER BLOOD!

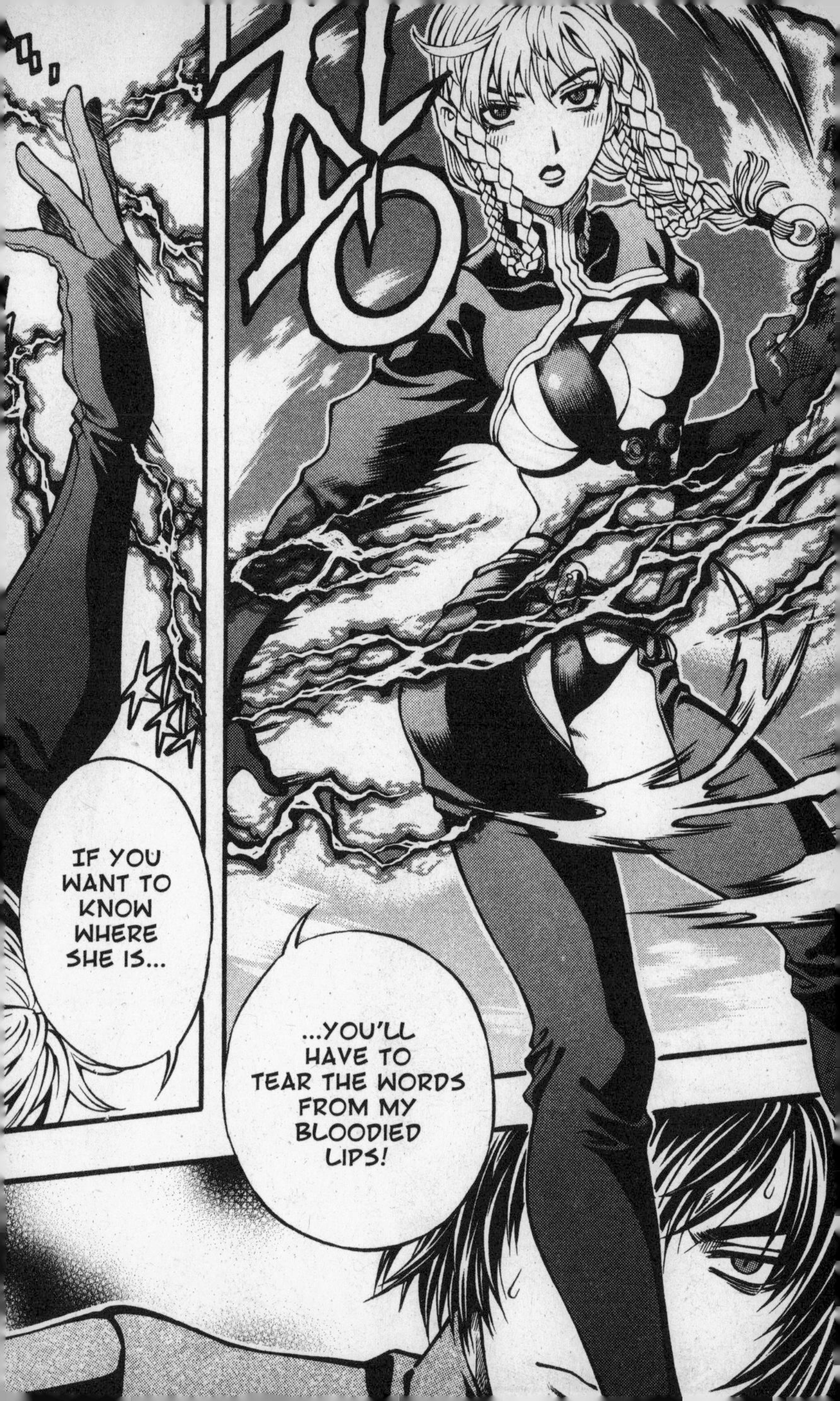
IF YOU WANT TO KNOW WHERE SHE IS...
...YOU'LL HAVE TO TEAR THE WORDS FROM MY BLOODIED LIPS!

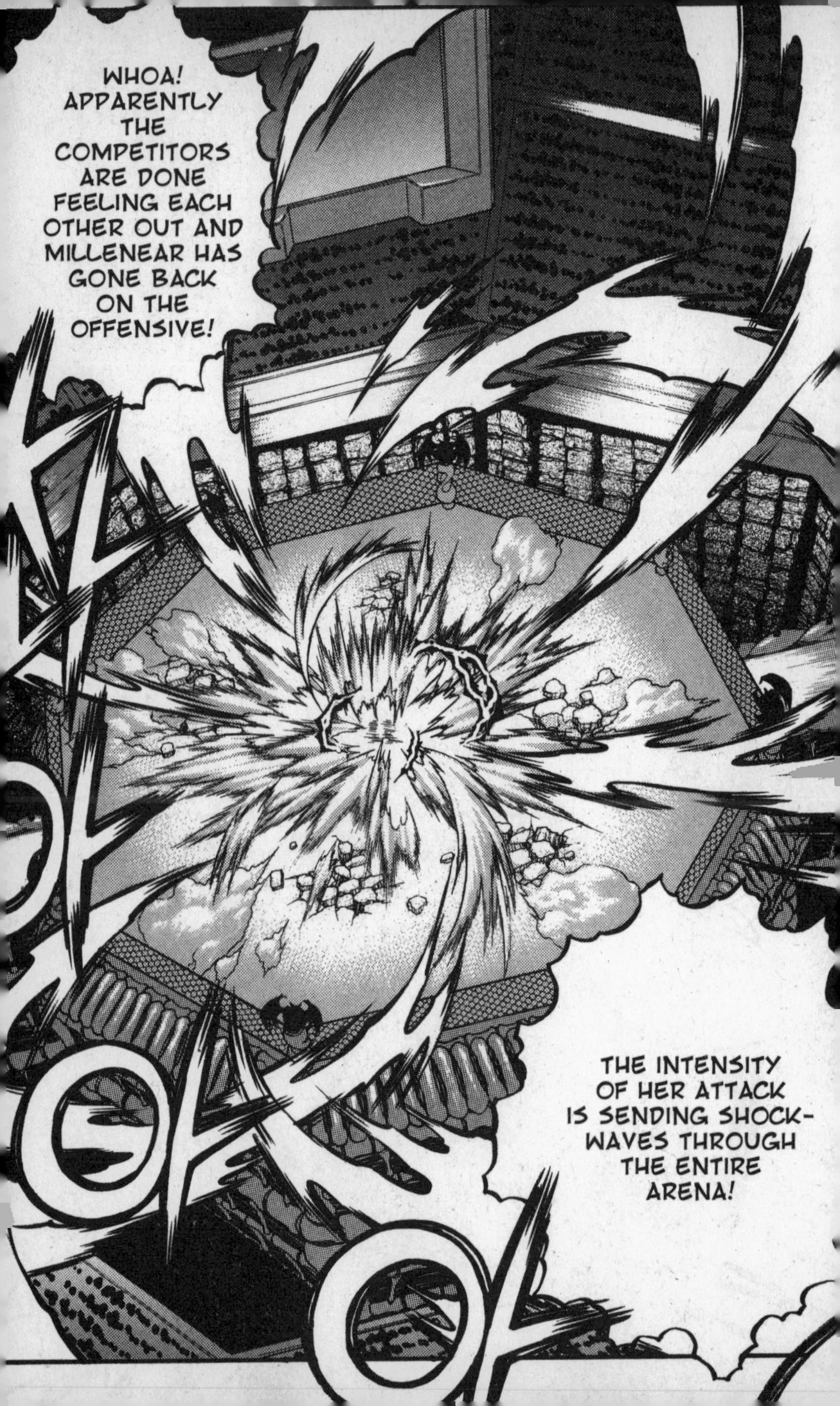
WHOA! APPARENTLY THE COMPETITORS ARE DONE FEELING EACH OTHER OUT AND MILLENEAR HAS GONE BACK ON THE OFFENSIVE!
THE INTENSITY OF HER ATTACK IS SENDING SHOCK-WAVES THROUGH THE ENTIRE ARENA!

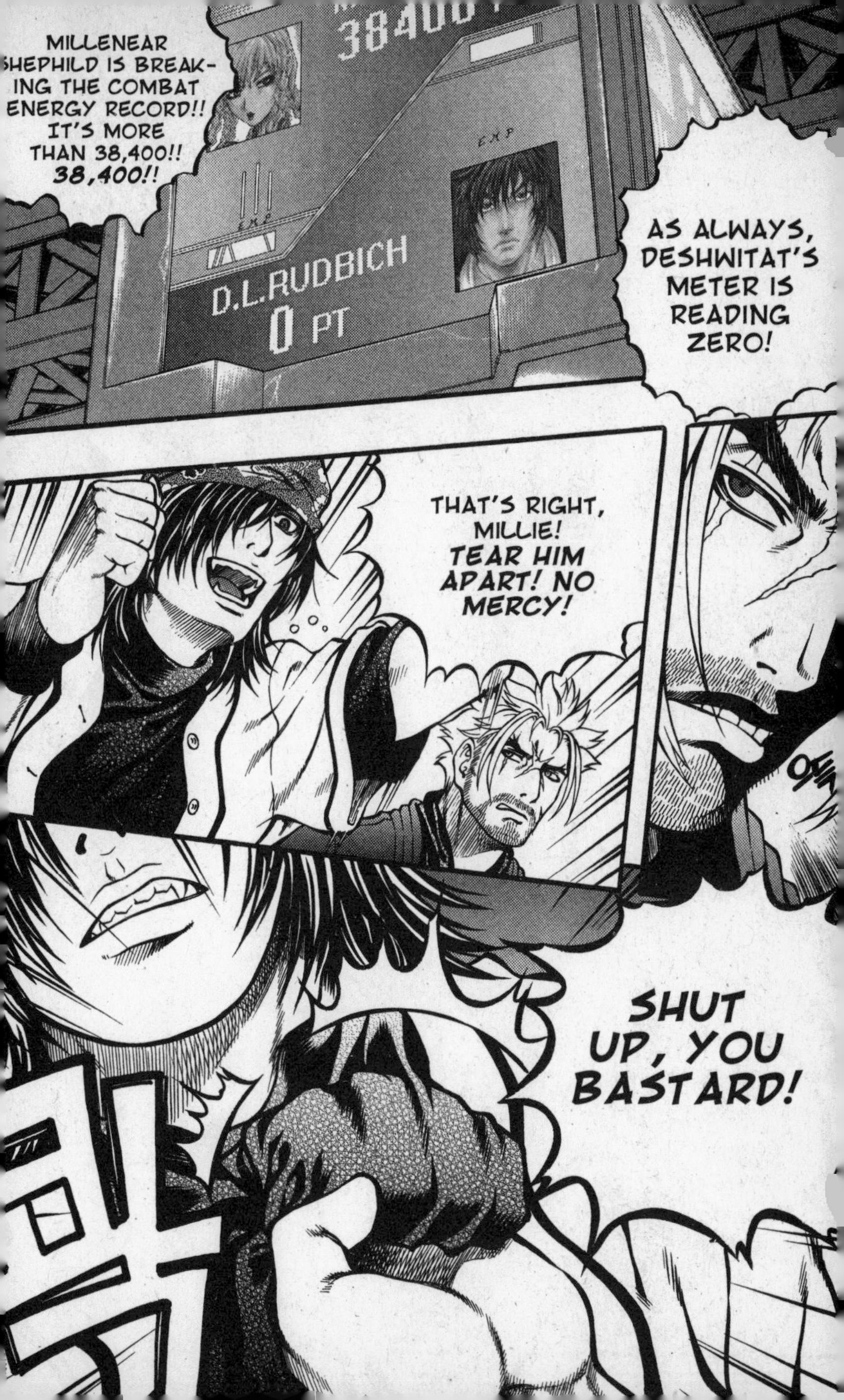
38400
MILLENEAR SHEPHILD IS BREAKING THE COMBAT ENERGY RECORD!! IT'S MORE THAN 38,400!! 38,400!!
D.L.RUDBICH
0 PT
AS ALWAYS, DESHWITAT'S METER IS READING ZERO!
THAT'S RIGHT, MILLIE! TEAR HIM APART! NO MERCY!
SHUT UP, YOU BASTARD!

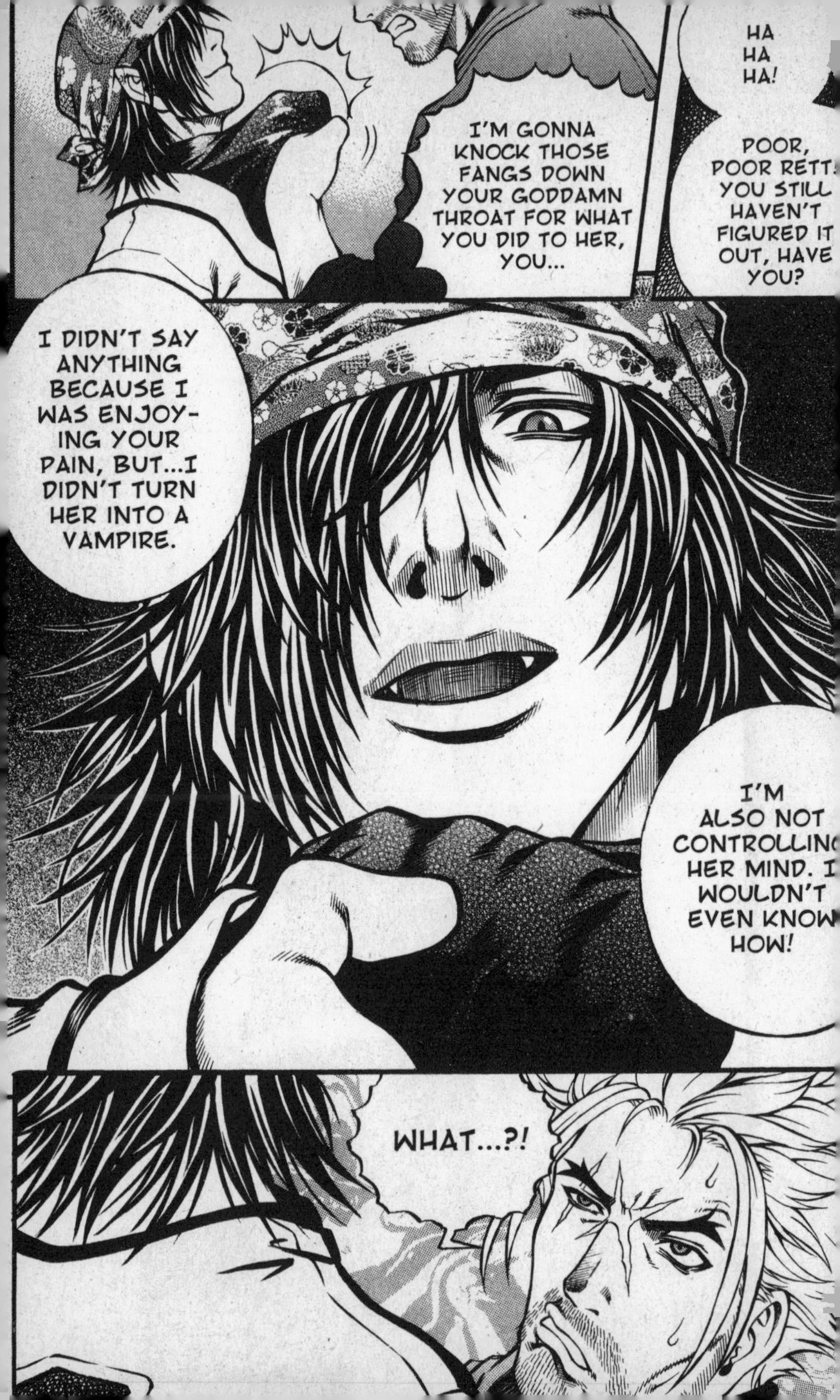
I'M GONNA KNOCK THOSE FANGS DOWN YOUR GODDAMN THROAT FOR WHAT YOU DID TO HER, YOU...
HA HA HA!
POOR, POOR RETT: YOU STILL HAVEN'T FIGURED IT OUT, HAVE YOU?
I DIDN'T SAY ANYTHING BECAUSE I WAS ENJOYING YOUR PAIN, BUT...I DIDN'T TURN HER INTO A VAMPIRE.
I'M ALSO NOT CONTROLLING HER MIND. I WOULDN'T EVEN KNOW HOW!
WHAT...?!

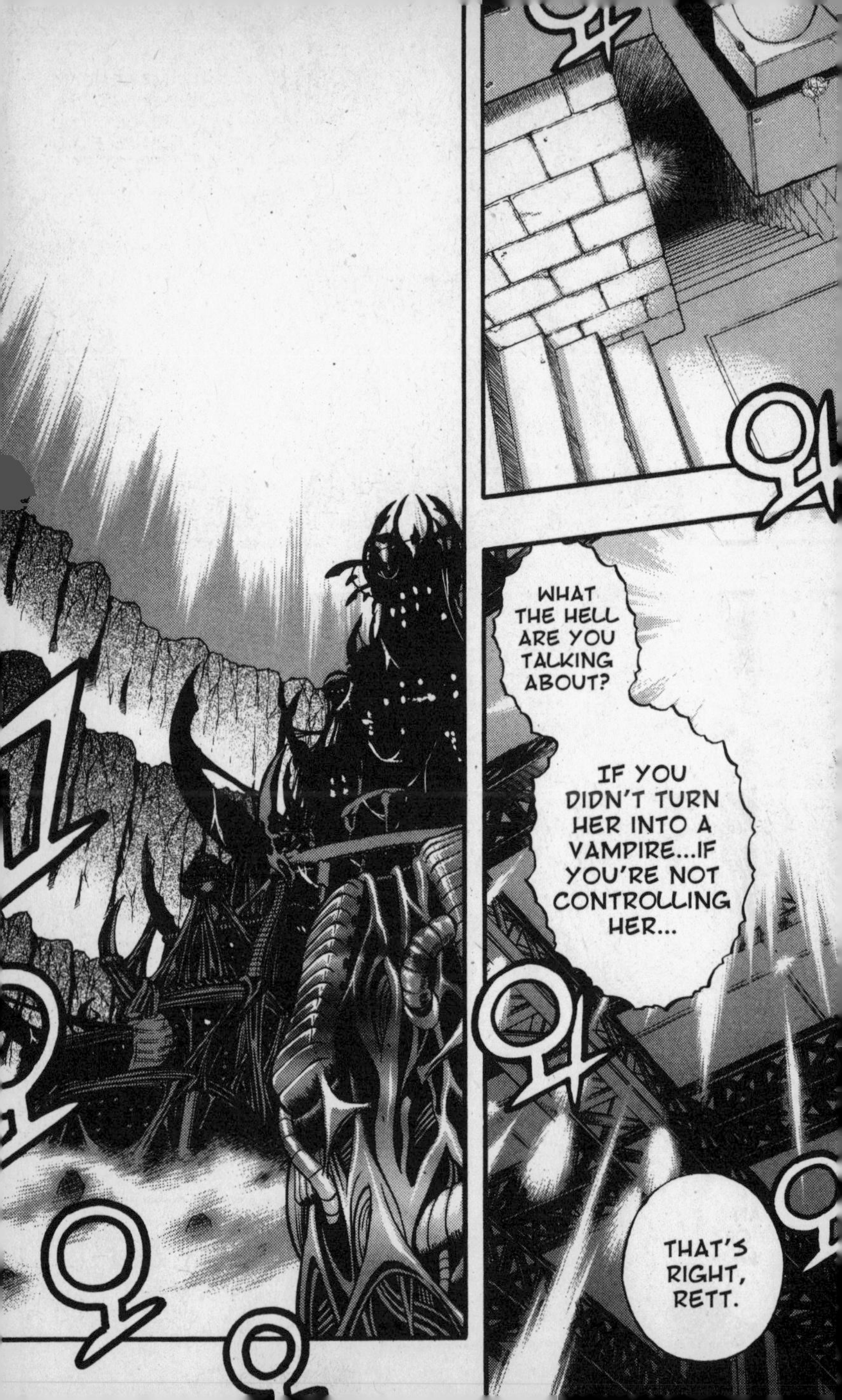
WHAT THE HELL ARE YOU TALKING ABOUT?
IF YOU DIDN'T TURN HER INTO A VAMPIRE...IF YOU'RE NOT CONTROLLING HER...
THAT'S RIGHT, RETT.

TH-THIS IS CRAZY! YOU'RE SAYING...WHAT? THAT MILLENEAR DID THIS OF HER OWN FREE WILL?

THAT MILLENEAR WAS SO TWISTED WITH JEALOUSY... NO! YOU'RE FULL OF SHIT, GREY!

WHETHER YOU BELIEVE ME OR NOT IS OF LITTLE CONSEQUENCE.

OH...AND YOU CAN LET GO OF ME NOW.

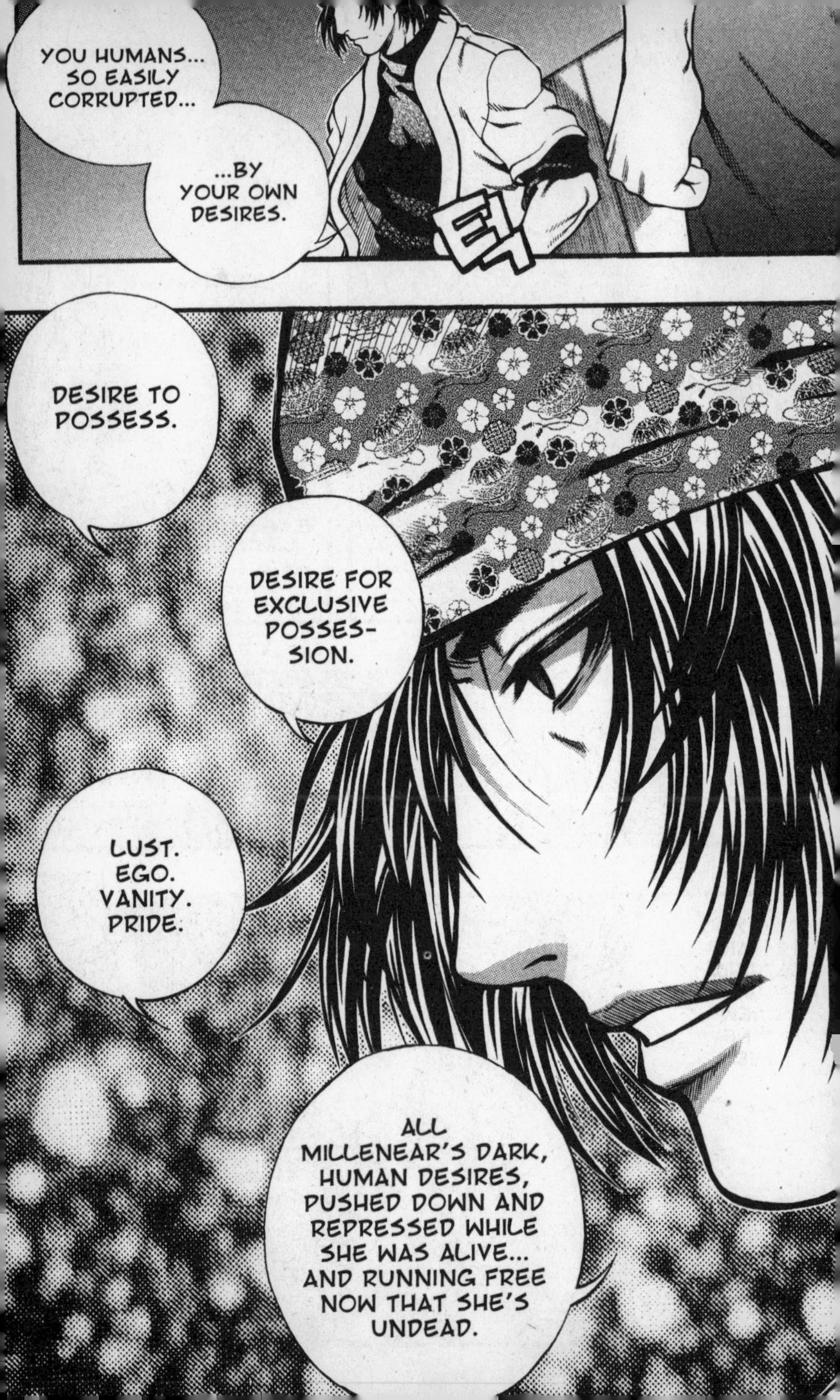
YOU HUMANS... SO EASILY CORRUPTED...
...BY YOUR OWN DESIRES.
DESIRE TO POSSESS.
DESIRE FOR EXCLUSIVE POSSES-SION.
LUST. EGO. VANITY. PRIDE.
ALL MILLENEAR'S DARK, HUMAN DESIRES, PUSHED DOWN AND REPRESSED WHILE SHE WAS ALIVE... AND RUNNING FREE NOW THAT SHE'S UNDEAD.

IF THIS WERE ANYONE ELSE, I MIGHT BELIEVE THIS BULLSHIT.

BUT NOT MILLENEAR. DO YOU EVEN KNOW WHAT KIND OF WOMAN SHE WAS?

SHE WAS INNOCENT... CARING... SHY.

AND YOU EXPECT ME TO BELIEVE THAT SHE BECOMES AN INCARNATION OF DESIRE OVERNIGHT? THAT GIRL DIDN'T HAVE A COVETOUS BONE IN HER BODY.

ALL HUMANS COVET. AND AS FOR BONES IN HER BODY...

...WELL, IT SEEMS THE ONE SHE DESIRED MOST BELONGS TO DESHWITAT.

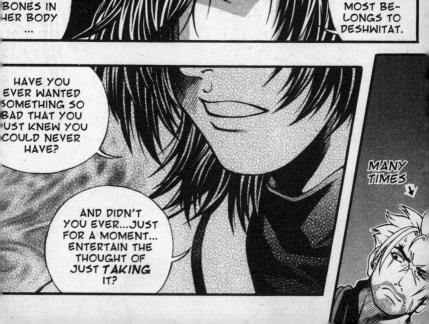

HAVE YOU EVER WANTED SOMETHING SO BAD THAT YOU JUST KNEW YOU COULD NEVER HAVE?

AND DIDN'T YOU EVER...JUST FOR A MOMENT... ENTERTAIN THE THOUGHT OF JUST *TAKING* IT?

MANY TIMES

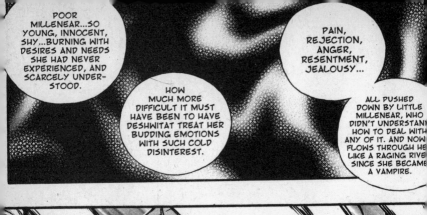

POOR MILLENEAR...SO YOUNG, INNOCENT, SHY...BURNING WITH DESIRES AND NEEDS SHE HAD NEVER EXPERIENCED, AND SCARCELY UNDER-STOOD.

HOW MUCH MORE DIFFICULT IT MUST HAVE BEEN TO HAVE DESHWITAT TREAT HER BUDDING EMOTIONS WITH SUCH COLD DISINTEREST.

PAIN, REJECTION, ANGER, RESENTMENT, JEALOUSY...

ALL PUSHED DOWN BY LITTLE MILLENEAR, WHO DIDN'T UNDERSTAND HOW TO DEAL WITH ANY OF IT. AND NOW FLOWS THROUGH HER LIKE A RAGING RIVER SINCE SHE BECAME A VAMPIRE.

IT'S ALWAYS THE QUIET ONES, YOU KNOW.

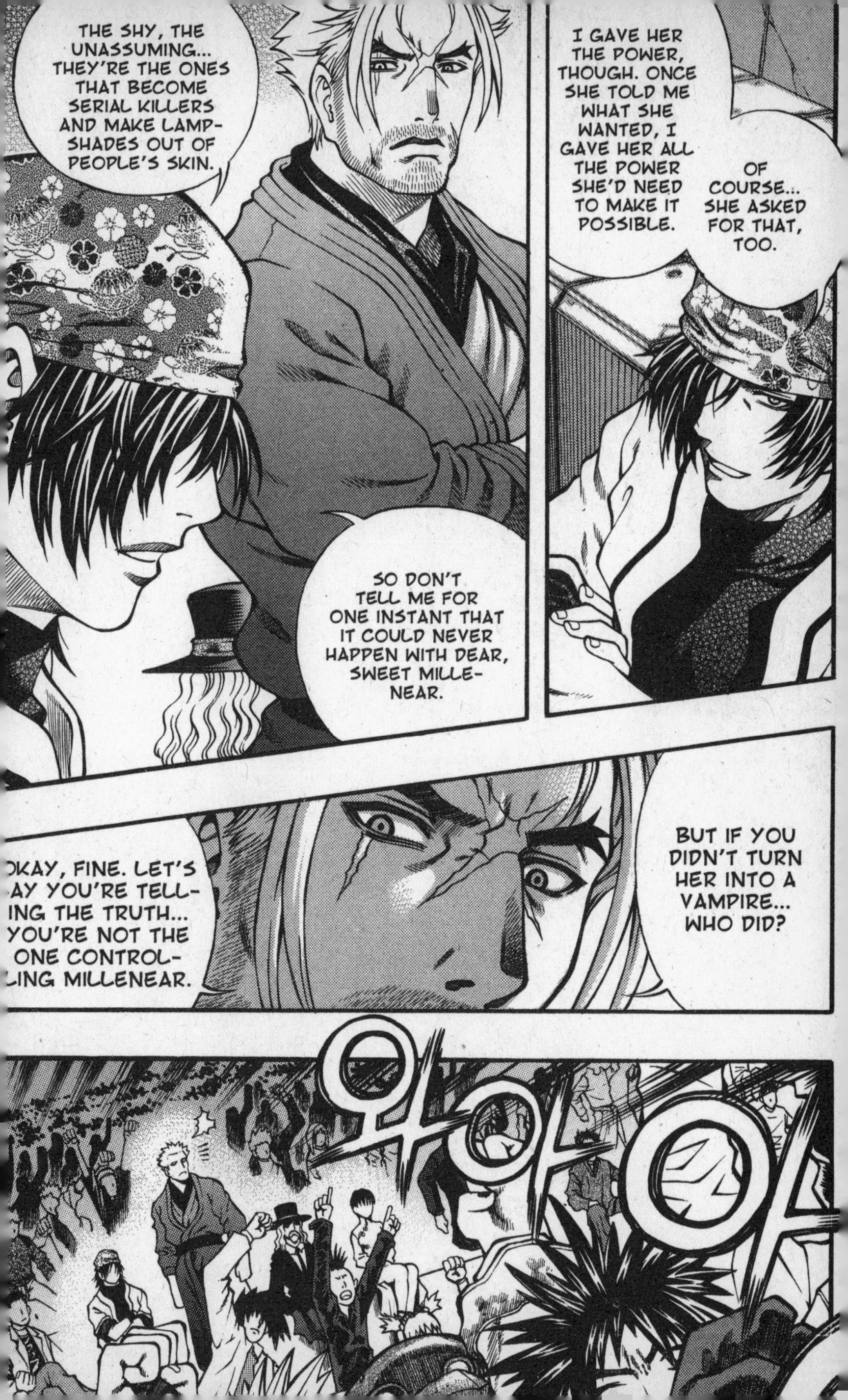
THE SHY, THE UNASSUMING... THEY'RE THE ONES THAT BECOME SERIAL KILLERS AND MAKE LAMP-SHADES OUT OF PEOPLE'S SKIN.
SO DON'T TELL ME FOR ONE INSTANT THAT IT COULD NEVER HAPPEN WITH DEAR, SWEET MILLE-NEAR.
I GAVE HER THE POWER, THOUGH. ONCE SHE TOLD ME WHAT SHE WANTED, I GAVE HER ALL THE POWER SHE'D NEED TO MAKE IT POSSIBLE.
OF COURSE... SHE ASKED FOR THAT, TOO.
OKAY, FINE. LET'S AY YOU'RE TELL-ING THE TRUTH... YOU'RE NOT THE ONE CONTROL-LING MILLENEAR.
BUT IF YOU DIDN'T TURN HER INTO A VAMPIRE... WHO DID?

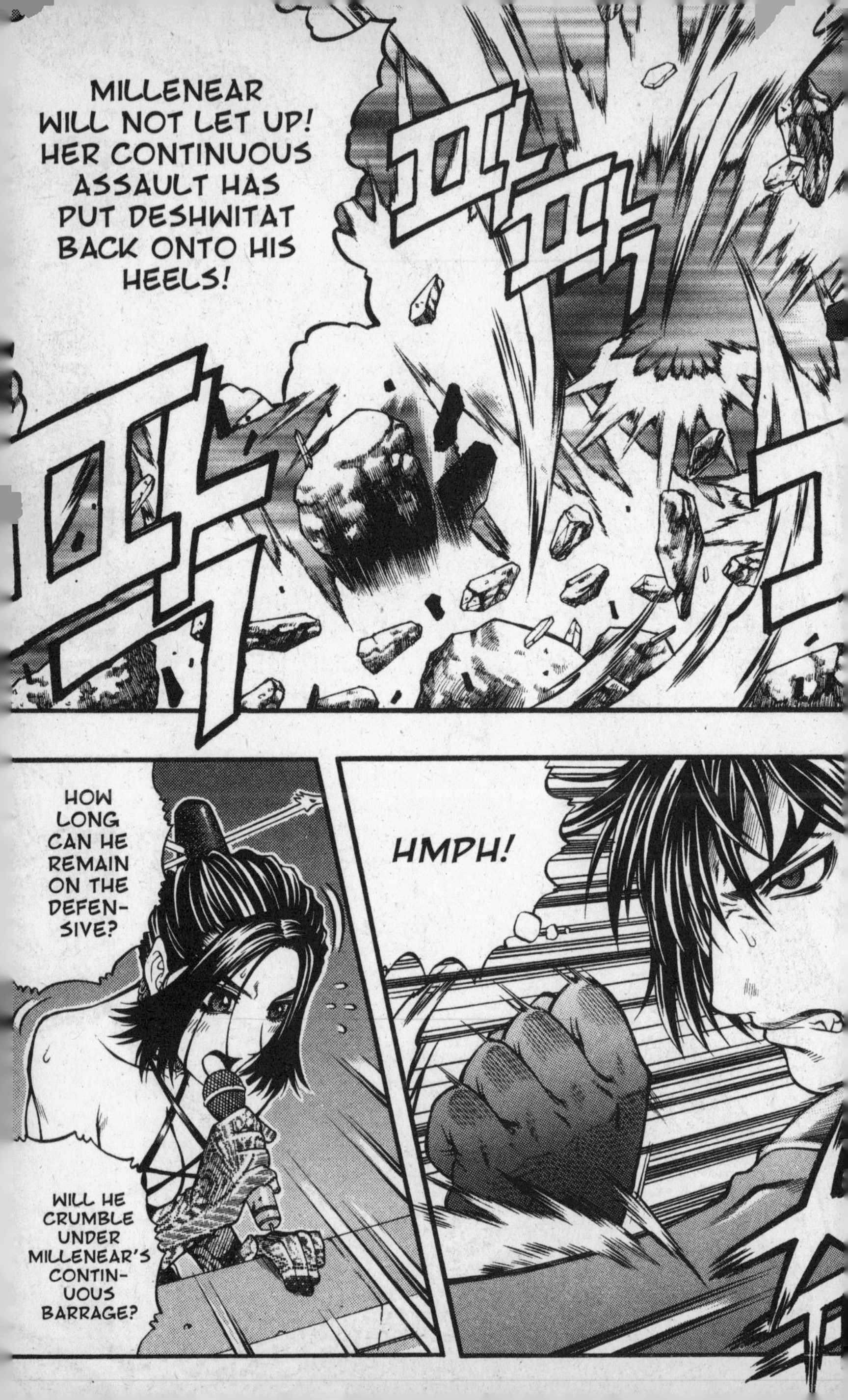
MILLENEAR WILL NOT LET UP! HER CONTINUOUS ASSAULT HAS PUT DESHWITAT BACK ONTO HIS HEELS!
HOW LONG CAN HE REMAIN ON THE DEFEN-SIVE?
HMPH!
WILL HE CRUMBLE UNDER MILLENEAR'S CONTIN-UOUS BARRAGE?

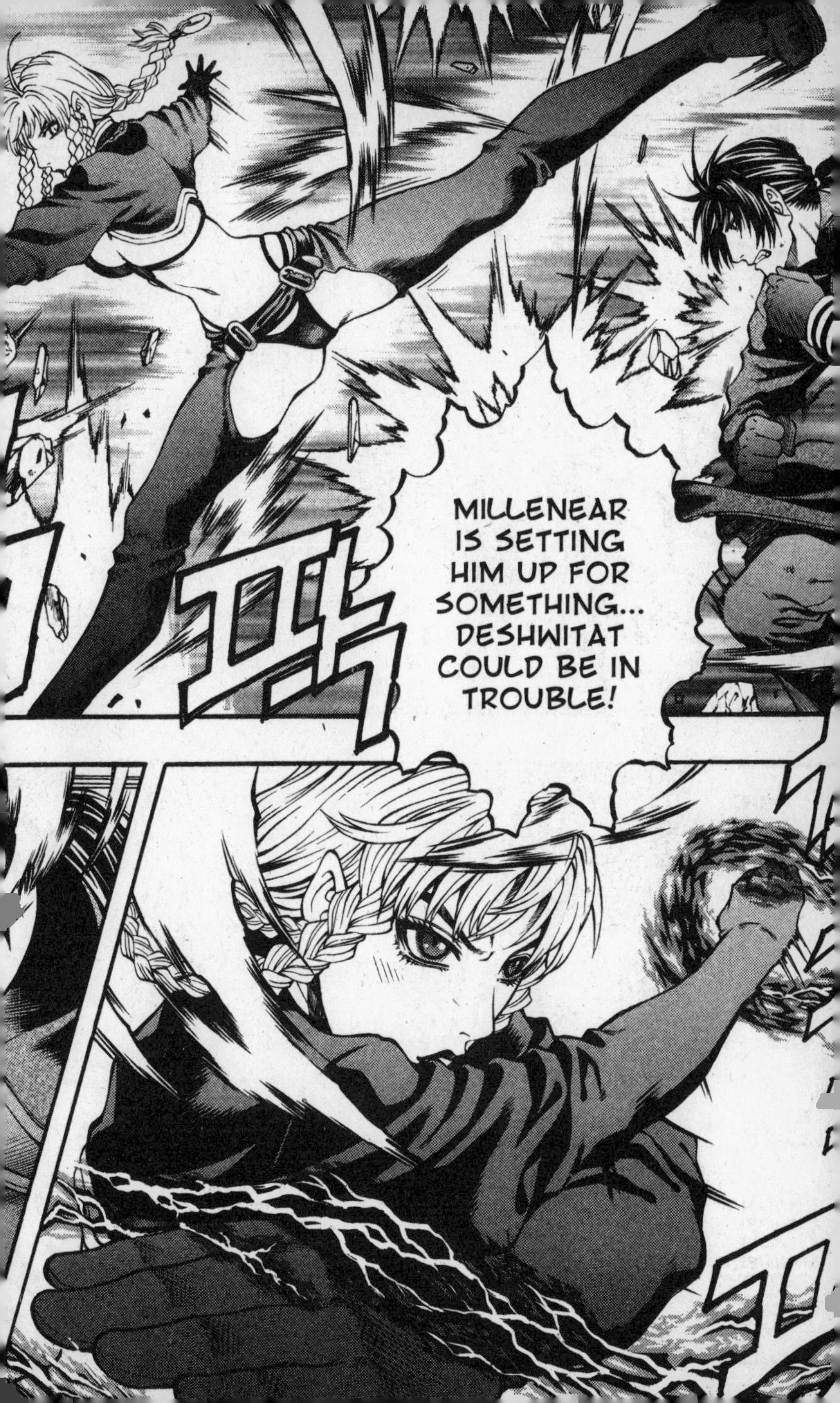
MILLENEAR IS SETTING HIM UP FOR SOMETHING... DESHWITAT COULD BE IN TROUBLE!

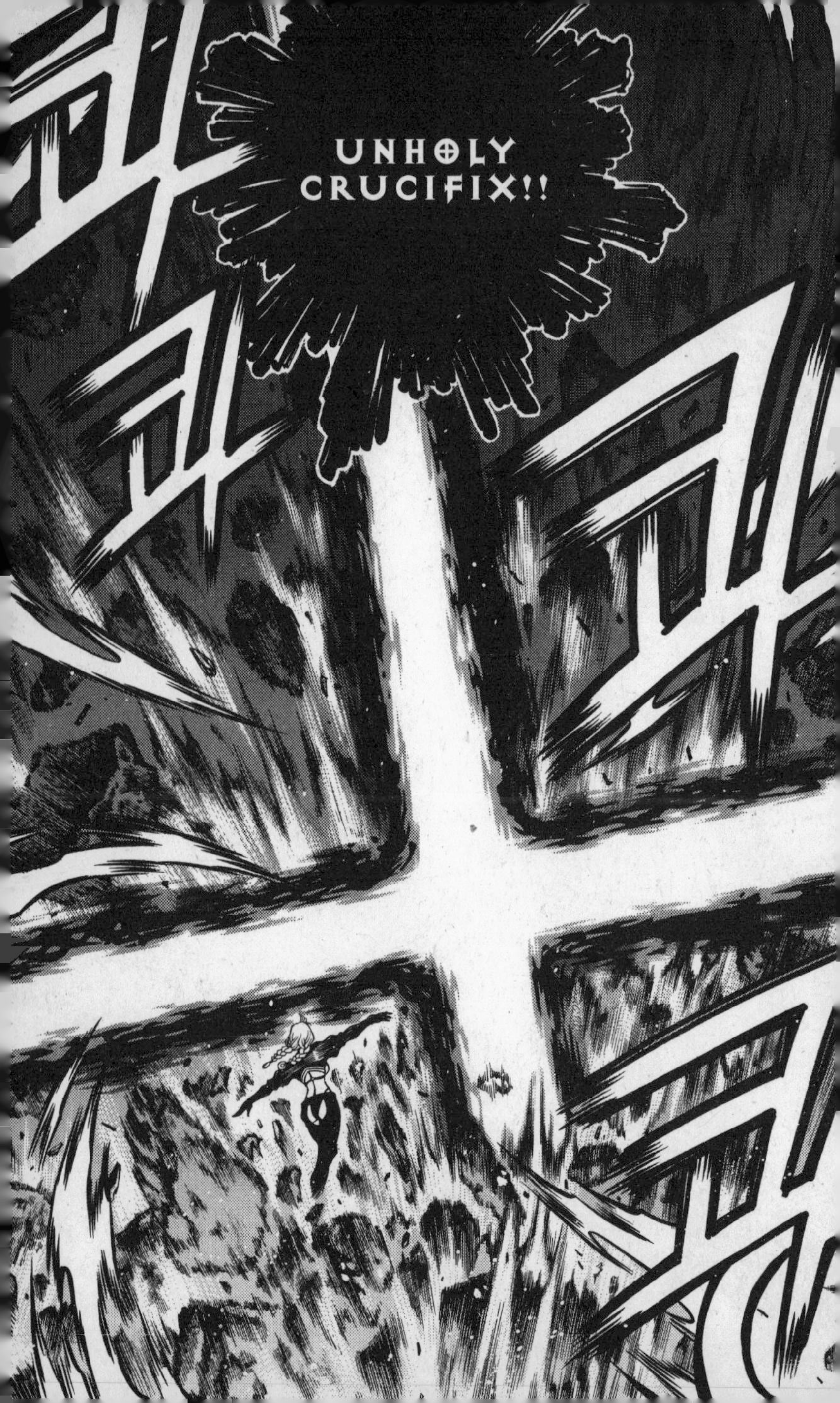
UNHOLY CRUCIFIX!!

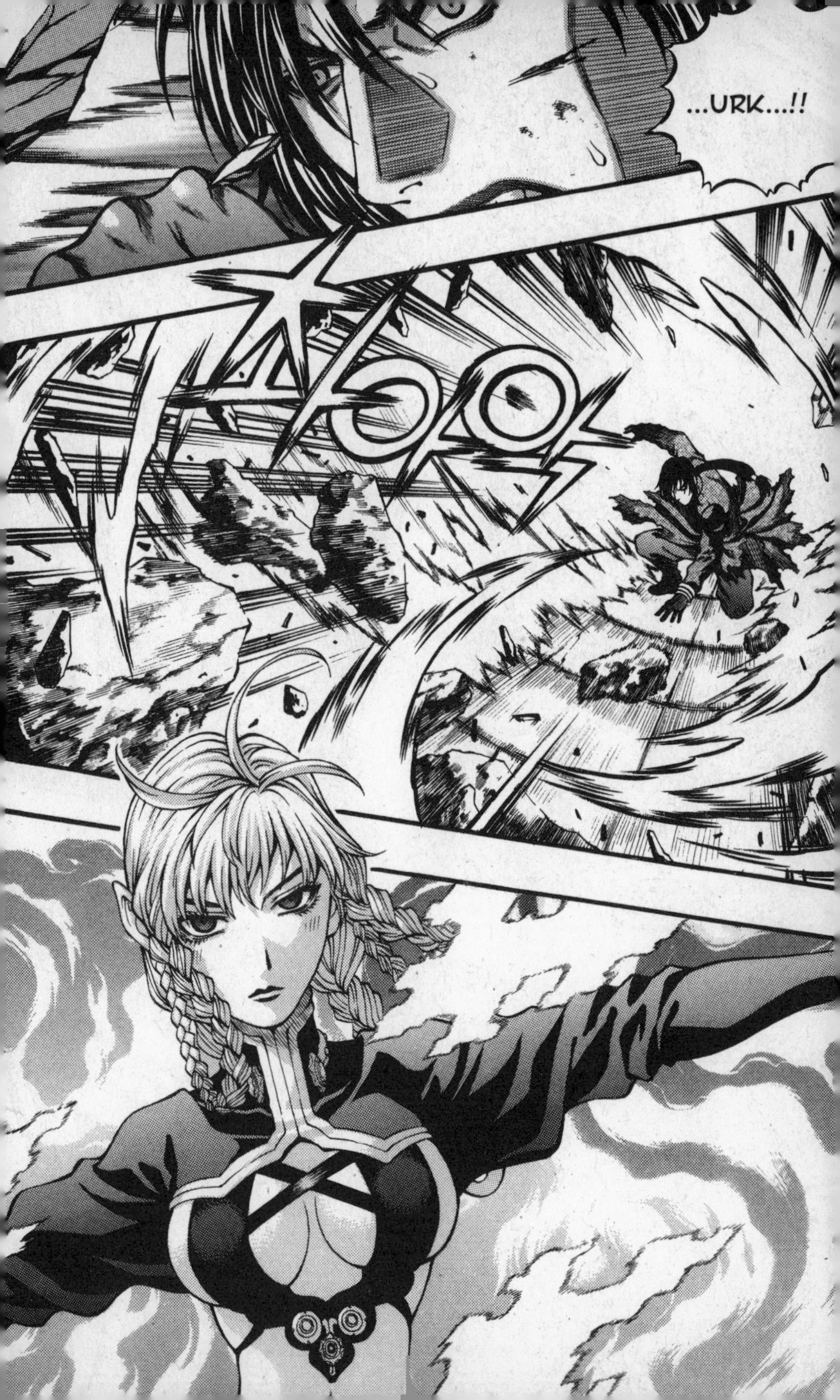
...URK...!!
DOOM

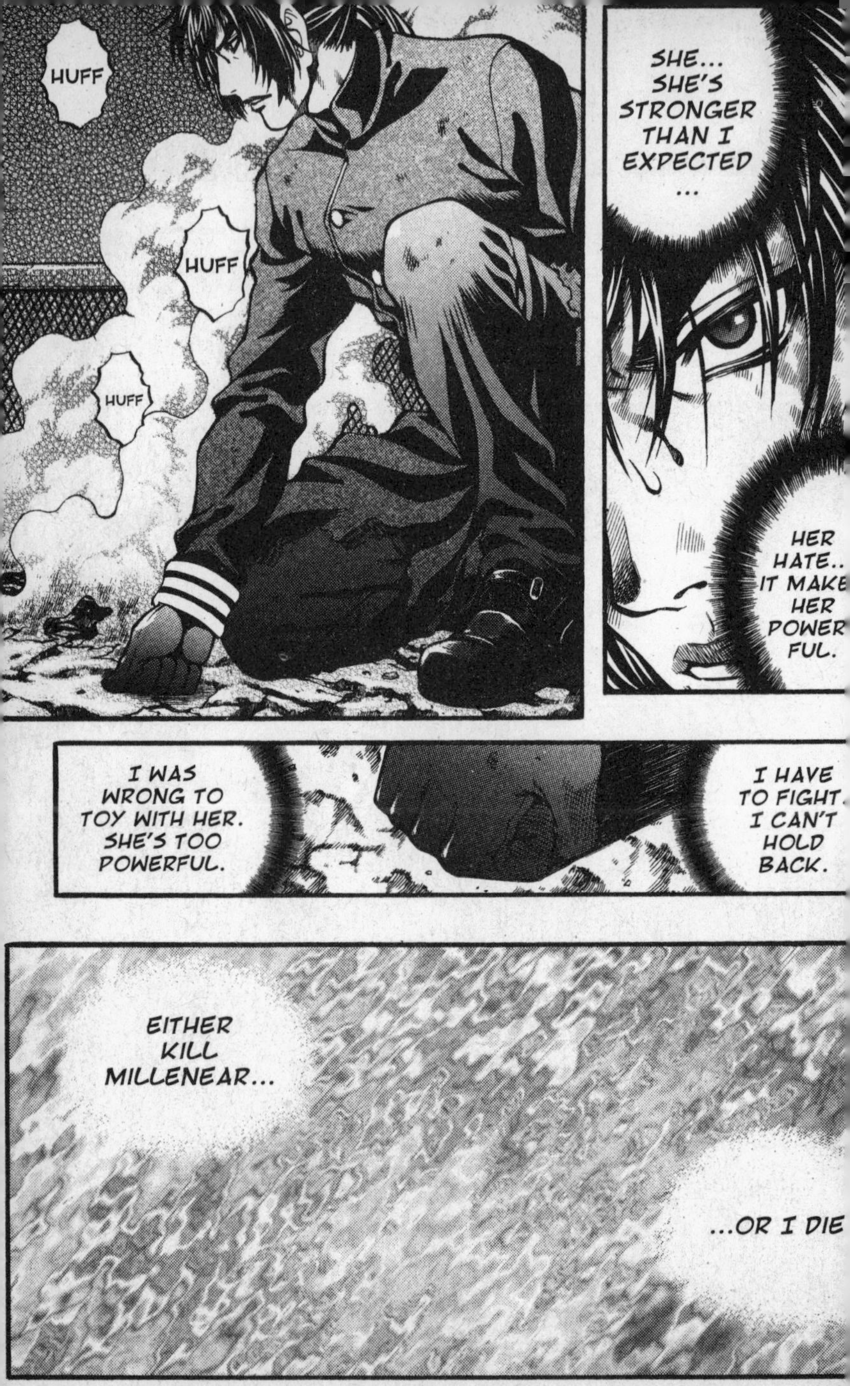

HUFF
HUFF
HUFF
SHE... SHE'S STRONGER THAN I EXPECTED ...
HER HATE.. IT MAKE HER POWER FUL.
I WAS WRONG TO TOY WITH HER. SHE'S TOO POWERFUL.
I HAVE TO FIGHT. I CAN'T HOLD BACK.
EITHER KILL MILLENEAR...
...OR I DIE

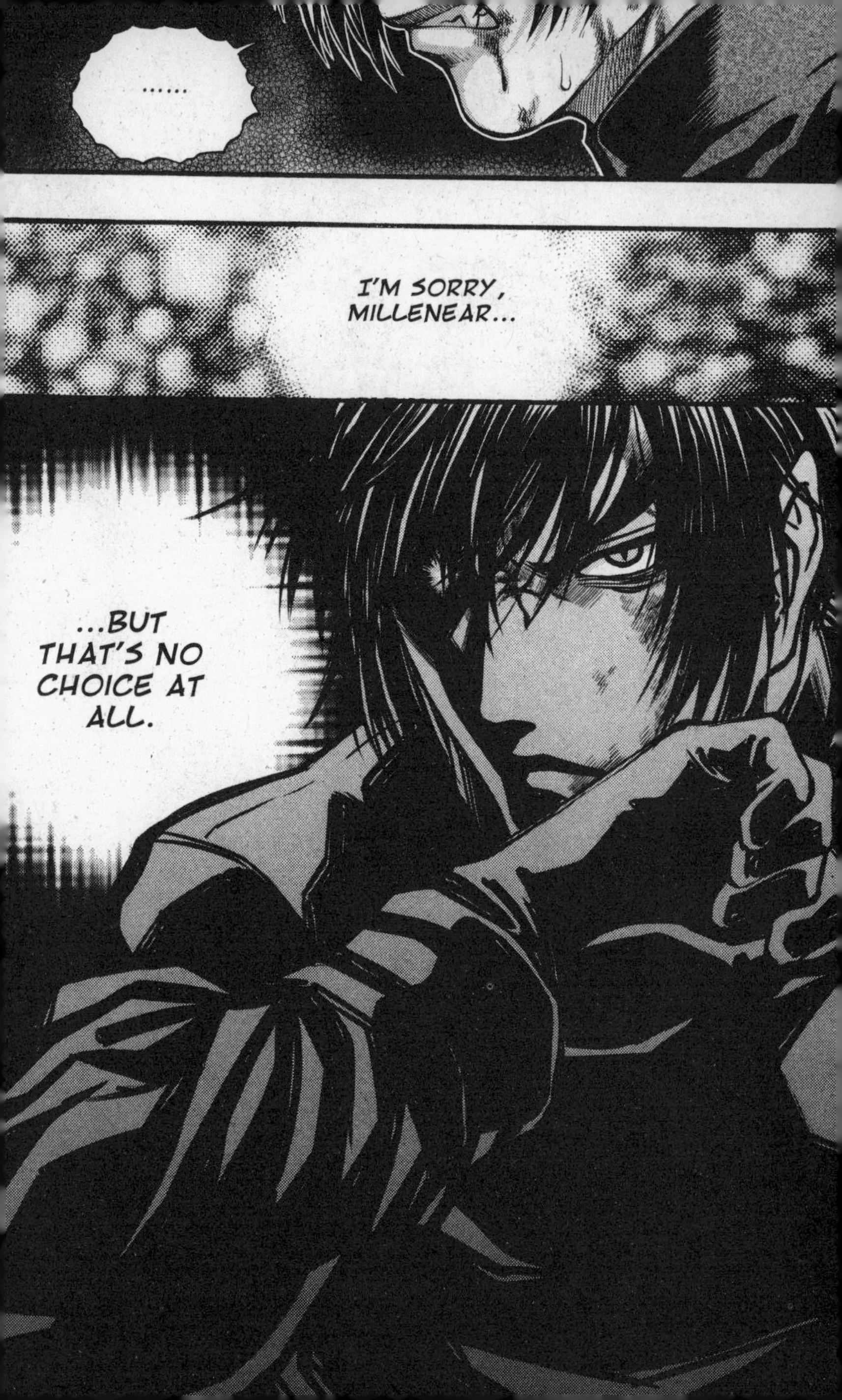
......
I'M SORRY, MILLENEAR...
...BUT THAT'S NO CHOICE AT ALL.

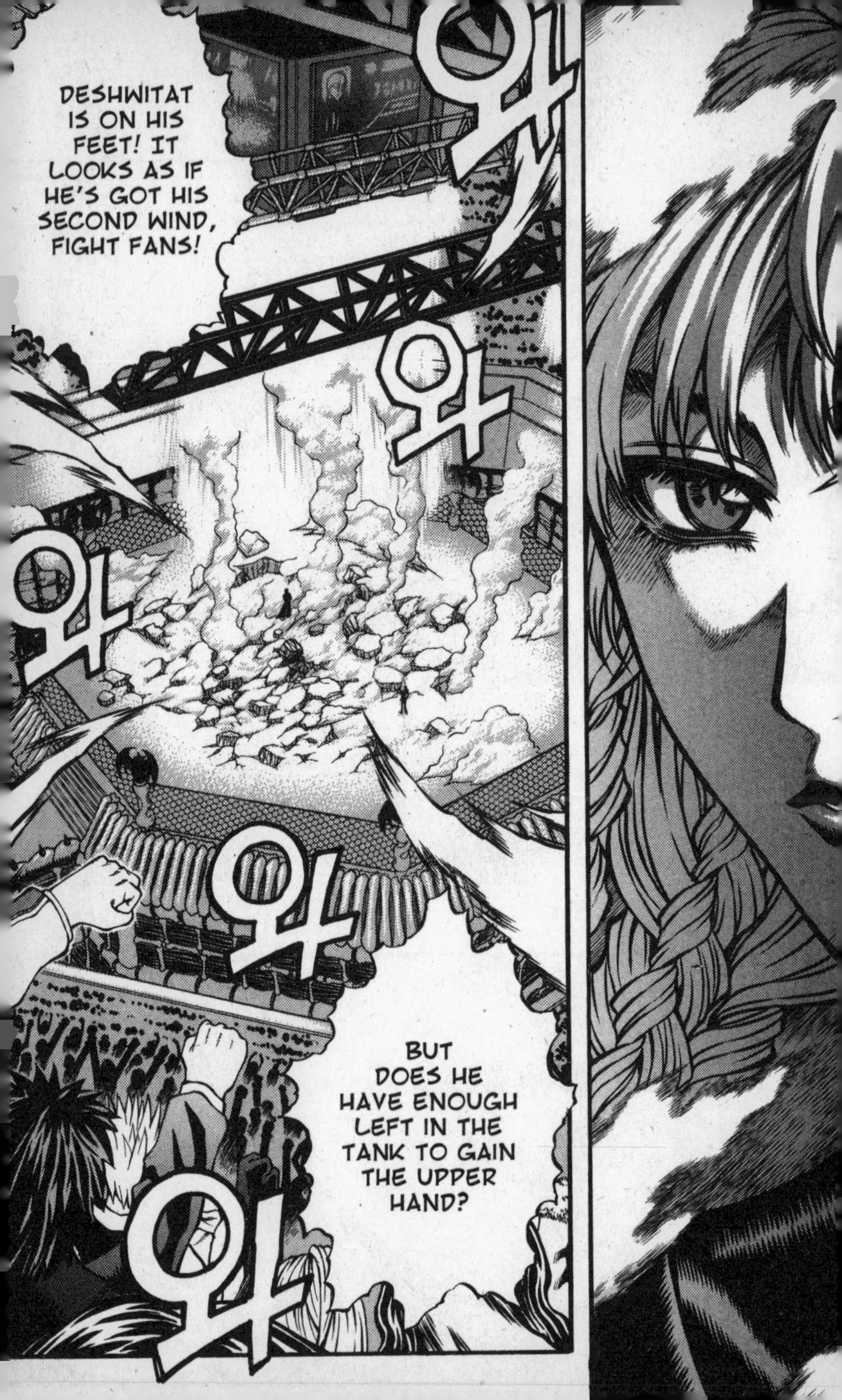
DESHWITAT IS ON HIS FEET! IT LOOKS AS IF HE'S GOT HIS SECOND WIND, FIGHT FANS!
BUT DOES HE HAVE ENOUGH LEFT IN THE TANK TO GAIN THE UPPER HAND?

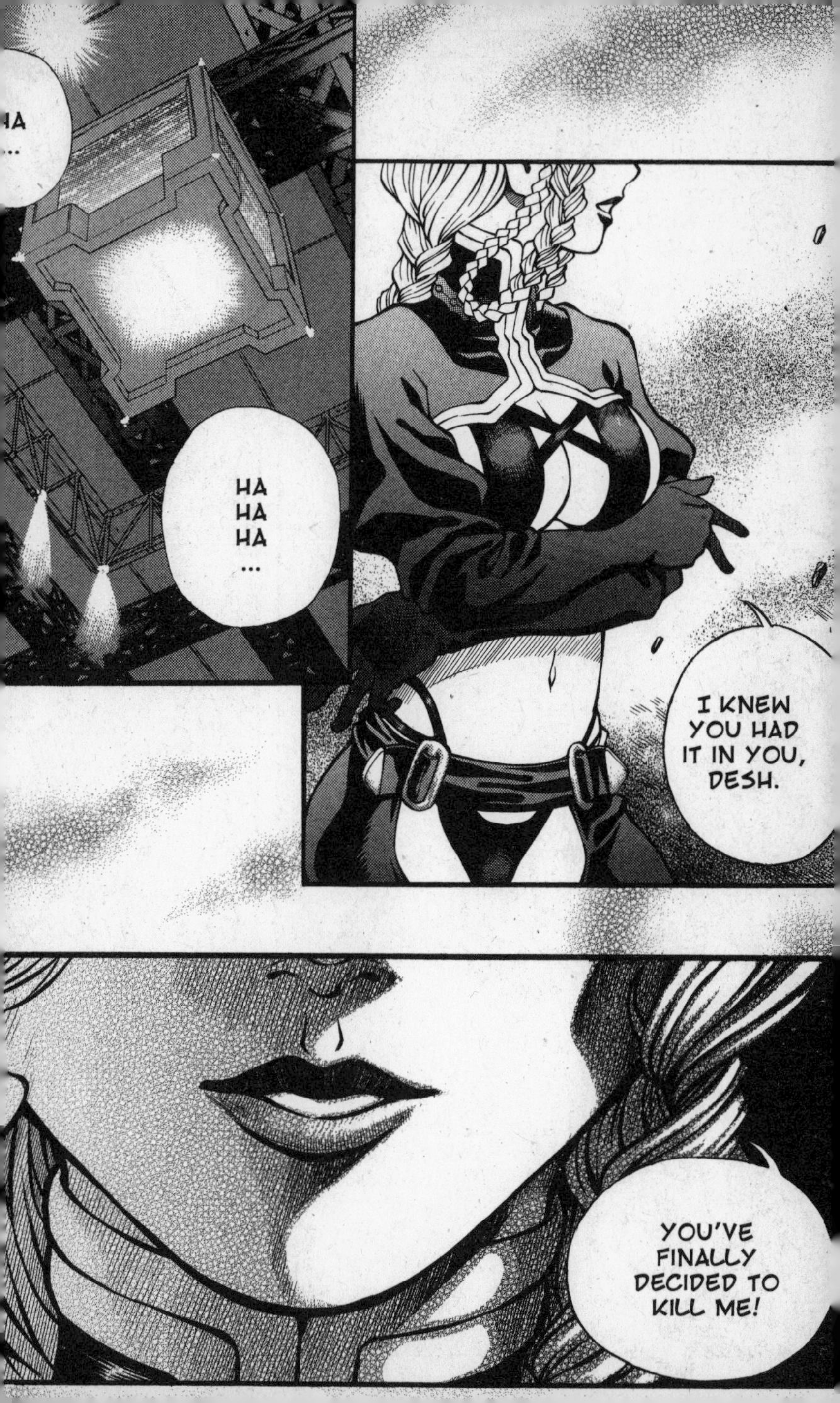
HA
...
HA
HA
HA
...
I KNEW YOU HAD IT IN YOU, DESH.
YOU'VE FINALLY DECIDED TO KILL ME!

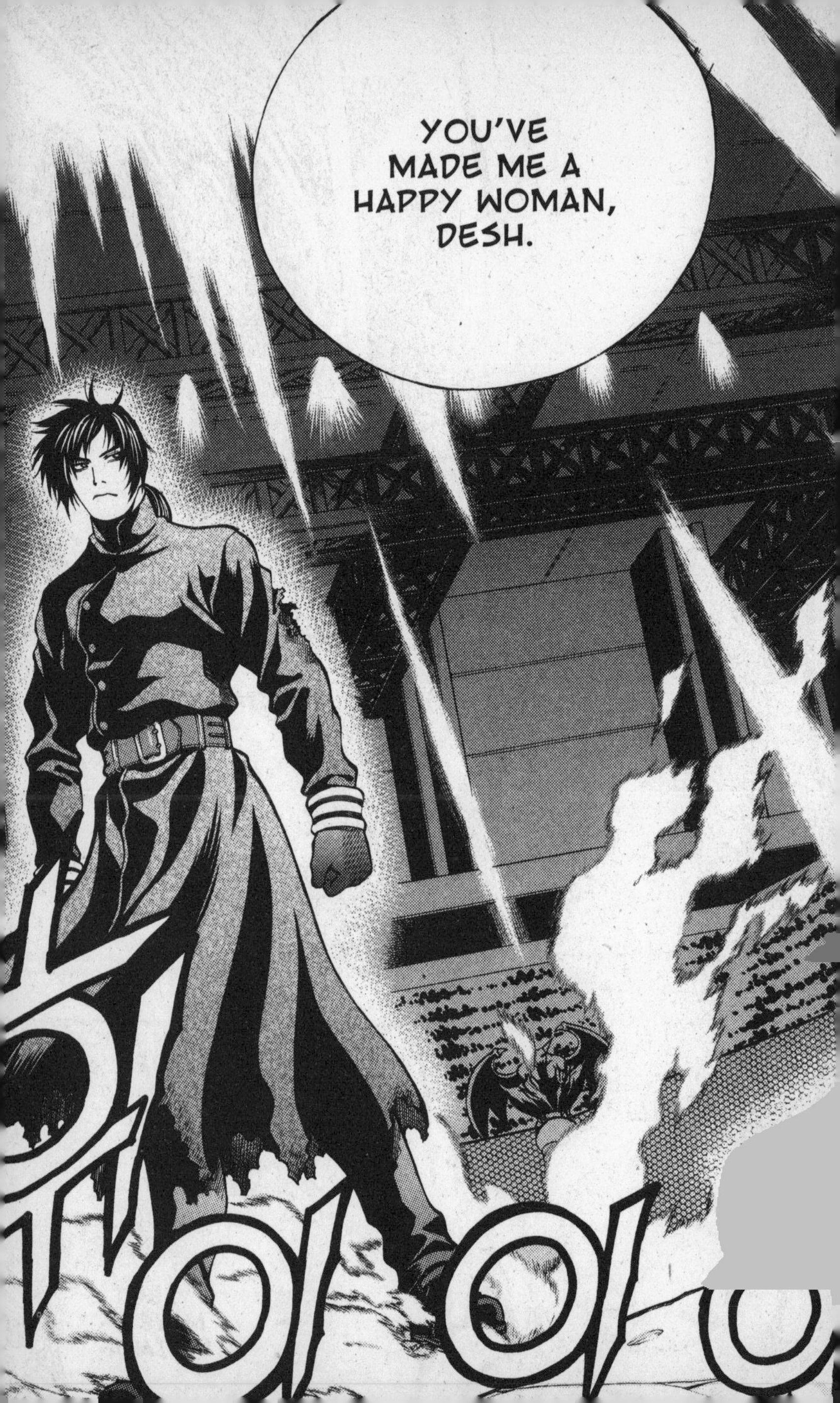
YOU'VE MADE ME A HAPPY WOMAN, DESH.

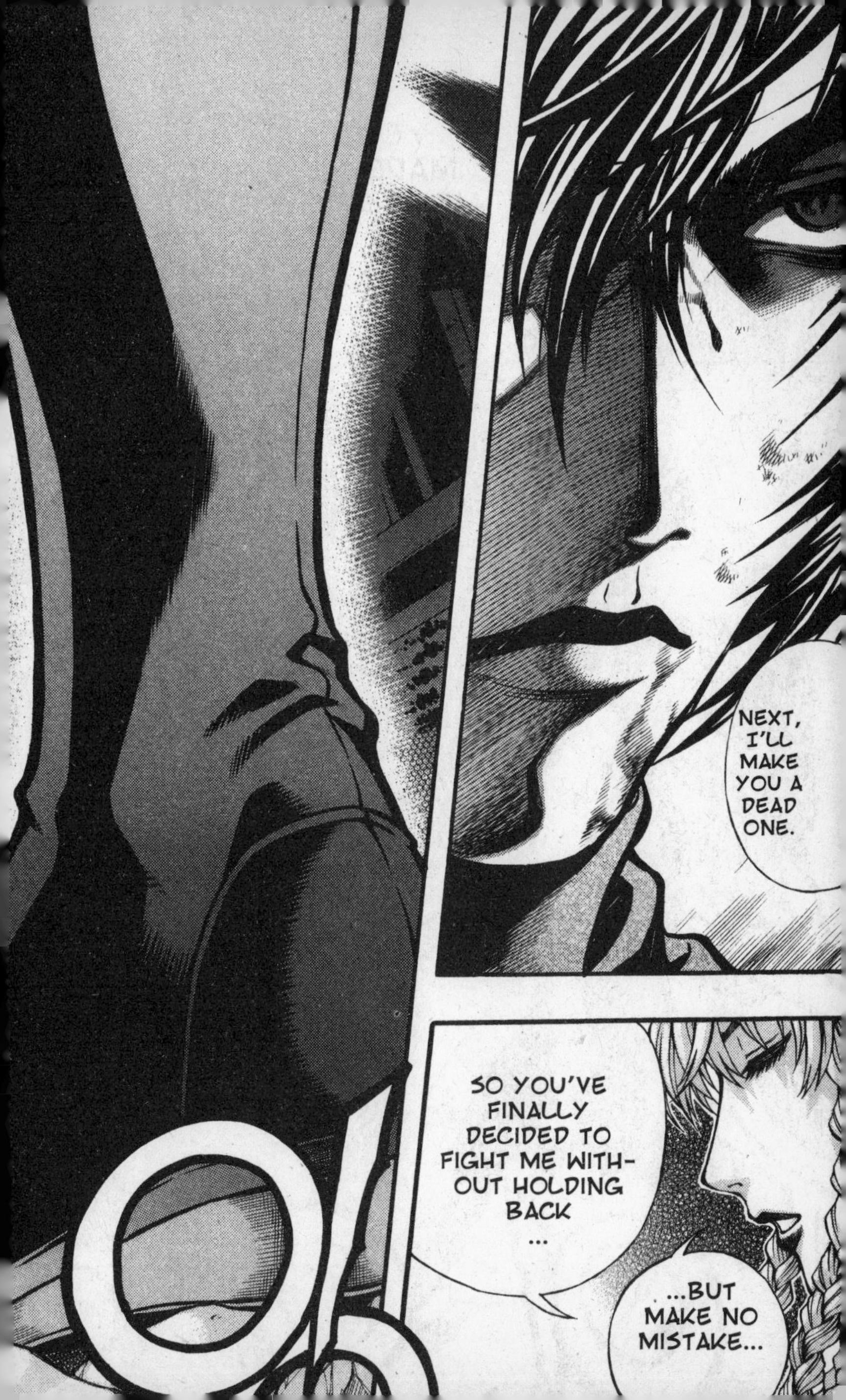
NEXT, I'LL MAKE YOU A DEAD ONE.
SO YOU'VE FINALLY DECIDED TO FIGHT ME WITH-OUT HOLDING BACK ...
...BUT MAKE NO MISTAKE...

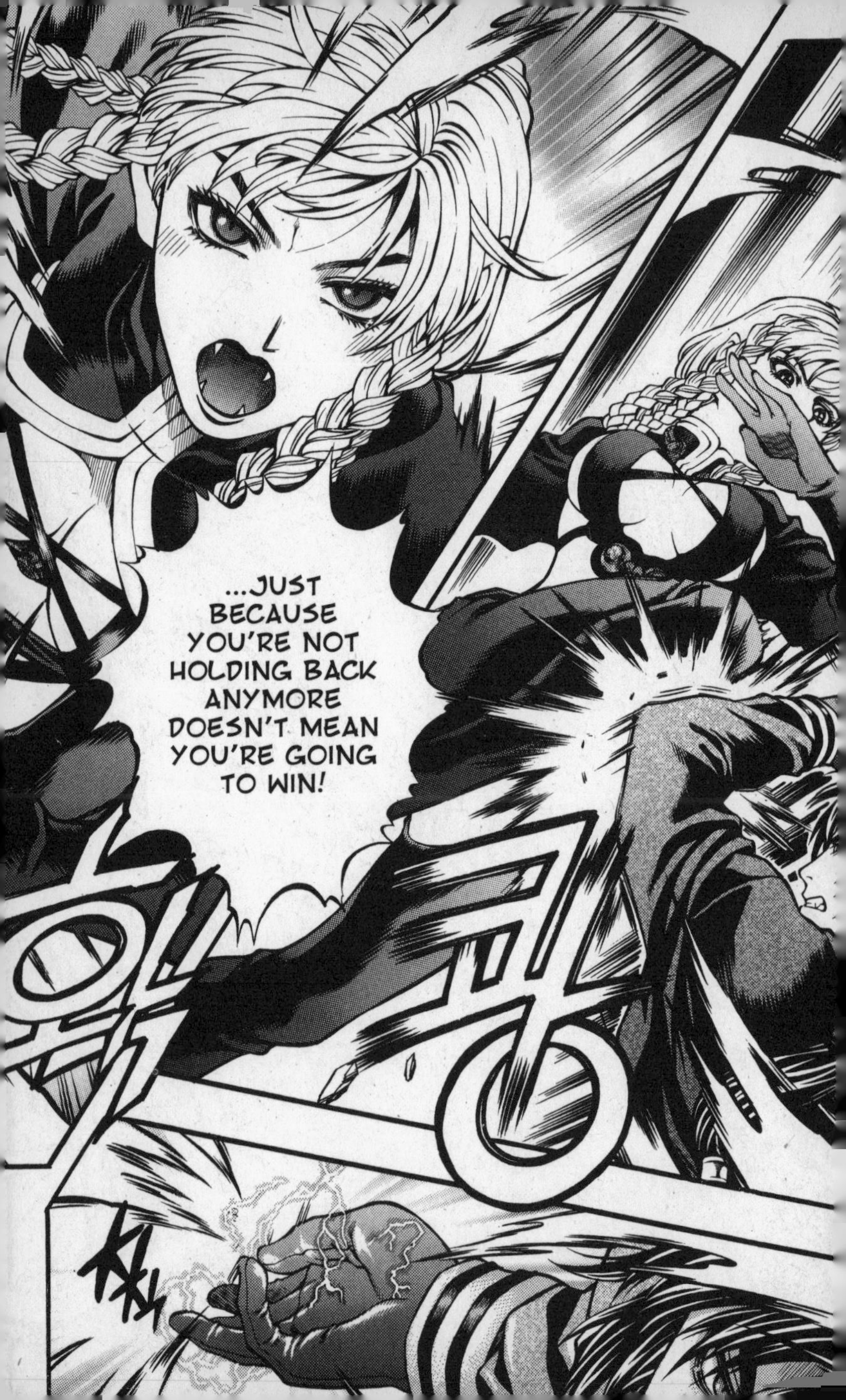
...JUST BECAUSE YOU'RE NOT HOLDING BACK ANYMORE DOESN'T MEAN YOU'RE GOING TO WIN!

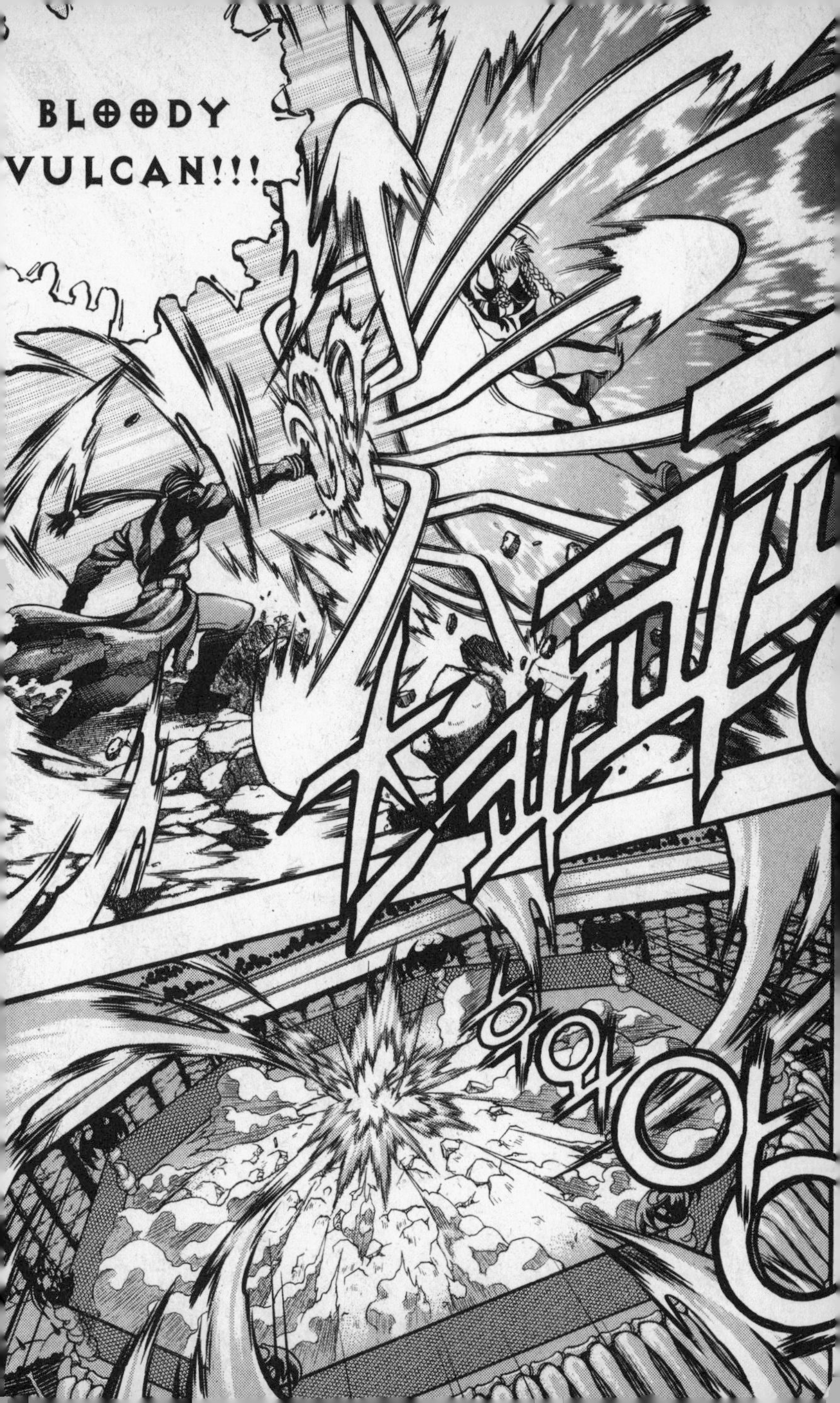
BLOODY
VULCAN!!!

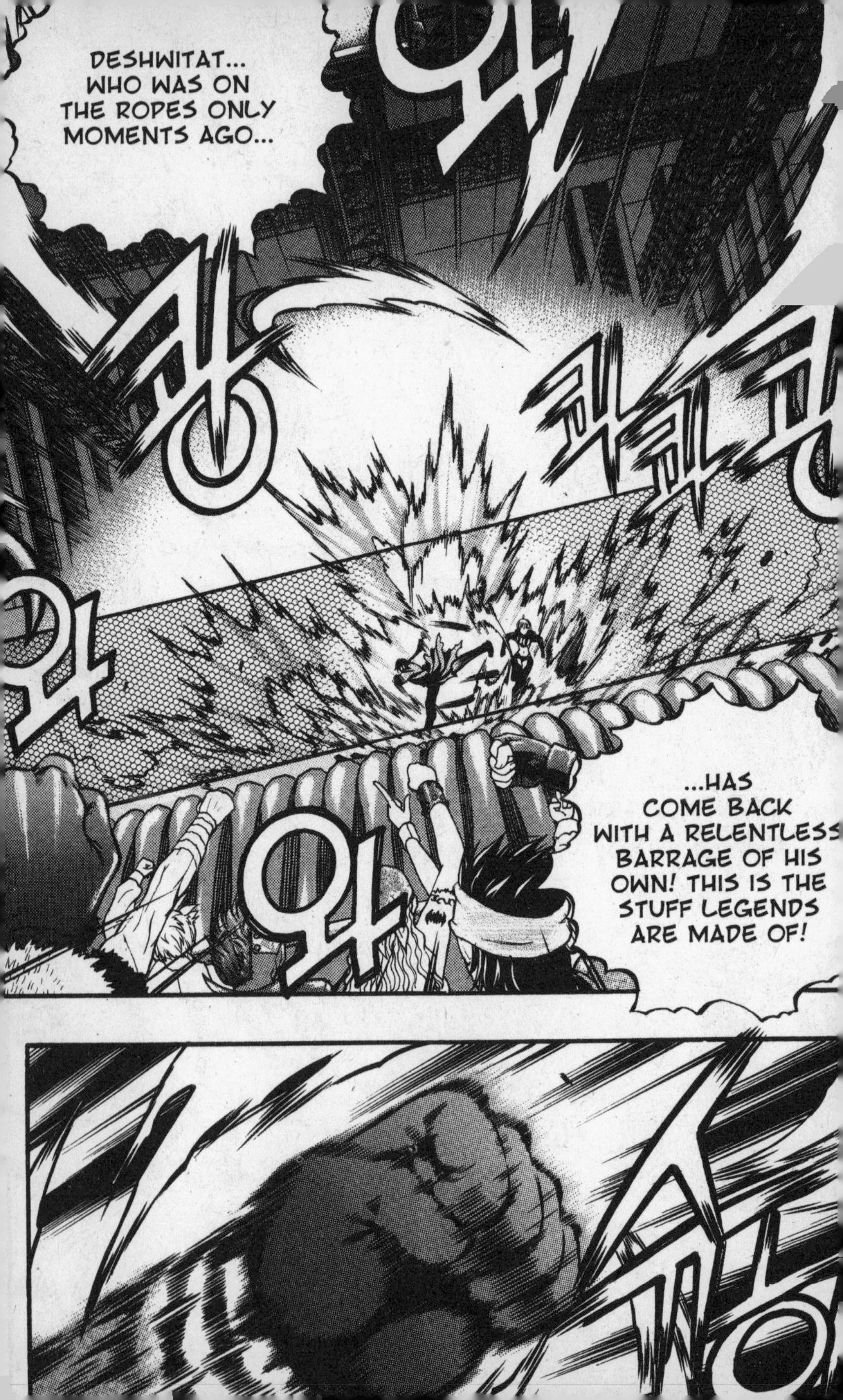
DESHWITAT... WHO WAS ON THE ROPES ONLY MOMENTS AGO...
...HAS COME BACK WITH A RELENTLESS BARRAGE OF HIS OWN! THIS IS THE STUFF LEGENDS ARE MADE OF!

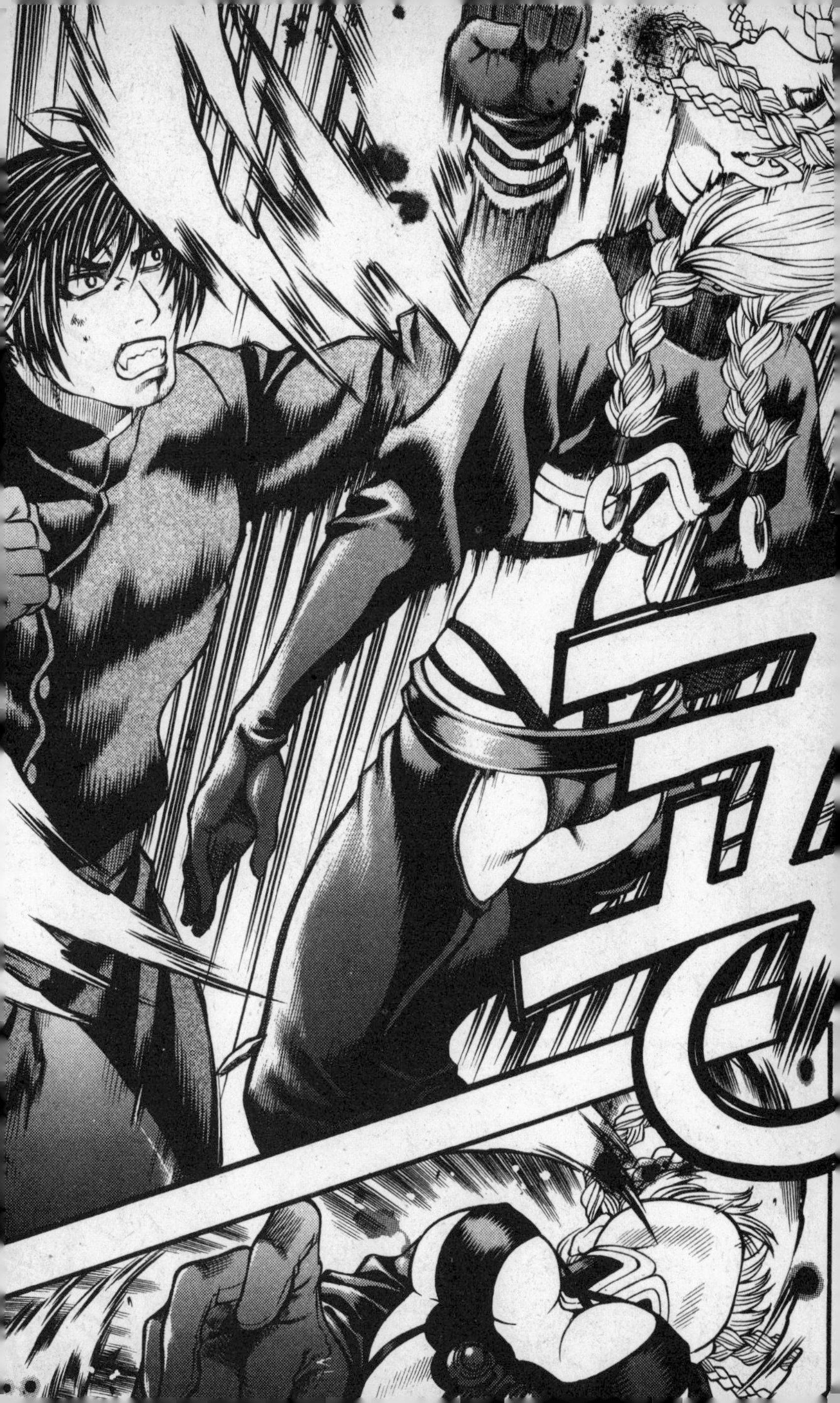

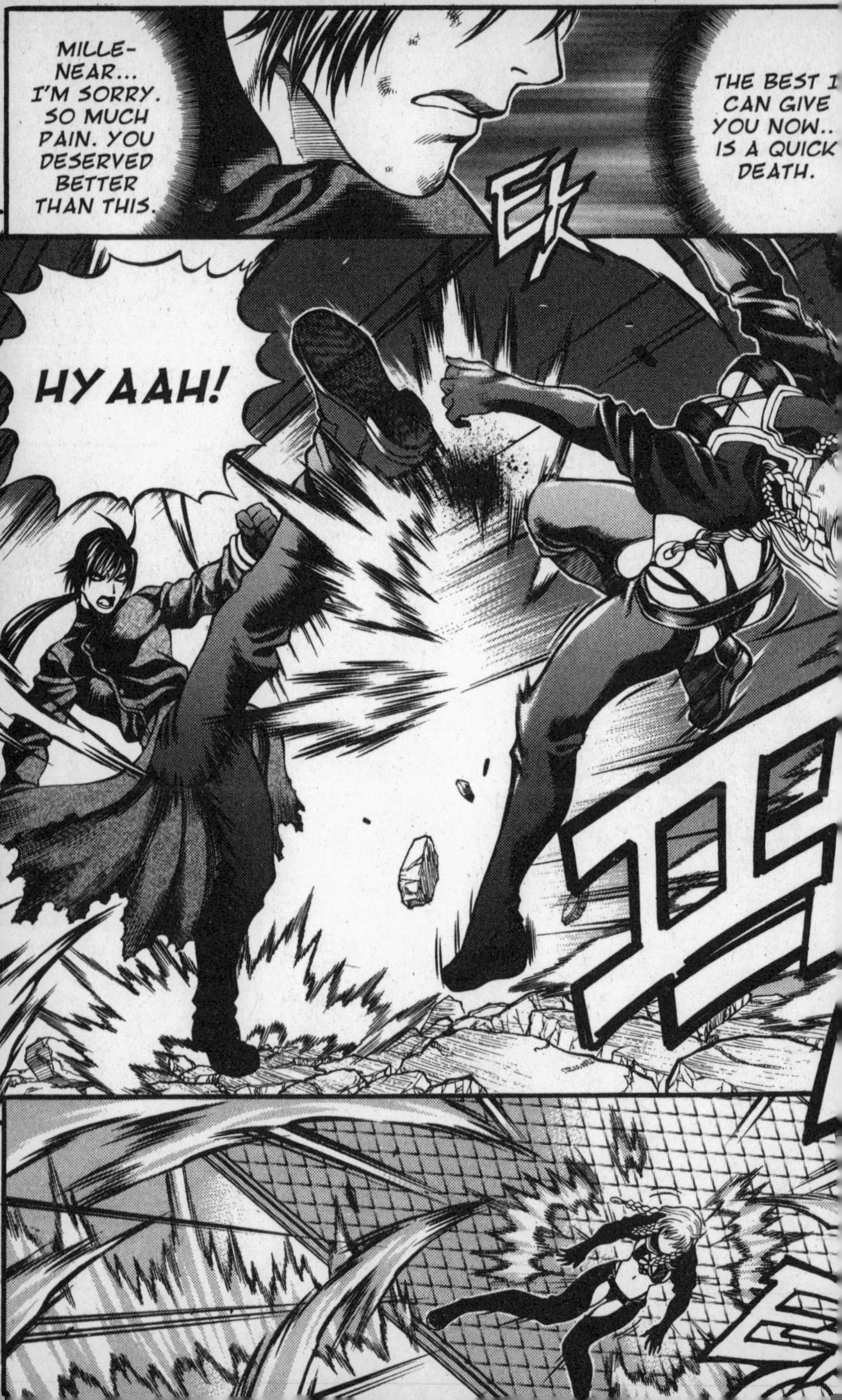
MILLE-NEAR... I'M SORRY. SO MUCH PAIN. YOU DESERVED BETTER THAN THIS.
THE BEST I CAN GIVE YOU NOW... IS A QUICK DEATH.
HYAAH!

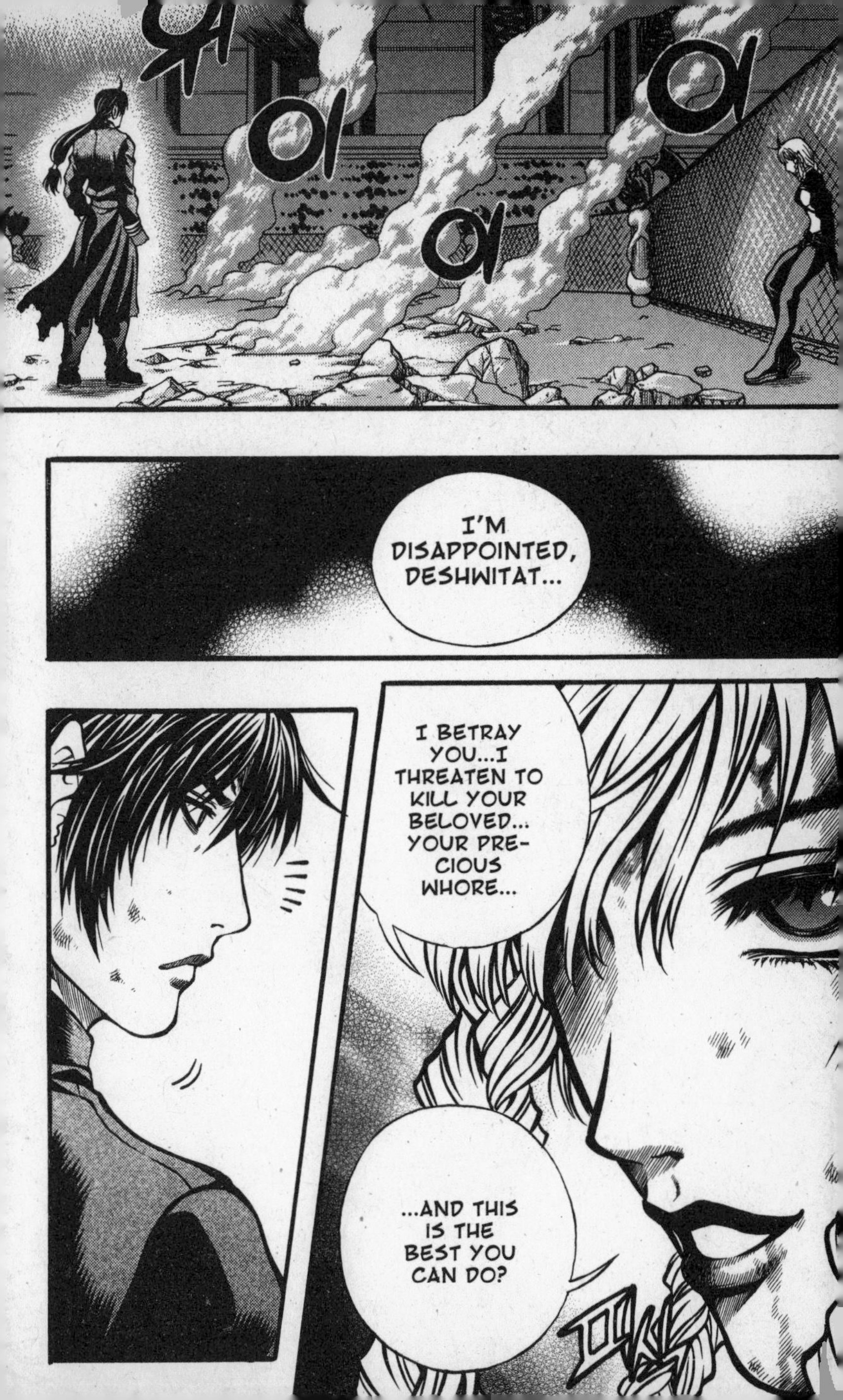

I'M DISAPPOINTED, DESHWITAT...
I BETRAY YOU...I THREATEN TO KILL YOUR BELOVED... YOUR PRECIOUS WHORE...
...AND THIS IS THE BEST YOU CAN DO?

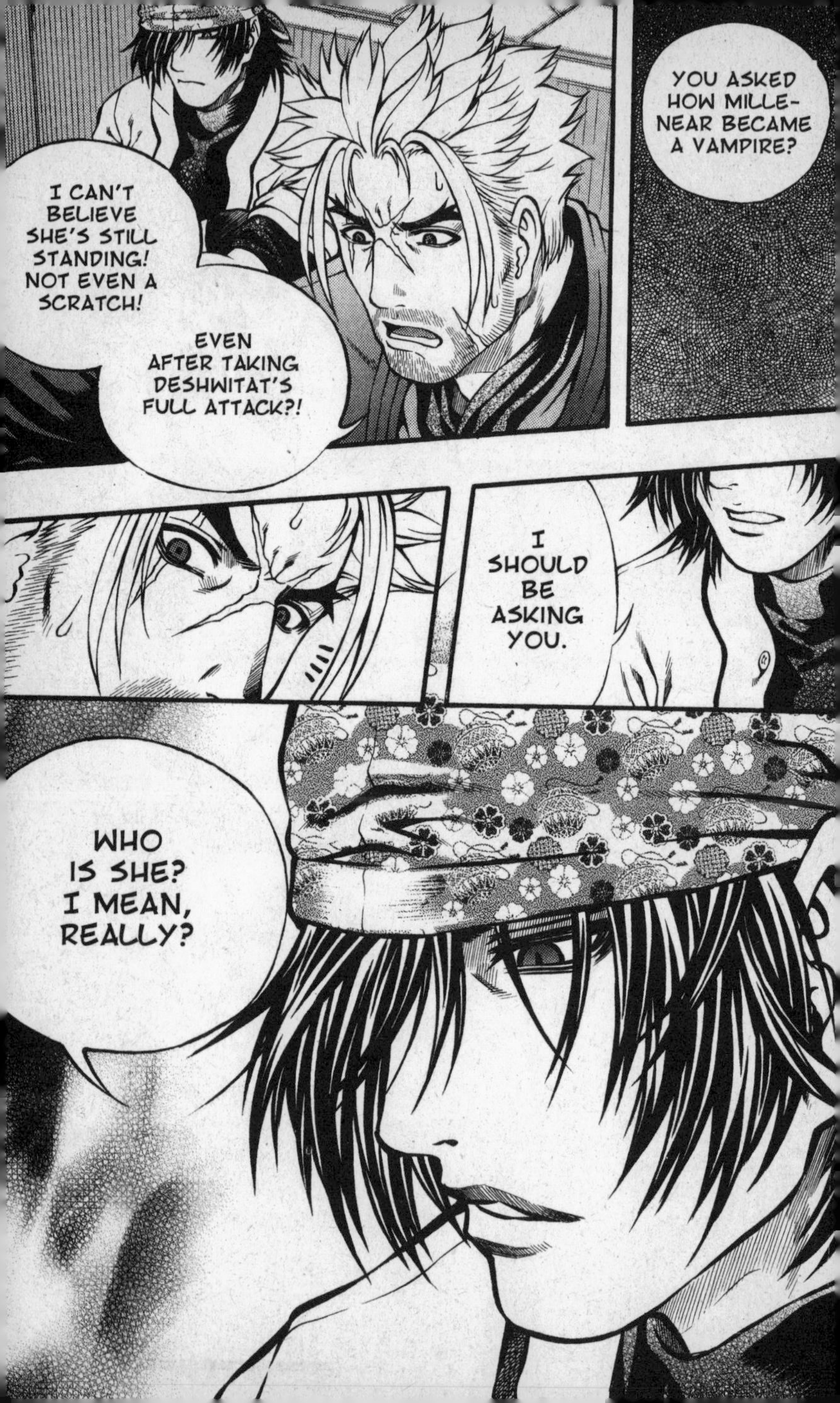

I CAN'T BELIEVE SHE'S STILL STANDING! NOT EVEN A SCRATCH!
EVEN AFTER TAKING DESHWITAT'S FULL ATTACK?!
YOU ASKED HOW MILLE-NEAR BECAME A VAMPIRE?
I SHOULD BE ASKING YOU.
WHO IS SHE? I MEAN, REALLY?

Chapter 73: Revelations

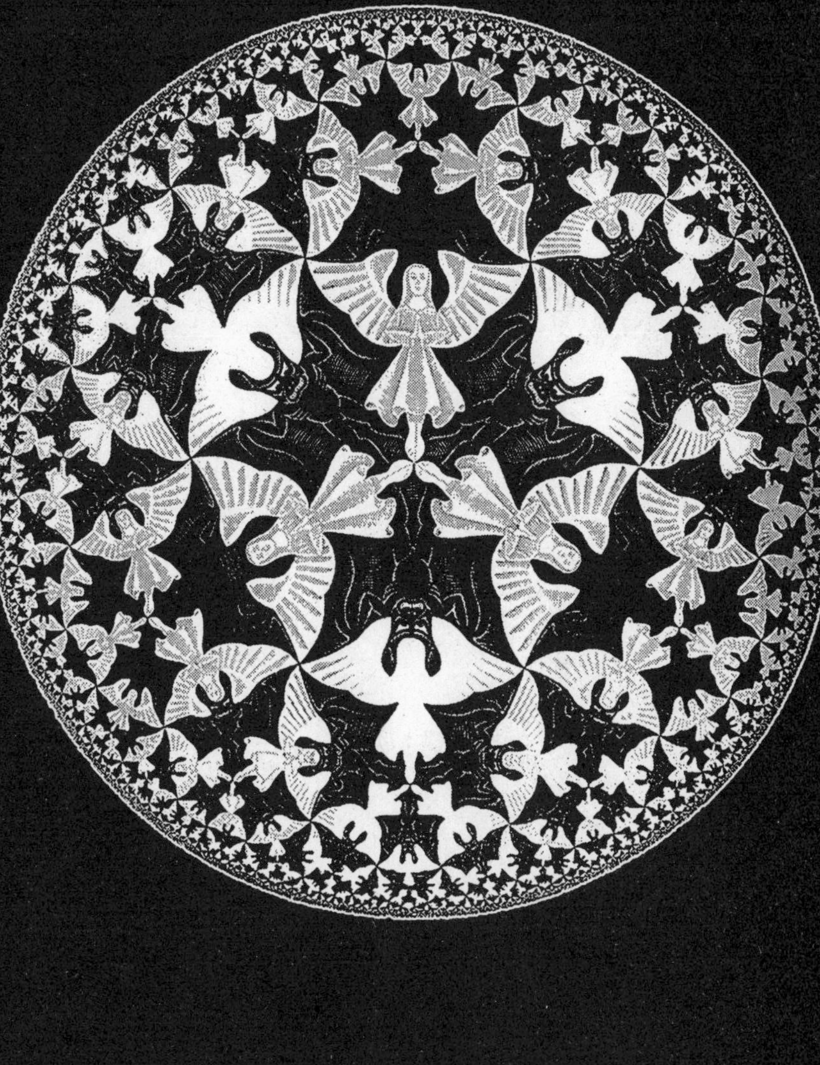

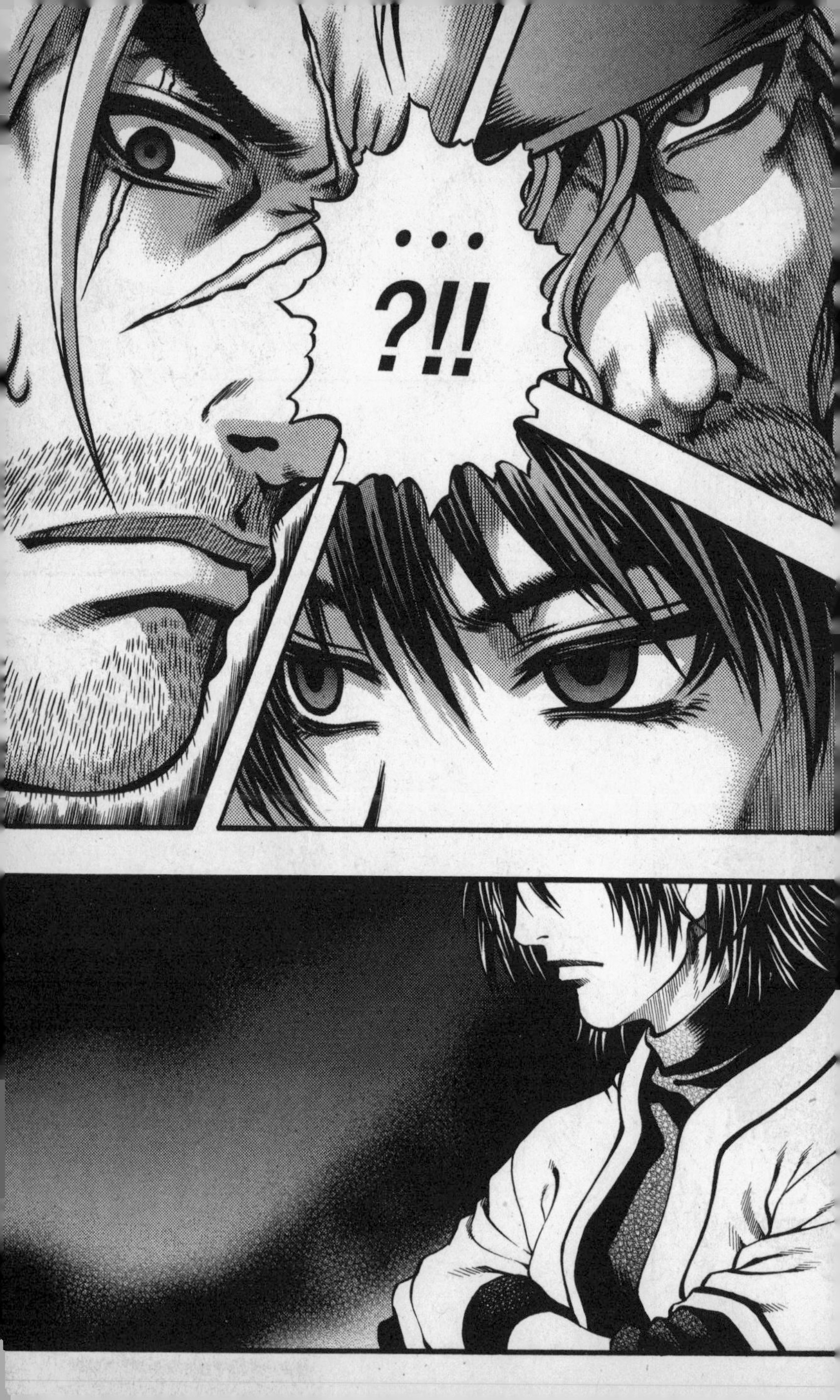
...
?!!

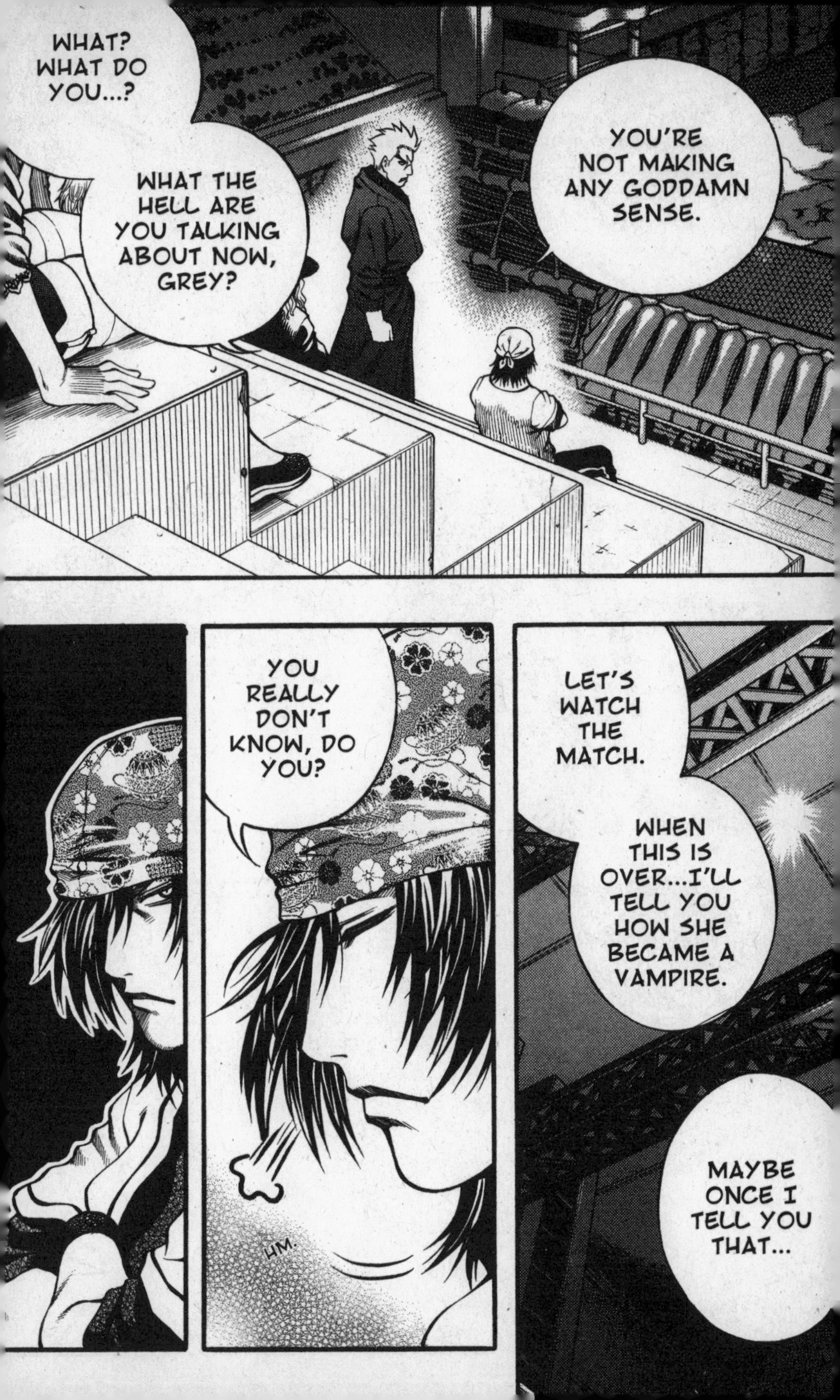
WHAT? WHAT DO YOU...?
WHAT THE HELL ARE YOU TALKING ABOUT NOW, GREY?
YOU'RE NOT MAKING ANY GODDAMN SENSE.
YOU REALLY DON'T KNOW, DO YOU?
HM.
LET'S WATCH THE MATCH.
WHEN THIS IS OVER...I'LL TELL YOU HOW SHE BECAME A VAMPIRE.
MAYBE ONCE I TELL YOU THAT...

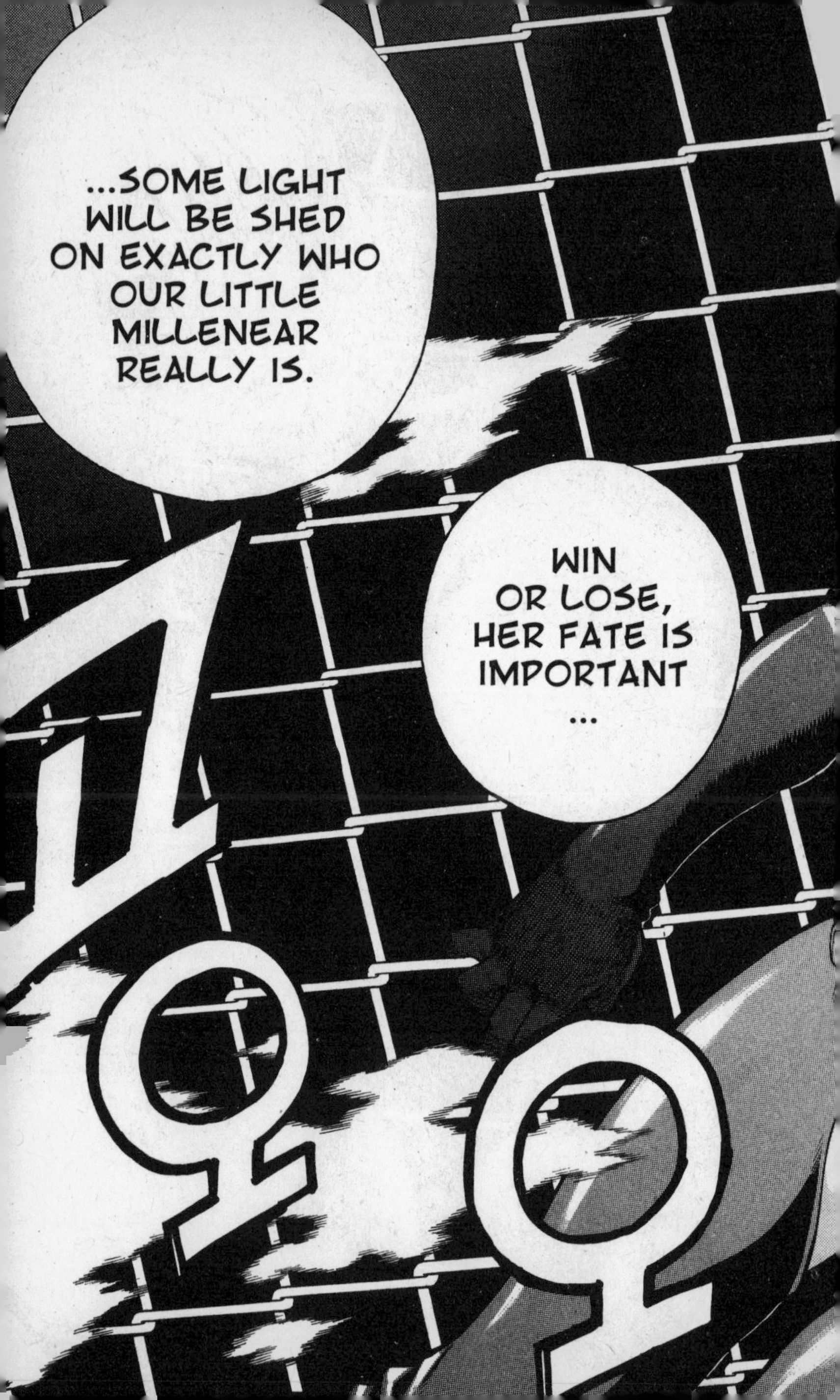
...SOME LIGHT WILL BE SHED ON EXACTLY WHO OUR LITTLE MILLENEAR REALLY IS.
WIN OR LOSE, HER FATE IS IMPORTANT ...

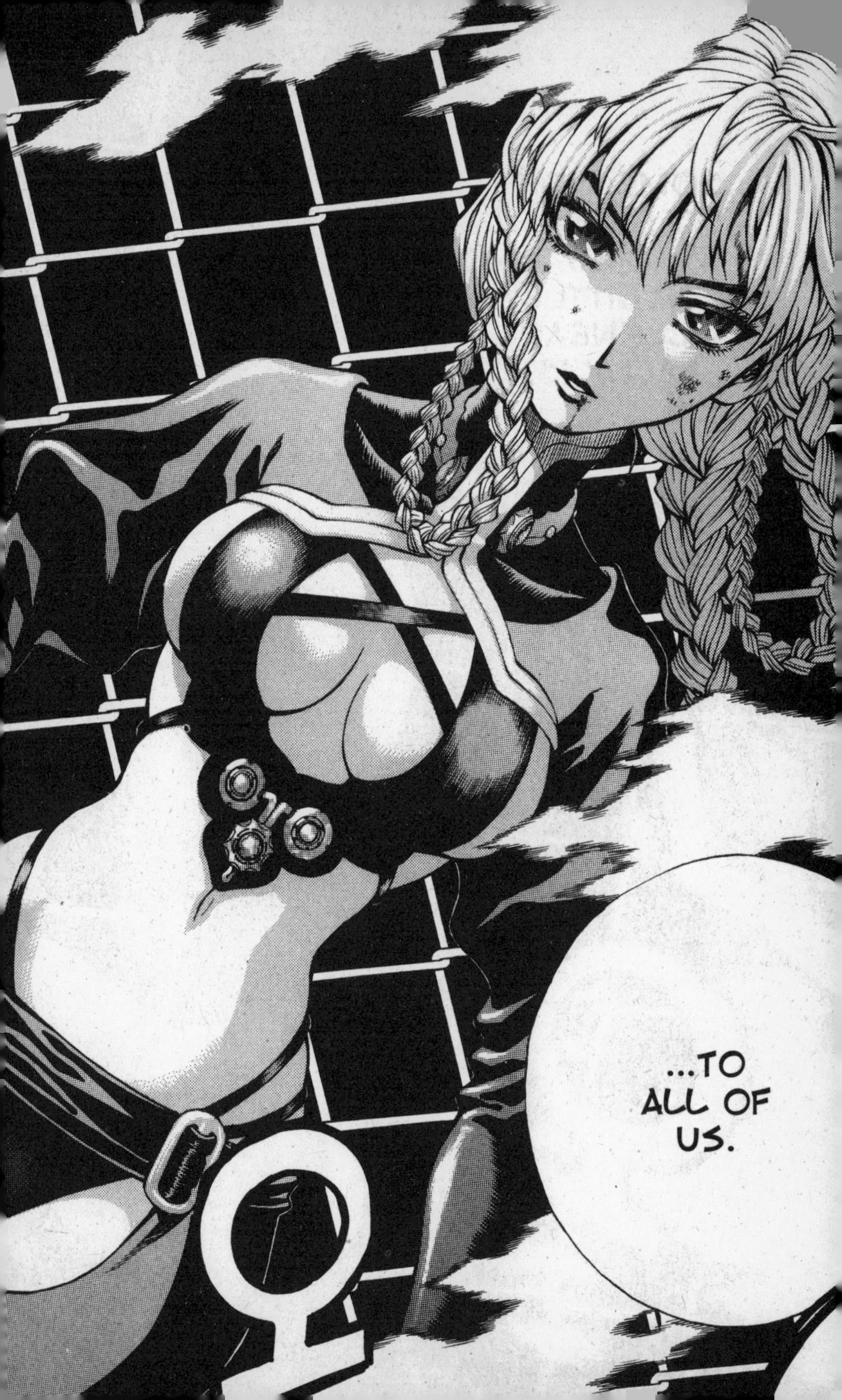
...TO
ALL OF
US.

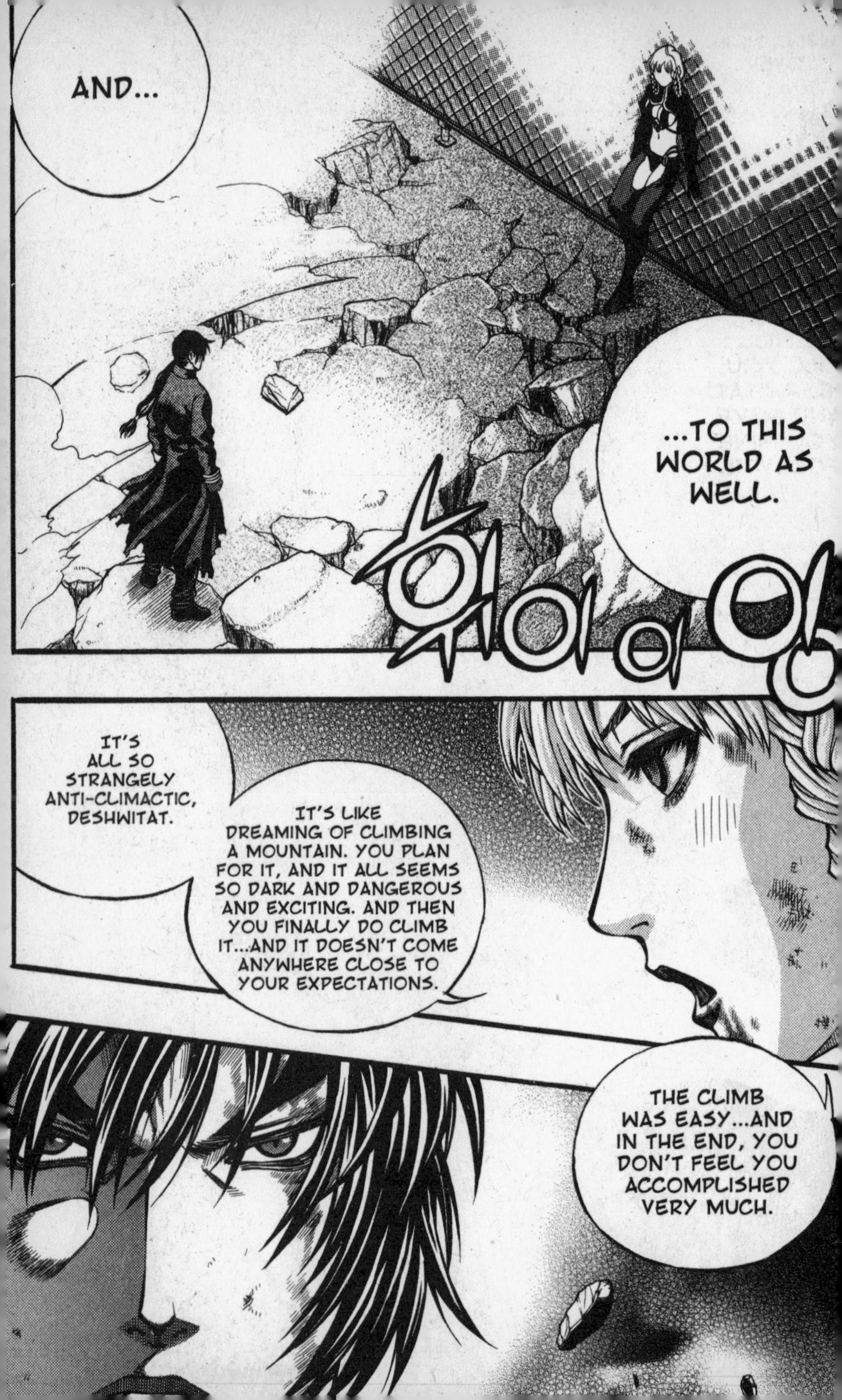
AND...
...TO THIS WORLD AS WELL.
IT'S ALL SO STRANGELY ANTI-CLIMACTIC, DESHWITAT.
IT'S LIKE DREAMING OF CLIMBING A MOUNTAIN. YOU PLAN FOR IT, AND IT ALL SEEMS SO DARK AND DANGEROUS AND EXCITING. AND THEN YOU FINALLY DO CLIMB IT...AND IT DOESN'T COME ANYWHERE CLOSE TO YOUR EXPECTATIONS.
THE CLIMB WAS EASY...AND IN THE END, YOU DON'T FEEL YOU ACCOMPLISHED VERY MUCH.

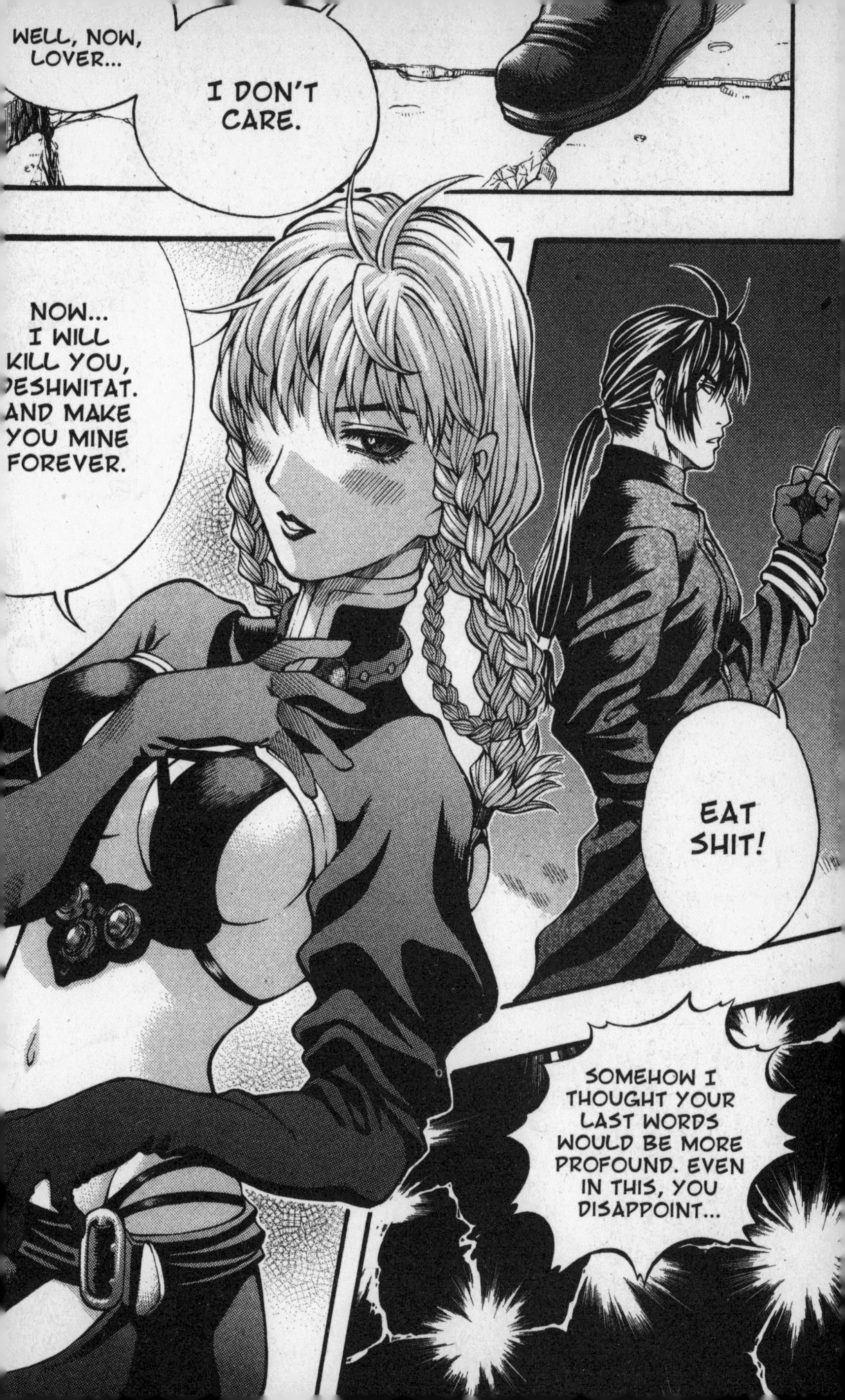
I DON'T CARE.
WELL, NOW, LOVER...
NOW... I WILL KILL YOU, ESHWITAT. AND MAKE YOU MINE FOREVER.
EAT SHIT!
SOMEHOW I THOUGHT YOUR LAST WORDS WOULD BE MORE PROFOUND. EVEN IN THIS, YOU DISAPPOINT...

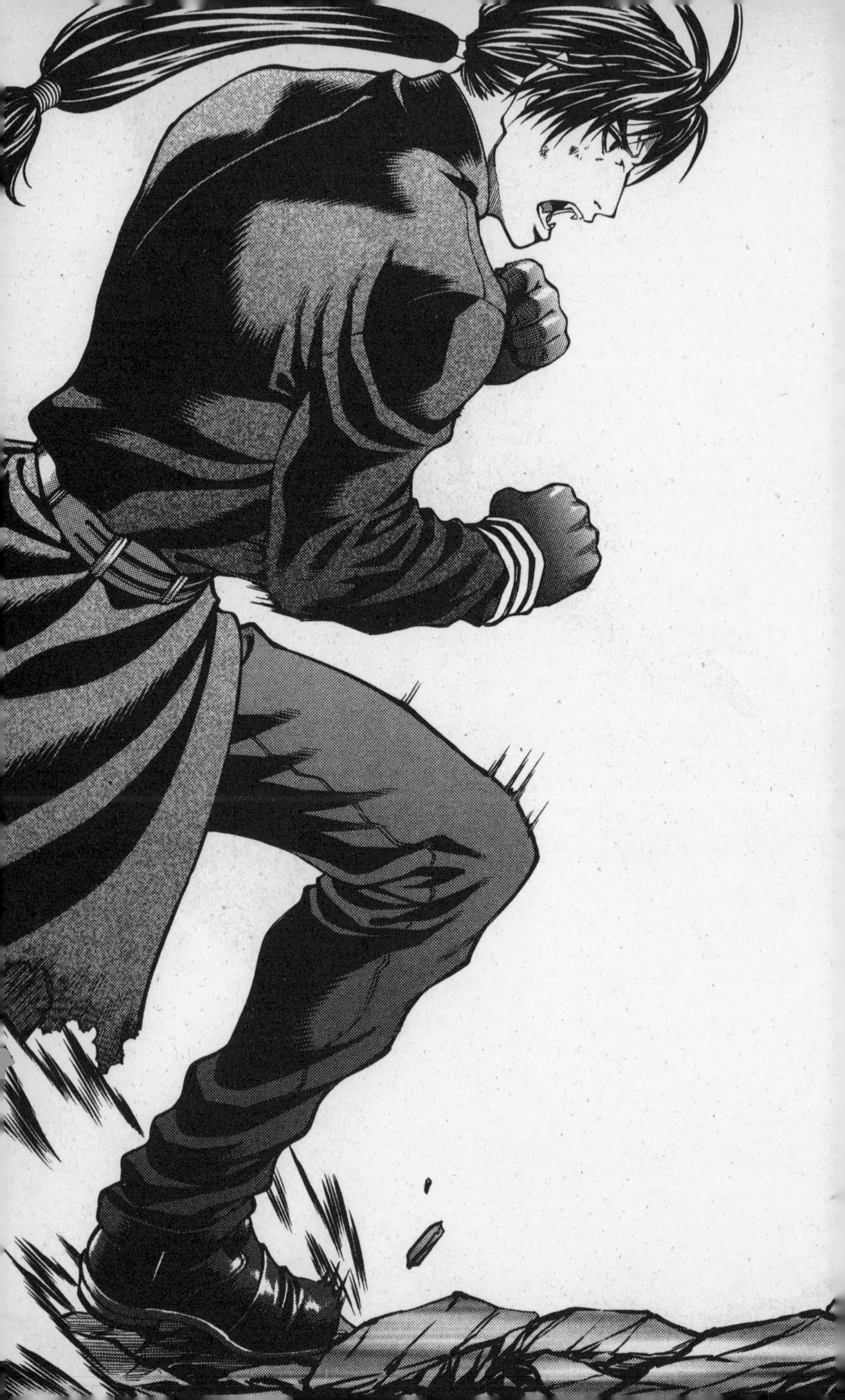

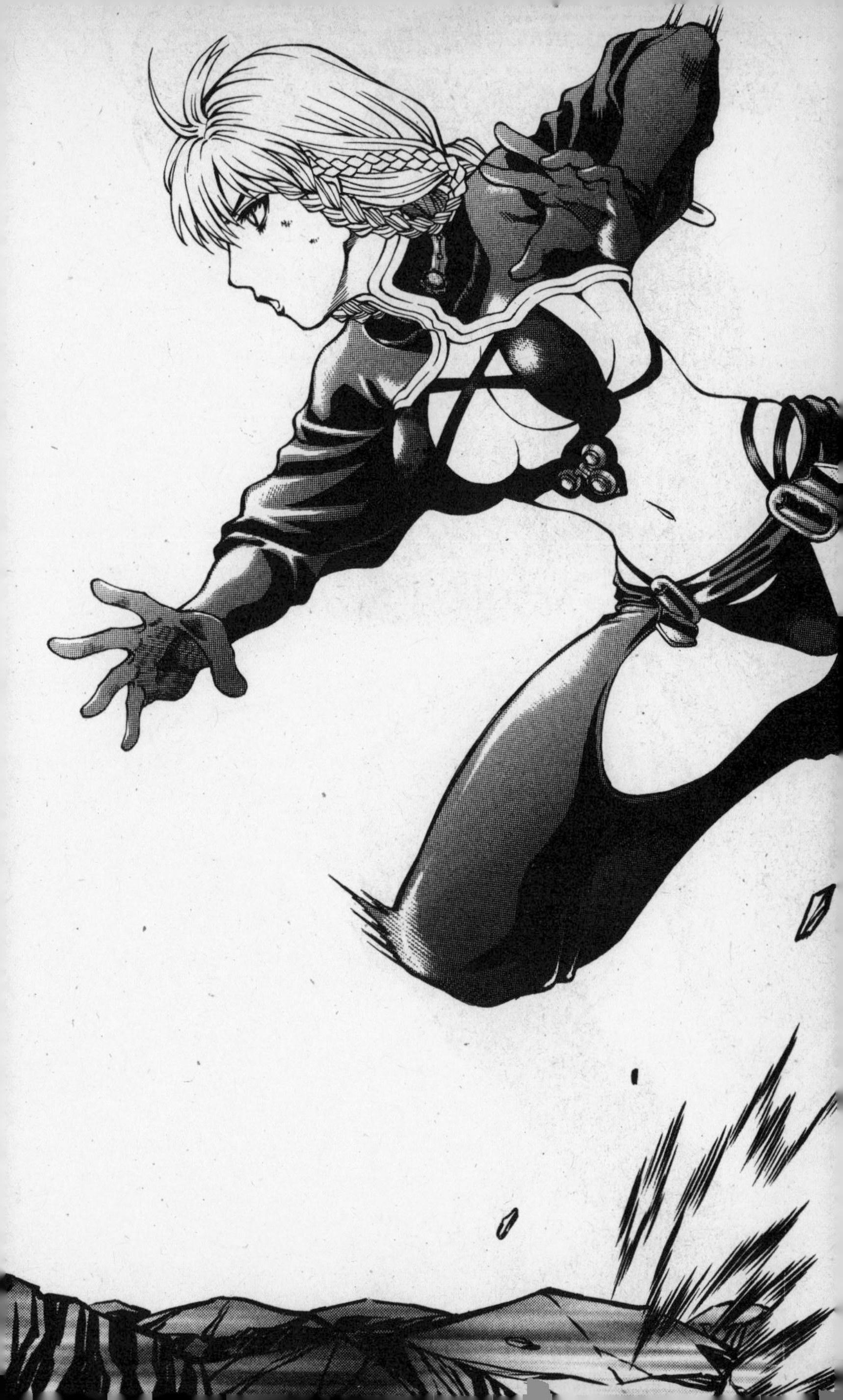

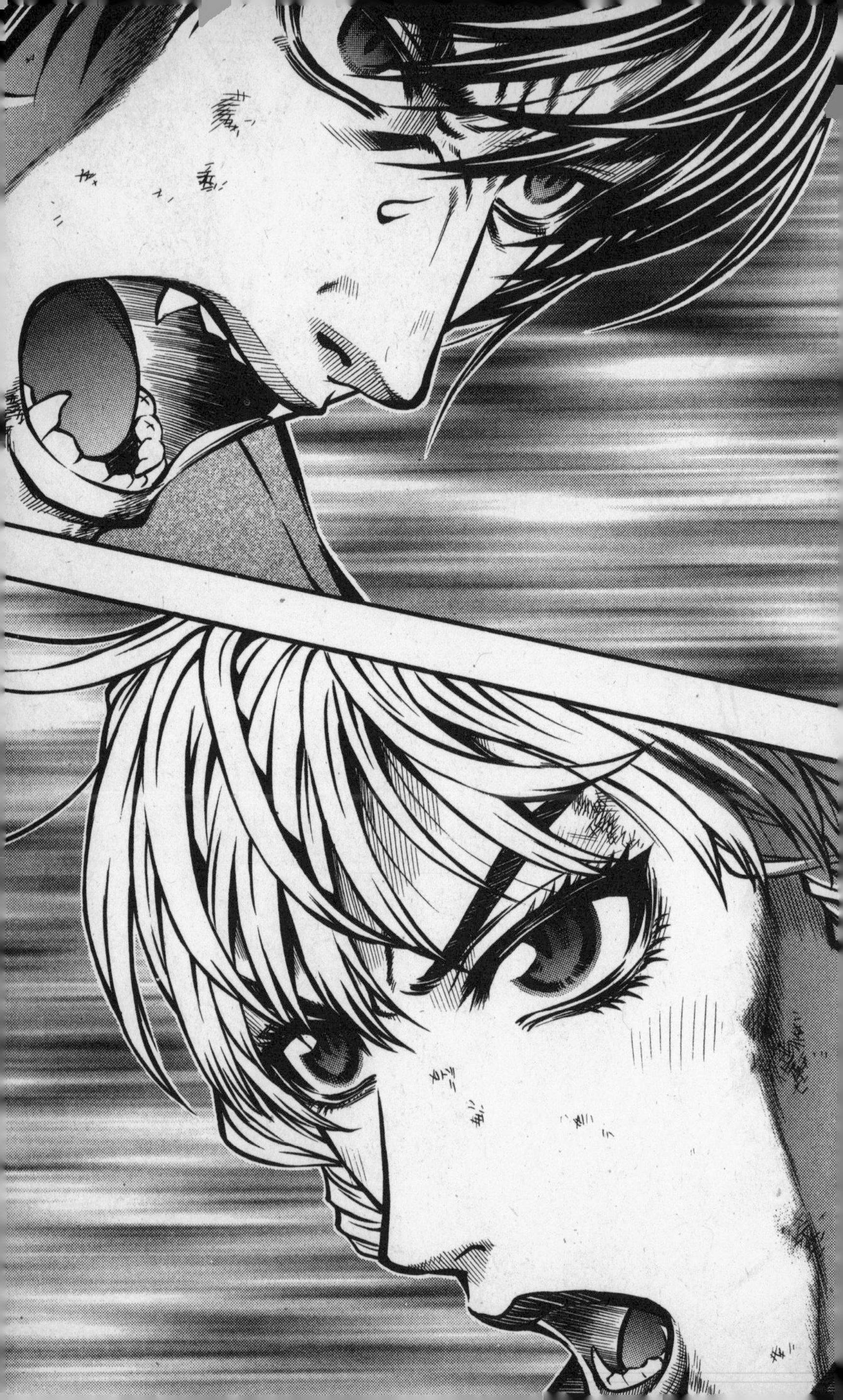

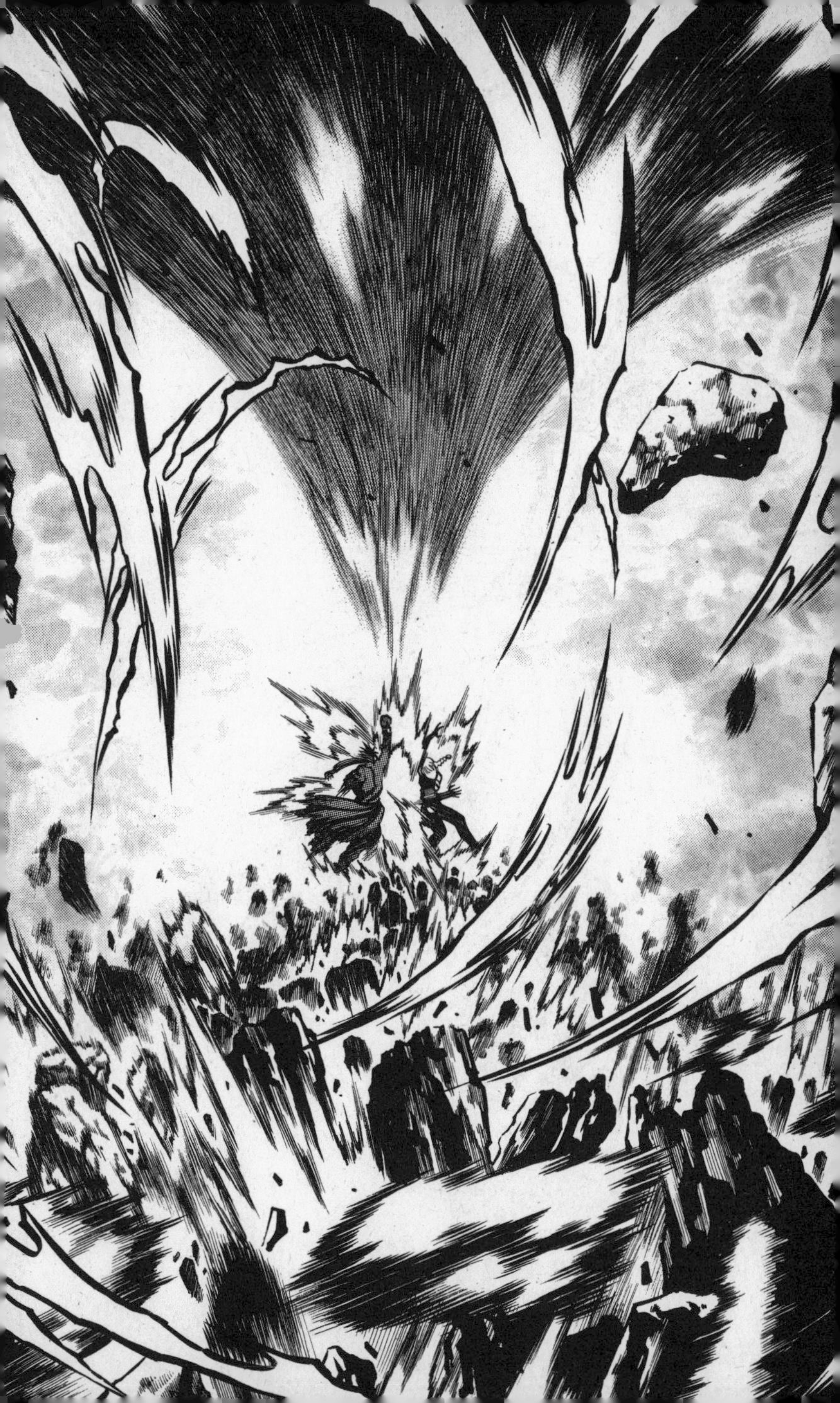

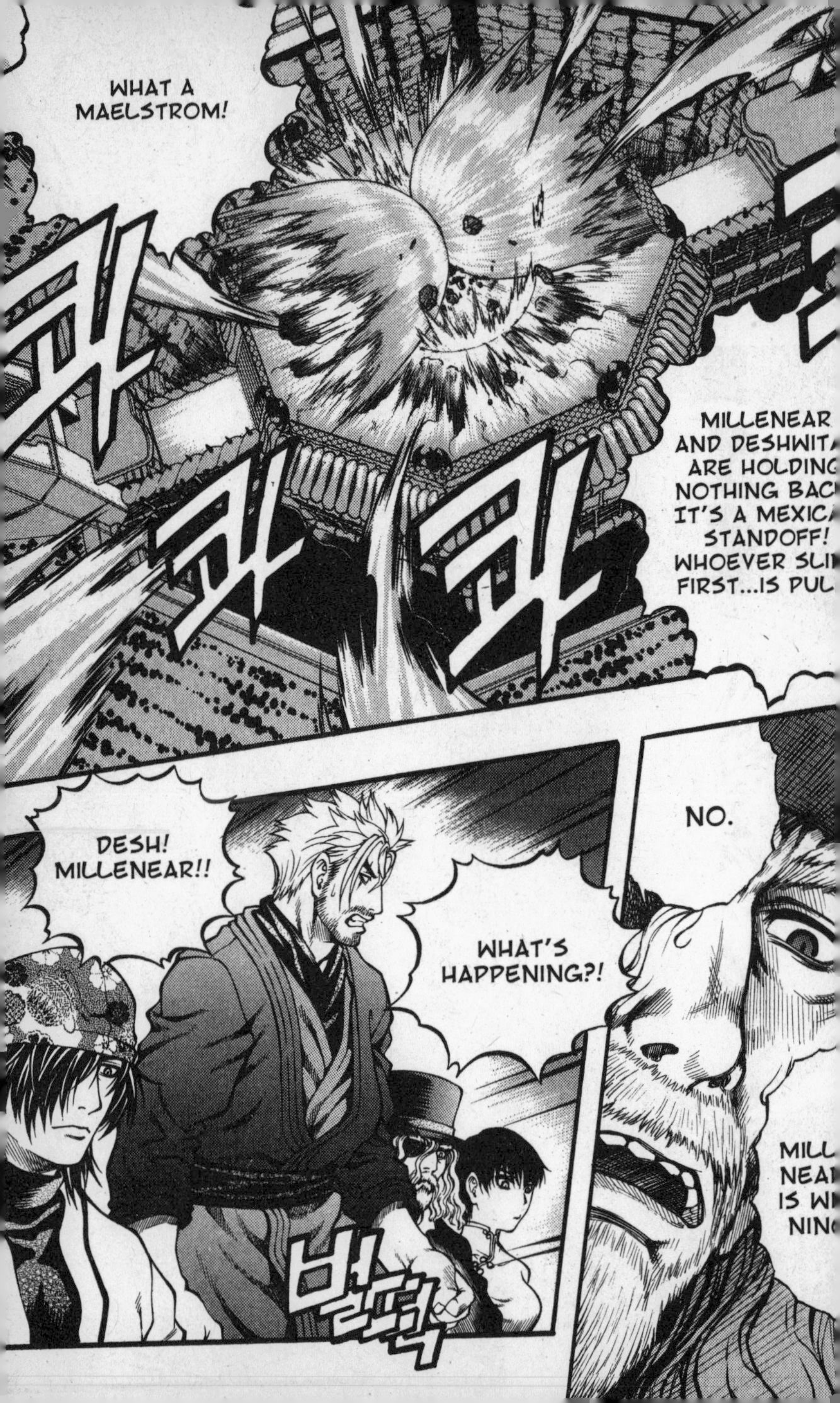
WHAT A MAELSTROM!
MILLENEAR AND DESHWITA ARE HOLDING NOTHING BAC IT'S A MEXICA STANDOFF! WHOEVER SLI FIRST...IS PUL
DESH! MILLENEAR!!
WHAT'S HAPPENING?!
NO.
MILL NEA IS WI NIN

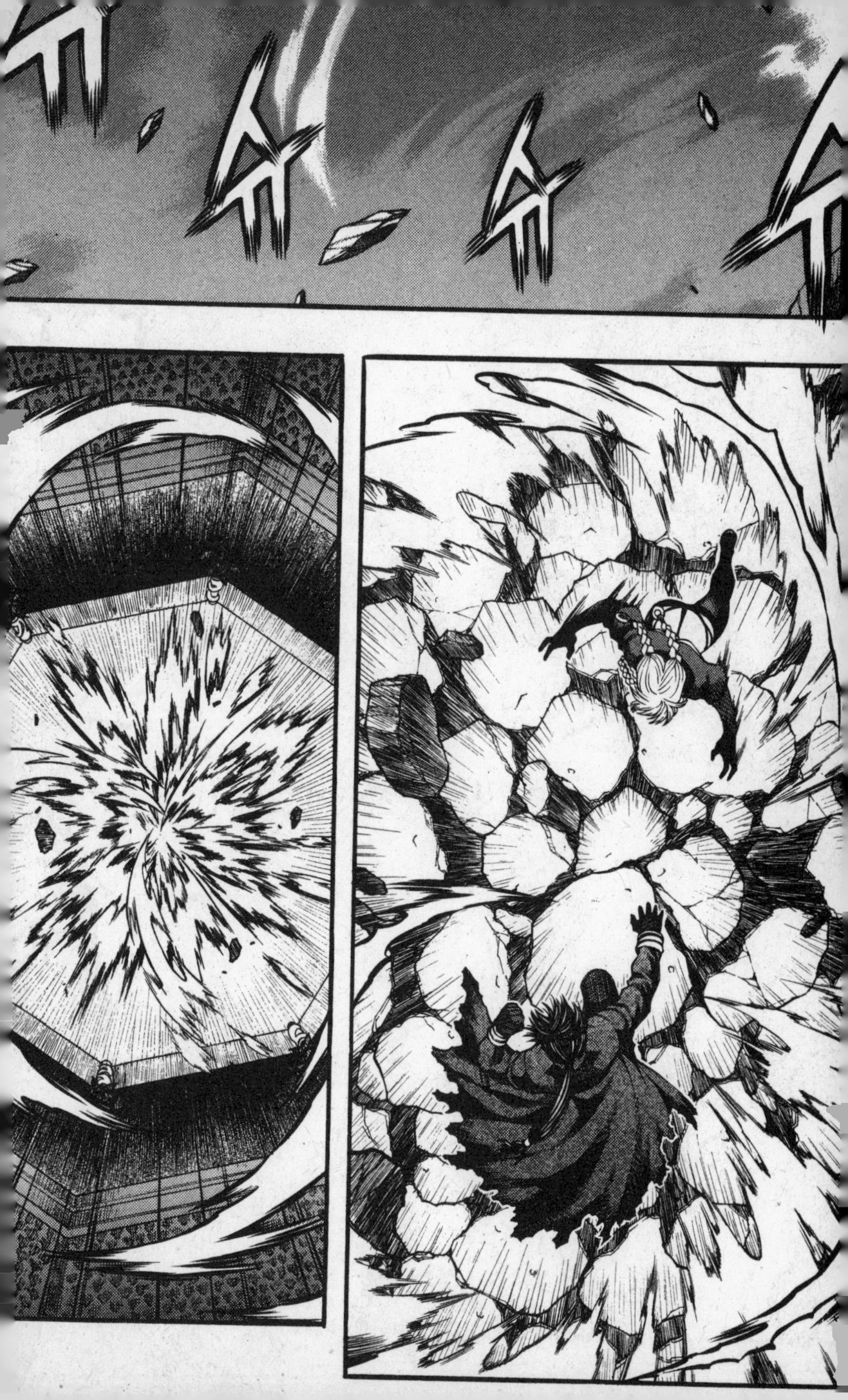

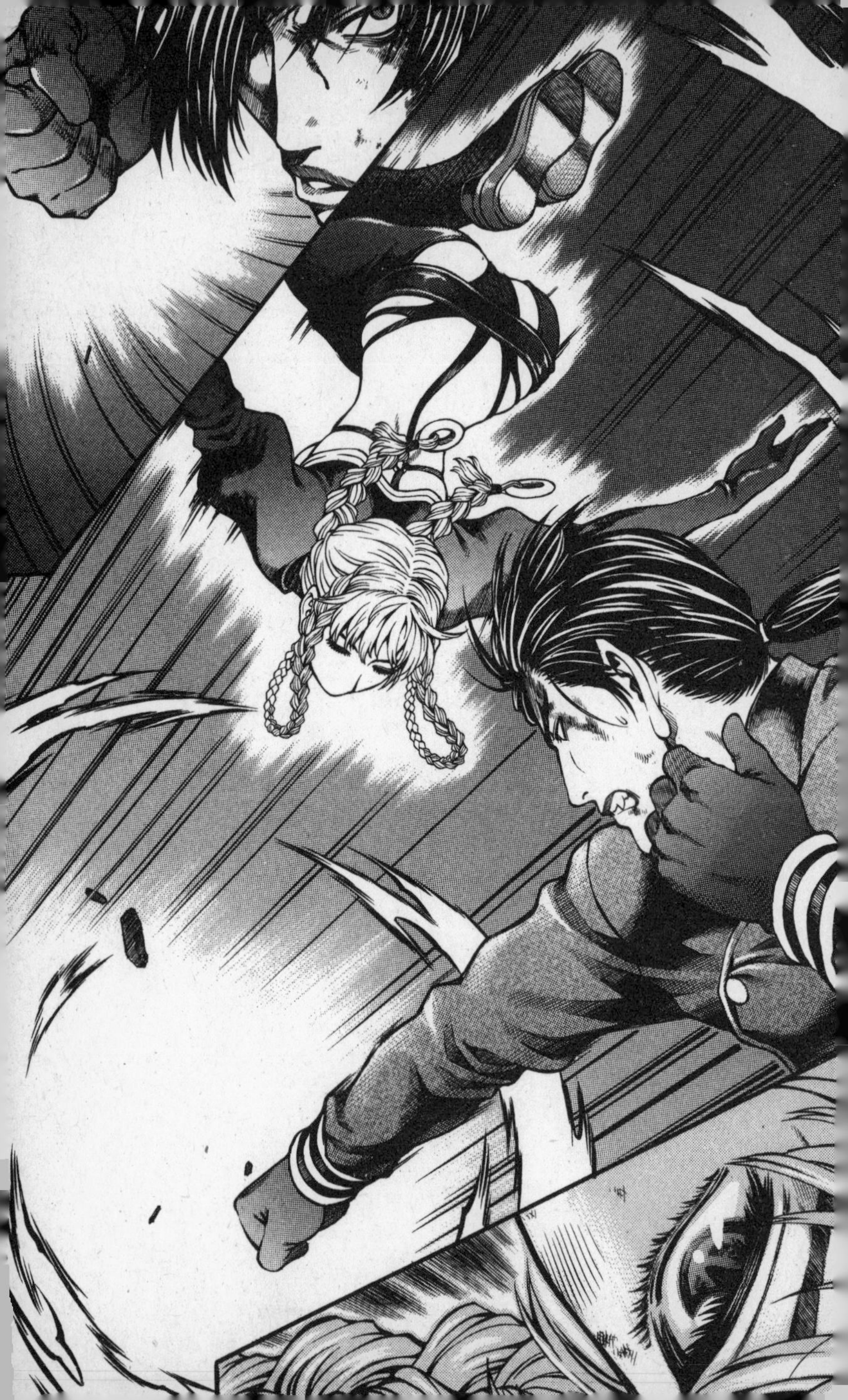

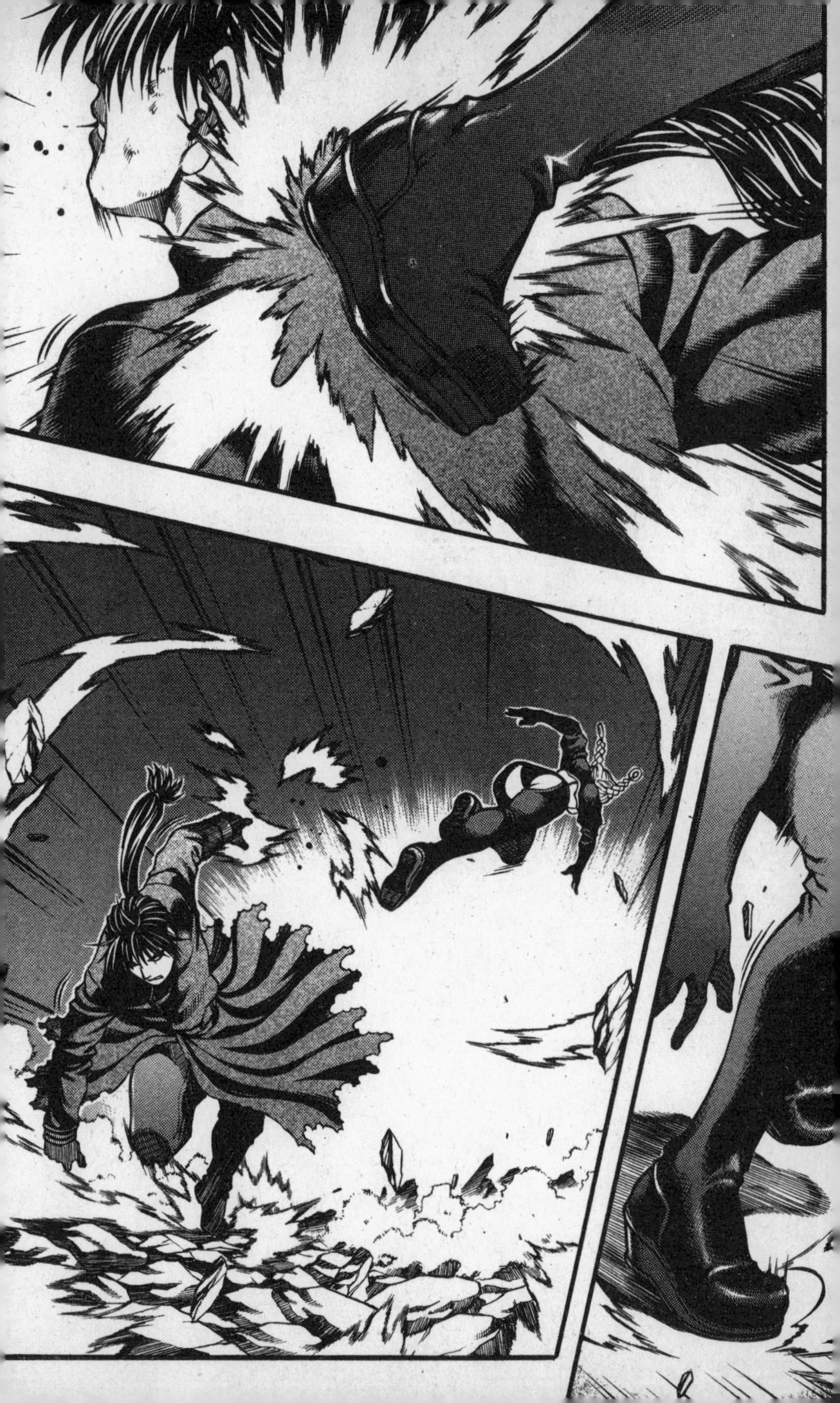

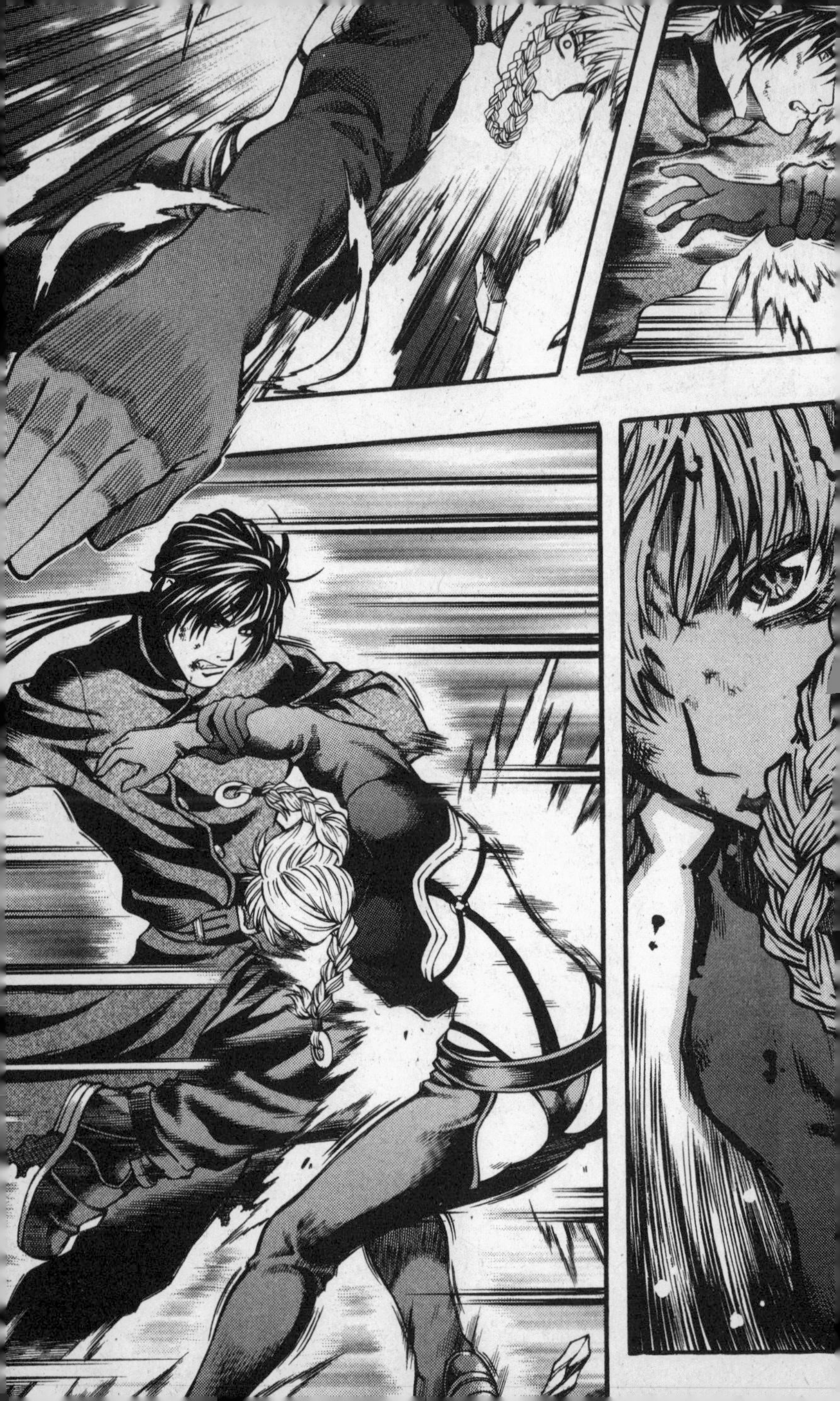

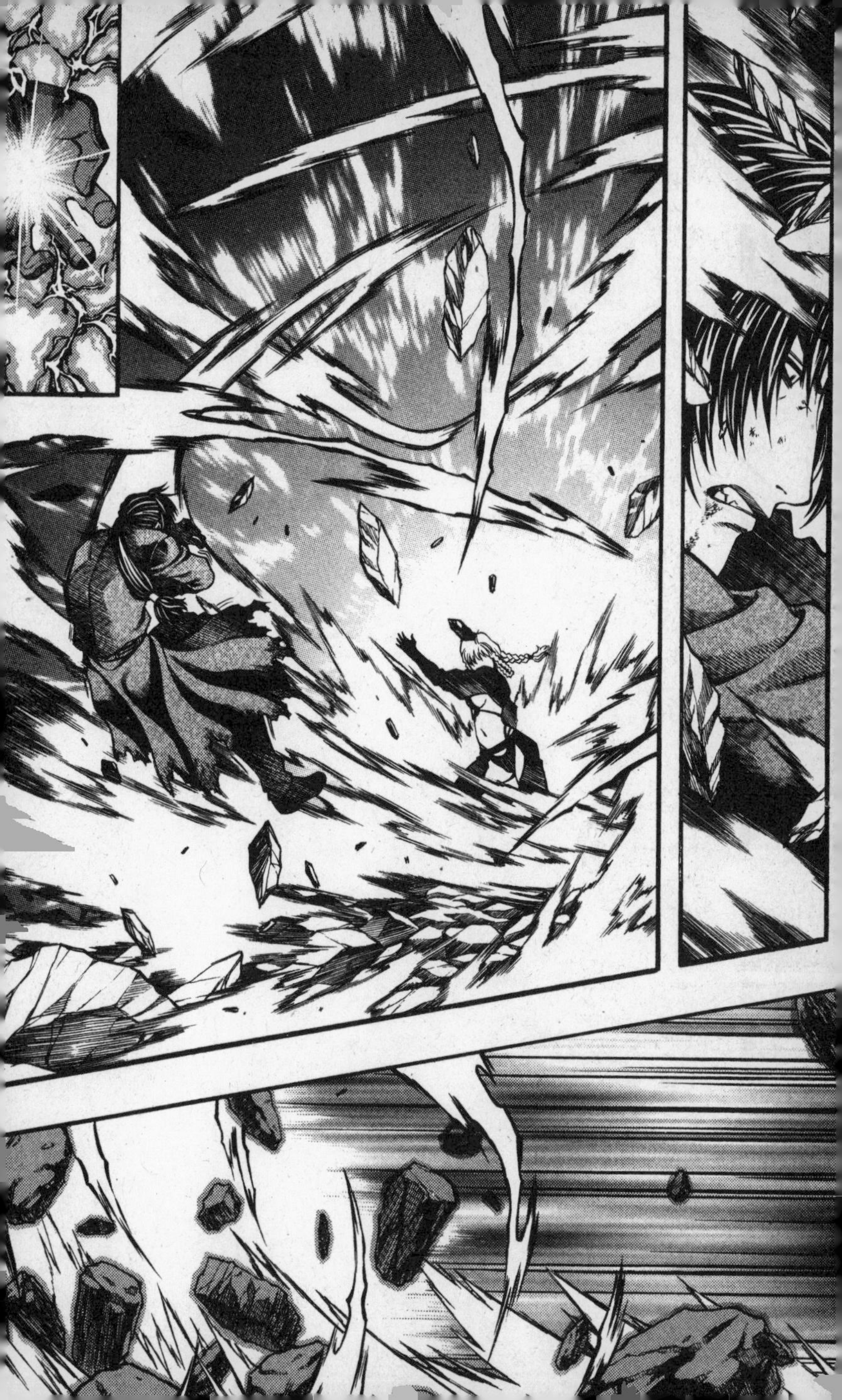

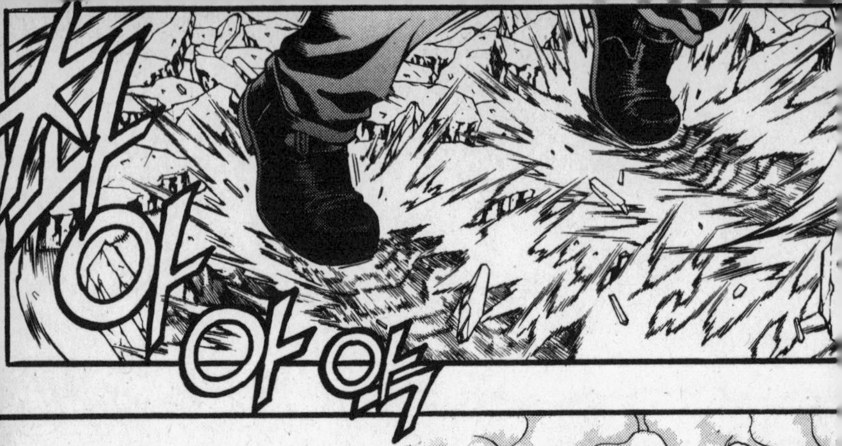
치아아악

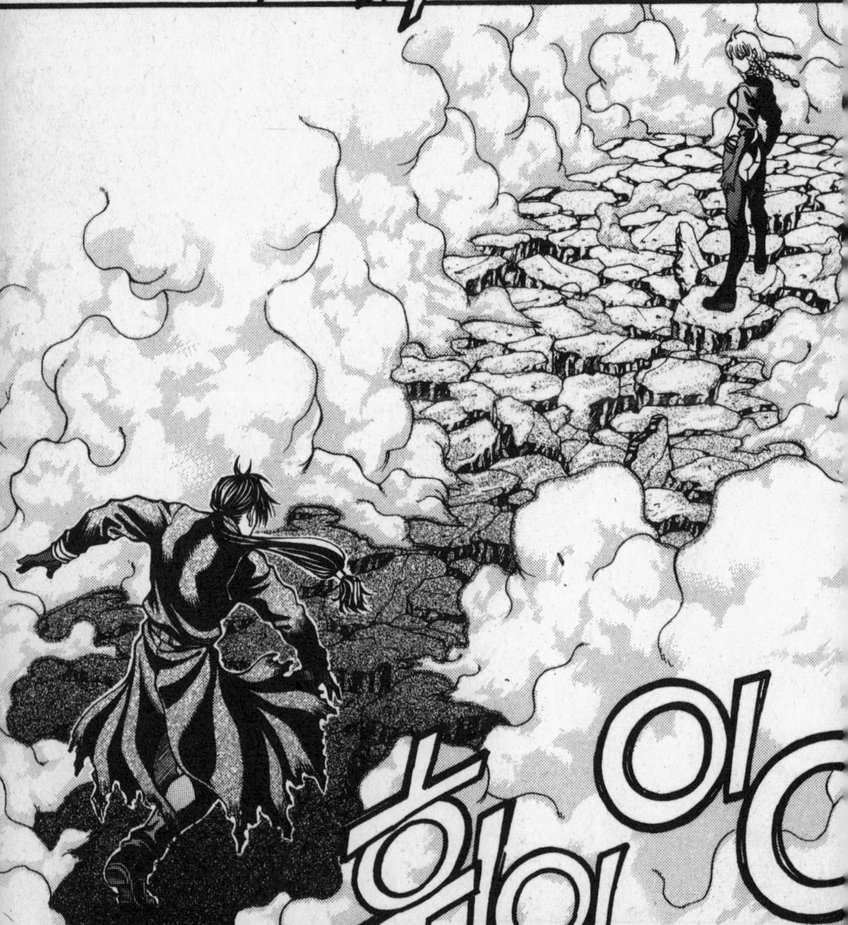

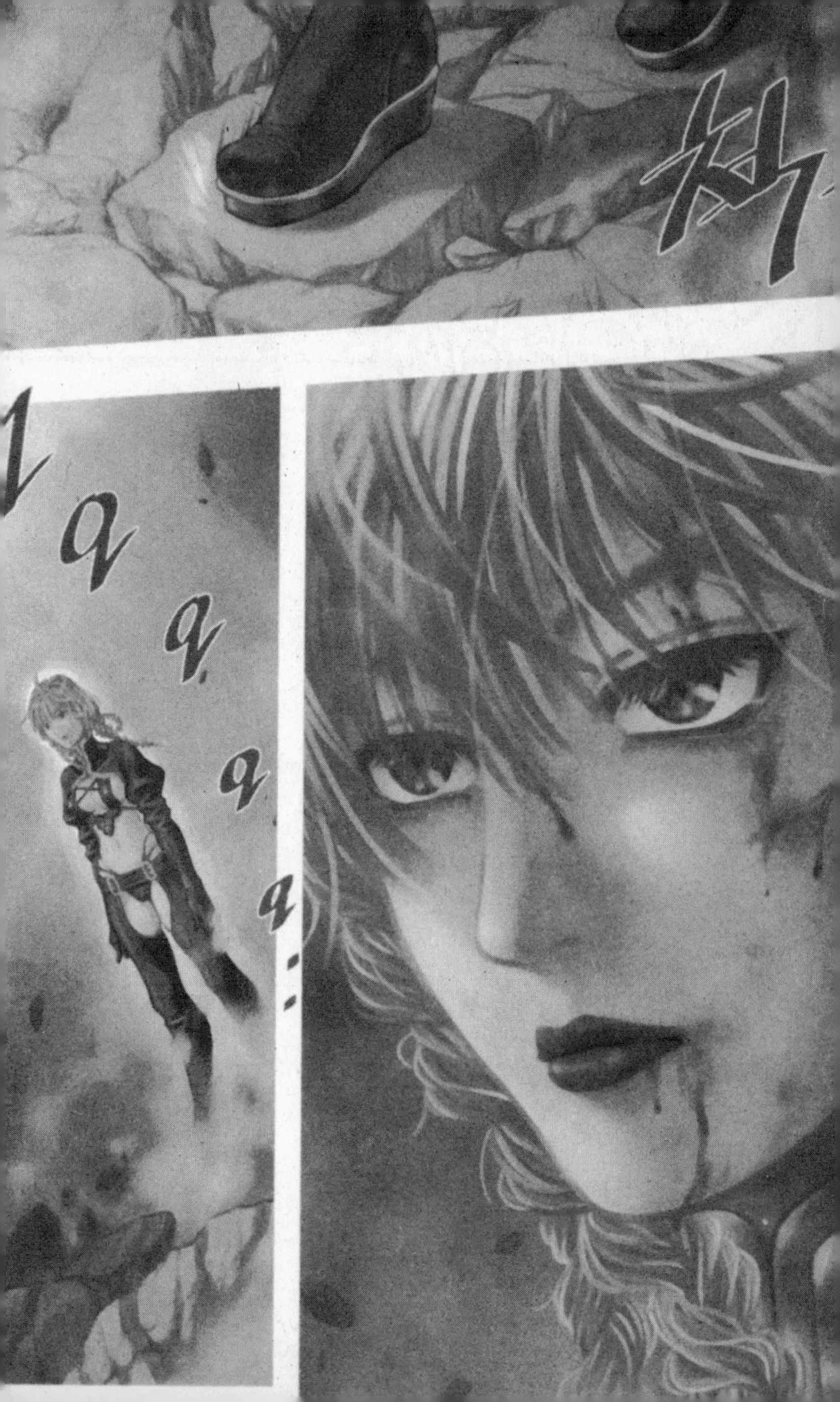

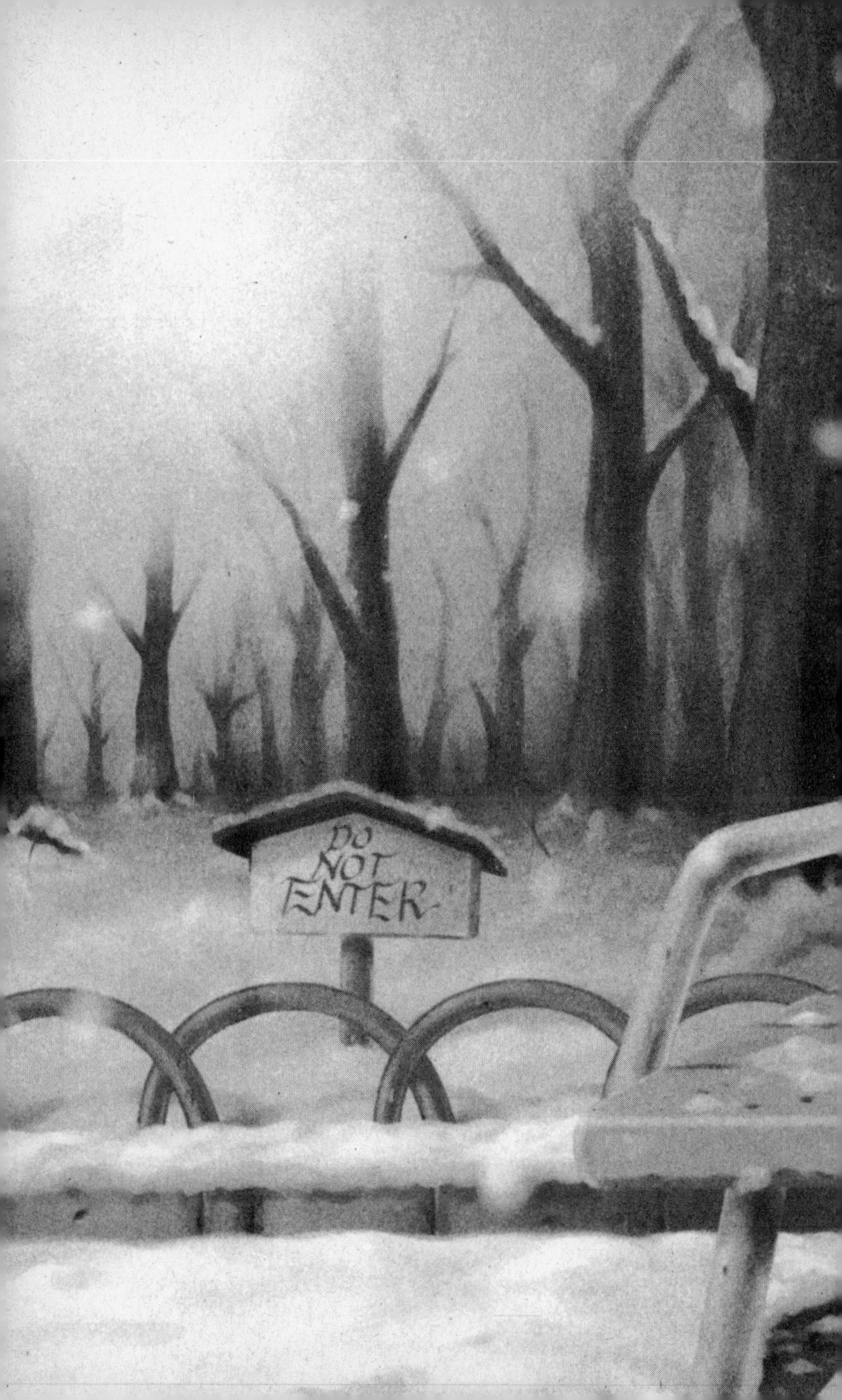
DO NOT ENTER

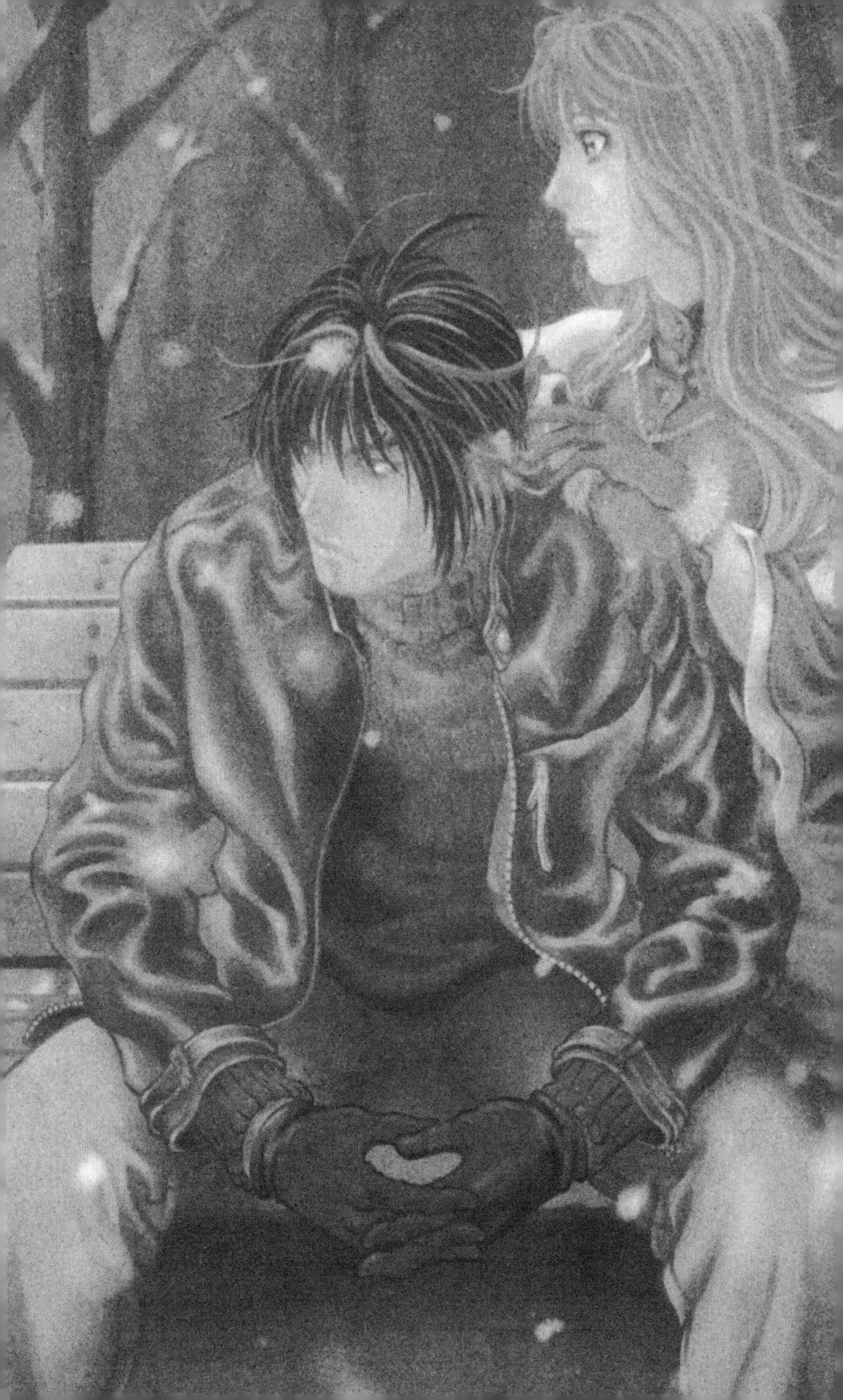

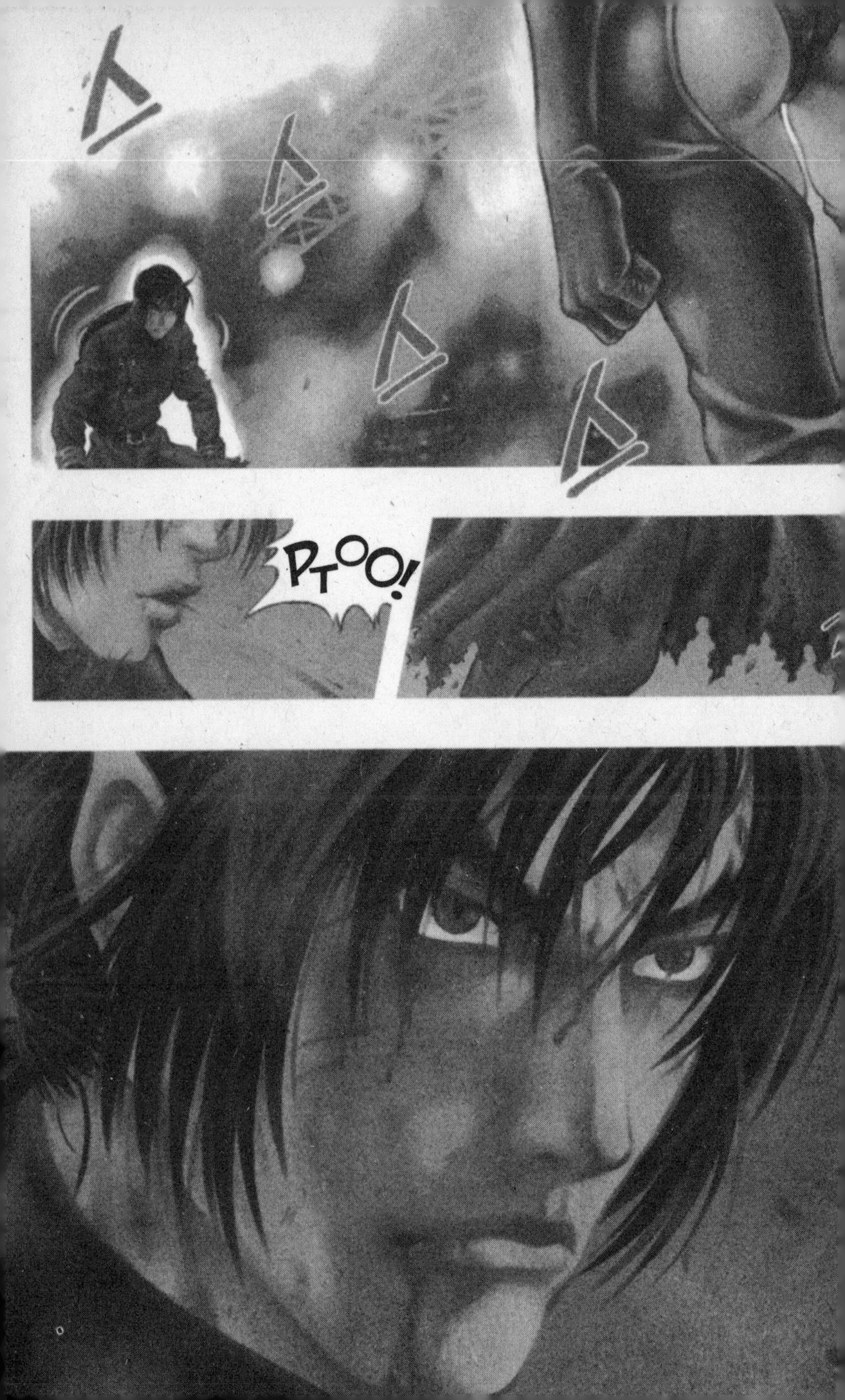
PTOO!

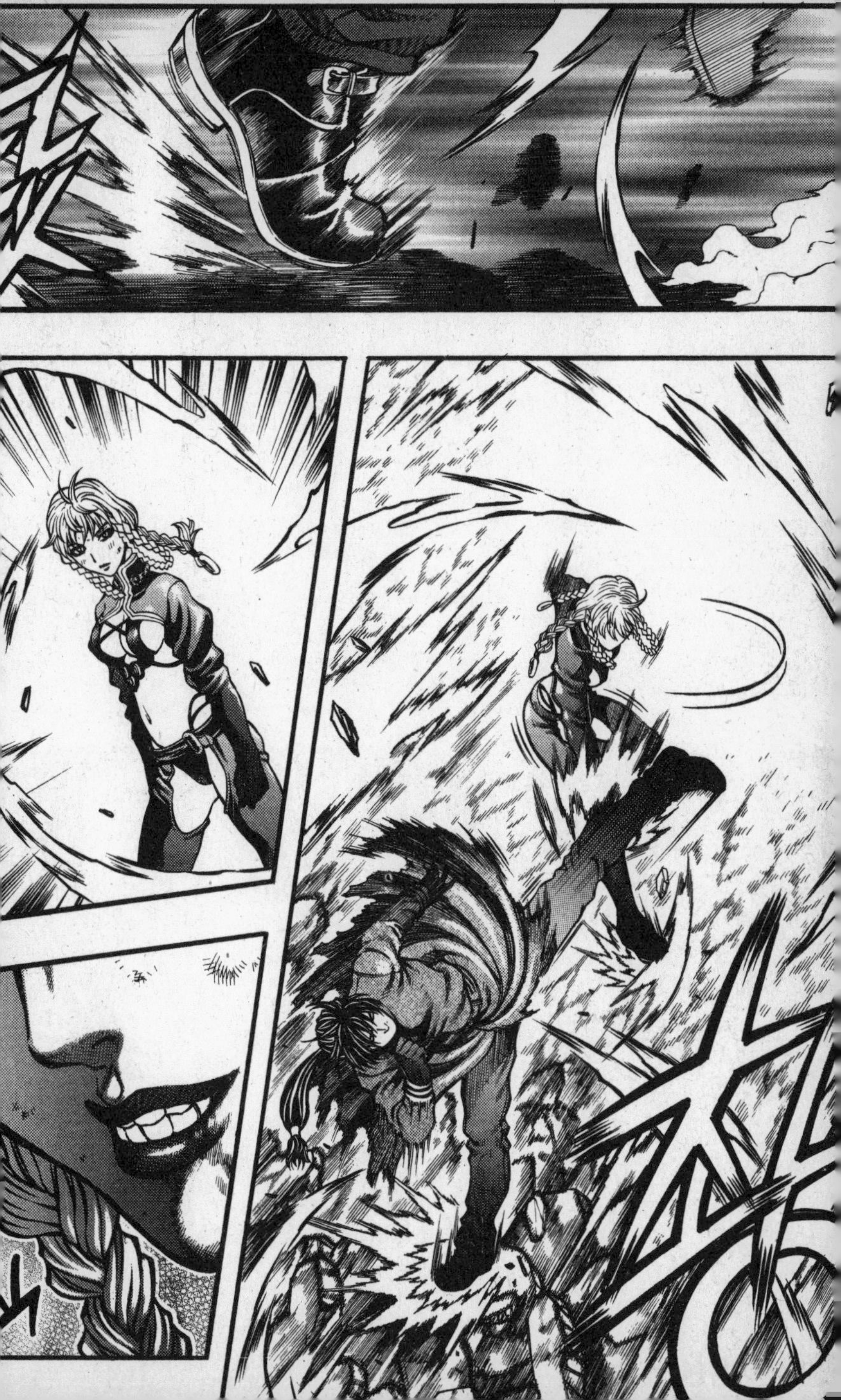

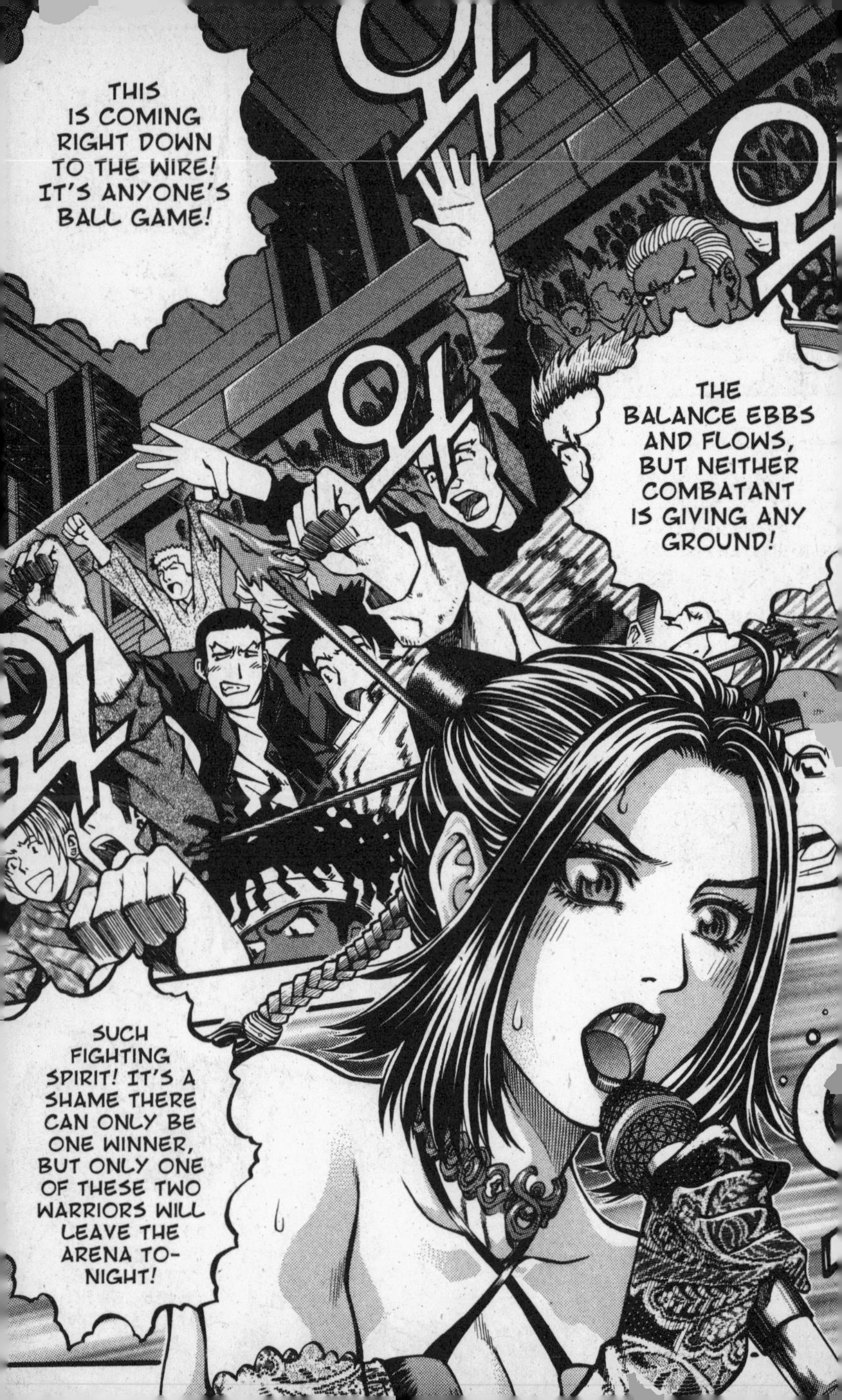
THIS IS COMING RIGHT DOWN TO THE WIRE! IT'S ANYONE'S BALL GAME!
THE BALANCE EBBS AND FLOWS, BUT NEITHER COMBATANT IS GIVING ANY GROUND!
SUCH FIGHTING SPIRIT! IT'S A SHAME THERE CAN ONLY BE ONE WINNER, BUT ONLY ONE OF THESE TWO WARRIORS WILL LEAVE THE ARENA TO-NIGHT!

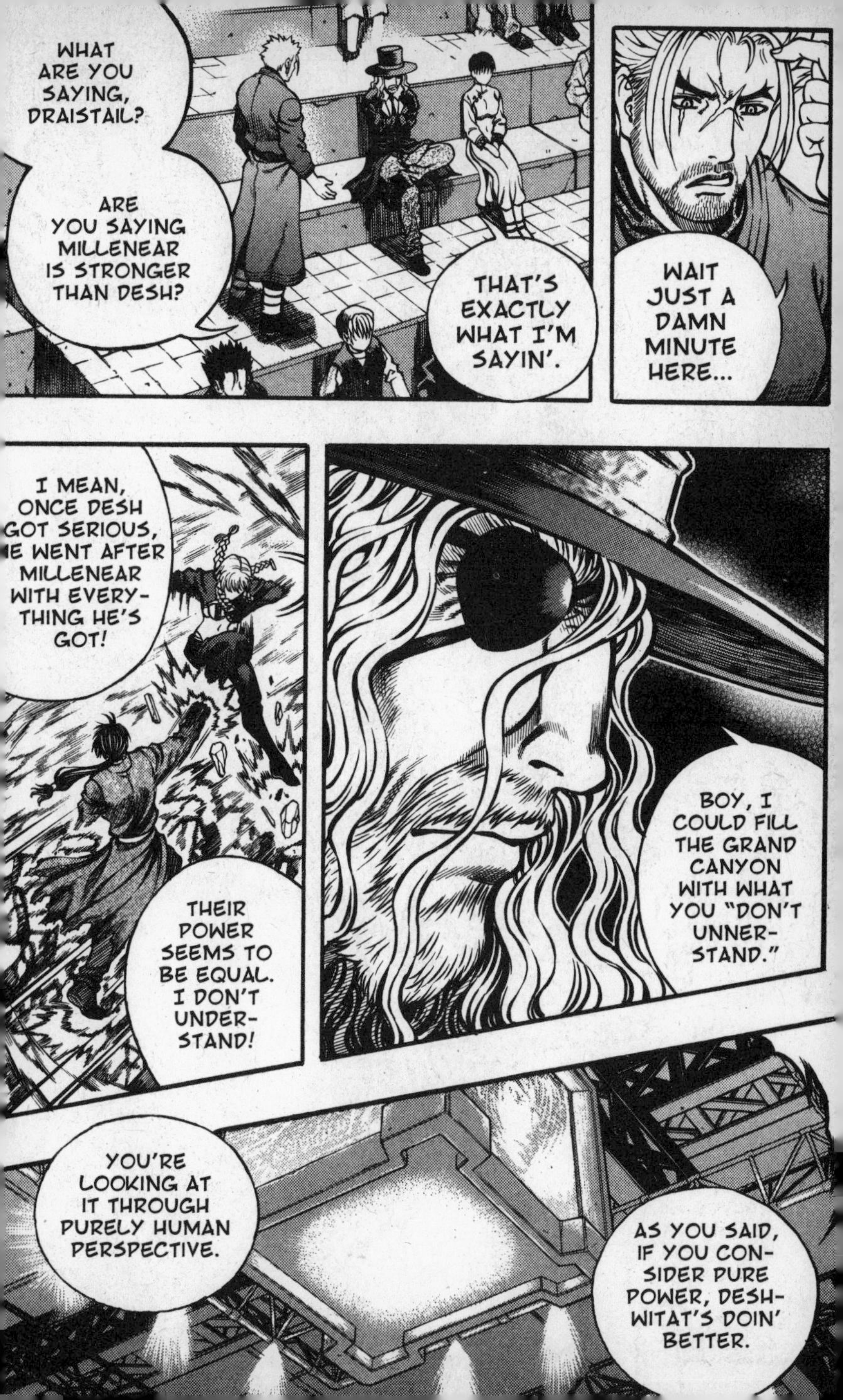
WHAT ARE YOU SAYING, DRAISTAIL?
ARE YOU SAYING MILLENEAR IS STRONGER THAN DESH?
THAT'S EXACTLY WHAT I'M SAYIN'.
WAIT JUST A DAMN MINUTE HERE...
I MEAN, ONCE DESH GOT SERIOUS, HE WENT AFTER MILLENEAR WITH EVERY-THING HE'S GOT!
THEIR POWER SEEMS TO BE EQUAL. I DON'T UNDER-STAND!
BOY, I COULD FILL THE GRAND CANYON WITH WHAT YOU "DON'T UNNER-STAND."
YOU'RE LOOKING AT IT THROUGH PURELY HUMAN PERSPECTIVE.
AS YOU SAID, IF YOU CON-SIDER PURE POWER, DESH-WITAT'S DOIN' BETTER.

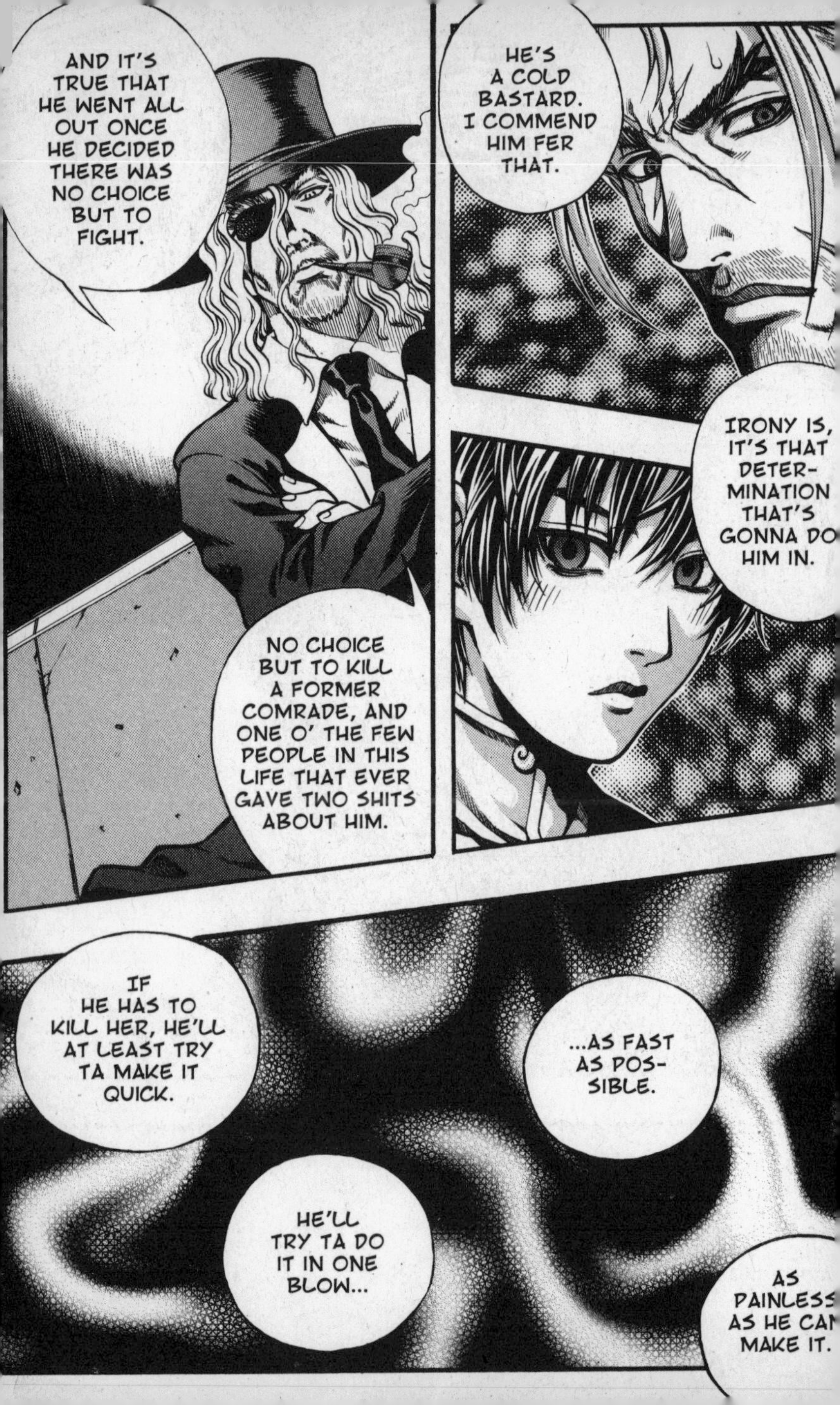
AND IT'S TRUE THAT HE WENT ALL OUT ONCE HE DECIDED THERE WAS NO CHOICE BUT TO FIGHT.
HE'S A COLD BASTARD. I COMMEND HIM FER THAT.
NO CHOICE BUT TO KILL A FORMER COMRADE, AND ONE O' THE FEW PEOPLE IN THIS LIFE THAT EVER GAVE TWO SHITS ABOUT HIM.
IRONY IS, IT'S THAT DETER-MINATION THAT'S GONNA DO HIM IN.
IF HE HAS TO KILL HER, HE'LL AT LEAST TRY TA MAKE IT QUICK.
...AS FAST AS POS-SIBLE.
HE'LL TRY TA DO IT IN ONE BLOW...
AS PAINLESS AS HE CAN MAKE IT.

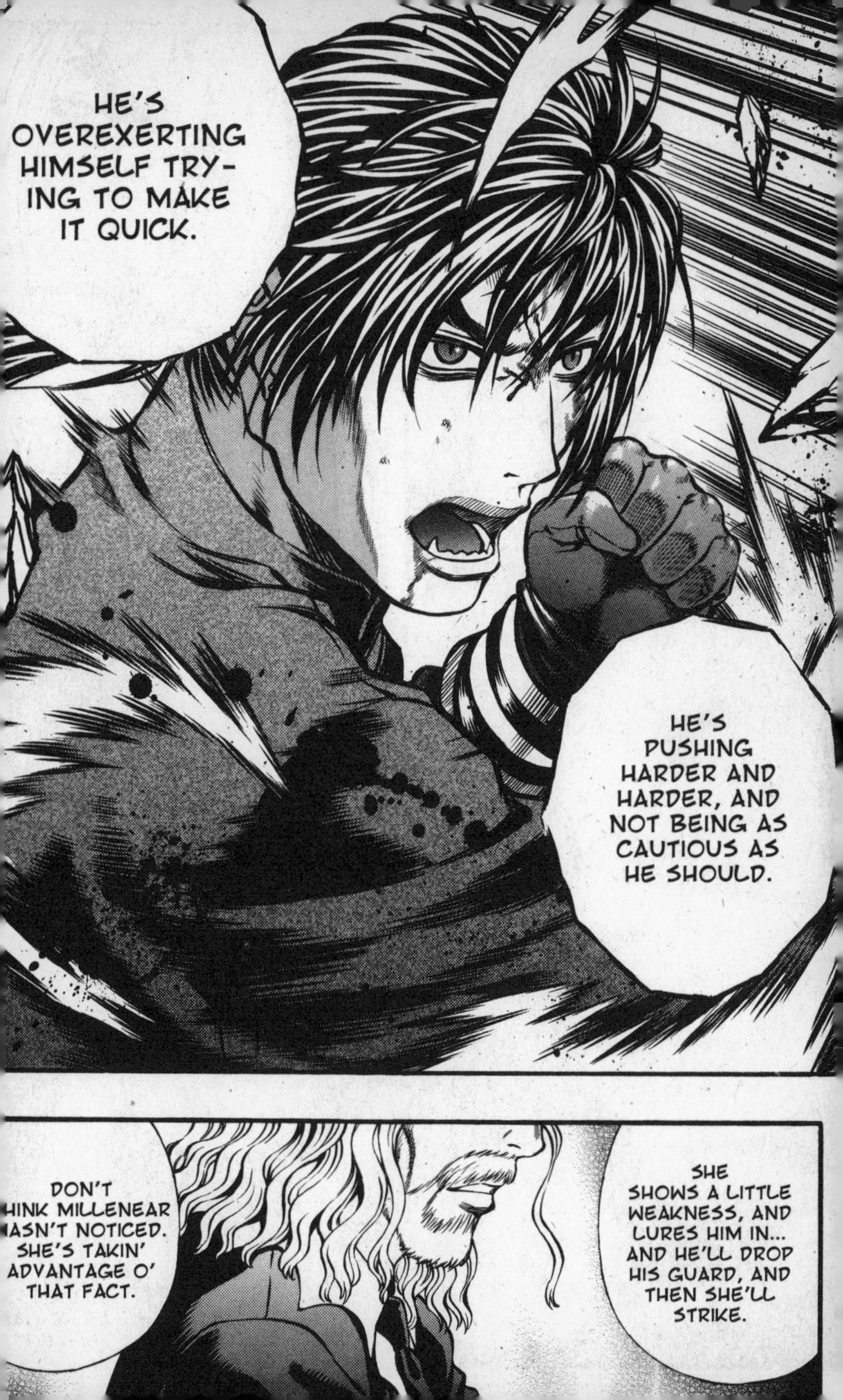
HE'S OVEREXERTING HIMSELF TRY- ING TO MAKE IT QUICK.
HE'S PUSHING HARDER AND HARDER, AND NOT BEING AS CAUTIOUS AS HE SHOULD.
SHE SHOWS A LITTLE WEAKNESS, AND LURES HIM IN... AND HE'LL DROP HIS GUARD, AND THEN SHE'LL STRIKE.
DON'T HINK MILLENEAR ASN'T NOTICED. SHE'S TAKIN' ADVANTAGE O' THAT FACT.

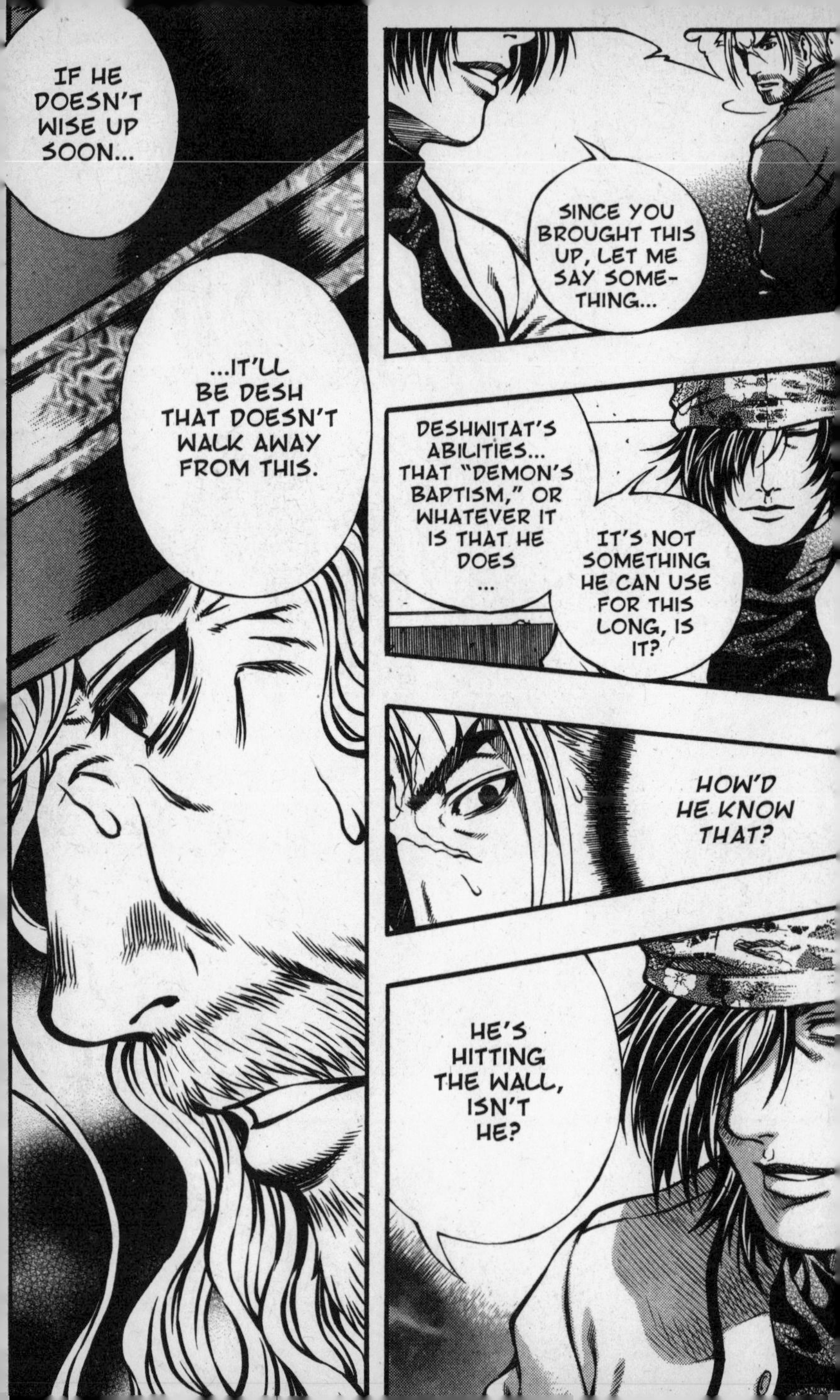
IF HE DOESN'T WISE UP SOON...
...IT'LL BE DESH THAT DOESN'T WALK AWAY FROM THIS.
SINCE YOU BROUGHT THIS UP, LET ME SAY SOMETHING...
DESHWITAT'S ABILITIES... THAT "DEMON'S BAPTISM," OR WHATEVER IT IS THAT HE DOES ...
IT'S NOT SOMETHING HE CAN USE FOR THIS LONG, IS IT?
HOW'D HE KNOW THAT?
HE'S HITTING THE WALL, ISN'T HE?

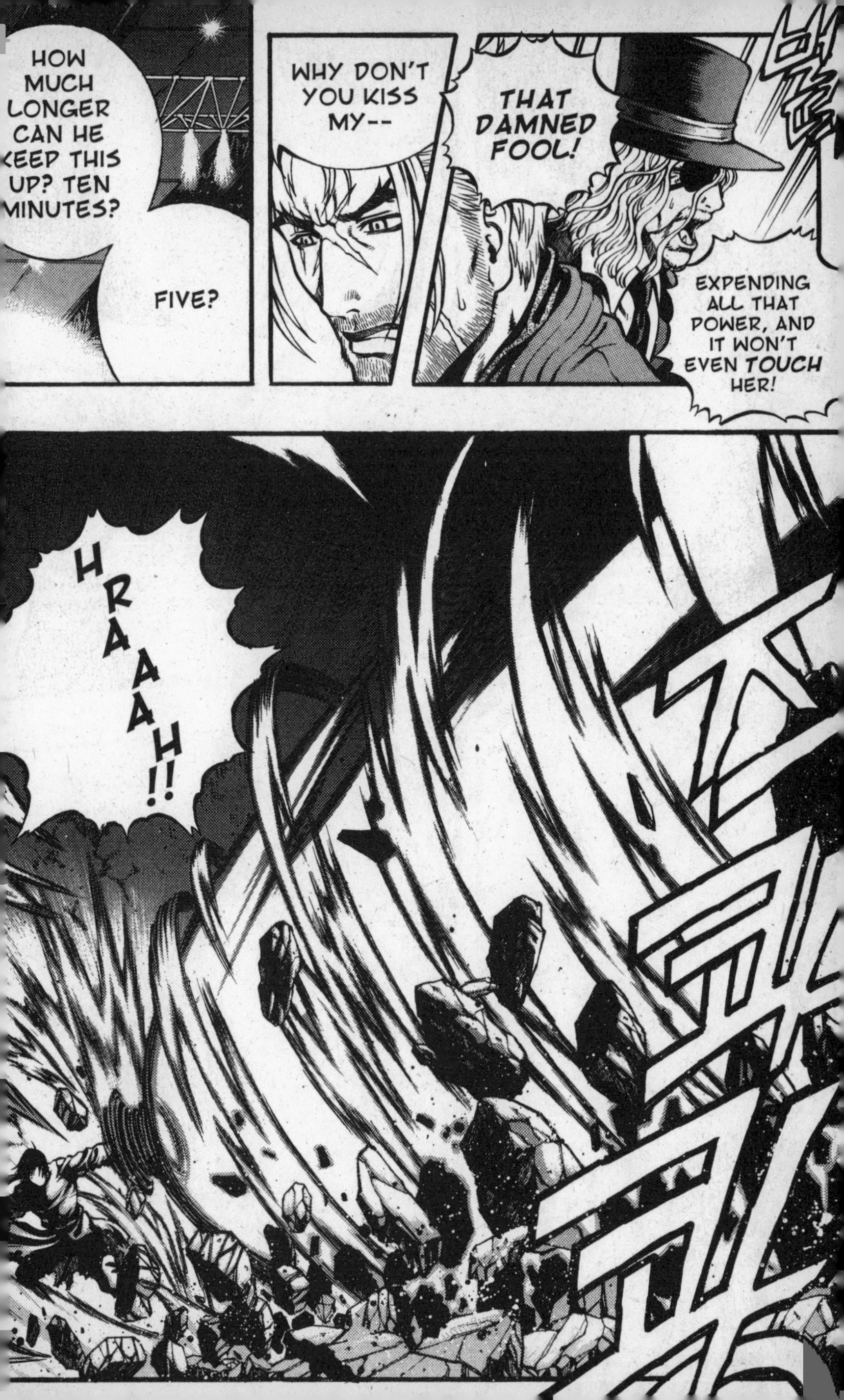
HOW MUCH LONGER CAN HE KEEP THIS UP? TEN MINUTES?
FIVE?
WHY DON'T YOU KISS MY--
THAT DAMNED FOOL!
EXPENDING ALL THAT POWER, AND IT WON'T EVEN TOUCH HER!
HRAAAH!!

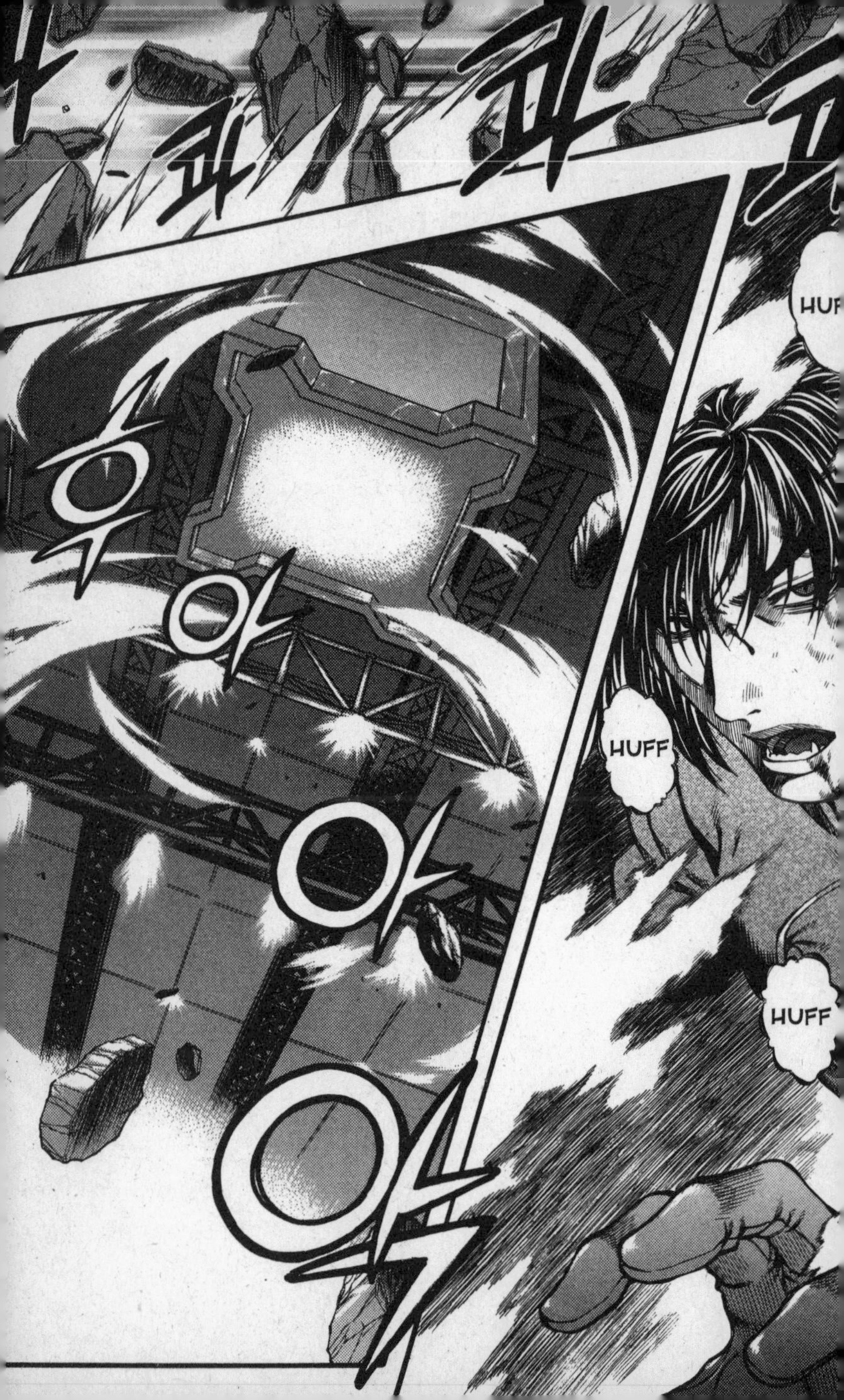

파 파
우아아아
HUF
HUFF
HUFF

CHAPTER 74:
CONCLUSION

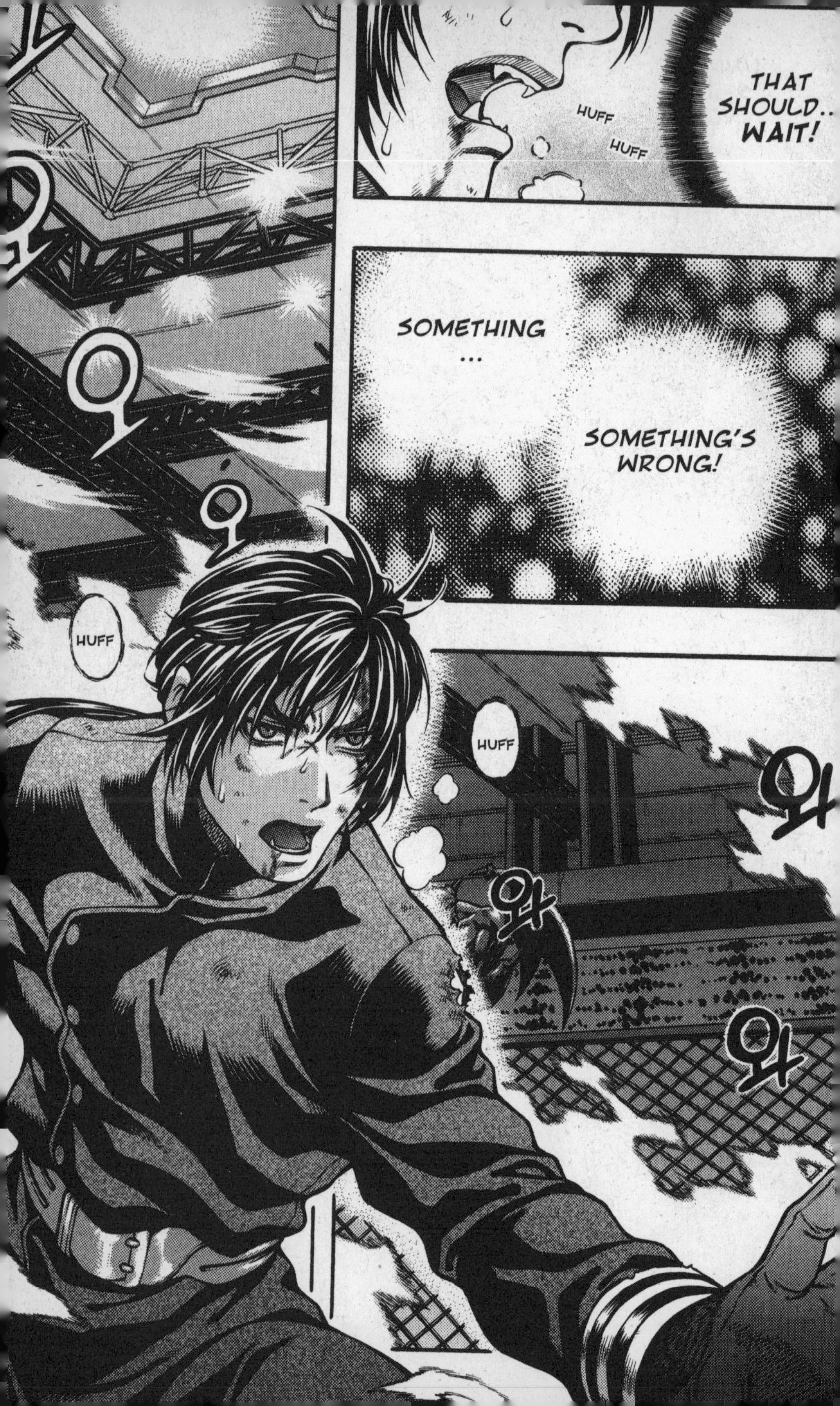
HUFF
HUFF
THAT SHOULD.. WAIT!
SOMETHING ...
SOMETHING'S WRONG!
HUFF
HUFF

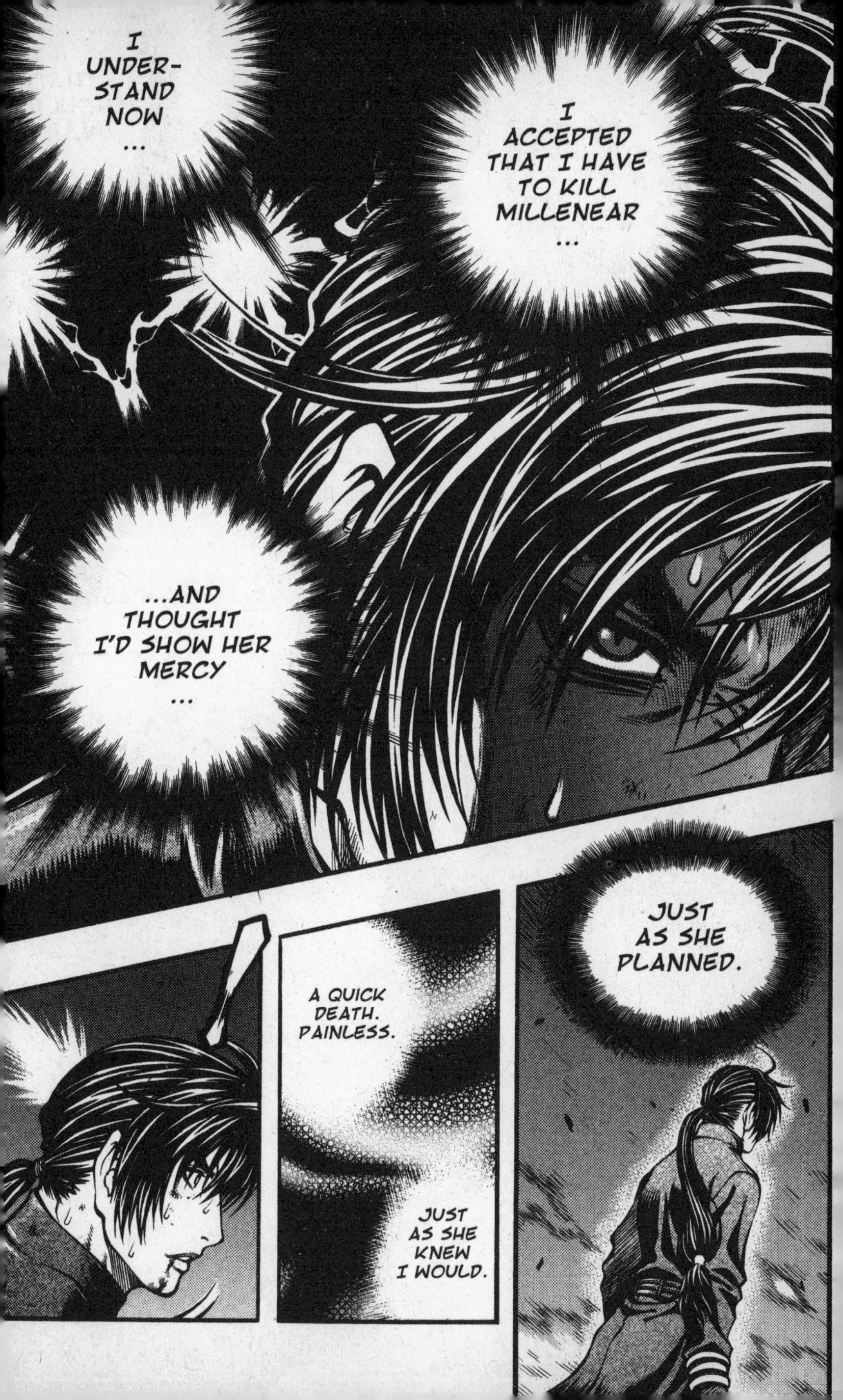
I UNDER-STAND NOW ...
I ACCEPTED THAT I HAVE TO KILL MILLENEAR ...
...AND THOUGHT I'D SHOW HER MERCY ...
JUST AS SHE PLANNED.
A QUICK DEATH. PAINLESS.
JUST AS SHE KNEW I WOULD.

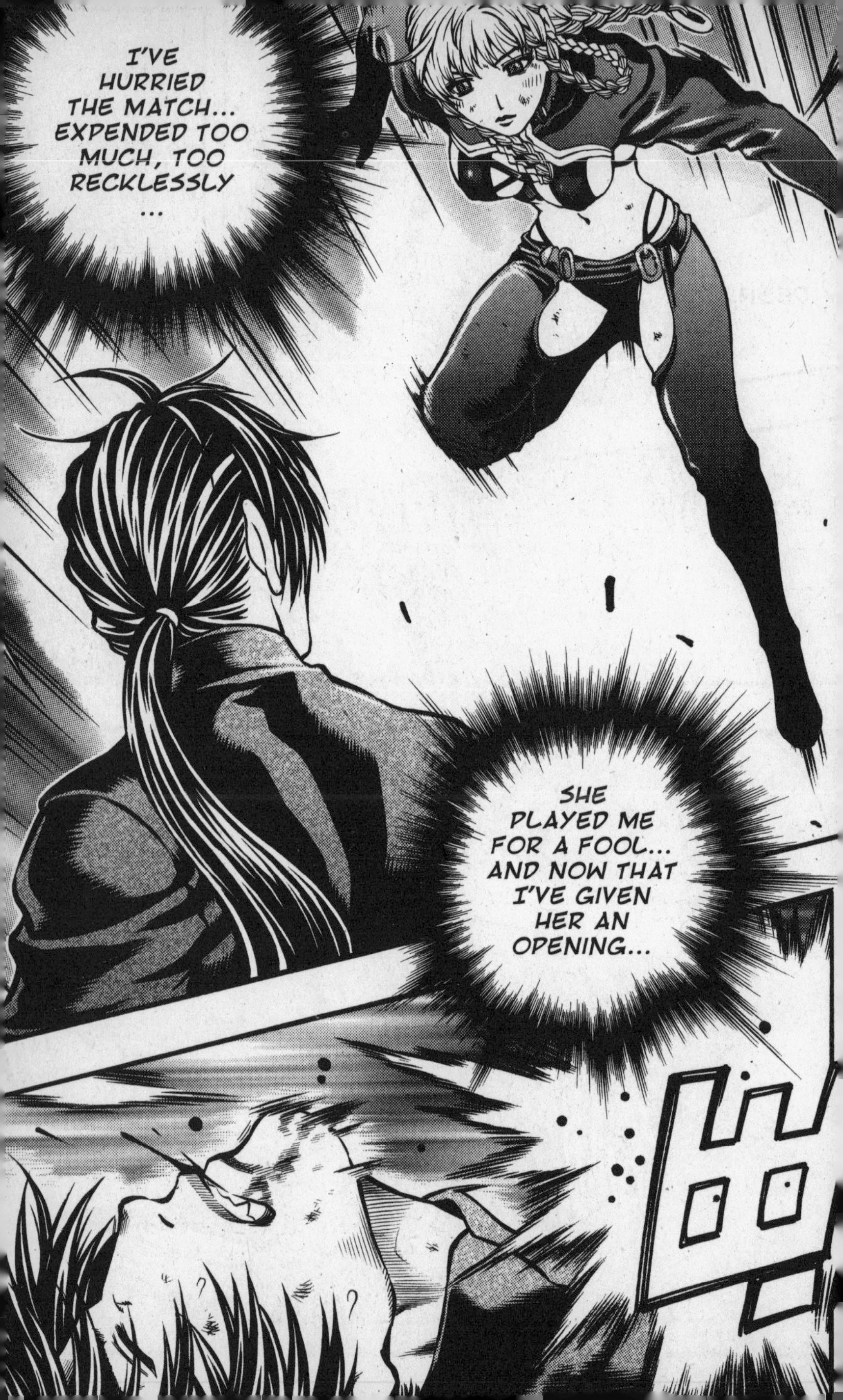
I'VE HURRIED THE MATCH... EXPENDED TOO MUCH, TOO RECKLESSLY ...
SHE PLAYED ME FOR A FOOL... AND NOW THAT I'VE GIVEN HER AN OPENING...

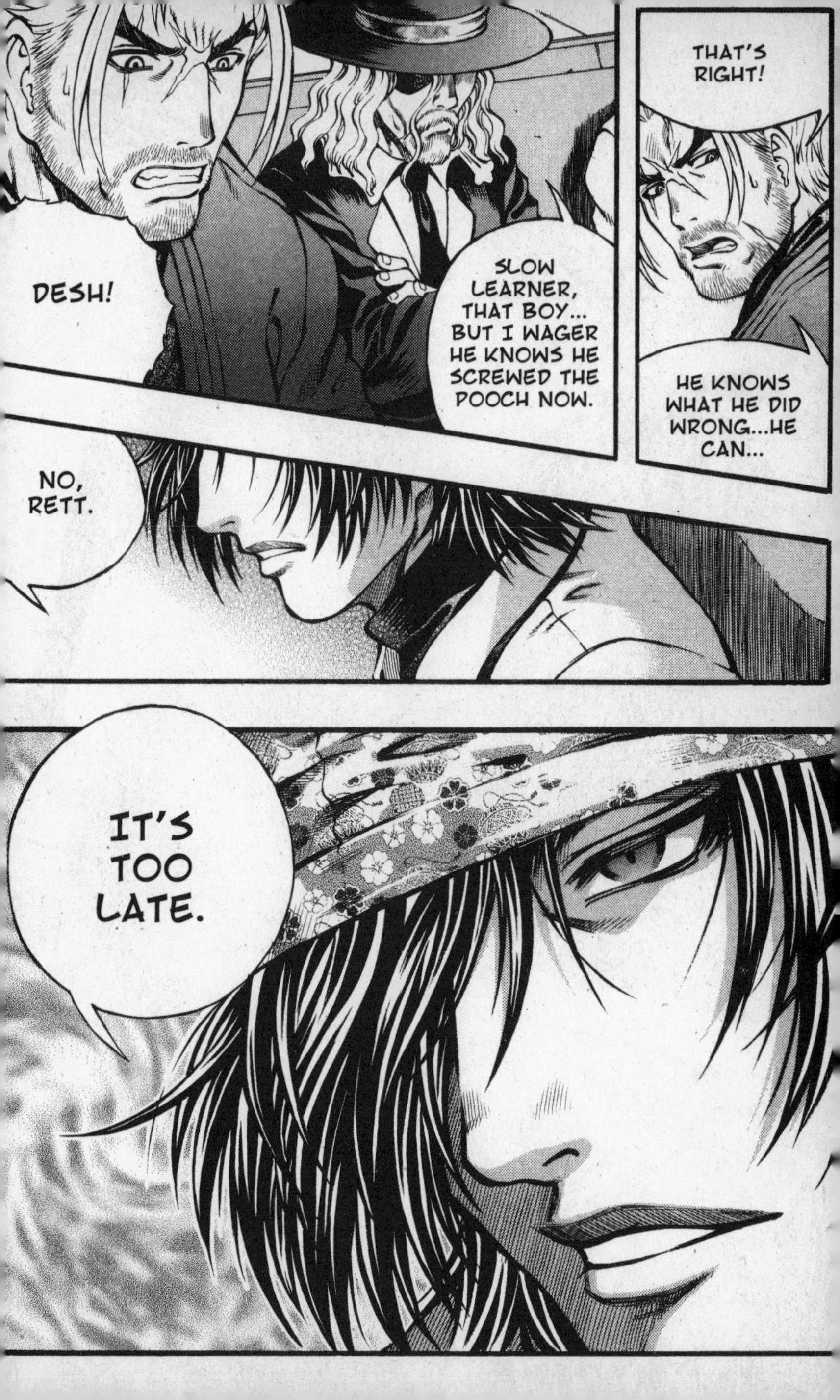
DESH!
SLOW LEARNER, THAT BOY... BUT I WAGER HE KNOWS HE SCREWED THE POOCH NOW.
THAT'S RIGHT!
HE KNOWS WHAT HE DID WRONG...HE CAN...
NO, RETT.
IT'S TOO LATE.

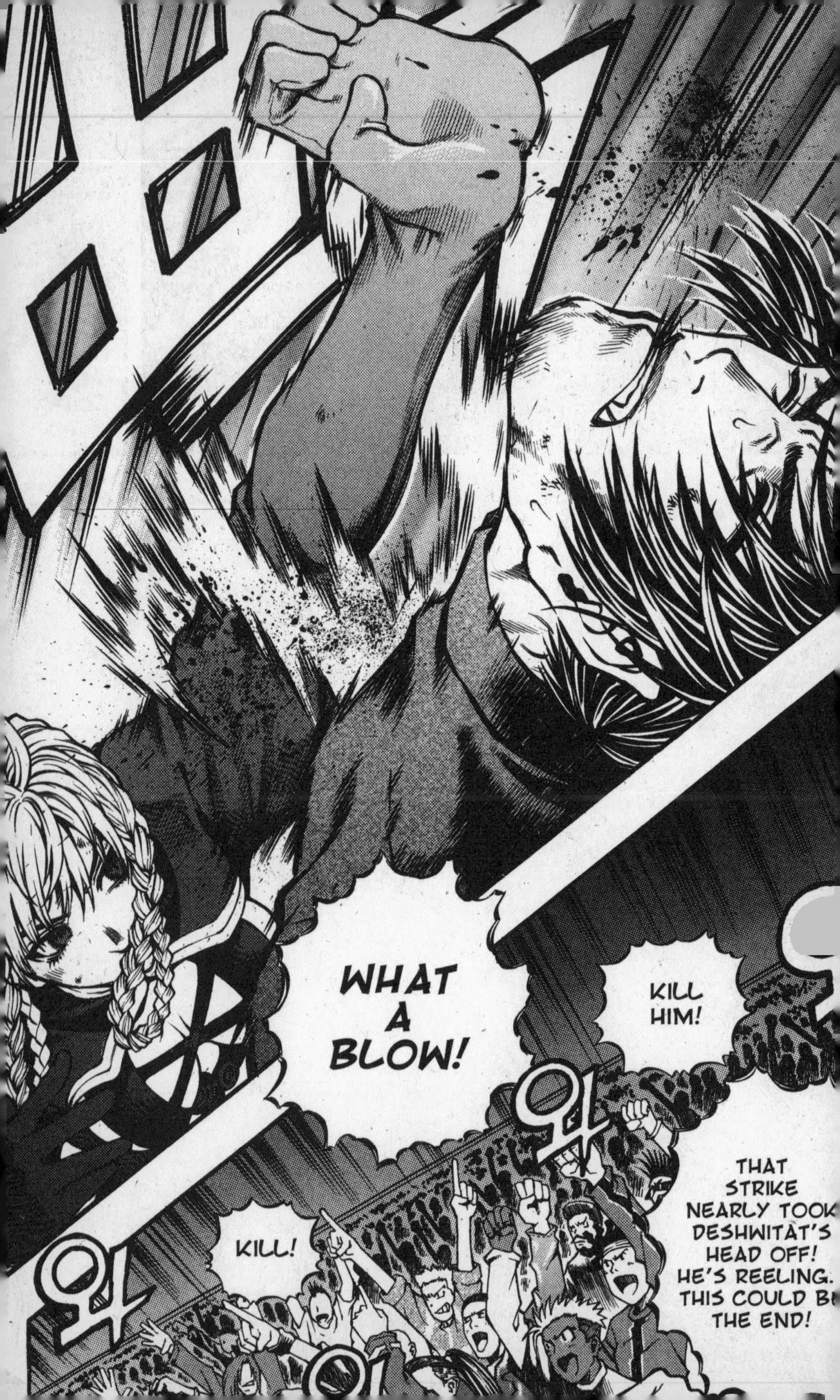
WHAT A BLOW!
KILL HIM!
THAT STRIKE NEARLY TOOK DESHWITAT'S HEAD OFF! HE'S REELING. THIS COULD B THE END!
KILL!

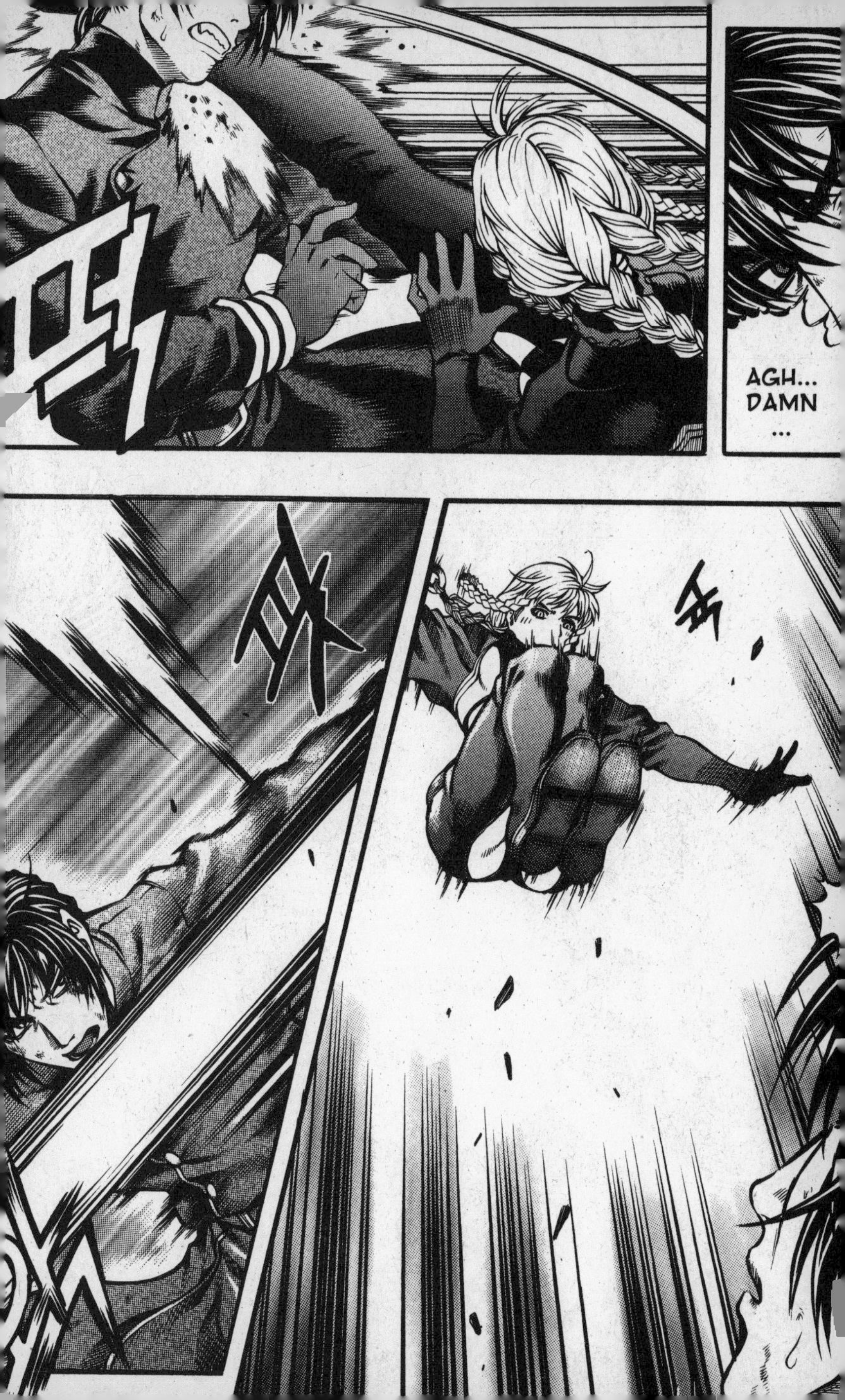
AGH... DAMN ...

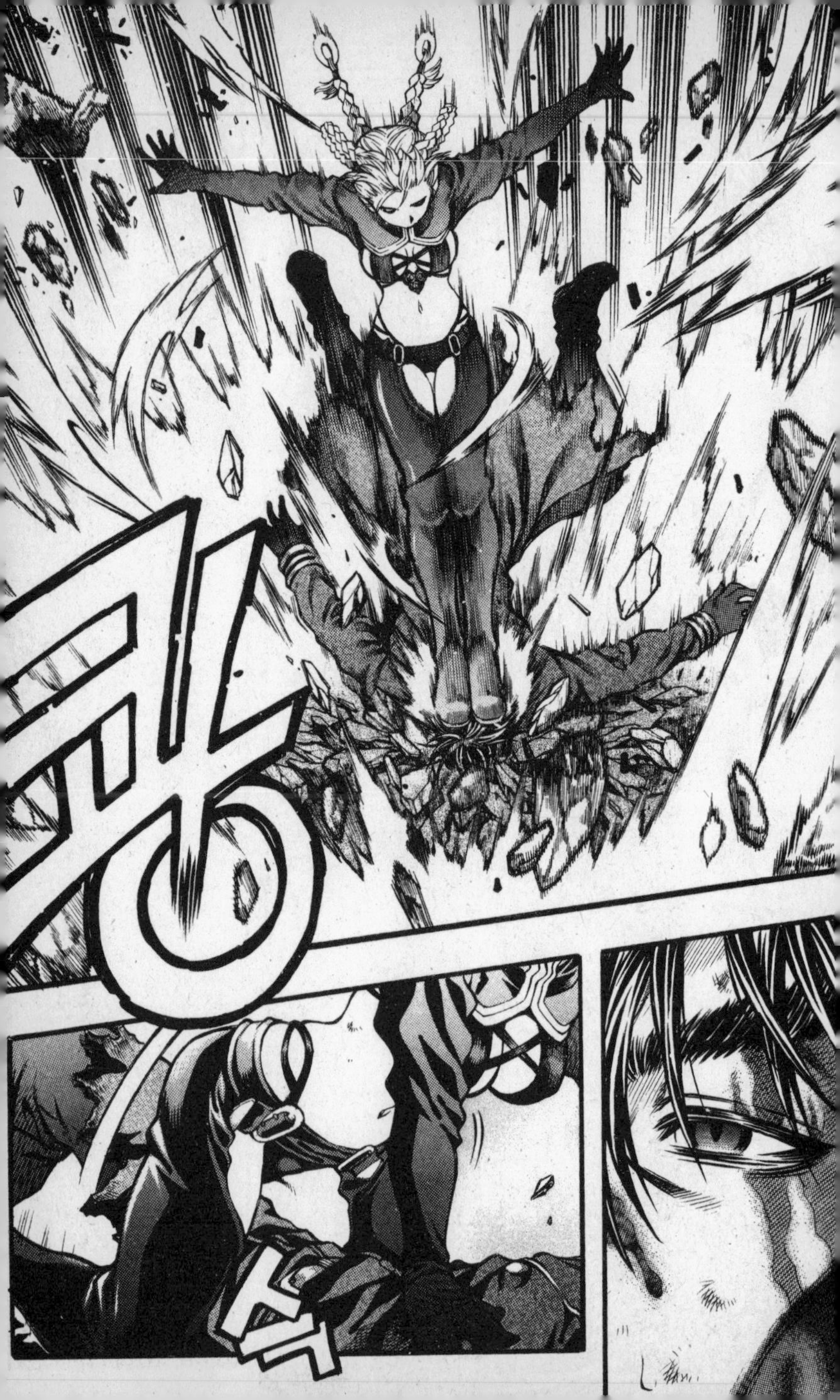

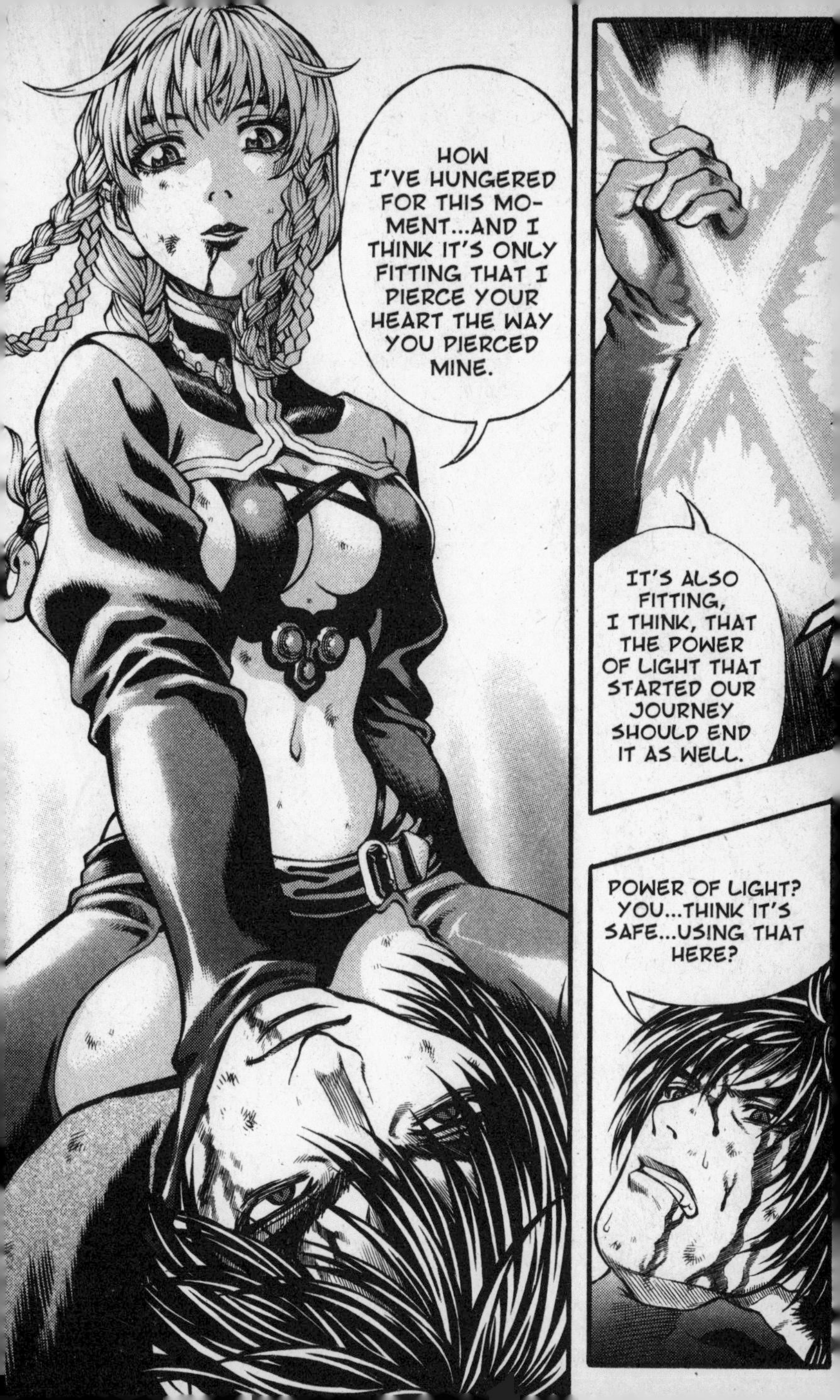
HOW I'VE HUNGERED FOR THIS MOMENT...AND I THINK IT'S ONLY FITTING THAT I PIERCE YOUR HEART THE WAY YOU PIERCED MINE.
IT'S ALSO FITTING, I THINK, THAT THE POWER OF LIGHT THAT STARTED OUR JOURNEY SHOULD END IT AS WELL.
POWER OF LIGHT? YOU...THINK IT'S SAFE...USING THAT HERE?

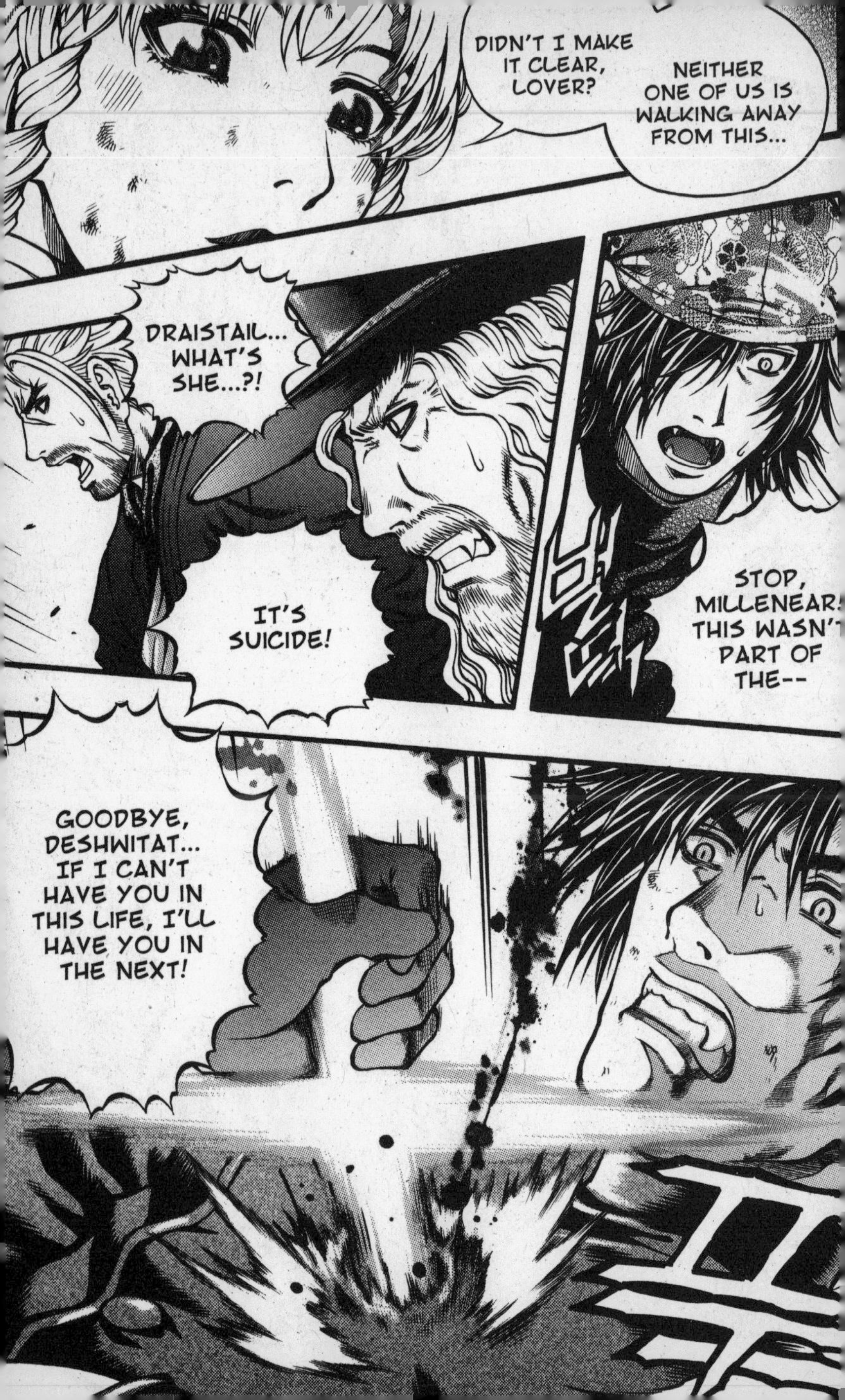
DIDN'T I MAKE IT CLEAR, LOVER?
NEITHER ONE OF US IS WALKING AWAY FROM THIS...
DRAISTAIL... WHAT'S SHE...?!
IT'S SUICIDE!
STOP, MILLENEAR! THIS WASN'T PART OF THE--
GOODBYE, DESHWITAT... IF I CAN'T HAVE YOU IN THIS LIFE, I'LL HAVE YOU IN THE NEXT!

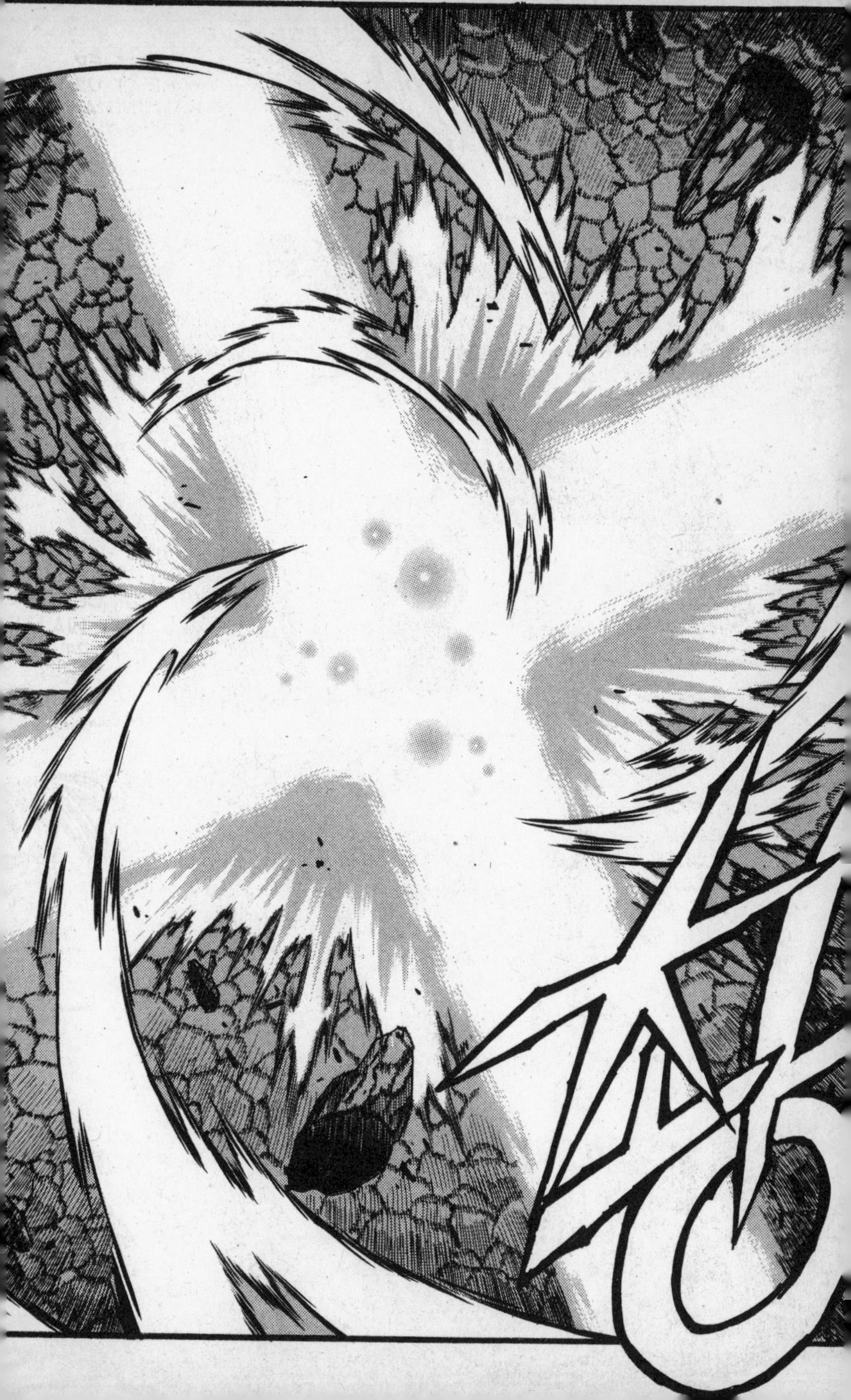

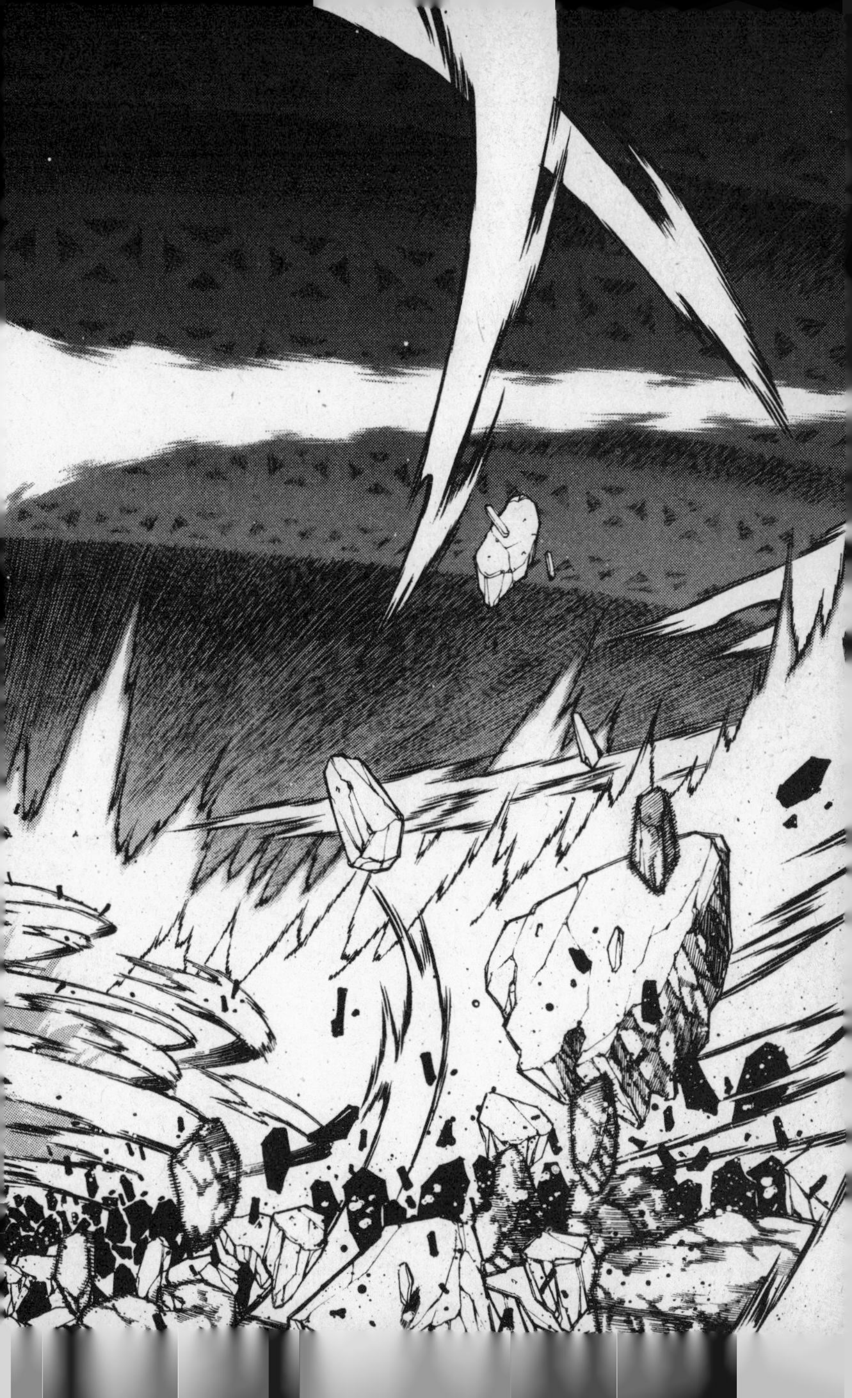

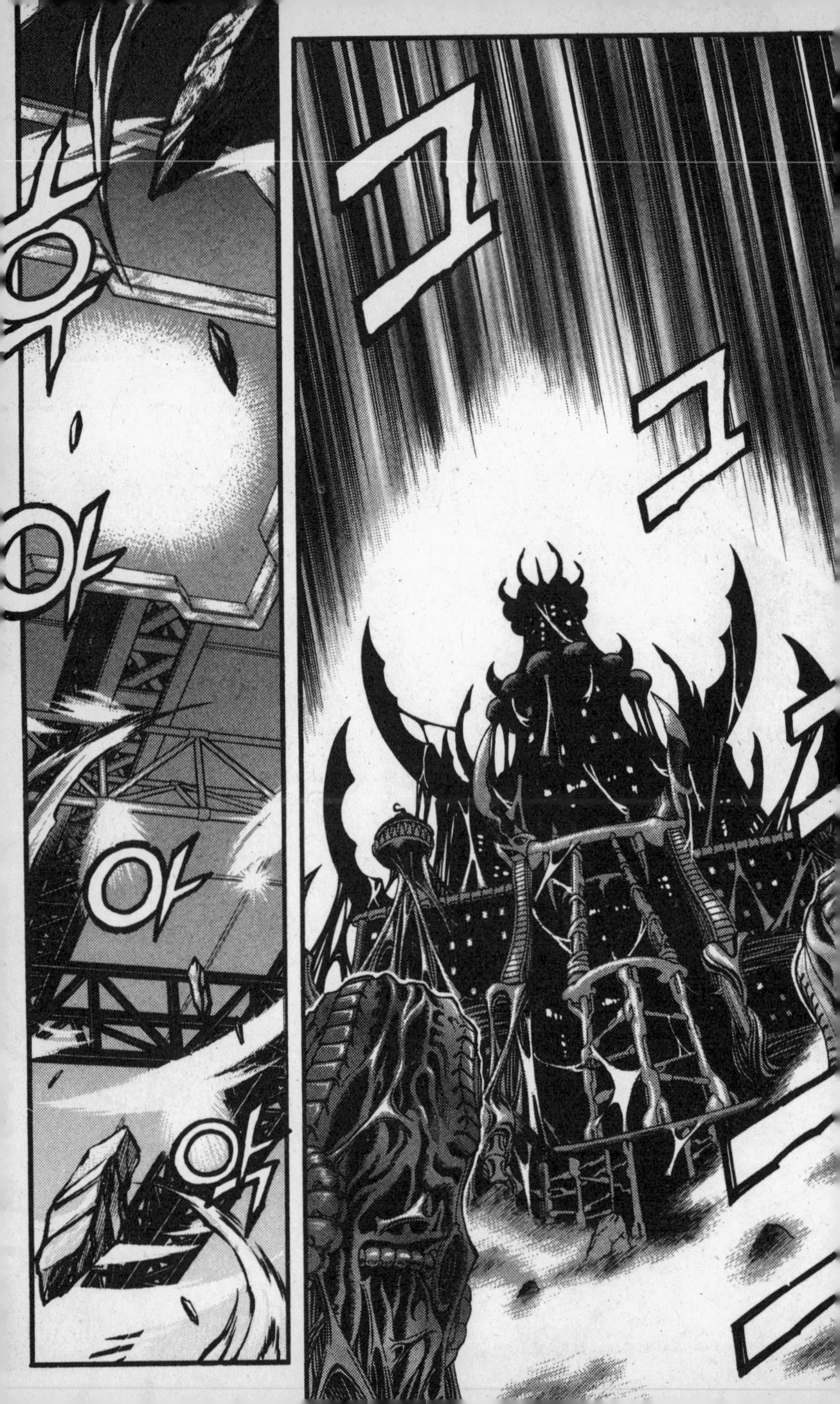
아
아
아
아
그
그

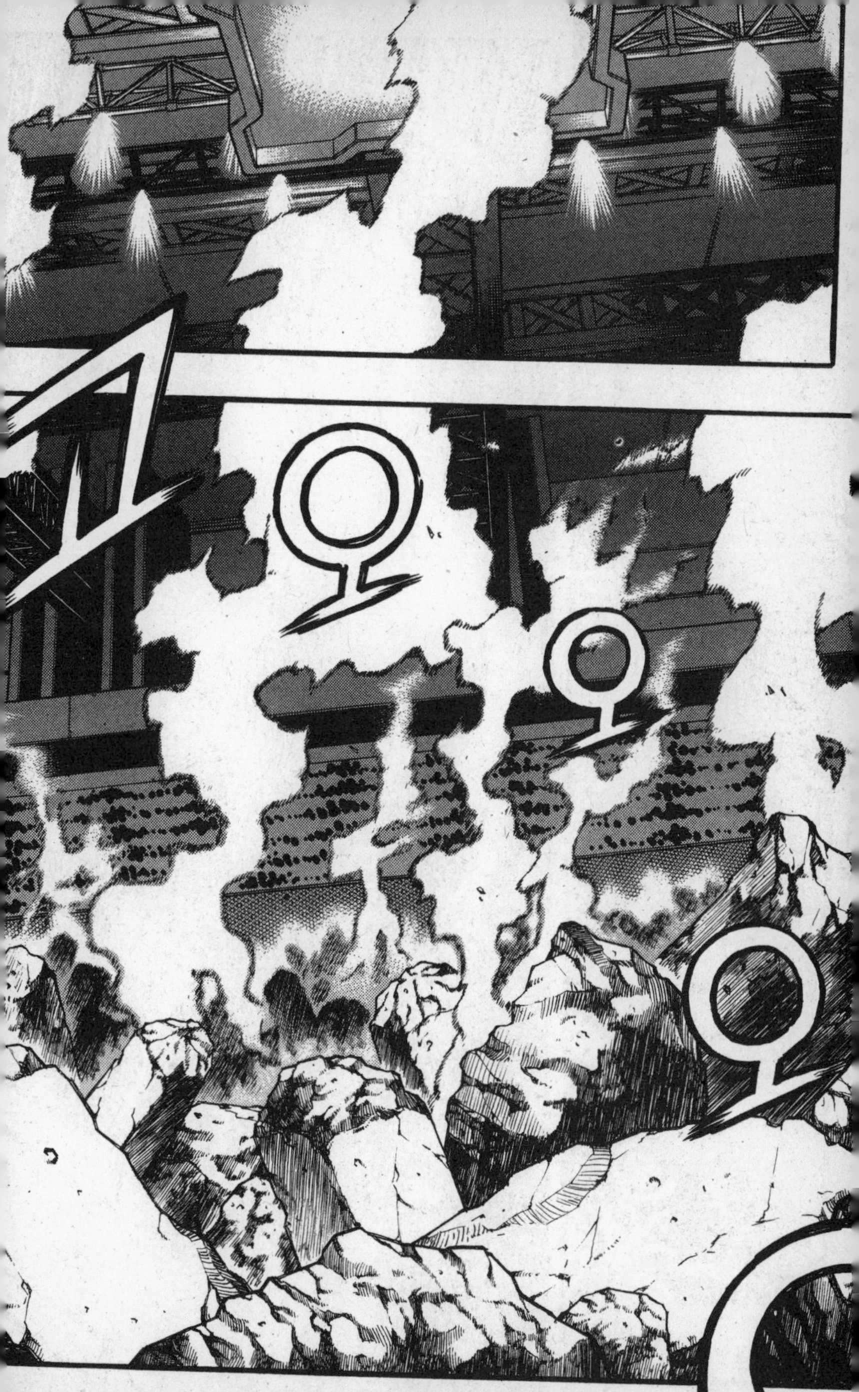

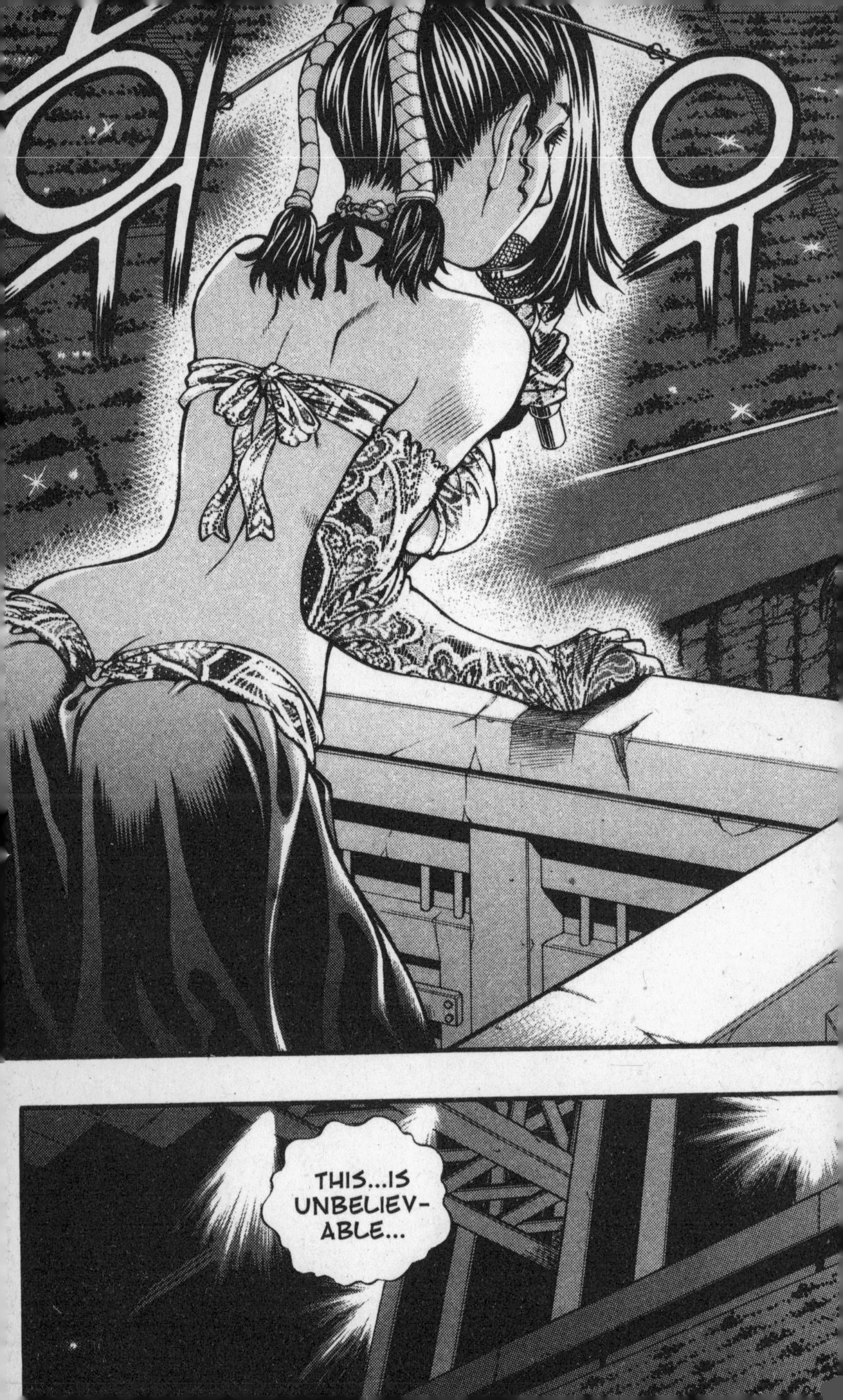
THIS...IS UNBELIEV-ABLE...

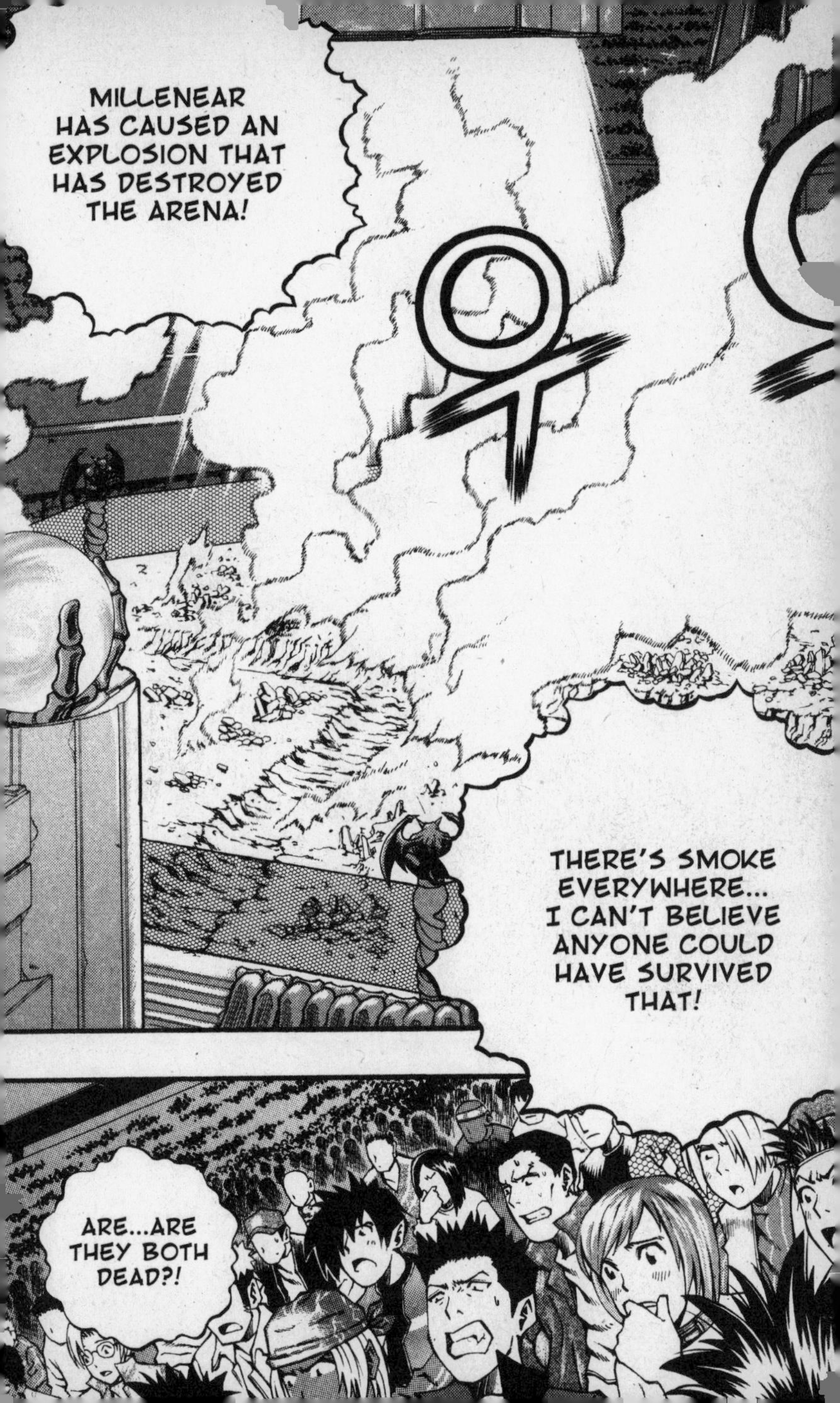
MILLENEAR HAS CAUSED AN EXPLOSION THAT HAS DESTROYED THE ARENA!
THERE'S SMOKE EVERYWHERE... I CAN'T BELIEVE ANYONE COULD HAVE SURVIVED THAT!
ARE...ARE THEY BOTH DEAD?!

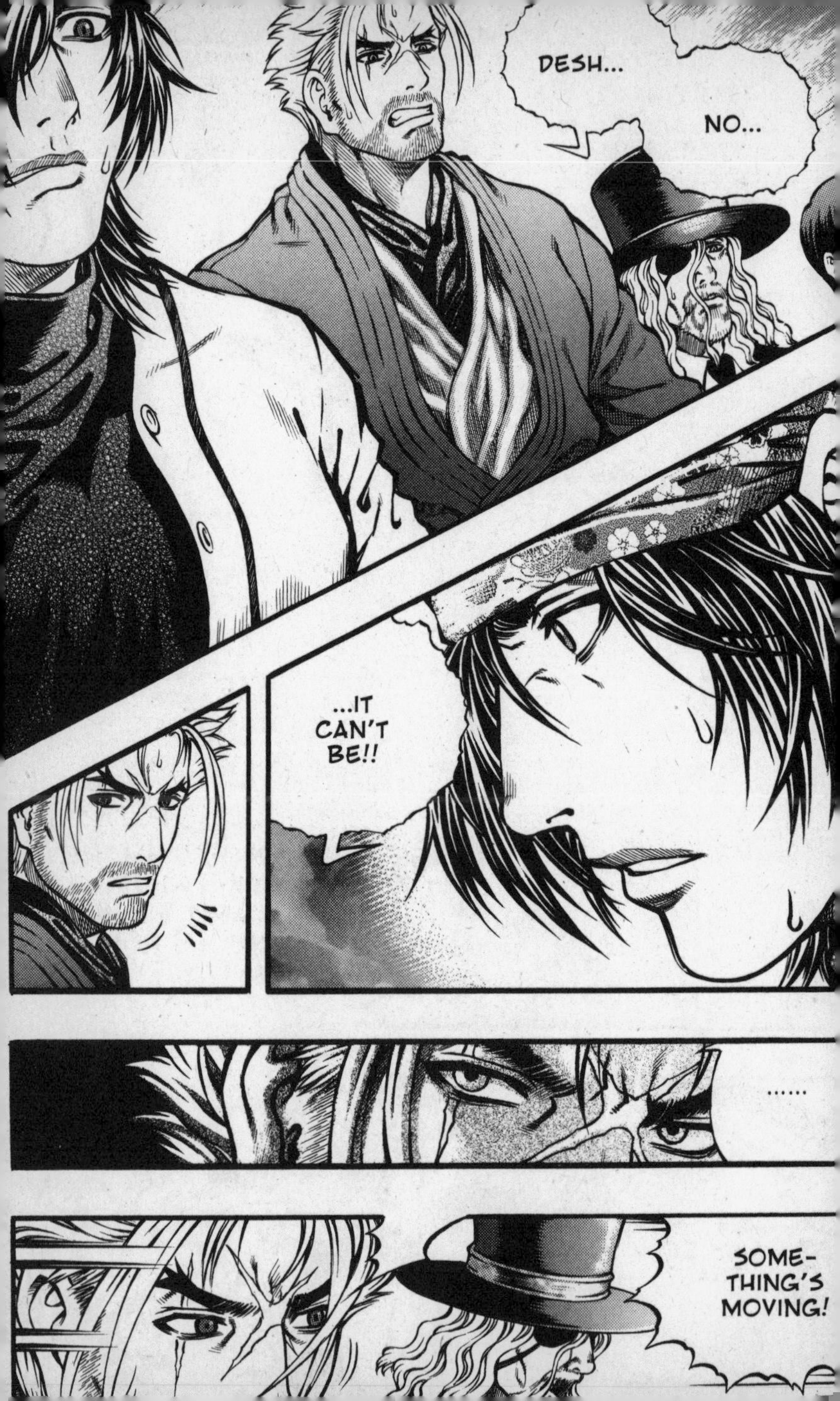
DESH...
NO...
...IT CAN'T BE!!
......
SOME-THING'S MOVING!

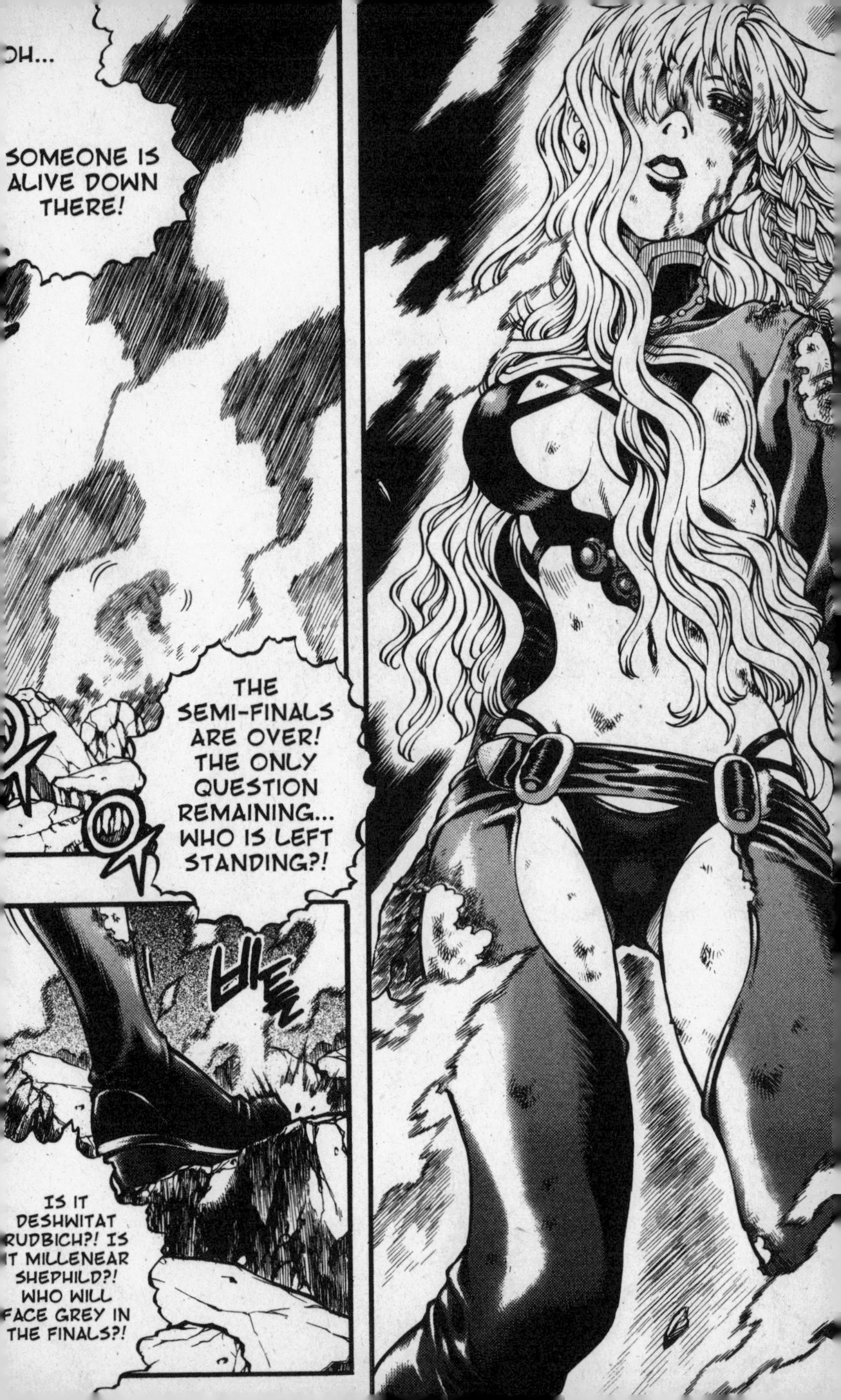

OH...
SOMEONE IS ALIVE DOWN THERE!
THE SEMI-FINALS ARE OVER! THE ONLY QUESTION REMAINING... WHO IS LEFT STANDING?!
IS IT DESHWITAT RUDBICH?! IS IT MILLENEAR SHEPHILD?! WHO WILL FACE GREY IN THE FINALS?!

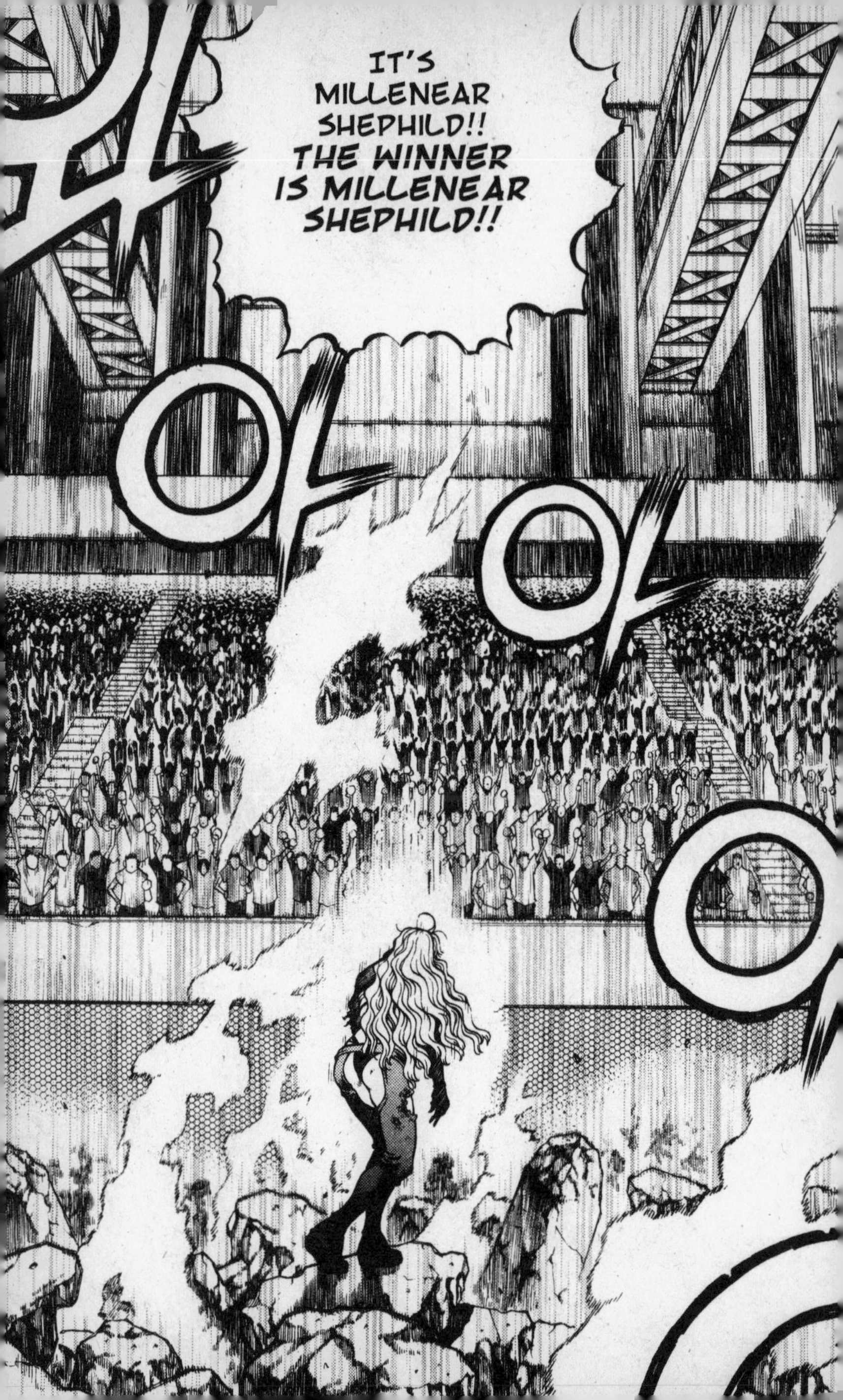
IT'S MILLENEAR SHEPHILD!! THE WINNER IS MILLENEAR SHEPHILD!!

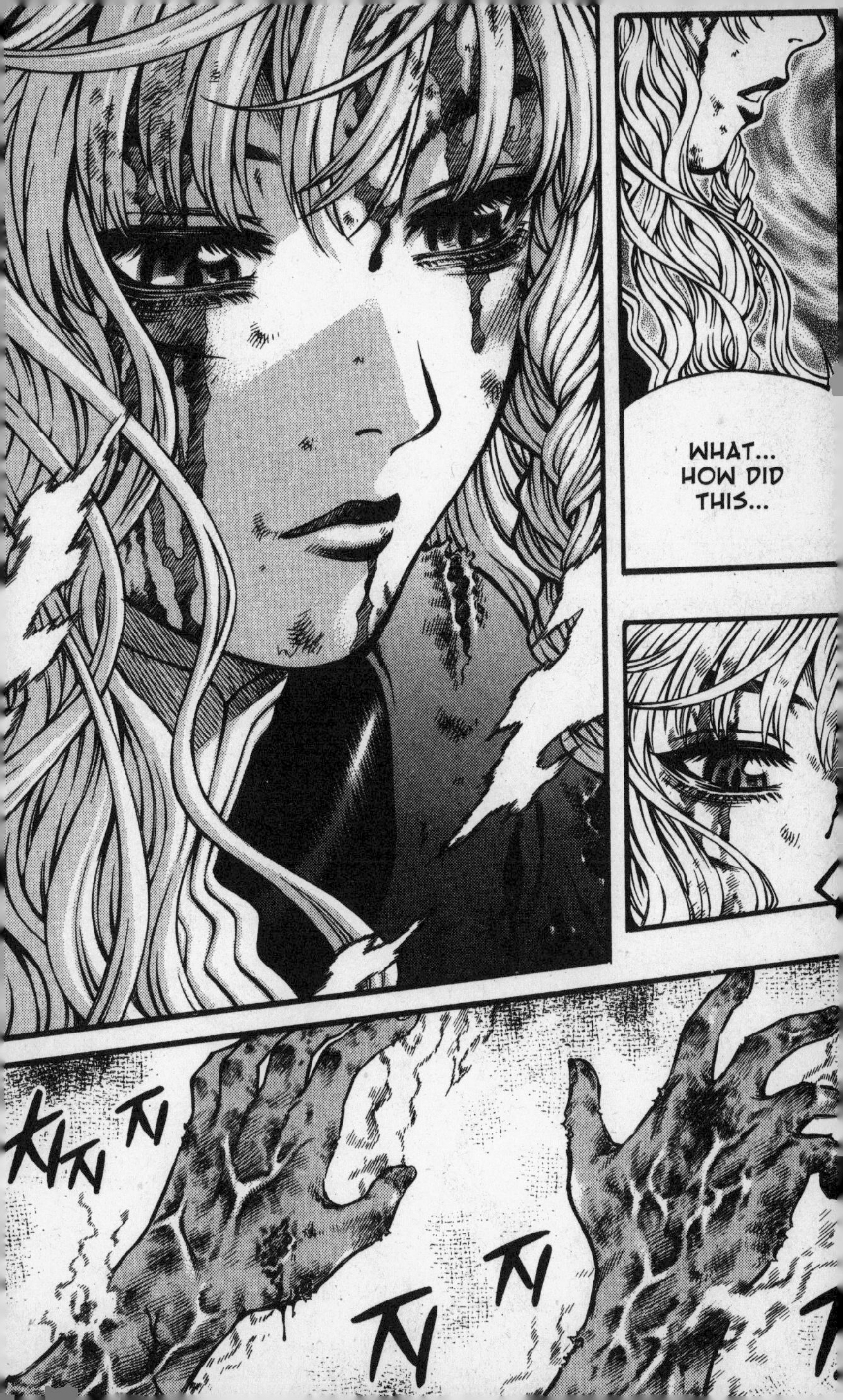
WHAT...
HOW DID
THIS...
KATATA
TATA

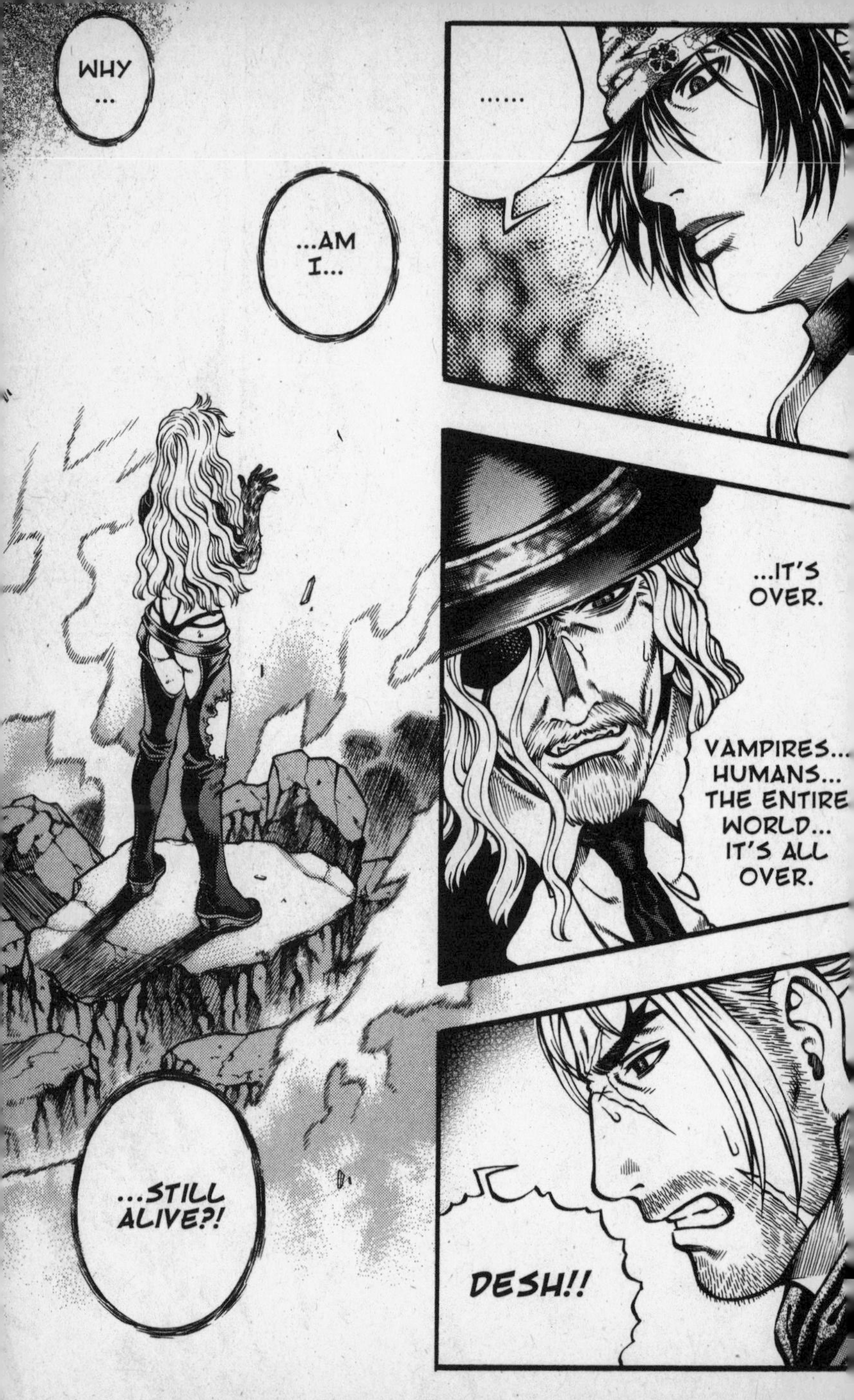
......
...IT'S OVER.
VAMPIRES... HUMANS... THE ENTIRE WORLD... IT'S ALL OVER.
DESH!!
WHY ...
...AM I...
...STILL ALIVE?!

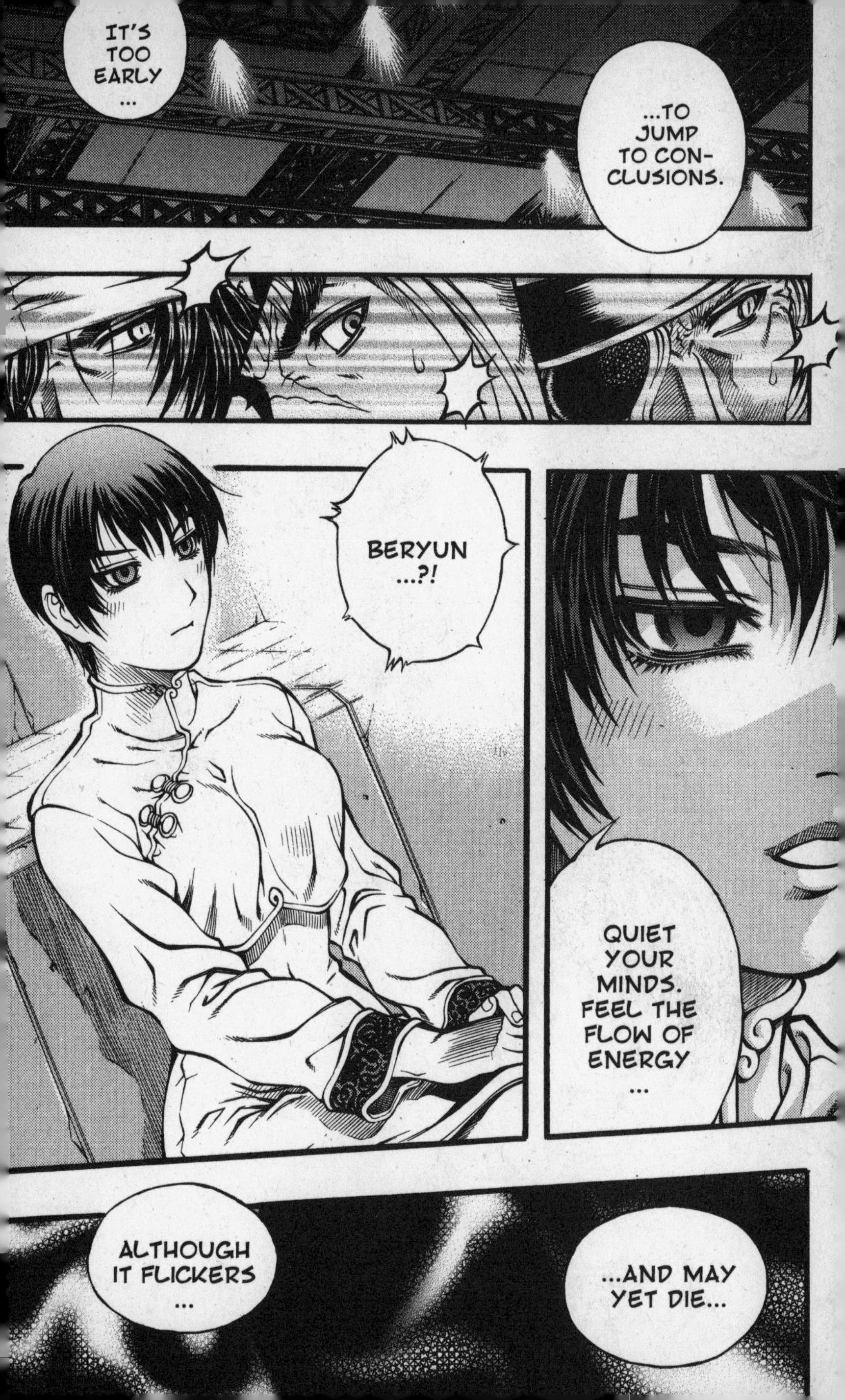

...TO JUMP TO CON-CLUSIONS.
IT'S TOO EARLY ...
BERYUN ...?!
QUIET YOUR MINDS. FEEL THE FLOW OF ENERGY ...
...AND MAY YET DIE...
ALTHOUGH IT FLICKERS ...

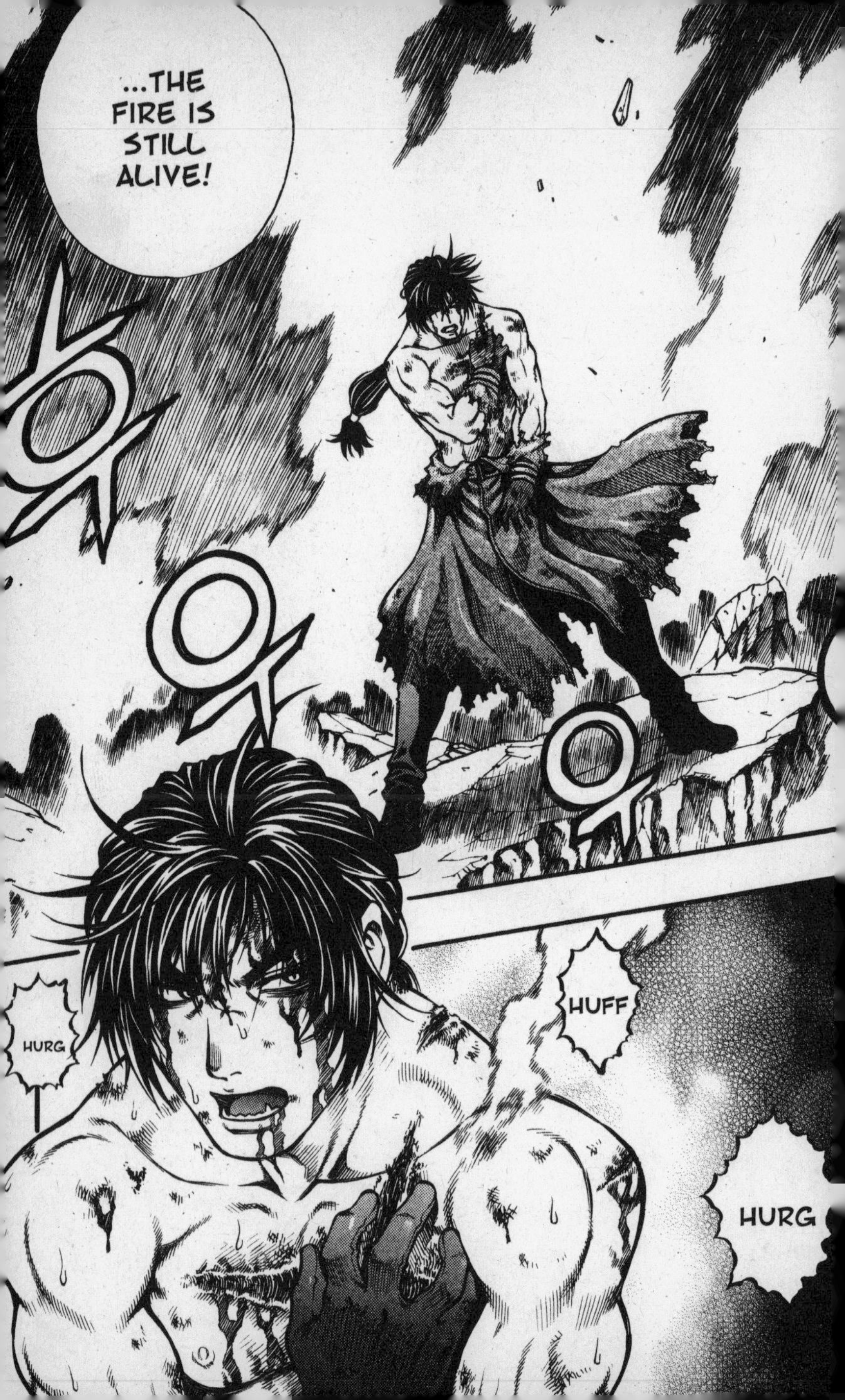
...THE
FIRE IS
STILL
ALIVE!
HUFF
HURG
HURG

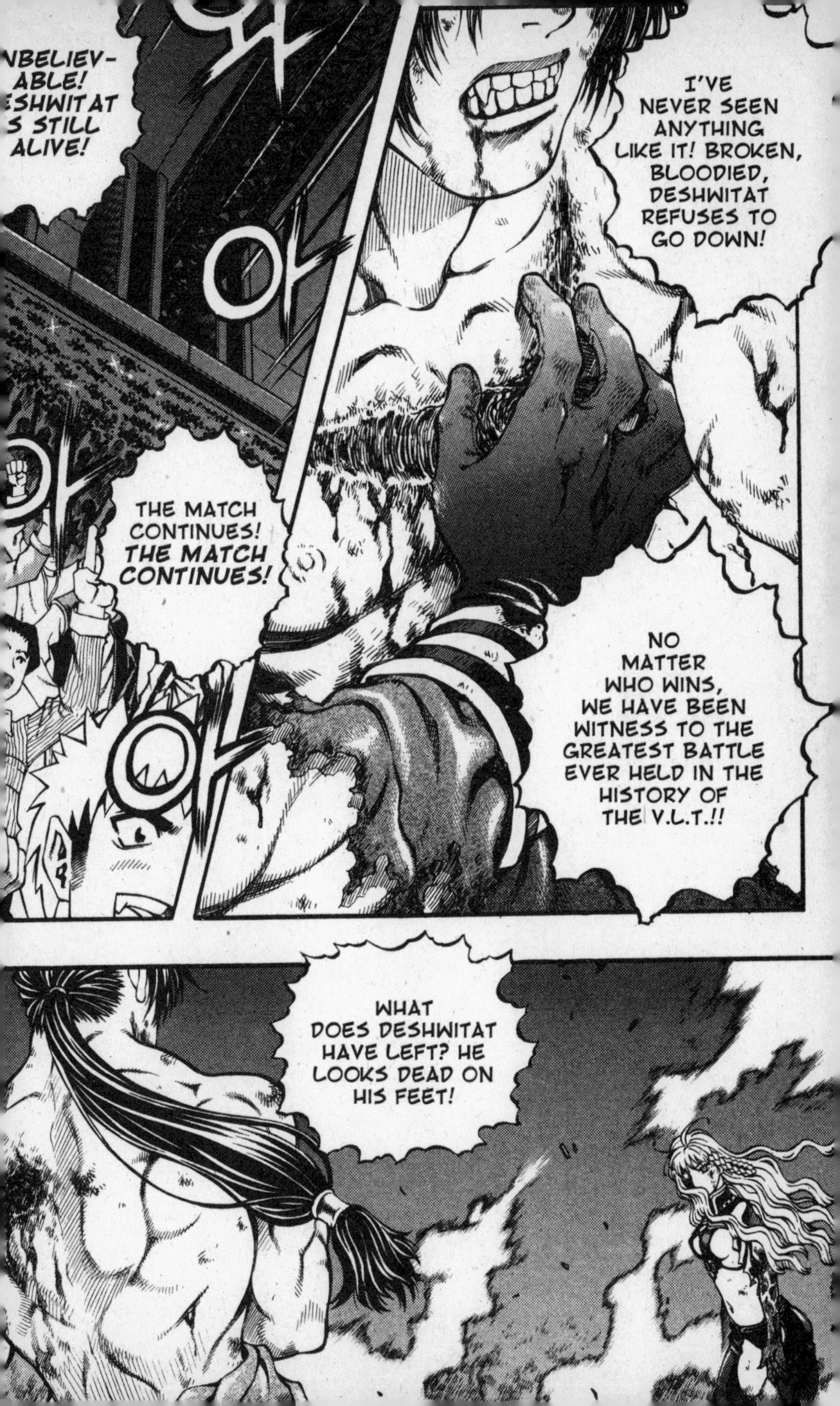

NBELIEV-ABLE! ESHWITAT S STILL ALIVE!
I'VE NEVER SEEN ANYTHING LIKE IT! BROKEN, BLOODIED, DESHWITAT REFUSES TO GO DOWN!
THE MATCH CONTINUES! THE MATCH CONTINUES!
NO MATTER WHO WINS, WE HAVE BEEN WITNESS TO THE GREATEST BATTLE EVER HELD IN THE HISTORY OF THE V.L.T.!!
WHAT DOES DESHWITAT HAVE LEFT? HE LOOKS DEAD ON HIS FEET!

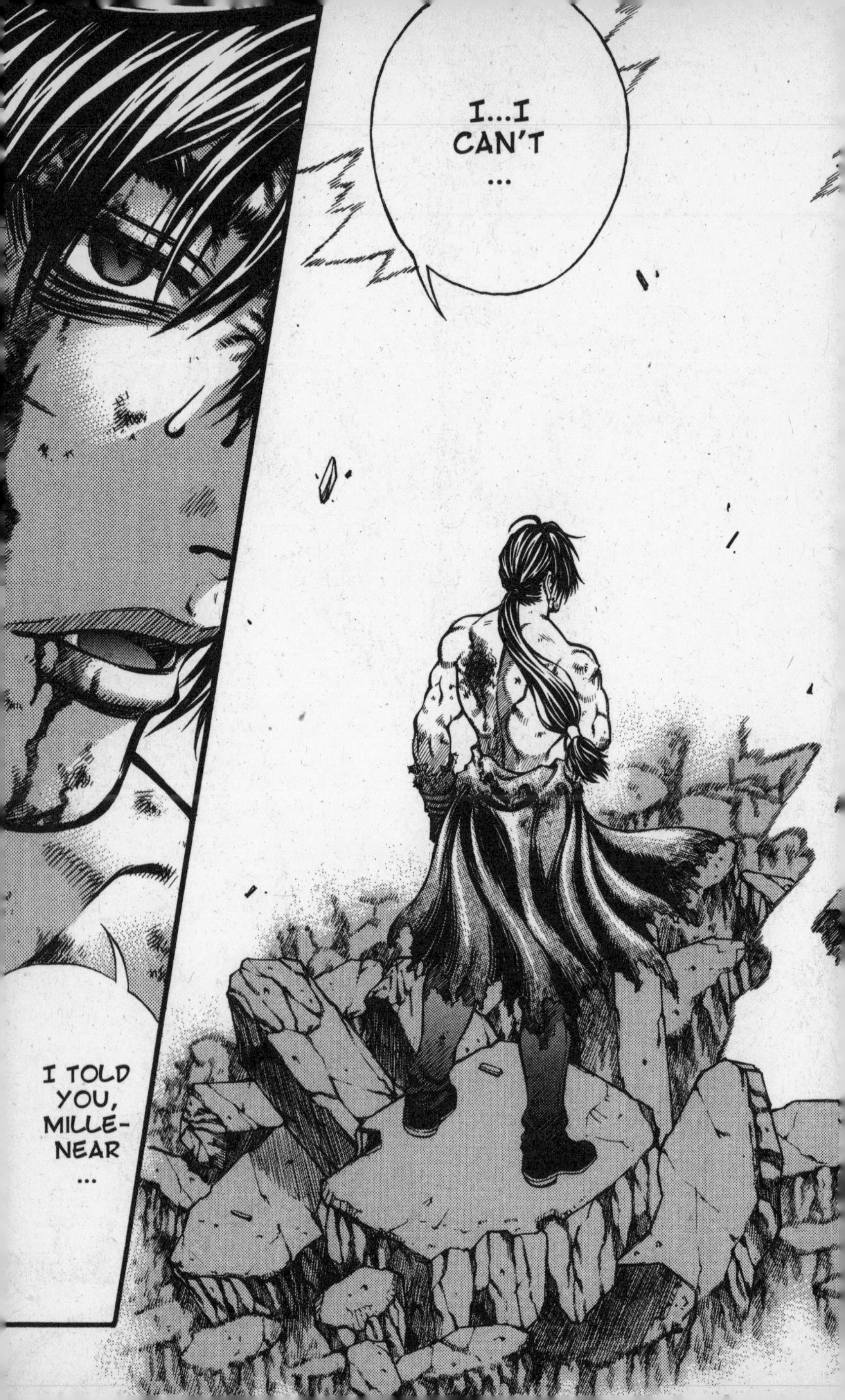
I...I CAN'T ...
I TOLD YOU, MILLE-NEAR ...

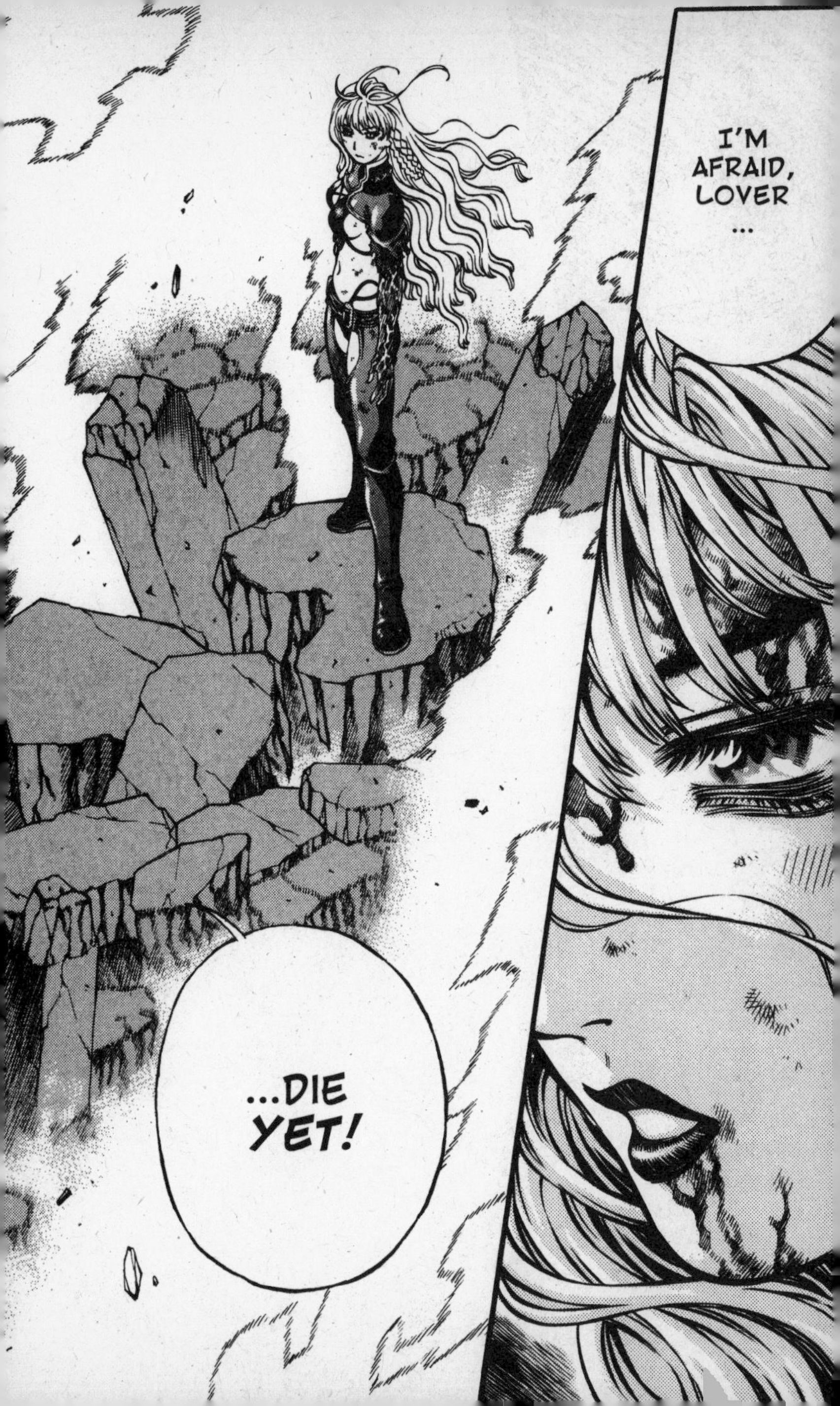
I'M AFRAID, LOVER ...
...DIE YET!

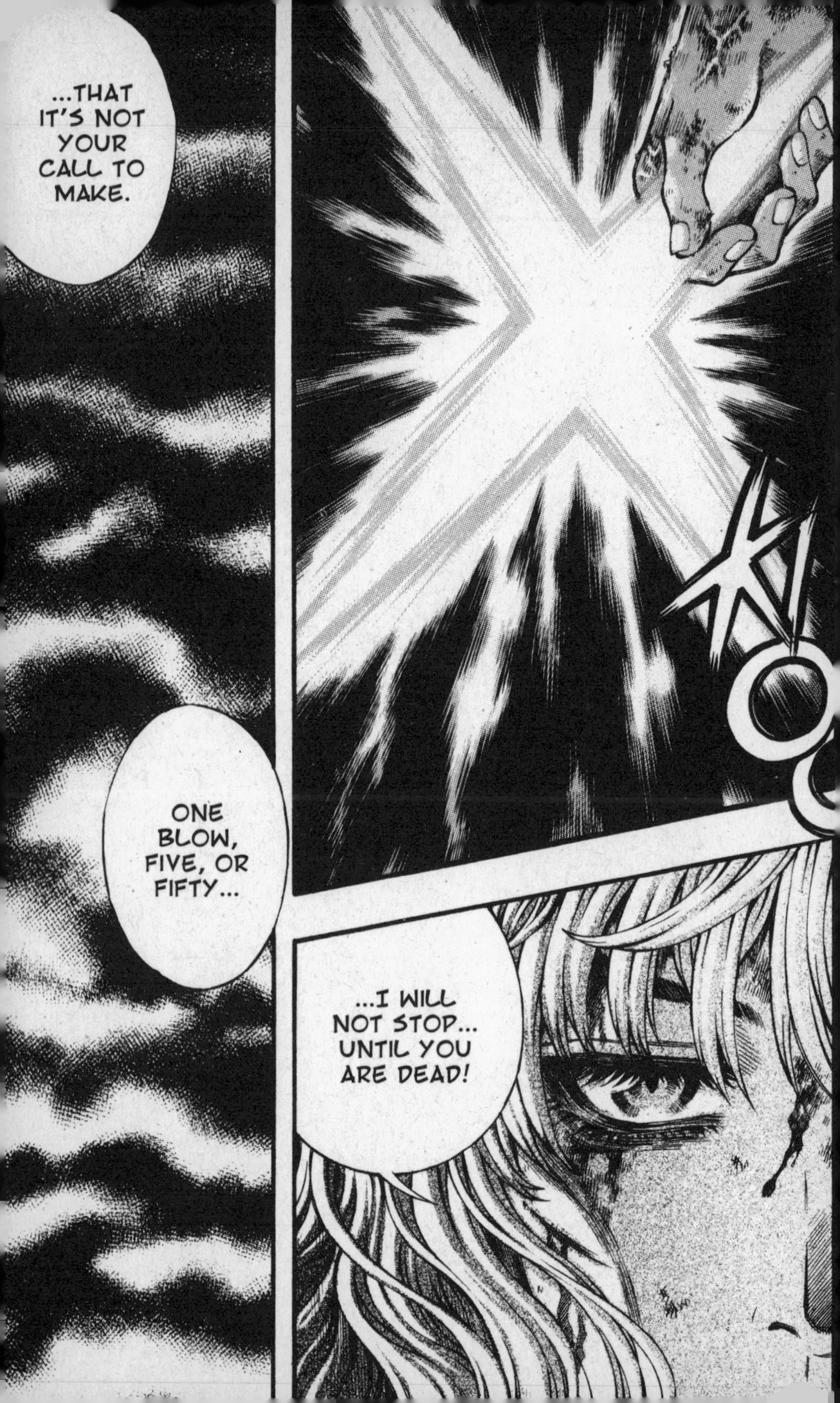
...I WILL NOT STOP... UNTIL YOU ARE DEAD!
...THAT IT'S NOT YOUR CALL TO MAKE.
ONE BLOW, FIVE, OR FIFTY...

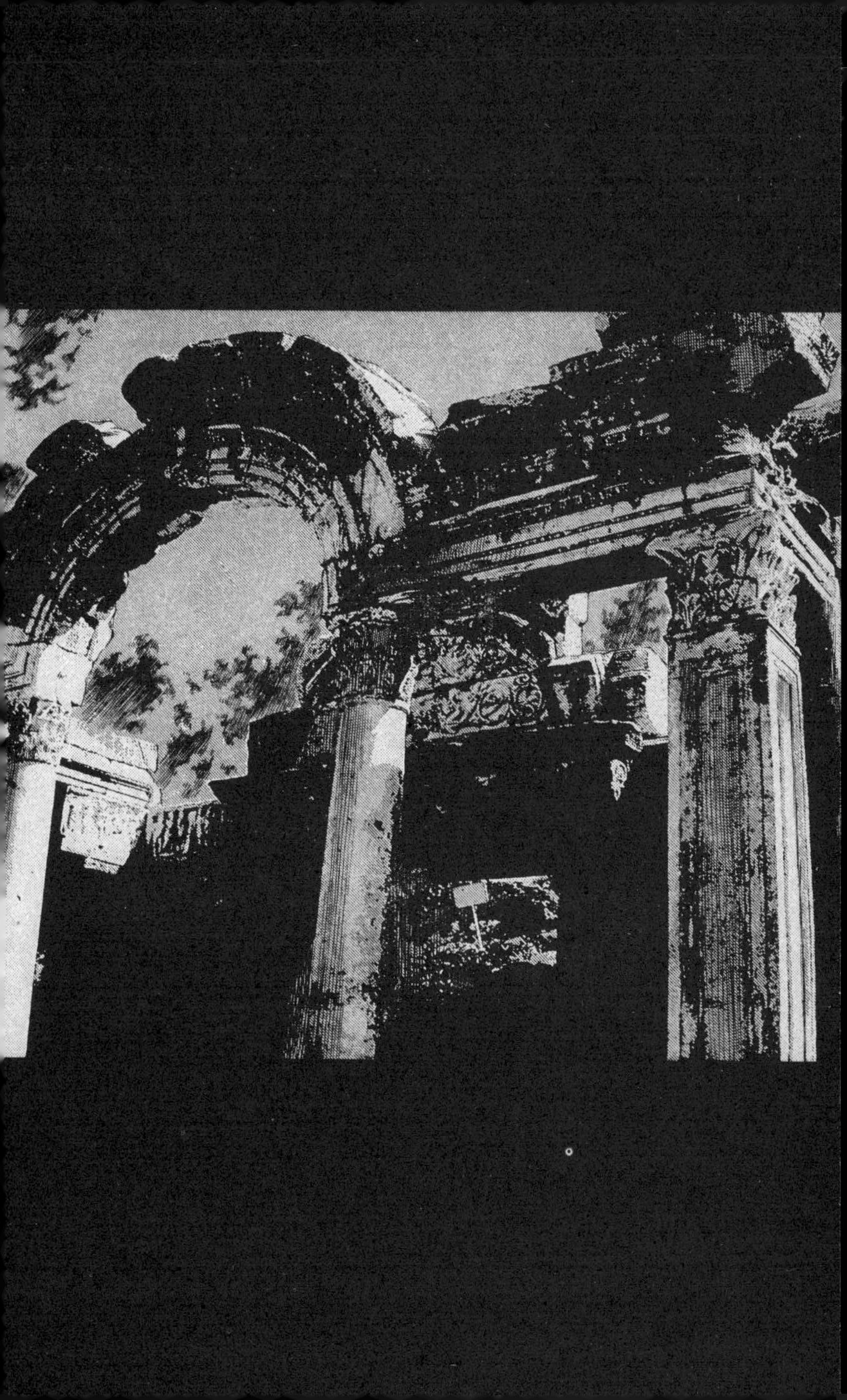

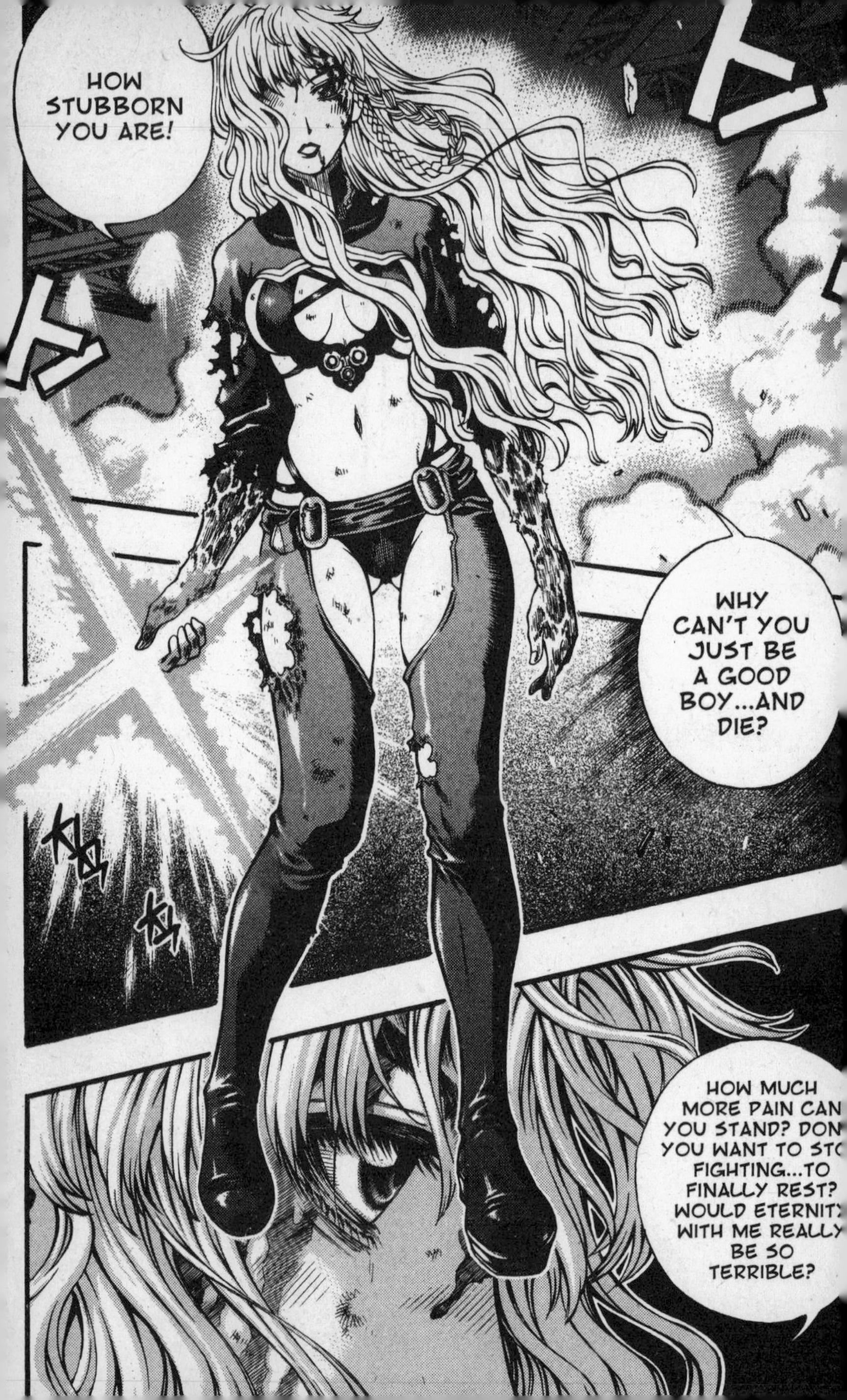
HOW STUBBORN YOU ARE!
WHY CAN'T YOU JUST BE A GOOD BOY...AND DIE?
HOW MUCH MORE PAIN CAN YOU STAND? DON YOU WANT TO STO FIGHTING...TO FINALLY REST? WOULD ETERNITY WITH ME REALLY BE SO TERRIBLE?

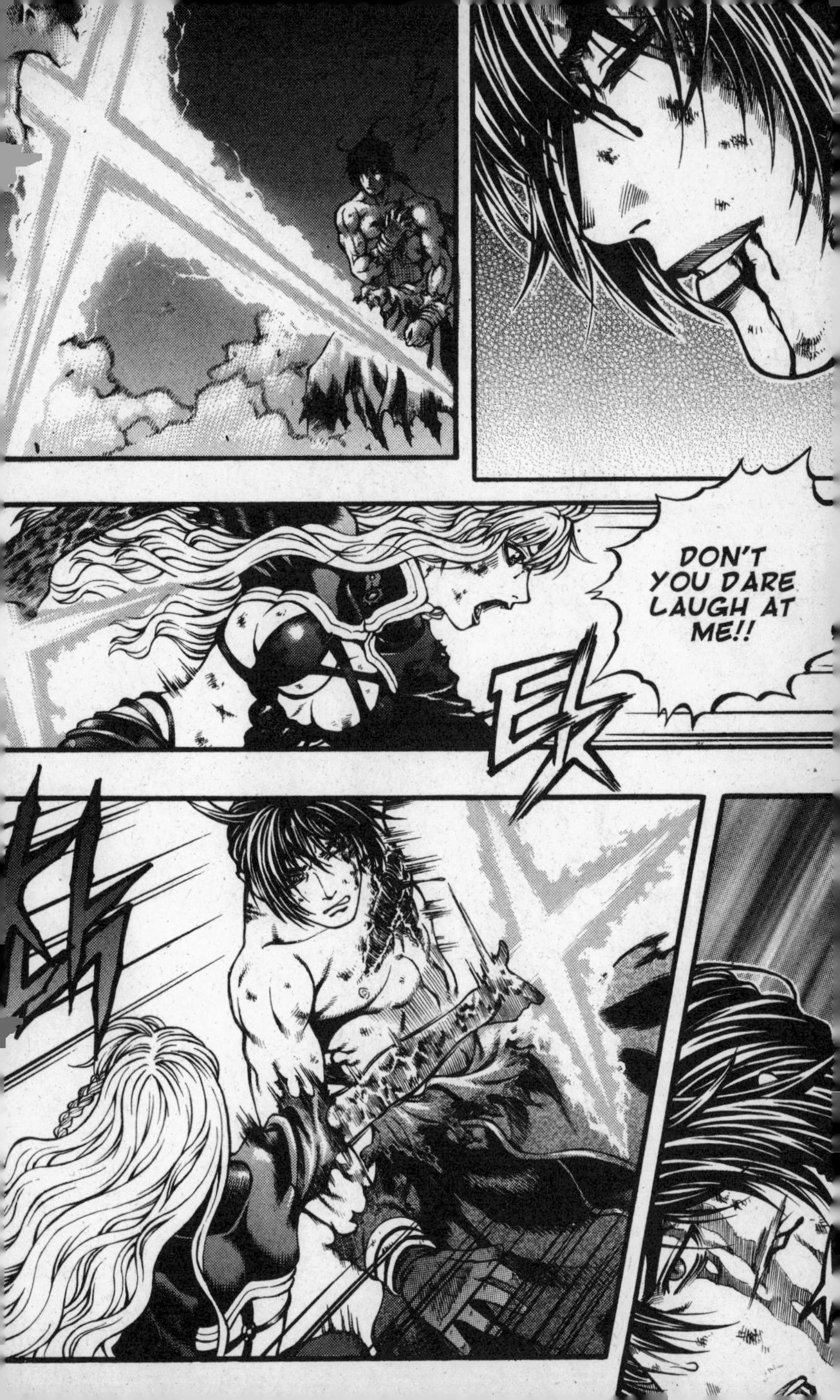
DON'T YOU DARE LAUGH AT ME!!

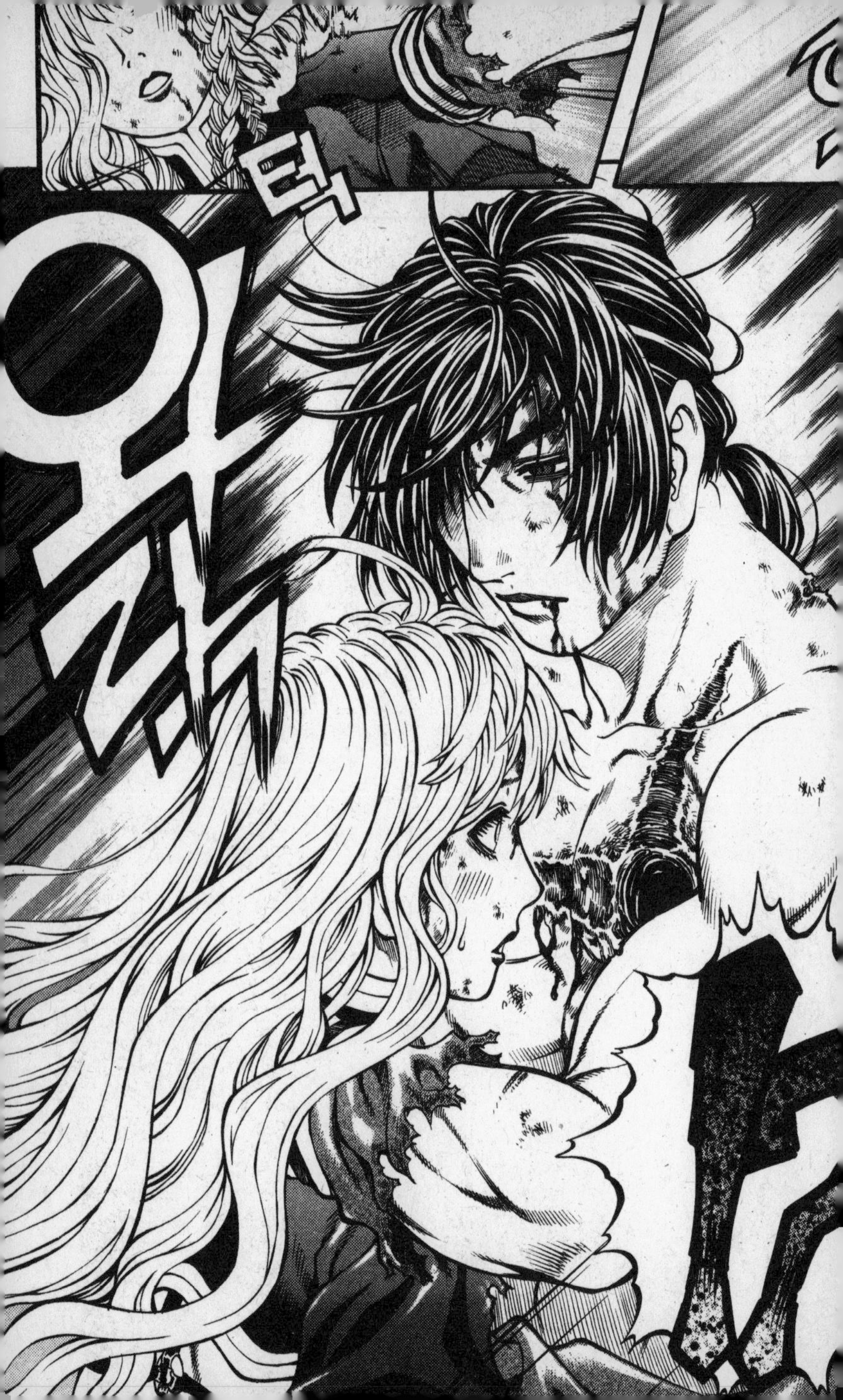

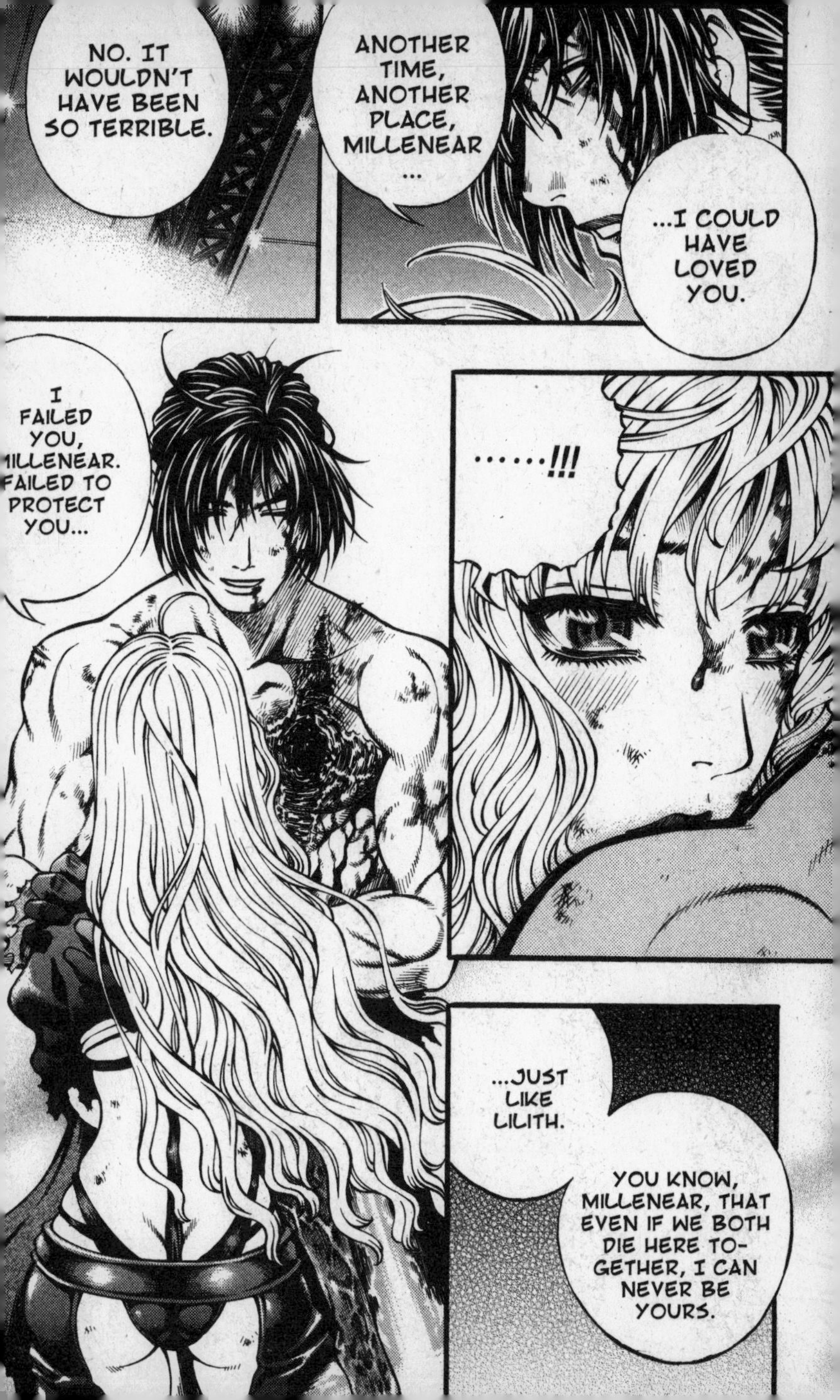

NO. IT WOULDN'T HAVE BEEN SO TERRIBLE.
ANOTHER TIME, ANOTHER PLACE, MILLENEAR ...
...I COULD HAVE LOVED YOU.
I FAILED YOU, ILLENEAR. FAILED TO PROTECT YOU...
......!!!
...JUST LIKE LILITH.
YOU KNOW, MILLENEAR, THAT EVEN IF WE BOTH DIE HERE TO- GETHER, I CAN NEVER BE YOURS.

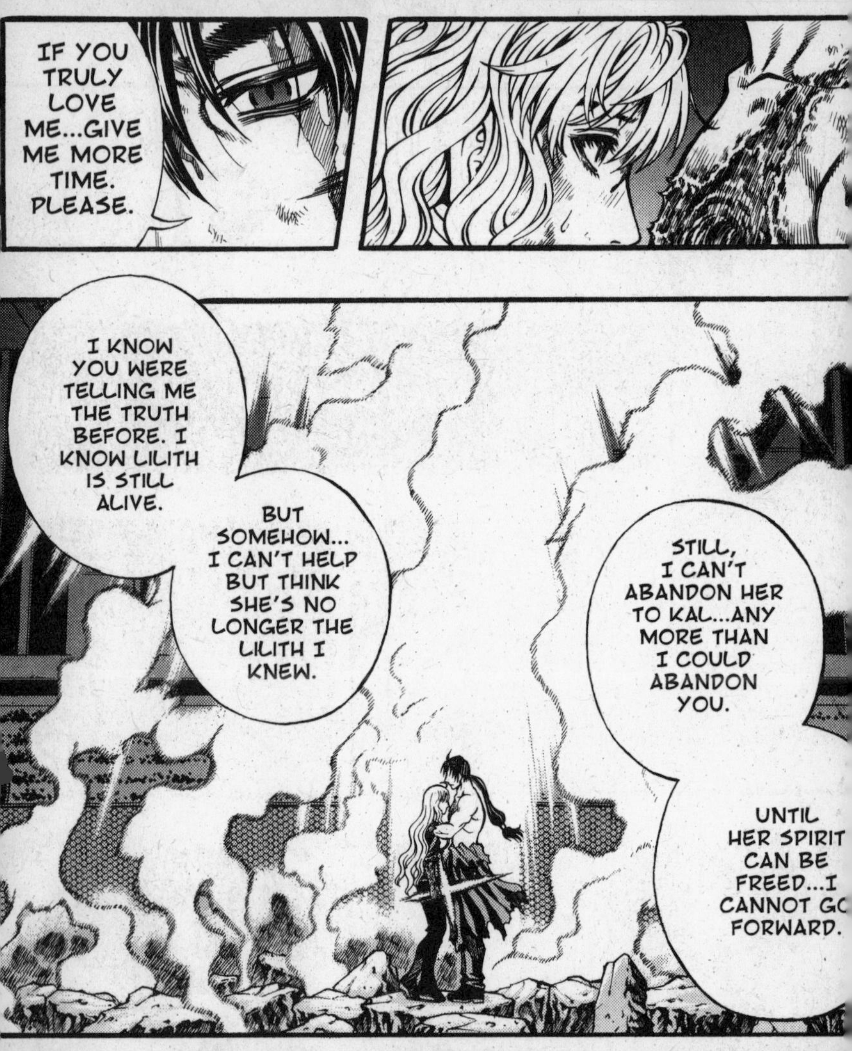
IF YOU TRULY LOVE ME...GIVE ME MORE TIME. PLEASE.
I KNOW YOU WERE TELLING ME THE TRUTH BEFORE. I KNOW LILITH IS STILL ALIVE.
BUT SOMEHOW... I CAN'T HELP BUT THINK SHE'S NO LONGER THE LILITH I KNEW.
STILL, I CAN'T ABANDON HER TO KAL...ANY MORE THAN I COULD ABANDON YOU.
UNTIL HER SPIRIT CAN BE FREED...I CANNOT GO FORWARD.

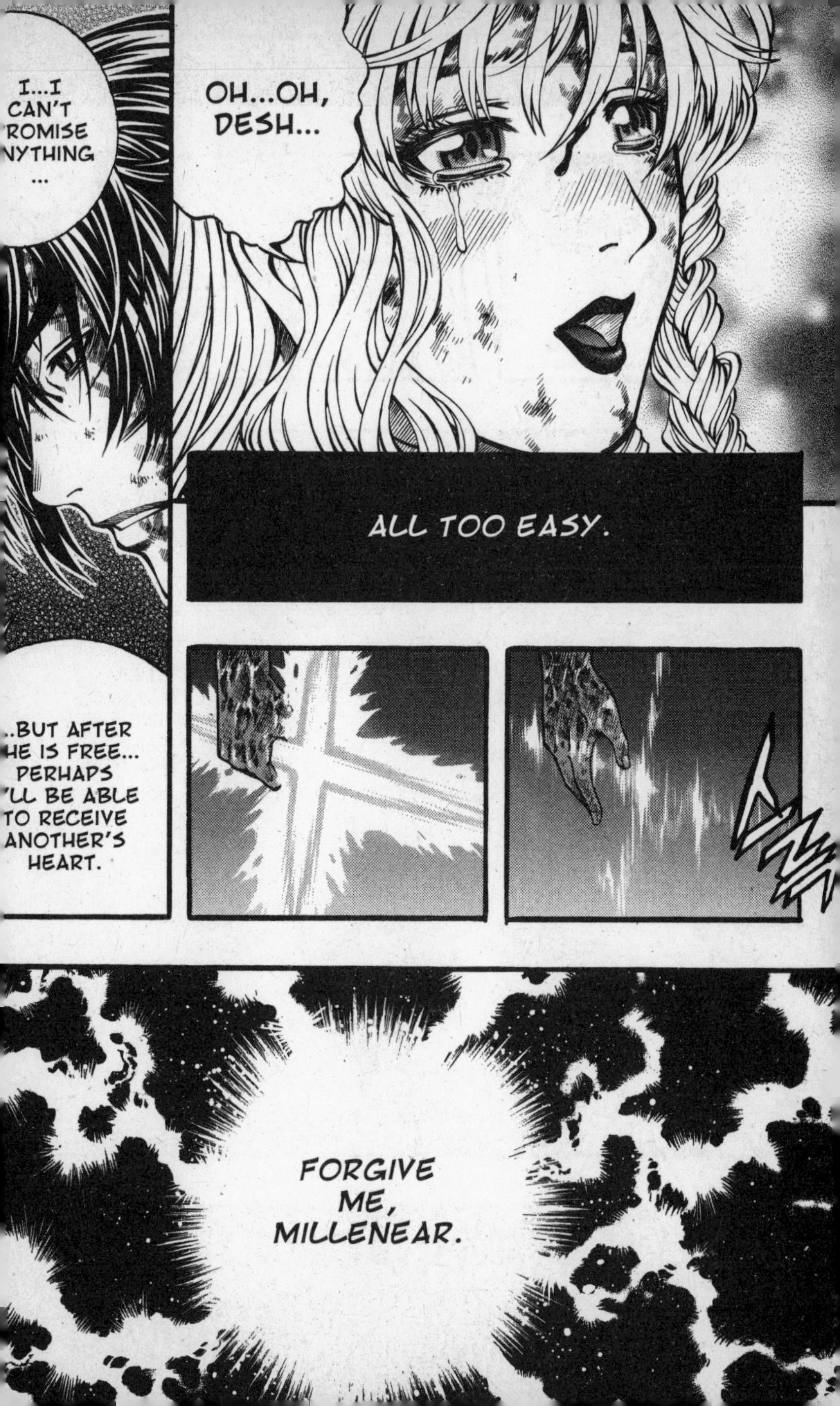

OH...OH, DESH...
I...I CAN'T ROMISE NYTHING ...
ALL TOO EASY.
..BUT AFTER HE IS FREE... PERHAPS 'LL BE ABLE TO RECEIVE ANOTHER'S HEART.
FORGIVE ME, MILLENEAR.

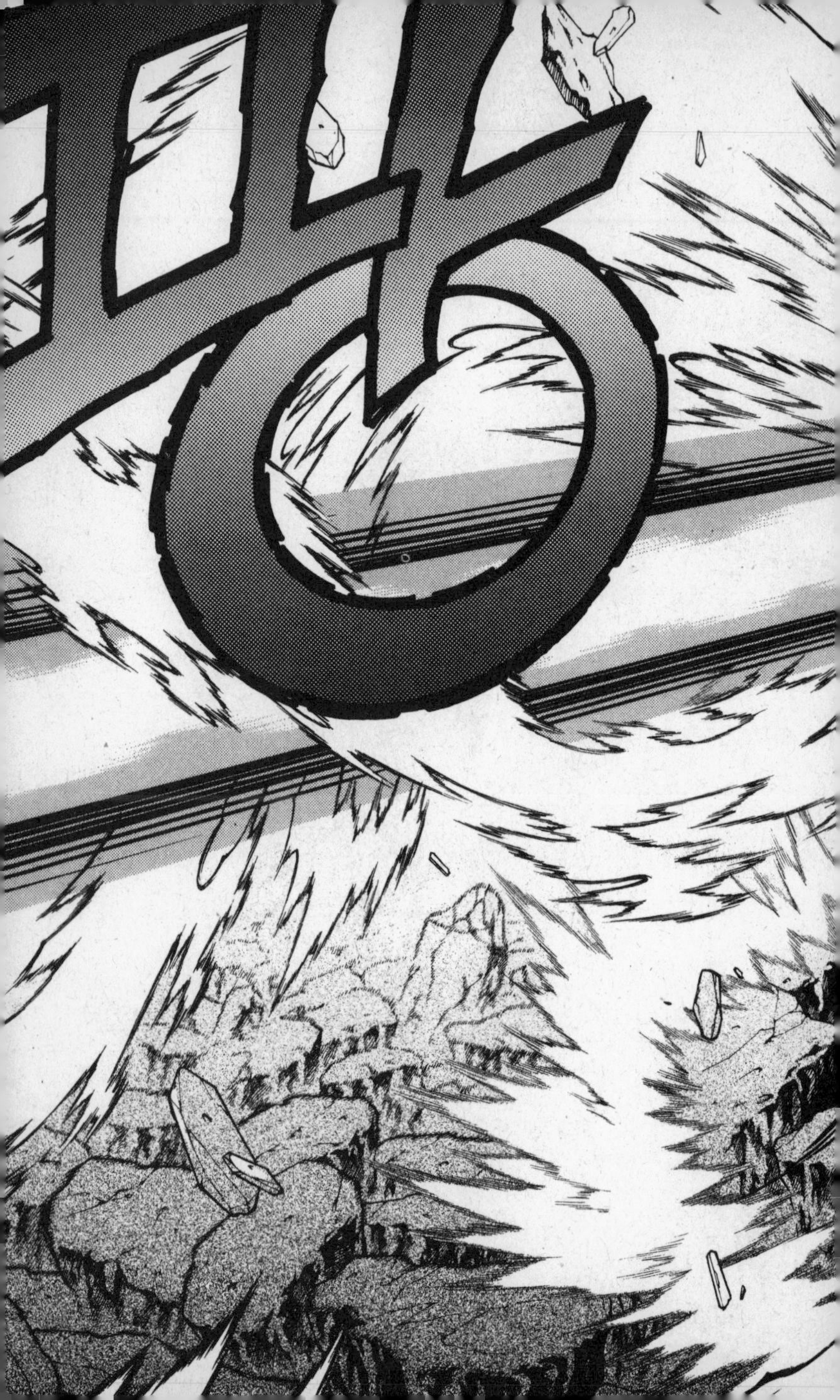

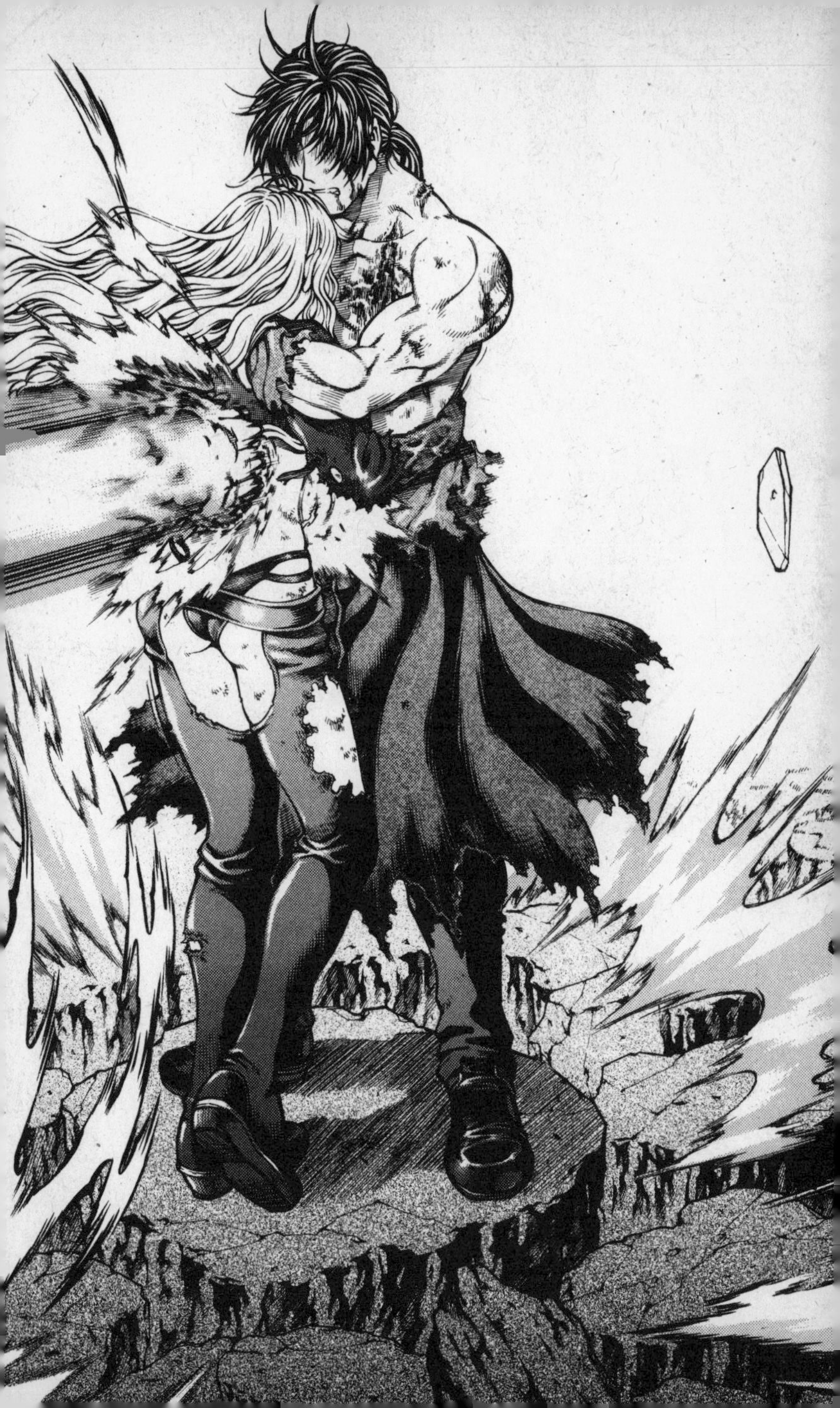

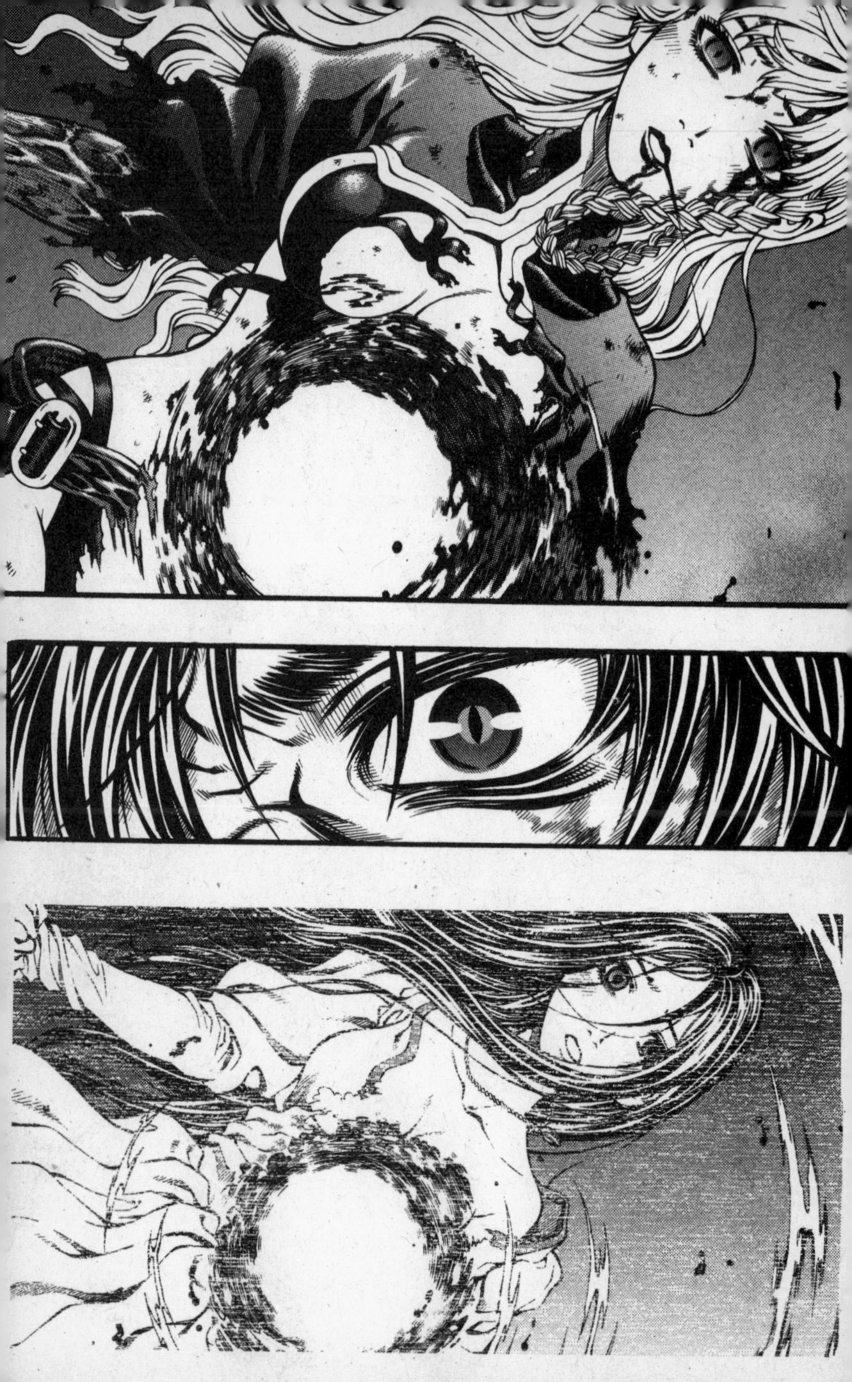

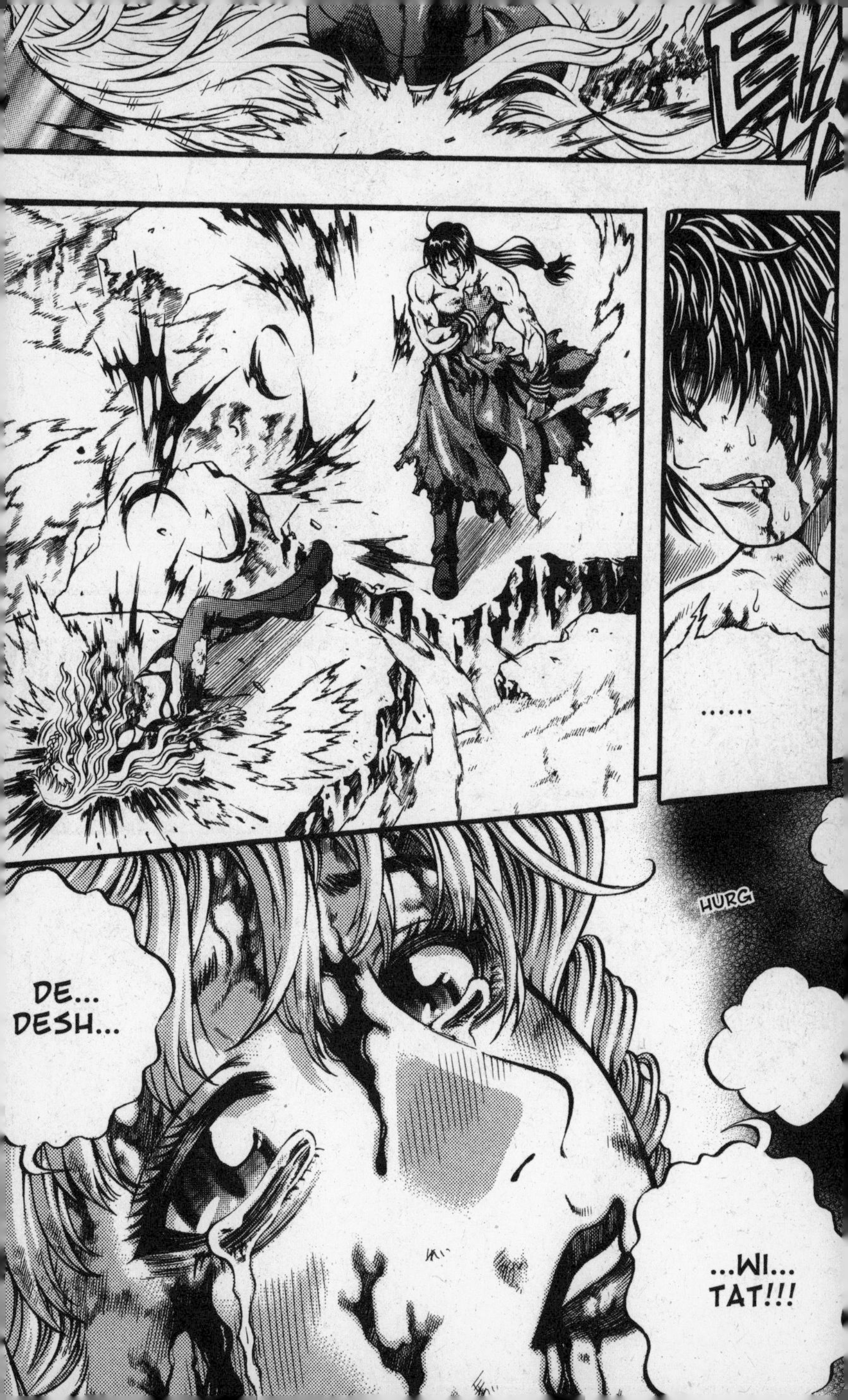
......
HURG
...WI...
TAT!!!
DE...
DESH...

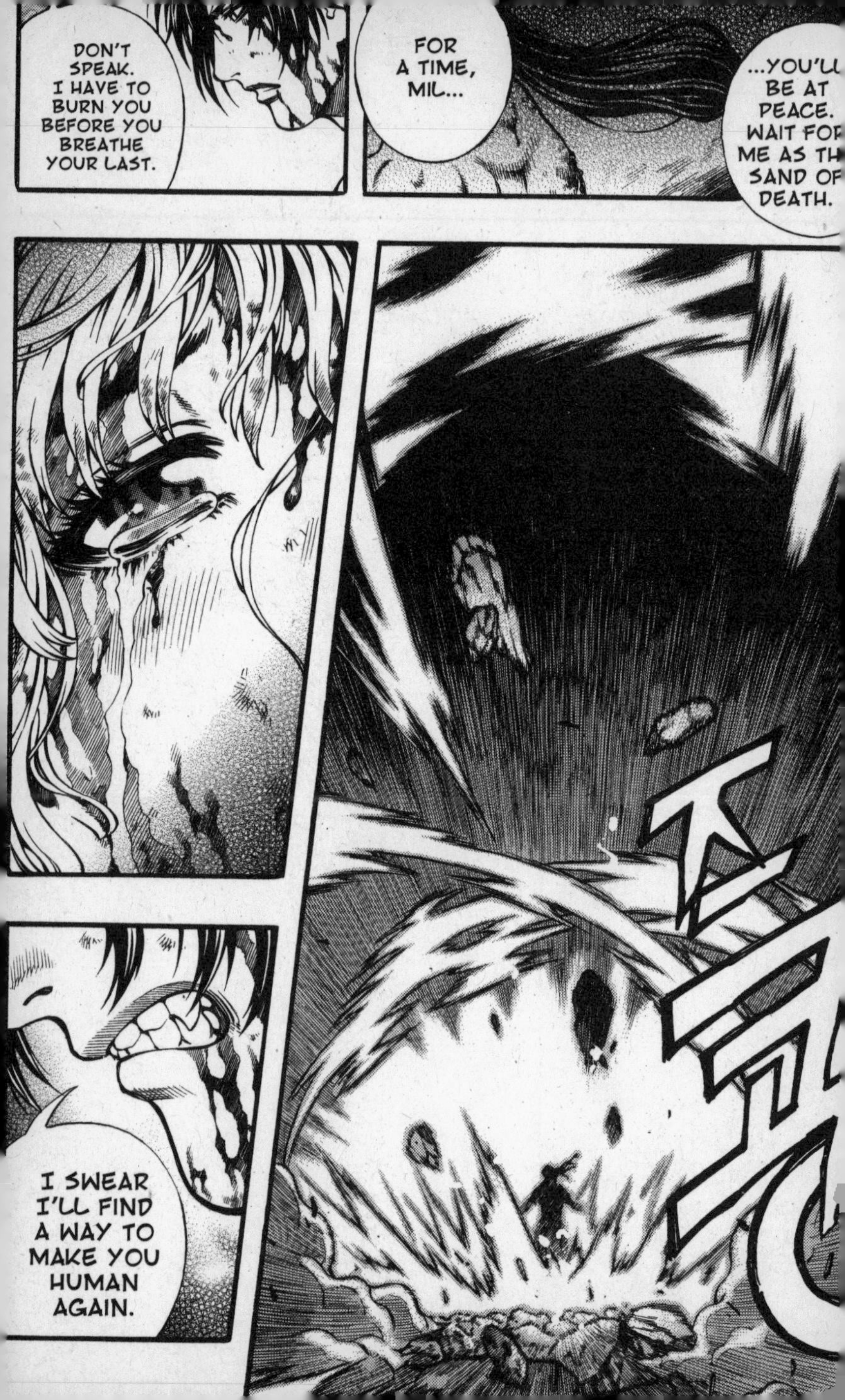
DON'T SPEAK. I HAVE TO BURN YOU BEFORE YOU BREATHE YOUR LAST.
FOR A TIME, MIL...
...YOU'LL BE AT PEACE. WAIT FOR ME AS TH SAND OF DEATH.
I SWEAR I'LL FIND A WAY TO MAKE YOU HUMAN AGAIN.

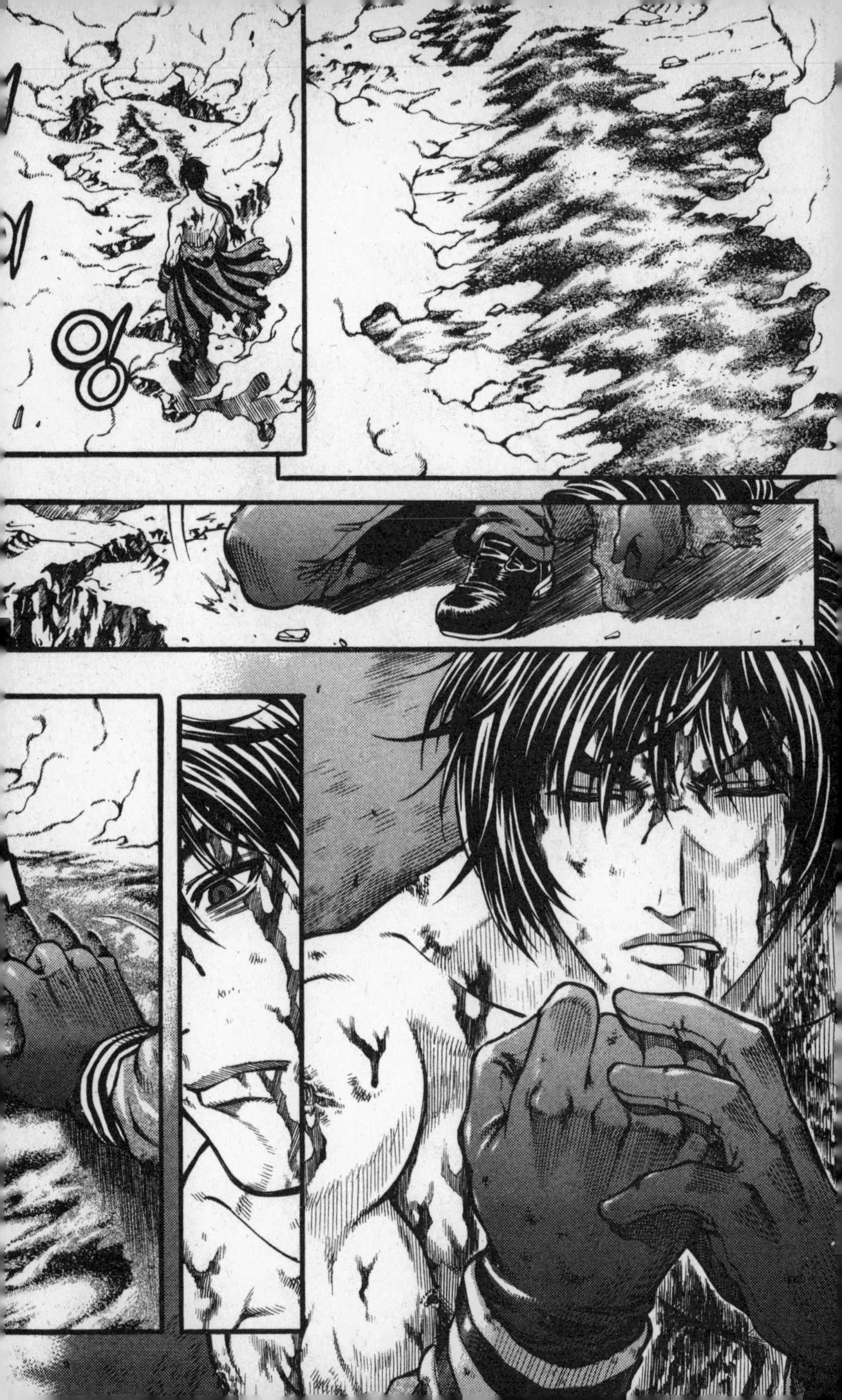

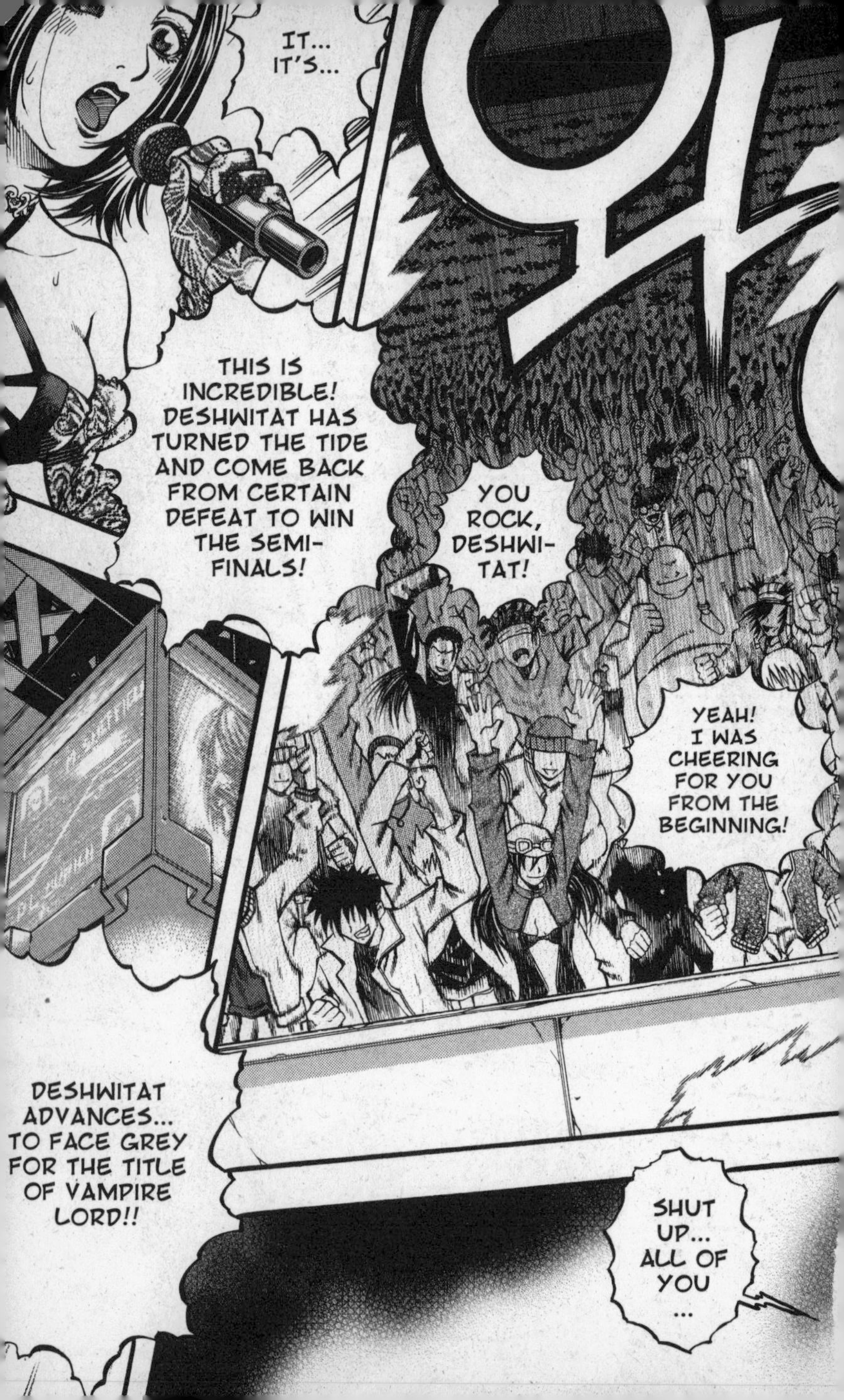
IT... IT'S...
THIS IS INCREDIBLE! DESHWITAT HAS TURNED THE TIDE AND COME BACK FROM CERTAIN DEFEAT TO WIN THE SEMI-FINALS!
YOU ROCK, DESHWI-TAT!
YEAH! I WAS CHEERING FOR YOU FROM THE BEGINNING!
DESHWITAT ADVANCES... TO FACE GREY FOR THE TITLE OF VAMPIRE LORD!!
SHUT UP... ALL OF YOU ...

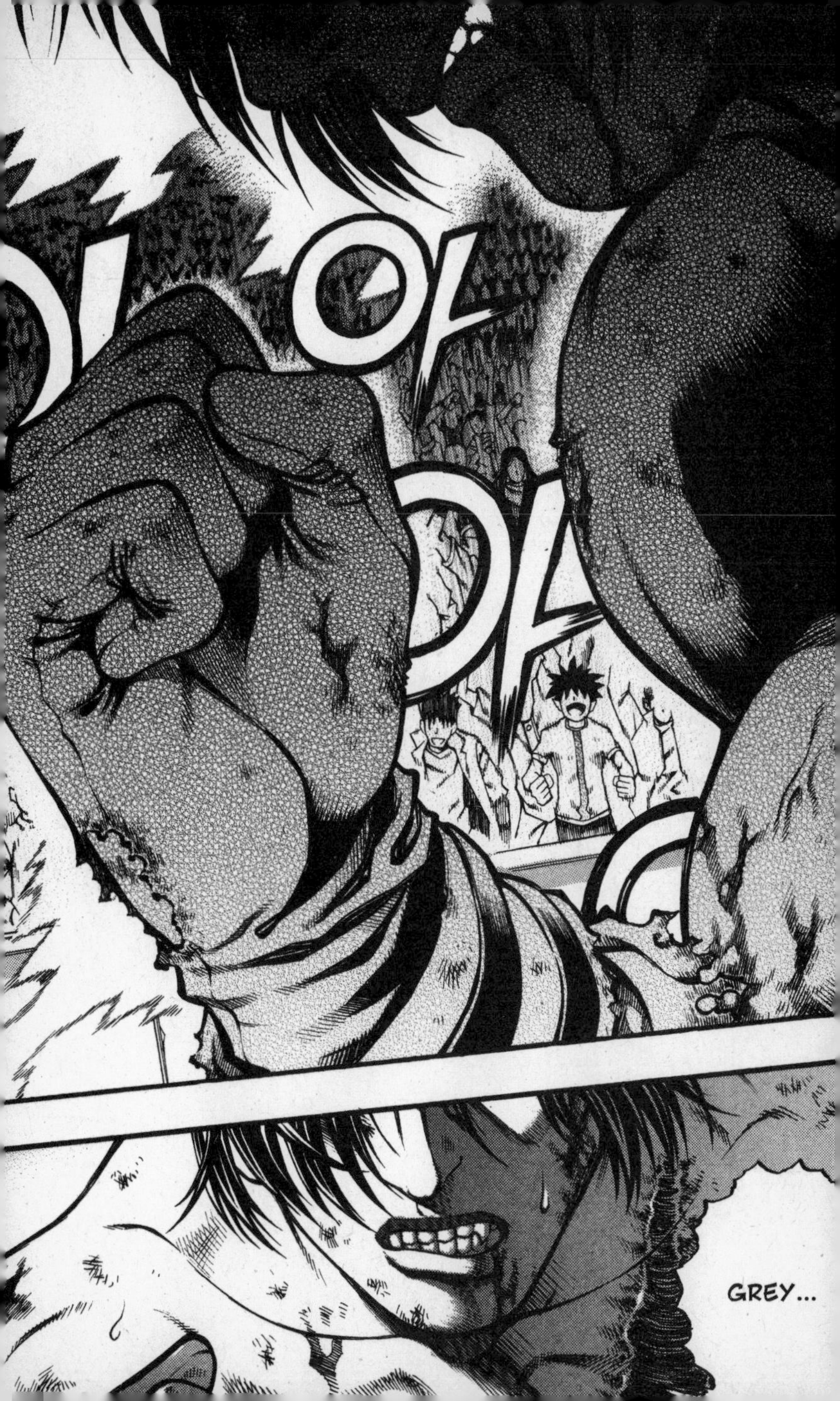
GREY...

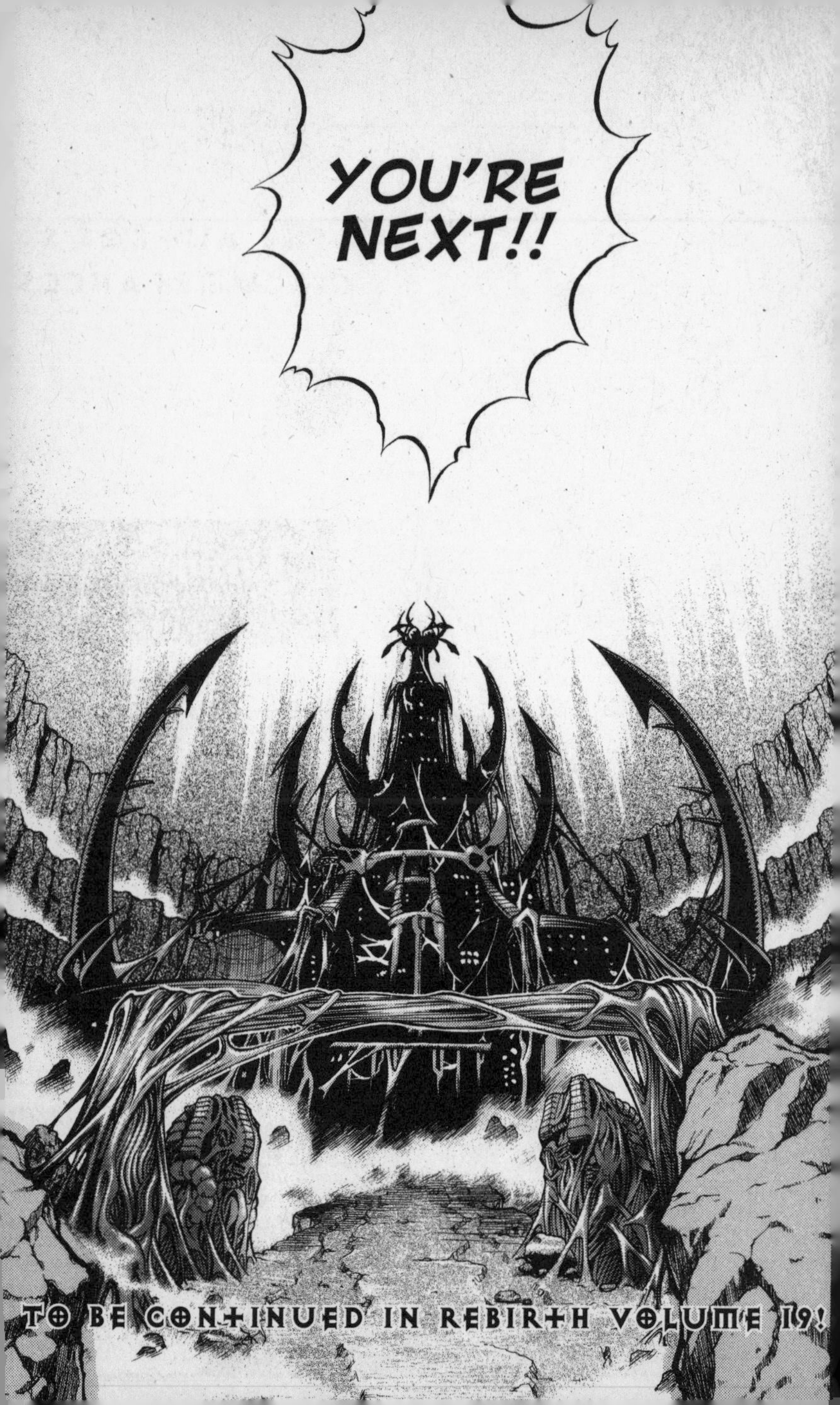
YOU'RE NEXT!!
TO BE CONTINUED IN REBIRTH VOLUME 19!

KYA HA HA!
FAN SERVICE!
AFTER THE DEADLINE
THE AUTHOR'S CIRCUMSTANCES
NO. 6 ISSUE: FOREIGN PUBLICATION OF "REBIRTH"
HELLO, EVERYONE. THIS IS THE REBIRTH PRODUCTION TEAM.
LOTTERY ADDICT HB 2nd
BUR-CHU-YAP-SAP KB
WOO
DARK SHADOW HB 1st
I'D LIKE TO INTRODUCE TO YOU TODAY THE FOREIGN PUBLICATIONS OF REBIRTH.
Spirit LOOSE
PRODUCTION TEAM
IN 1998, REBIRTH WAS BORN, WIDE-EYED INTO KOREA ...
...AND IS NOW FORTUNATE ENOUGH TO BE PUBLISHED ALL OVER THE WORLD!

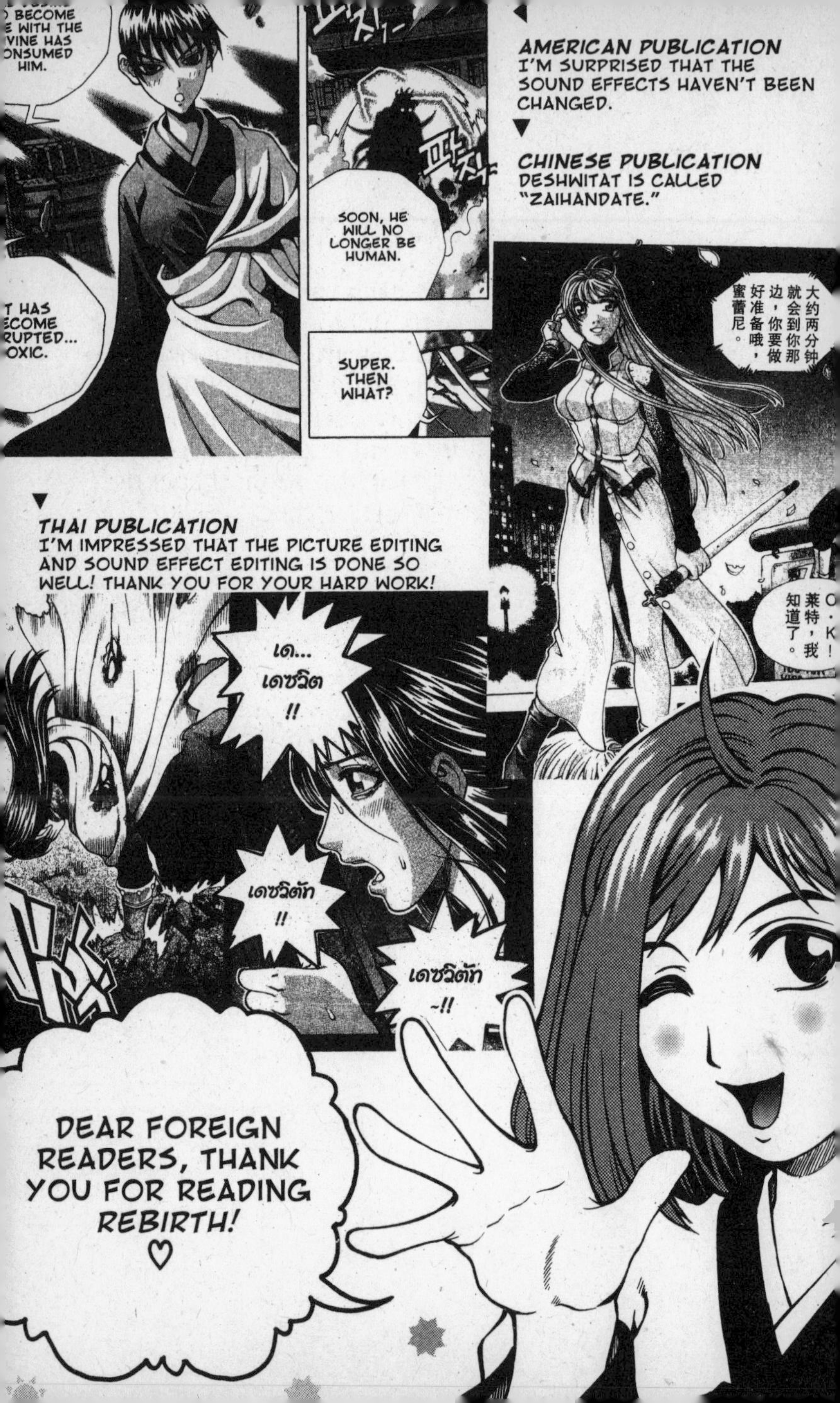

O BECOME
E WITH THE
VINE HAS
ONSUMED
HIM.
T HAS
ECOME
RUPTED...
OXIC.
SOON, HE WILL NO LONGER BE HUMAN.
SUPER. THEN WHAT?
AMERICAN PUBLICATION
I'M SURPRISED THAT THE SOUND EFFECTS HAVEN'T BEEN CHANGED.
CHINESE PUBLICATION
DESHWITAT IS CALLED "ZAIHANDATE."
大约两分钟就会到你那边，你要做好准备哦，蜜蕾尼。
O·K！莱特，我知道了。
THAI PUBLICATION
I'M IMPRESSED THAT THE PICTURE EDITING AND SOUND EFFECT EDITING IS DONE SO WELL! THANK YOU FOR YOUR HARD WORK!
เด... เดซวิต !!
เดซวิตัท !!
เดซวิตัท ~!!
DEAR FOREIGN READERS, THANK YOU FOR READING REBIRTH! ♡

Preview: Vol. 19

As Deshwitat struggles with his conscience in the aftermath of his battle with Millenear, Grey reveals the truth of how she became a vampire to a stunned Rett. And in the bowels of the terrifying Tower of Trials, Remi and Eiji battle creatures more horrifying than anything from their worst nightmares—all in a last ditch effort to rescue the elite covert exorcism team known as... The Order of St. Michael!

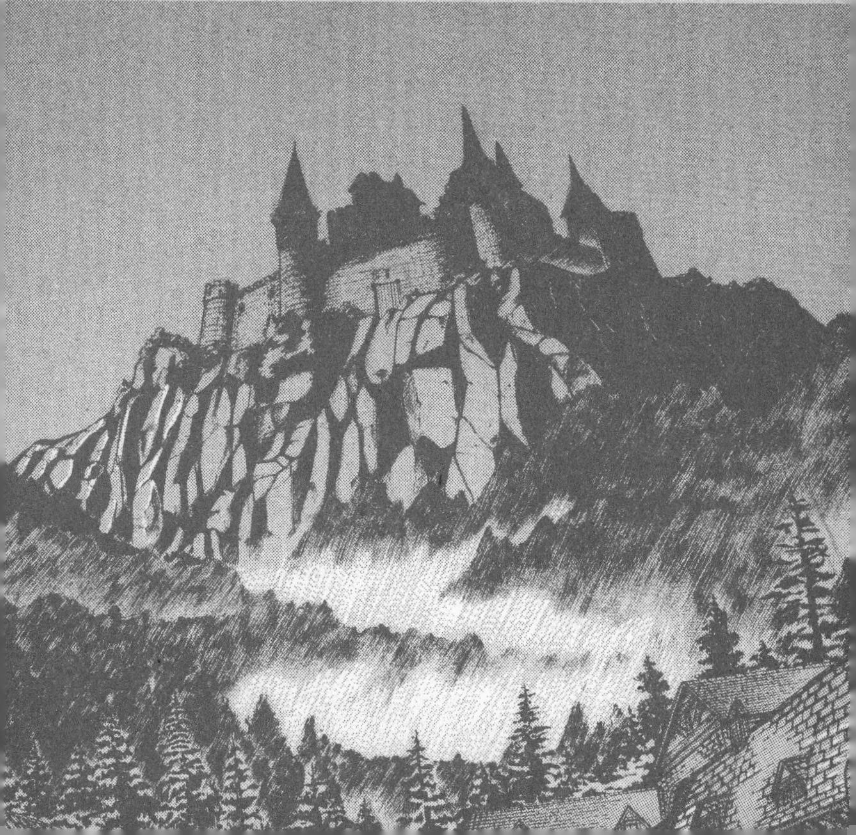

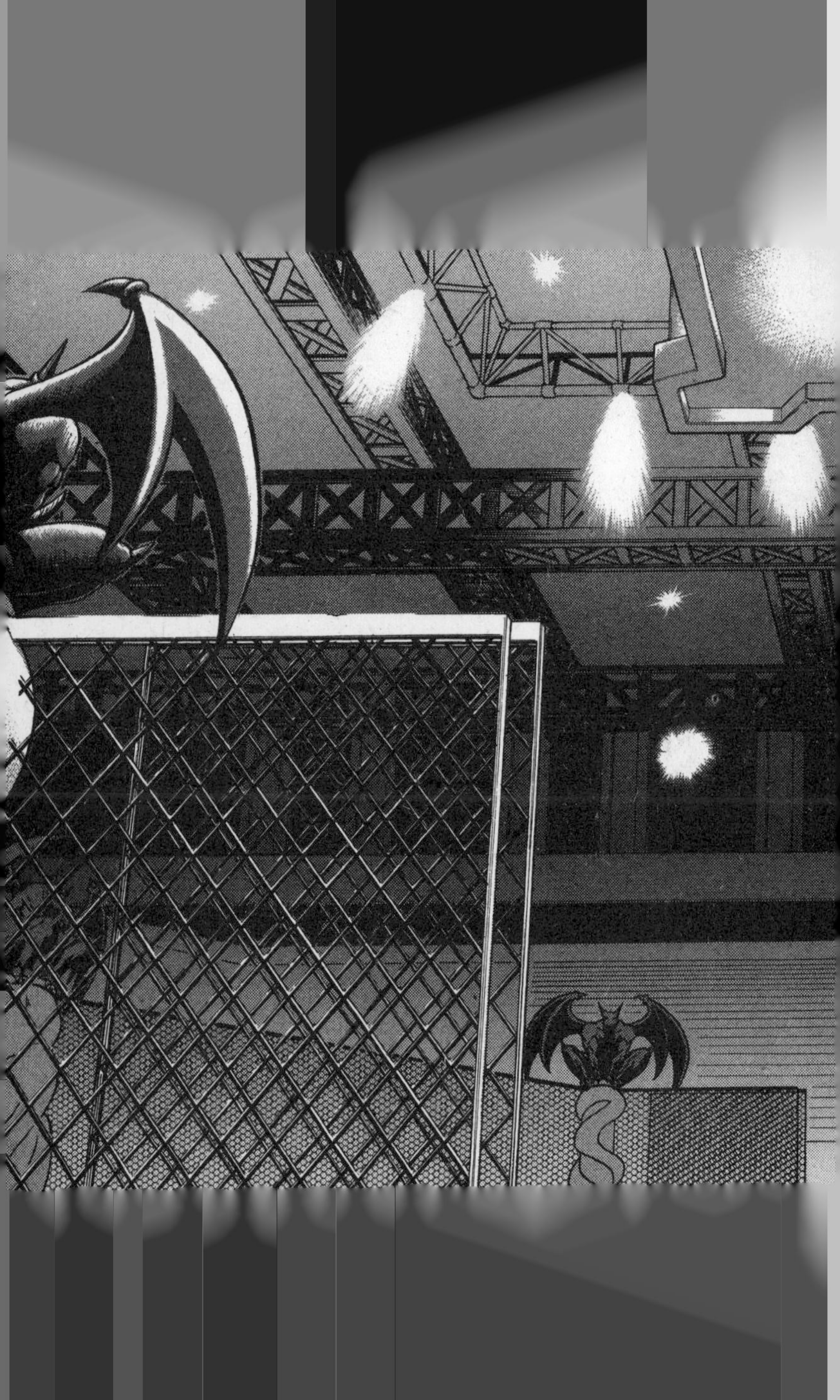

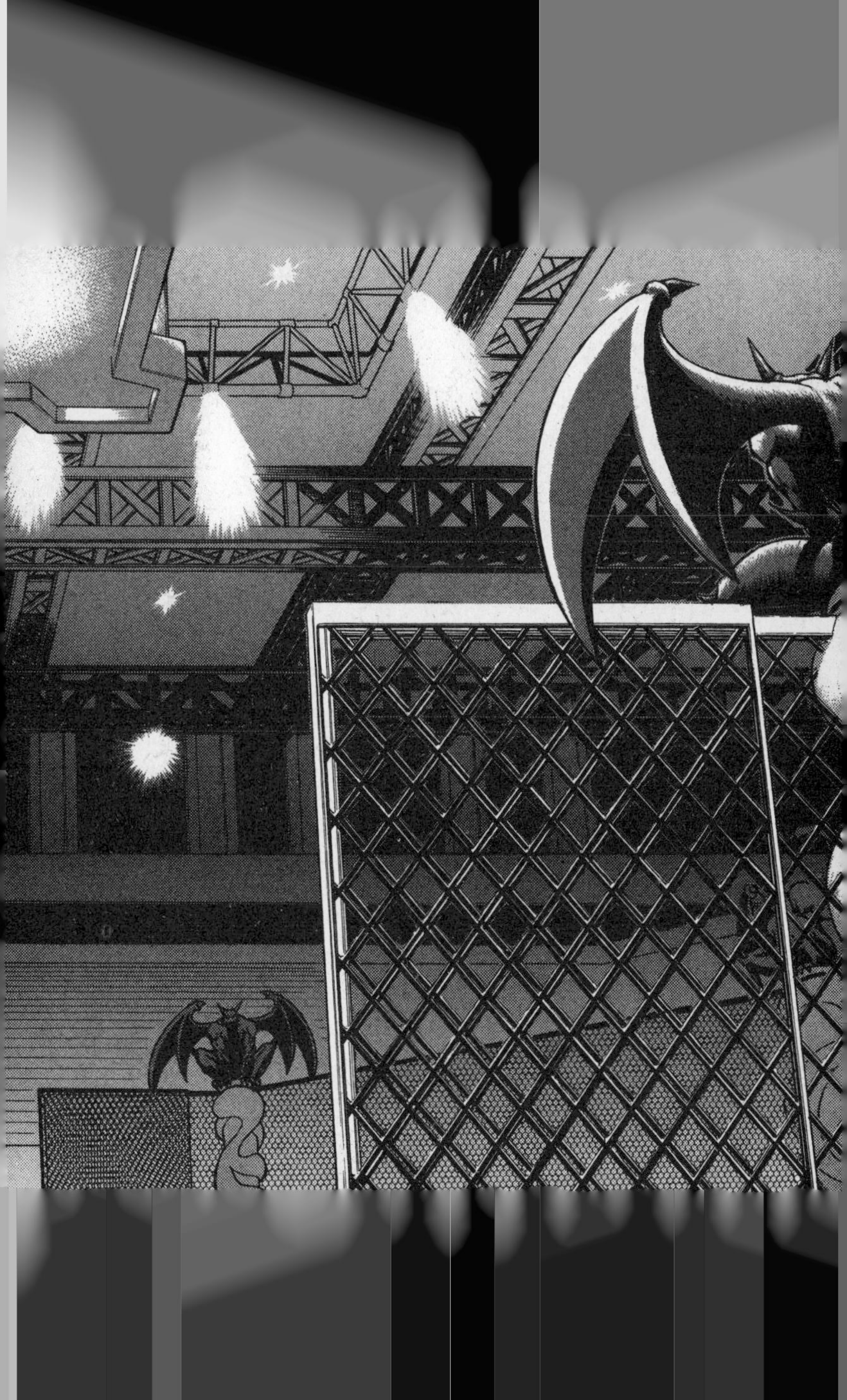

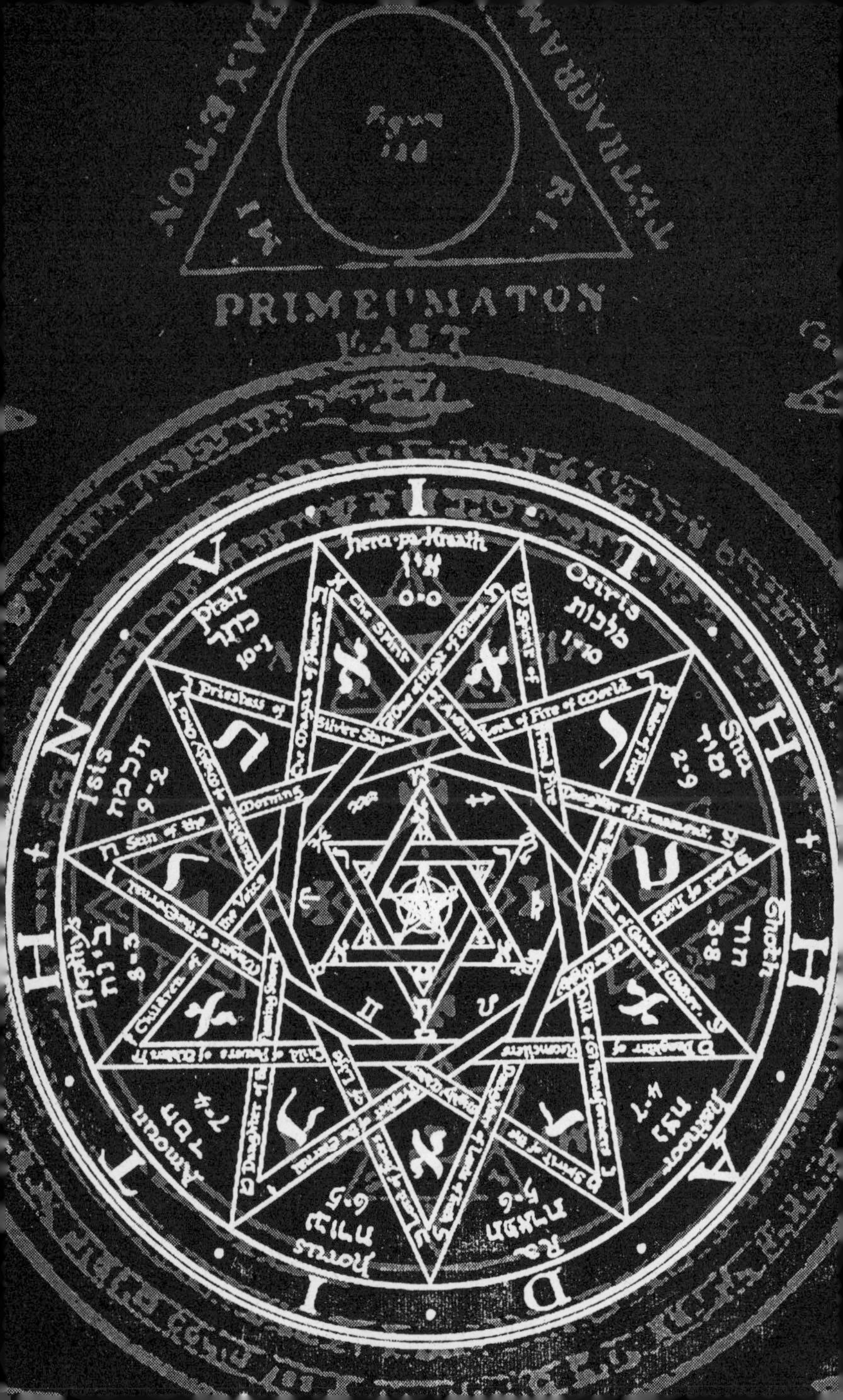

PRIMEUMATON
Heru-pa-Kraath
Osiris
Ptah
Isis
Thoth
Nephthys
Amoun
Horus
Priestess of Silver Star
Son of the Morning
Lord of Fire of World

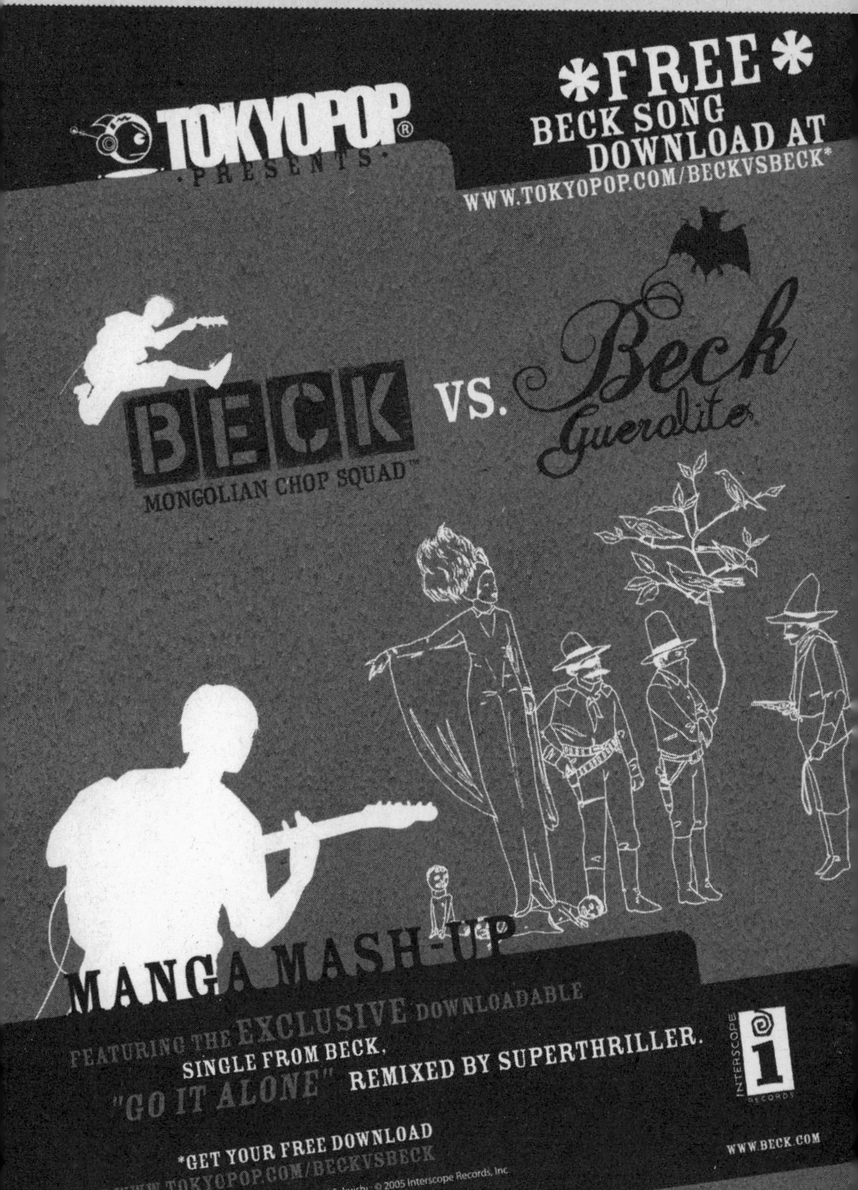
TOKYOPOP®
PRESENTS
FREE
BECK SONG
DOWNLOAD AT
WWW.TOKYOPOP.COM/BECKVSBECK*
BECK
MONGOLIAN CHOP SQUAD™
VS.
Beck
Guerolito
MANGA MASH-UP
FEATURING THE EXCLUSIVE DOWNLOADABLE
SINGLE FROM BECK,
"GO IT ALONE" REMIXED BY SUPERTHRILLER.
INTERSCOPE RECORDS
*GET YOUR FREE DOWNLOAD
AT WWW.TOKYOPOP.COM/BECKVSBECK
© 2006 Harold Sakuishi; © 2005 Interscope Records, Inc.
WWW.BECK.COM

FOR MORE INFORMATION VISIT: WWW.TOKYOPOP.COM

GRENADIER

CREATED BY: SOUSUKE KAISE

TWO BIG GUNS CAN BRING PEACE TO THE WORLD...

Rushuna is a golden-haired Senshi—a gunslinger who travels the land with one purpose: to make the world a peaceful place with her high-caliber revolver and enchanting smile. However, her journey of nonviolence won't be easy and she may have to display her amazing gun skills and talent for reloading on the bounce.

THE MANGA THAT SPARKED THE POPULAR ANIME!

ACTION

OT OLDER TEEN AGE 16+

© SOUSUKE KAISE.

FOR MORE INFORMATION VISIT: WWW.TOKYOPOP.COM

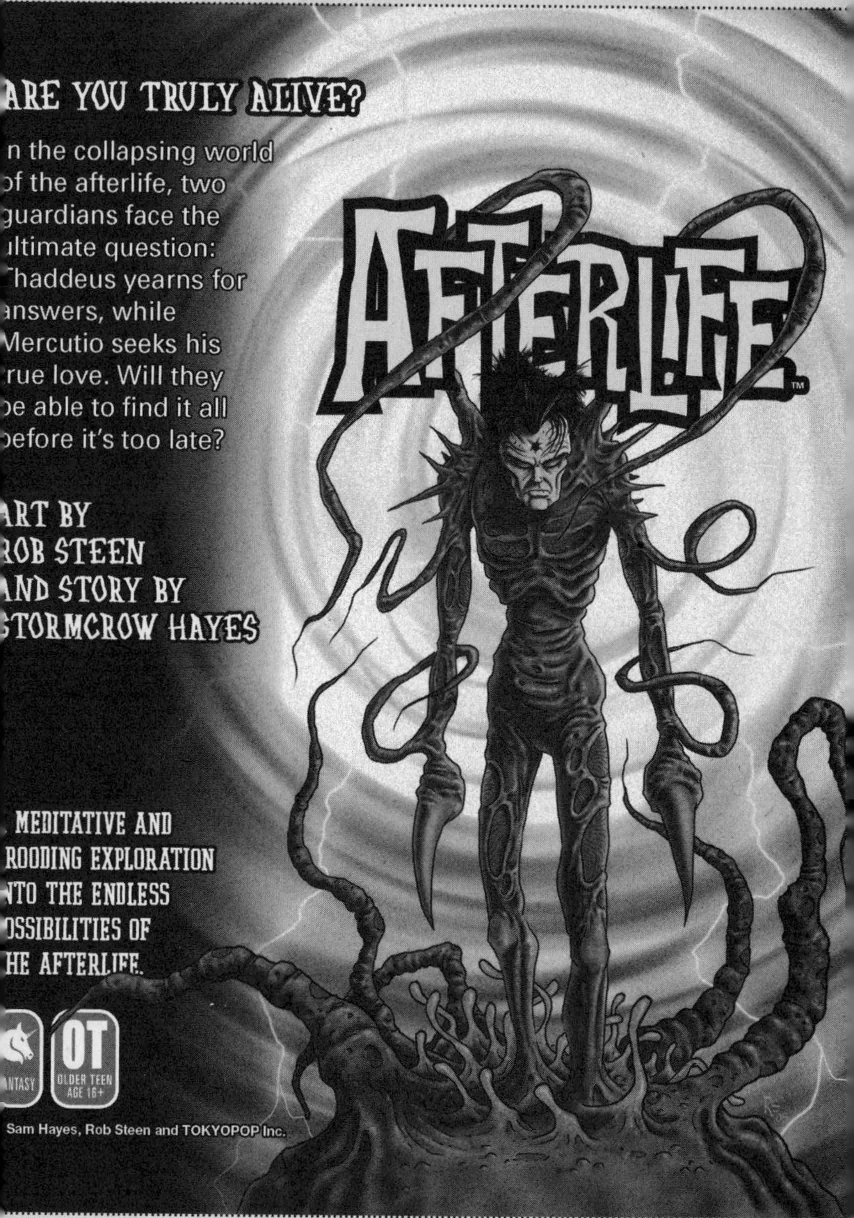
ARE YOU TRULY ALIVE?
n the collapsing world
of the afterlife, two
guardians face the
ltimate question:
Thaddeus yearns for
answers, while
Mercutio seeks his
rue love. Will they
be able to find it all
before it's too late?
AFTERLIFE™
ART BY
ROB STEEN
AND STORY BY
STORMCROW HAYES
MEDITATIVE AND
ROODING EXPLORATION
NTO THE ENDLESS
OSSIBILITIES OF
HE AFTERLIFE.
NTASY
OT
OLDER TEEN
AGE 16+
Sam Hayes, Rob Steen and TOKYOPOP Inc.

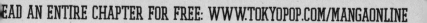

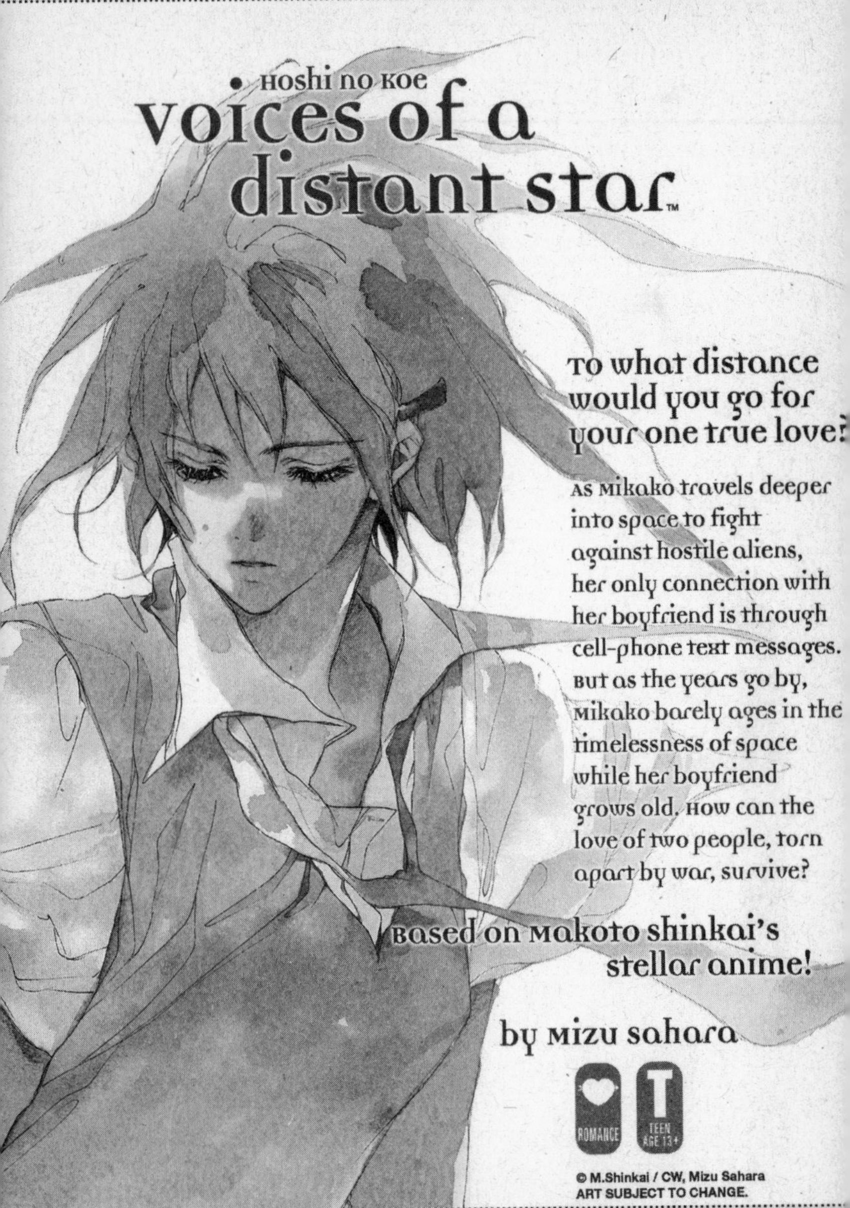
HOSHI NO KOE
voices of a distant star™
To what distance would you go for your one true love?
As Mikako travels deeper into space to fight against hostile aliens, her only connection with her boyfriend is through cell-phone text messages. But as the years go by, Mikako barely ages in the timelessness of space while her boyfriend grows old. How can the love of two people, torn apart by war, survive?
Based on Makoto Shinkai's stellar anime!
by Mizu Sahara
ROMANCE
T
TEEN AGE 13+
© M.Shinkai / CW, Mizu Sahara
ART SUBJECT TO CHANGE.

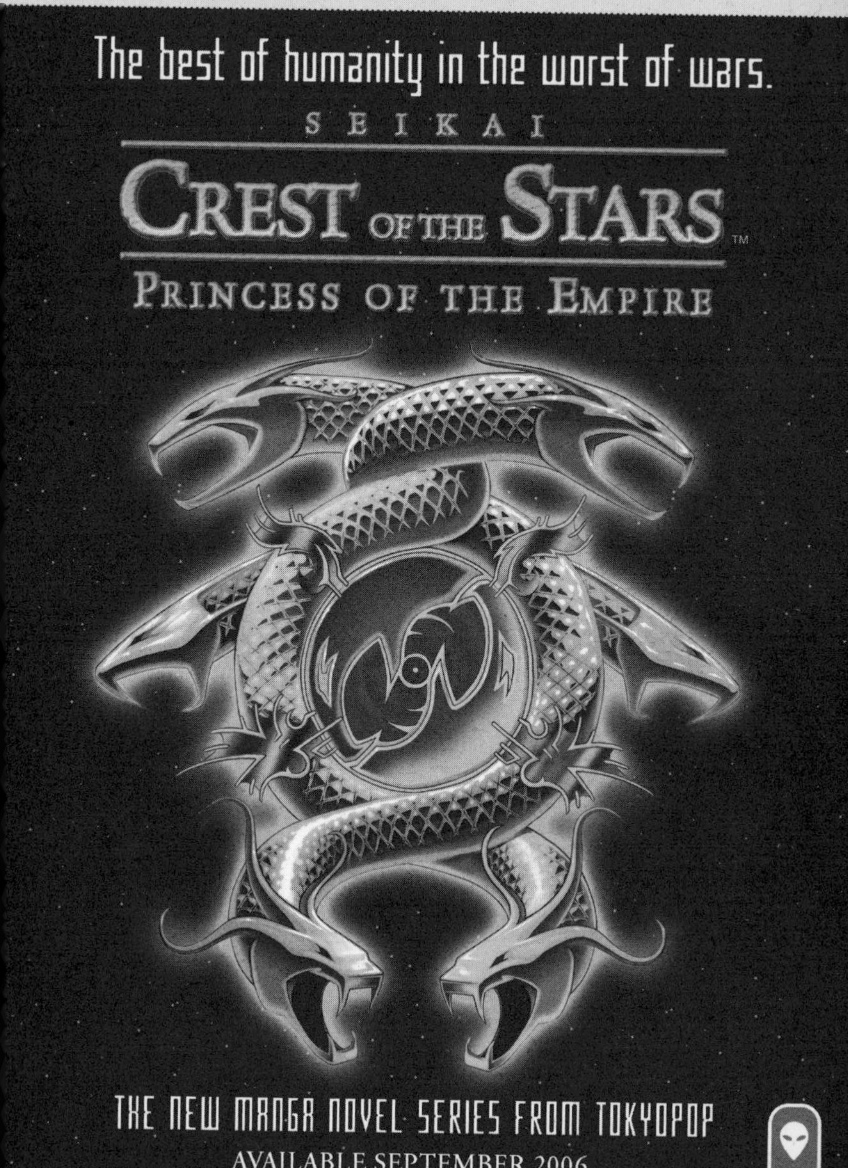
The best of humanity in the worst of wars.
SEIKAI
CREST OF THE STARS™
PRINCESS OF THE EMPIRE
THE NEW MANGA NOVEL SERIES FROM TOKYOPOP
AVAILABLE SEPTEMBER 2006
© 1996 • Hiroyuki Morioka All Rights Reserved • First published in Japan by HAYAKAWA PUBLISHING CORPORATION
SCI-FI

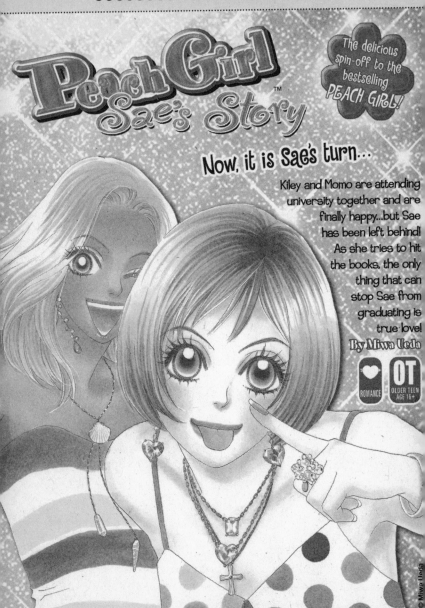